G000149373

38
SLEEPS

Published in the UK in 2021 by Boomsong Publishing

Copyright © Michael Bacon 2021

Michael Bacon has asserted their right under
the Copyright, Designs and Patents Act, 1988,
to be identified as the author of this work.

All rights reserved. No part of this book may be reproduced,
stored in a retrieved system or transmitted, in any form or by
any means, electronic, mechanical, scanning, photocopying,
recording or otherwise, without the prior permission of the
author and publisher.

This book is a work of fiction, and except in the case of
historical or geographical fact, any resemblance to names,
place and characters, living or dead, is purely coincidental.

Hardback   ISBN 978-1-7399452-2-0
Paperback ISBN 978-1-7399452-0-6
eBook   ISBN 978-1-7399452-1-3

Cover design and typeset by SpiffingCovers
Boomsong Publishing logo by Andrew Summers

38
SLEEPS

NOT ALL PARTNERSHIPS ARE EQUAL

MICHAEL
BACON

For Tracey

x

ONE

Friday, April 3

IT was frustrating, but not unusual.

People often cancelled appointments. But most at least had the courtesy to let the dental surgery know in good time. One hour was *not* 'good time'. Still, if people were rude, then they were just plain rude, it wasn't going to ruin Tom's day. And anyhow, he was going to the theatre with Polly that evening.

'Open wide. Let's take a shufty in the gods, a shufty downstairs.' Tom leant forward and stared into the dark chasm that was Mr Summers' mouth.

'All looking good to me. Don't think we'll need the periodontal probe, you'll be pleased to know. Perhaps a quick polish would be in order. Rinse out.' Tom turned away and looked outside the window of his surgery. Blue sky and the street below was busy. He liked being in the centre of the city. Norwich was just perfect, just as London had been all those years go.

Mr Summers was no different to the majority of Tom's patients. Most had little wrong with their teeth and few required treatment. A quick brush and polish — 40 quid — see you in six months. *'Only bookmakers and kebab houses make easier money,'* his friends were always telling him.

'Glad things are okay old chap.' Mr Summers relaxed in the chair. 'Had enough probing with me old prostate recently, wouldn't want any probing on my teeth. Bloody painful, I can tell you. You had yours checked, Tom lad?'

'What my teeth or my prostate?'

'Your prostate, man'

'Um, well, not really. I am only 33, not quite sure I should be worrying about that just yet.'

'Never be too careful. My pal Reggie at the golf club had a touch of gout. Before you know it, they're talking of amputating his foot. Bad job, bad job. Didn't have to in the end, but unpleasant business. Never be too careful. He hasn't played golf for a year, even sold his clubs. I told him not to, he could always have got one of those prostrate legs to get about.'

'You mean prosthetic!' Tom smiled at Emily, his assistant, who wasn't really paying attention. She was too busy piecing together the tools for the polish.

Mr Summers wasn't finished. 'Well, whatever they're called. And get that cholesterol checked, and your blood pressure. Stressful job this I imagine. And keep off the cheese, frightful stuff.'

Tom smiled. 'I will, don't worry. Open wide again please.'

Mr Summers did as instructed. Brush and polish. He would soon be on his way.

It had taken Tom Armstrong 11 years to get to this point in his professional career. Five years of university, a year learning with Mr Freeman, in Chelsea — 'hatchet man Freeman' — as he was known in local circles in the West End. It had been a long road, exams, pressure, more exams and more pressure. It hadn't always been easy but he had got through. He was confident in his own shell now. The 75K he had splashed out on his surgery was starting to pay dividends.

Now well established, patient numbers were up. He could clear £66K a year, enjoy time away at the apartment he and his wife Polly had in Spain, as well as loving his Audi TT. And a season ticket at Arsenal.

Tom was the first dentist in his family. His parents, Doreen and Colin were teachers in Reading, where he was born and raised. He had one brother, Joe, and the pair had always been close, playing football together, listening to the same type of music, collecting football stickers and racing bikes.

His childhood had been a happy one. The family had been surrounded by neighbours with nice cars and mowed gardens, long summer holidays, cosy winter nights. After getting a host of GCSEs and three 'A' levels, Tom had headed off to the University of Glasgow to study dentistry.

These days, his ducks were all lining up in a row. Life was good, work was good, he and Polly were happy, finances stable, and improving. He had good friends, a nice house, great social life, flash car.

He just wished people wouldn't cancel so late.

'So, who was I supposed to be seeing at 4.30?' Tom had headed downstairs and was turning to talk to Jill having just seen Mr Summers off the premises. He was a tad irritated. His next appointment wasn't now until 5.05pm – and that was the cantankerous Mr Jenkins who hardly had any of his own teeth.

'A Mrs Harding cancelled', said Jill. 'An hour ago. Said she was very sorry but one of her boys had been taken ill at school, so she had picked him up, but couldn't come in to the surgery.'

'Bloody kids!' Tom shook his head. 'Can we get hold of Harry Jenkins and tell him to come in now, he only lives in the Cloisters. Who is Mrs Harding anyhow?'

'I don't know,' shrugged Jill. 'She's a new patient – well, would have been. She called up last week to make an appointment. I know, I took the call. I did try to get hold of Mr Jenkins to see if he could come in earlier, but he hasn't got a mobile and no-one answered his home line. He's probably in the pub.'

'Well if Mrs bloody Harding calls again, get her to sign up on the scheme and get some commitment off her.' Tom picked up one of the newspapers on the table in the middle of reception and began to look at it. 'Remember, only my wife is allowed to do things like that. Call off at the last moment and make out she's done you a favour.'

'Oh, hi Polly,' Jill looked behind Tom at the surgery door. He spun round, then realised no-one was there. Jill laughed out loud.

'I can see who wears the trousers in your house.' Jill raised her eyebrows and smiled.

'You must be joking. I wear the trousers, don't you worry about that.'

'Of course you do, Tom.'

Jill was one of two receptionists who had been with Tom since he opened the practice four years ago. Susan was the other, but she only worked Tuesdays. Jill was cosy in a motherly sort of way, had a great sense of humour, spoke her mind, which he liked, and Tom valued her work. She was married to Robert but heaven knows what she had ever seen in him. Jill was mid-50s, slim and strikingly attractive with short bobbed hair and dark brown eyes.

Robert resembled more ape than human and worked 'in security'. Tom had never seen so much hair on one set of forearms; the man had huge teeth as well which required plenty of work. But he liked Jill, so gave them both complimentary treatments, which was just as well as Bob's treatment bills alone would have seen them need to take out a second mortgage.

At least Harry Jenkins was on time. A former WW2 veteran he had owned a shoe shop for many years in the city, he had retired at 66 after a mild heart attack, but he hadn't let that stop him and here he was 16 years later still looking in good shape. And still argumentative.

'You still voting for that Tory lot? Bunch of tax dodgers and takers they are.' Harry had only just got to the top of the stairs before he'd started ranting at Tom, who was holding out his hand, waiting for Harry's firm shake. 'Posh boy like you, blue through and through I bet?'

'Hello Harry, how are you? You won't believe this but I'm a Green Party man now. Signed up last month. Got fed up of the mainstream parties.'

That took the wind out of Harry's sails. He couldn't think of a repost and sure enough his teeth were in good shape – the few he had left.

Tom looked at his watch, it was 5.25. He knew Polly would not be impressed if he came home late. They had to be at the theatre by 7. She was not a good person to be late for.

'See you Harry.' Tom almost pushed him out of the surgery door before turning to Jill.

'You okay to lock up aren't you? If I make us late for the bloody theatre, you know what will happen? And I've only just sewn them back on from the last time I pissed Pol off.'

'Go on, get going, Emily and I will lock up, see you tomorrow.'

Tom ran back upstairs and grabbed his coat before running out of the door and jumping in his car. There was a private car park at the back of the surgery that he shared with a solicitor and law firm. There were 10 spaces, of which the surgery had three.

The traffic on the ring road was heavy, not helped by an accident involving two cars, which appeared no more than a shunt. It was 5.45pm and the small village of Melsham, where they lived, was still eight miles away. He had said he'd be home by now. At least the traffic was flowing freely again but he'd have to put his foot down.

He was going to be late....

TWO

POLLY Armstrong prided herself on many things. Looking good, earning good, being in control and being punctual were four of them. There were many more.

She had little time for people who didn't make an effort, no time for scroungers and certainly no time for people who were late. And her husband was set to push the *'late button'* right now. Okay, so a trip to the theatre wasn't his cup of tea, but it was hers, and musicals even more so. The tickets for *'Bring It On – The Musical'* had been booked months ago. She looked at her Gucci watch, an 18th birthday present from her parents; *'Where the hell was he?'*

The last words she had uttered to him as he walked out of the house that morning had been not to forget they were going to the theatre. She was sure he would be back in good time, not after what happened the last time he was late. That was two years ago when they almost didn't get to an awards ceremony in Ilford that Polly 'plus one' had been invited to. She was up for an award that evening, which she duly won.

But, because Tom had been late home from the football, they almost didn't make it. As he raced along the motorway to get there in time, she had given him the 'silent treatment'. She'd then picked up her award, got pissed, spent all night laughing and giggling with clients while Tom sat on his own like Billy no-mates, before chewing his ear off all the way home.

Polly thought he'd learned his lesson.

'Sorry, sorry, sorry, I know what you are going to say.' Tom burst through the front door and threw his briefcase down. It was

6.05pm and the doors at the Theatre opened at 7. They still had to drive back into the city.

'Traffic was hell love, sorry.'

'Where have you been?' Polly had her hands on her hips. 'I told you to get away early, so what do you do? Get home the latest you have all week. You know I hate being late and we've got to get across town and find a bloody parking space. This really pisses me, you know it does. I've put a curry on in the slow cooker, help yourself, I've had some already. *'Traffic was hell love'.* Is that the best you can come up with? Why couldn't you have arranged to close the surgery early? You own the bloody thing. Sometimes I could just, oh, I don't know, brain you! I'm going to finish getting ready.'

Tom had prepared himself for the barrage.

'Keep your hair on, Pol. Jesus, how long does it take for me to get ready? Five minutes. I'll be ready before you.'

He knew his sarcasm wouldn't go down well as Polly continued shouting as she got to the top of the stairs.

'Just get ready and shut the smartarse comments up. If we're late, I won't be happy. Fuck you Tom. You know I've looked forward to this for ages, and where exactly are we going to park? It's Friday night, Norwich will be heaving, God, I can't believe you have done this. When's the last time we went to the theatre? If it was a bloody shitty football match you wouldn't be late would you?'

She went into the bedroom to finish getting ready, slammed the door, leaving Tom flailing in the hallway. It had been no more than he expected, he knew he would still be ready before she was. It took most blokes five minutes to chuck some clothes on. He smiled to himself as he spooned out some curry from the slow cooker. In a perverse way, he kind of liked it when Polly was cross. They'd get there on time. The curry was decent.

'How long you going to be in the toilet?' Tom walked into the bedroom.

'Go in the other bloody toilet. Are you trying to go out of your way to piss me off, or what? What's wrong with you?'

'No, sorry darling, nothing, it's just I need a wee. I'm as good as ready to go.'

There was silence from inside the toilet.

Polly emerged a few seconds later having flushed the loo

and put on some perfume. She sat on the bed putting her hair straighteners to good use. She looked at her watch, they had 25 minutes to get there.

'Don't keep looking at me.' Tom was walking around the bedroom doing up his shirtsleeves admiring her. 'Just get ready will you?'

'I am ready, I'm wondering how long you're going to be?'

She turned round on the bed and stared at him. 'Have you been drinking or something?'

'No, why?'

'Don't wind me up, Tom. If we're late for this show, I'm going to kill you!'

'Wow! That's a bit heavy. But, seriously, how long are you going to be, love? We could do with getting going.'

With that Polly picked up her hairbrush and threw it in Tom's direction. It missed as he ducked and it thudded against the door. Tom laughed and picked it up.

'Don't call me 'love'. You know I hate that.'

He grinned and blew her a kiss. 'Love you to.'

She tried hard to hide not to smile. 'Just shut up and let me get ready.'

Polly was an only child. Her love of musicals began in London, during her three-year stay at London Metropolitan University, where she got a 2:1 in Marketing & Business. She and many of her fellow students would venture up to the West End and take in shows – all sorts of shows – at all times of the day and night. And although it wasn't cheap, it was her only real social activity of the week, aside from the 'Thursday Night Girls' Club', that often descended into an evening of drinking and batting away the attentions of groups of lads.

So, when she moved in with Tom, she was glad to find Norwich enjoyed fine theatres and occasionally featured shows she had not seen before in the Capital.

The pair had met 10 years ago while on holiday. Both a few years out of university, they were bright and sparky, and single. Polly the pretty blond with the English Rose skin, the wavy hair and a figure to die for, the girl every boy dreamed of dating at university. But she was choosy. Yes, there were a few 'flings', a few long romances. Polly was impulsive and two years older than Tom, who was far from her first lover, but he had been the only man to pin her down for any length of time. She had fallen head over heels with him.

Tom, dark hair, blue eyes, cheeky grin. At 6ft, he was taller than her. Menorca had proved the perfect setting for the soon-to-be Mr and Mrs Armstrong. Lazy summer days, long boozy nights, Spain had worked its magic on them.

Both had the jobs, the money and the confidence, and the idea of marriage didn't worry them. There was never any danger they were going to be 'left on the shelf'. It was just a case of finding the right jar on the shelf.

Once back from Spain their relationship developed. Even though Polly was living with friends in Brighton after her university days, and Tom in Norwich at the surgery, trips up and down the motorways became regular for both. And it was no surprise when she announced to her flat-mates she was making the move to Norfolk permanent. Finding a job in PR and Marketing in her new home county proved a doddle for a girl with her credentials.

They were married in great pomp three years later. Her father Jonathan was so determined his daughter would enjoy the full works of a grand wedding experience, he paid for the lot and even coughed up half the money for the pair to put towards their honeymoon – a three-week all-inclusive trip to the Maldives.

'My little girl deserves the best, the very, very best, you both do,' he had slurred to Tom late on at the wedding reception. Tom wasn't one to protest.

But, Polly could be complicated.

It didn't take much to set her off. As fun-loving, gregarious and attractive as she was, the life and soul of any party, you didn't want to cross her. She could be very feisty. Only Tom, and Polly's best friend, Jody, knew her inside out, back to front. Everyone else learnt as they went along.

'I'll start the car up. Hurry up.' Tom went out of the front door and got into the Audi. He turned the radio on and looked at the clock. It was 6.35pm. Polly came flying out and whipped her seat belt on.

'Now, before we go, have you got everything?' He turned to look at his wife who was looking stunning, as usual, in a short white skirt and orange blouse.

'Yes. Unlike you I got myself prepared hours ago,' Polly said with another hint of martyrdom in her voice.

'Excellent, well, let's go. We don't want to be late.' He winked. She pinched him hard on the leg.

Sitting in the Huddleston Road car park at 6.49pm, Tom grinned.

They had made it to the theatre in time, well the car park. But the theatre was only a two-minute walk away. Norwich must have been having a night off, or at least the traffic was. They sailed around the ring road and into the city with no problems.

'Told you we need not have rushed, why do you make such a fuss? You wouldn't make a very good dentist getting yourself all flustered like that, Pol. One needs to be calm, composed under pressure.' He raised his eyebrows, she pinched his leg again, and pinched it hard! 'Shut up, Tom!'

'Oi. That hurt. Remember I've got cataracts and you could damage me for life.'

She gave a sarcastic grin, but Tom's smug look was beginning to grate.

The clock in the car said 6.51pm.

'You've always made a fuss about keeping time,' he said looking forward.

'We were always going to be okay and now look, we're early. We'll have to sit here like a couple of lemons waiting for the doors to open. Just as well we did get here early though, there's only about 150 parking spaces left.'

'*Norwich will be heaving tonight.*' How did you work that out? Let me guess, you asked Jody? She'd know.' He laughed and turned the radio down. Tom hated the Beach Boys. Polly didn't look at him. She tried to hide a smile. He could be such a smart shit sometimes.

'And while we're sitting here doing Jack nothing because you insisted on us leaving the house early, don't use such bad language, Mrs Potty mouth. You swore at least twice at me when I got in tonight. What would your dad say if he heard you talk like that?

He thinks butter wouldn't melt in your mouth. Just as well he's not there to watch some of your terrible behaviour in the bedroom after a few G&Ts!' He grinned.

'You wish. Anyway, who's being rude now?'

A couple of minutes passed and a few people began getting out of their cars. The first ones to make a move were an elderly couple getting out of a Range Rover with a personalised number plate. Tom was straight on his soap box.

'Why on earth do people that age want a car that big? And with a personalised number plate?

'A Citroen or Fiat or one of those little Smart cars, is enough for anyone over 70, bloody absurd. This is why the Government is making us get electric cars, so old people don't keep buying bloody great SUVs and 4x4s. What do they need all the seats for?'

'Listen to you.' Polly pushed him on the shoulder. 'I'll remind you of that when you're 70. You'll be the first to moan you've paid your taxes so you can have however big a car you want. Anyway, isn't the size of a man's car supposed to represent the size of his manhood? I can see now why we have this tiny little Audi.' It was Polly's turn to laugh.

'Tiny, little Audi,' he snorted. 'Tiny, little Audi. It's a bloody Audi TT, fast as fuck Audi. Anyhow, car sizes have nothing to do with a bloke's willy — and how would you know anyway?'

'Oh, I do know. Before you came on the scene, I went out with a guy who drove a Range Rover. We are talking big, huge, bloody Range Rover. That's all I'll say.'

He looked at her and shook his head. 'You're disgraceful.' She smiled.

A group of four girls got out of a VW Golf. They were giggling and lighting up cigarettes as soon as they hit the fresh air. Polly and Tom looked at each other and sighed. A few moments later they got out of the Audi. Polly linked her arm in his as they strode towards the Theatre.

'I love you,' Polly looked into his eyes, which always seemed to sparkle. 'You do make me laugh, even if you are late and I hate you for it.'

'Don't come that with me now after all the names and bad words you have called me tonight, as well as the nipping. And that not very funny joke about the size of my manhood and the bloke with the huge Range Rover. Who was he, by the way? Please don't tell me I knew him.

'Of course you didn't. Some posh idiot at Uni, I think his name was Paul, or it could have been Richard, or John, or Philip.' She flicked her eyebrows.

'Ha, ha, ha,' said Tom.

Polly continued: 'His dad owned a flash garage, so he let him have the Range Rover for the summer semester. But as I found out, it's no good having a thing that big if you don't know what to do with it. He didn't know how to drive the Range Rover, either.'

She flashed a cheeky smile and raised her eyebrows again. Tom shook his head. 'You're not funny.'

Ten years together and the magic was still there. They had no jealousies, they had no envy. For both of them, their past was their past, their future was ahead. As a couple they enjoyed each other's company to the full, they could laugh at each other and with each other.

'Oh, I forgot to say by the way, I spoke to Jody today.' Polly was taking her coat off as they sat down into their seats in the theatre.

'Oh yeah, what did she have to say? Let me guess, poor old Craig has been told to move the house a little to the left.'

'Don't say that. Jody's my 'bestie'. They're our friends.'

Tom pulled a resigned face.

'Anyway, Jody's had some bad news. But don't mention it to Craig unless he mentions it to you.

'Her IVF has failed again.'

THREE

'COME on, get up here.' Polly was frantically waving at Tom as she jigged around in the aisles.

It had only taken the cast of *'Bring It On'* to shout out; *'Come on guys and girls, let's get up and dance'*, and Polly was up. More than 100 people were bobbing about in the aisles and Polly was one of the first half-dozen to get up. She was that type of girl. 'Taking a back seat' was not in her dictionary. For Tom however, when it came to pulling dance moves, it was all rather cringe worthy.

'Quick, come on. Come up and dance.' She held her hands out to him. He knew better than not to join her. As much as he hated dancing, his wife was looking stunning with her blond hair ringlets bouncing up and down on her shoulders, her hips moving to the beat.

'I love this song.' She smiled and did a 360 degree spin in front of him, as he tried to put one foot in front of the other without tripping over. She pointed to the stage. 'See that lead singer. He reminds me of Andy'

'Andy who?' Tom leaned forward and shouted in her ear as he continued to shift about uncomfortably.

'Andy, my boss Andy, at the gym.' It was Polly's turn to raise her voice above the music. 'He looks just like him. Spitting image. I'll have to ask him on Monday if he's moonlighting.'

Tom didn't know Andy that well, so didn't comment. All he did know is that Polly enjoyed her job and anyone who could make his wife as happy as she was in her work, was alright by him.

The aisles were not very wide and bumping into others was par for the course. Tom was smiling but still feeling uncomfortable. Surely this couldn't go on for much longer, he thought, as he looked across to see the couple from the car park, the ones with the Range Rover, pulling some sort of move that would not have looked out of place in an aqua aerobics class for the over 90s.

The singing stopped, as did the dancing, as the show came to a finale, much to Tom's relief. The cast went through a second curtain call, most of the audience on their feet applauding, none more so than Polly. He wondered if she was ever going to stop.

'Come on Pol, let's go. I think they know you enjoyed it. Anyhow, we'll need to get back to the car to avoid the queue to get out.' His sarcasm went unnoticed.

They headed back to their seats and sat and relaxed for a couple of minutes. It had been a fun night. 'We did pay for the parking, didn't we? Because I didn't see you put the ticket on the windscreen.' Tom looked at Polly.

She picked up her coat. 'What ticket? I didn't get a ticket. Don't tell me we needed a ticket. I thought it was free parking in the evenings. Well, tough shit, I'm not paying any fine, you never told me we needed a ticket. You better not be messing me about.'

'I'm not messing about. I thought I left you to sort the ticket out, remember? I said get the ticket just after you had a go at me about that old couple's car.'

She shook her head. 'You didn't say anything of the sort. Look don't fool around, did we have to pay or not? Come on, let's go just in case.'

'*Let's go just in case*'. It's a bit late for that. Ah, don't worry, the council laid off two traffic wardens last week. Hopefully they're understaffed! If not and we get a fine, you will have to go without your five bottles of Prosecco this week.'

He smiled and nudged her. It was free parking. He got another pinch, but this time harder on the arm. 'I didn't believe you, anyway.'

Tom smiled again… 'Really?'

The cold air hit them as they made their way back to the car and Polly snuggled in close to him. Even if Tom had seemed sceptical beforehand, he seemed to have enjoyed it.

'Okay, that was decent, I'll let you off.' He kissed her on the side of the head before aiming his key fob at the Audi from about 20 yards away. The lights flashed to open the car doors. He looked at her once more. 'Did you see the old couple in the Range Rover get up and dance? It was like a re-enactment of *'Night of the Living Dead'*. I thought I hardly moved when I danced. They were almost motionless. And what's all this about a resemblance between the singer in the play and Andy, that singer must have been about 20 years old. You told me Andy was in his 40s. Don't tell me you fancied that singer, you're a right cougar. You're almost old enough to be his mum. Or is it Andy you fancy?'

She ignored him. Polly didn't fancy the singer, or Andy. Her boss was 44 and married.

'Fancy a Maccie D and thick shake?' Tom went to start the car up. He knew he didn't likely need to ask. If Pol was hungry, she would eat anything. She was no food snob.

She could get down and dirty with the best on many levels. And fast food was one of them. Pizzas, kebabs, Maccie D's, KFC, she was more than capable of showing a different side to the prawn sandwich and orange juice brigade she shared her life with during her day job at the corporate and team meetings she had to go to.

'Where is there a drive-thru near here?' Polly looked at him as he pulled away.

'I know where,' he replied. 'You leave it to me. You just make sure we can get out of this bloody car park first. We could be here all night, there must be at least five cars in here now.'

'Ha, ha. Very funny, you're getting boring now. Did you enjoy the show?' Please say you did.'

'Yeah, I did. I've been to worse. I hope you noticed when you got up to dance, those girls sitting in front of us were staring. Can't imagine what for, perhaps it was your short dress. What's the phrase? Mutton, lamb, dressed up and something.'

'You are so funny,' she held out her hands and grinned. 'For someone whose jokes are always so shit, you are excelling yourself tonight. More likely the girls were wondering why I was calling out to my dad to come up and dance with me.

Polly kissed him on the cheek.

'Touché, my darling!'

It was 11.15pm by the time they pulled up at the drive-through. Typically for a Friday night there were plenty of cars in the queue. Smoke billowed out of the driver's window from the car in front as the driver vaped out so much smoke, it looked like his car was about to go up in flames. Slowly they crept forward before arriving at the two-way microphone.

'Can I help you?' said the rather bored-sounding girl in the booth.

'I'll have two thick shakes, vanilla and strawberry, a double cheeseburger and wrap of the day please, which is what?' Tom said quickly.

'Sweet chilli', came the response.

'Yep, okay, one of them.'

'That will be seven pounds, 69p, drive round to the next booth.'

Sitting in the car park, the pair tucked in. It had been five hours since they had last eaten, and a late-night burger and wrap was hitting the mark.

'You never said anymore about Jody.' Tom was munching his burger. 'You said she called about her IVF failing. I suppose she is in a bit of a state.'

'It's awful,' Polly said. 'I feel so sorry for her. I want to go up to Chester and see her. She was in tears on the phone, it's their third time and they are so desperate to have kids. Apparently Craig hasn't taken it that well, but he's putting on a brave face, you know what he's like? So, if he does mention it, talk to him, but knowing him, I don't reckon he will, do you?'

'Doubt it,' Tom replied, as he glanced at a pretty girl walking across the front of the car sipping what looked like a coffee. 'He plays a pretty straight bat does Craig. Then again, I don't know, depends how he's feeling. I'm sure he'll be just as upset, even if he doesn't show it. When you thinking of going up to see Jody?'

'I can get a Friday off in the next week or so. I'm owed some time. I can make a long weekend of it. You come as well. Come on, see if you can get away early on a Friday for a change. Even if you can't leave off till, say 4, we can be up there by 8. You and Craig can take in a football match on the Saturday and we can all go out for a meal. It would be nice, we always have good fun together and you know how much Jody loves to see us.'

Polly and Jody had been friends for years. They were like sisters. It always felt as though they came as a package. 'Eggs and bacon', 'salt and pepper', Tom called them. Friends from their days in Brighton, Polly had moved to Norwich when she met Tom, before Jody moved to Chester a year later after she had met Craig at a 'yoga retreat' in Manchester.

Jody had a degree in fashion and owned a small retro clothes shop in Chester. From being live-in buddies and best friends since they were in their early 20s, Polly and Jody were now hundreds of miles apart but with a friendship that was as strong as ever. They spoke almost every day, they knew everything about each other. Nothing was a secret. Friends and family, work, jobs, holidays, kids – or the thought of having kids – sex, drugs, alcohol, one-night stands, nothing was off limits. Neither had a sister, neither needed one, they had each other.

Craig was a director of a shipping company. It clearly paid well if Craig's two properties in Spain, a brand new bright red BMW Z4 and plethora of houses he rented over Boston way, was anything to go by. Tom and Craig had lots in common. They had become good pals. Both loved a drink. Both were Tories. Both were Arsenal fans and both liked fast cars.

'Okay, I'll see what I can do. I'll get some time off.' Tom got out of the car and put their rubbish in a bin, before getting back in.

He was about to pull out of the car park when he caught sight of a group of boys, two on push bikes, one walking, heading towards the parking bays he and a few other cars were in. With scarves wrapped around their mouths and the bicycle boys pulling 'wheelies', they looked the type you didn't want to bump into at this time of night. Certainly not the lad walking, he was older and shouting.

All three had baseball caps on.

Despite the parking area being a good size, the two lads on the bikes continued to pull stunts and make loud noises, egged on by the older boy, as they performed tricks ever closer to the cars around them. Tom looked in the rear mirror as they went past. He put the Audi into reverse and went back a couple of yards. *'Bang!'*

He felt a bump. Either he had hit something, or something had hit him.

'What was that?' Polly was concerned.

'I don't know.' Tom got out of the car and was confronted by two of the gang at the rear of the vehicle, one of the boys on the bikes and the older boy. The third boy was on the ground.

'Shit man, what you doing?' said the older boy. The lad on the floor had his bike sprawled on top of him. He was groaning and moaning. 'You reversed into him dickhead.'

Tom could see the boy who spoke was likely in his 20s. He wasn't tall, but looked menacing with a dark complexion and goatee beard, bandana and bright green trousers. Tom looked at the boy on the floor.

'Goatee' had shades on which was absurd at this time of night. He was carrying some sort of drink, likely alcohol, in his left hand. Tom had to get a grip of the situation. He wasn't sure what had happened, but from what he could see of the boy on the floor, he could only assume two things. Either he hadn't seen him and reversed into him or one of the tricks the boy was pulling hadn't come off and he had veered into the back of his car.

It didn't look like the boy was in any trouble. He was thrashing about and trying to get the bike off himself, while swearing. Tom lent over to see if he was okay, but 'goatee' stepped in his way.

'Watch your back man,' he said aggressively. 'You think you a flash bastard with this car, don't you? You hit my friend and no-one's laughing. You see what I'm saying. Now get some money out and pay for the damage.'

The guy was looking for trouble. He was close enough for Tom who could smell the alcohol on his breath. He had taken his shades off and his eyes were wide open. Probably high as well.

'Look mate. I didn't see him. He went into the back of me, didn't he? Pulling a wheelie was he? I didn't hit him. He looks okay to me, so let's all move on.' Tom tried to calm things down.

'You okay, mate?' Tom spoke to the lad who had been on the floor but had now struggled to his feet and was standing a few metres back, as was his mate. The force of the impact had been minimal.

The boy just looked back at him but didn't answer.

'Goatee' moved forwards and put his hand on Tom's throat, holding it there, squeezing slowly, before letting go. This lad was trouble. He was very strong and Tom was caught off-guard. Things were spiralling out of control.

'You a flash boy.' 'Goatee' was becoming more menacing. 'You knocked my mate off so what you going to do? It will cost to put that bike proper again. You got money bro, you know you have, so cough up fucker and we'll be done here. You heard me, now give us some fucking money, or that watch.' The lad had clocked Tom's Tag Heuer wrist piece. 'That watch, will do.'

Tom knew he had to get out of this. 'Goatee's' two young pals were backing off. He sensed they didn't like where this was going, either.

'Come on JJ, leave it man.' The boy who had been knocked off the bike started to move away. 'Let's go. You're cool JJ, he's scared, let's leave it. My bike's fine, I'm cool.'

But 'Goatee', aka JJ, was not backing down. There were only a few cars in the car park and no-one seemed to be noticing what was going on. He upped the stakes, getting out a small flick-knife from his pocket which he began waving in front of Tom.

'Give us the fuckin' watch, man or I'll cut it off your fucking wrist if you don't give it to me.'

He pushed Tom back. They were now leaning against the boot of the car.

Polly had been watching the whole thing through her wing mirror. She had seen Tom talk to the lads, and she had watched as the boy got up from his bike. He seemed okay and Polly had assumed that would be that. But Tom had been grabbed around the throat. She had gone to get out of the car then, but didn't, now she saw the knife, Polly was up and out. 'What's going on?'

Tom flicked a glance at his wife. 'Get back in the car Pol. It's fine. Just get back in the car.' This was getting out of hand. The last thing he wanted was Polly getting involved.

JJ's face lit up as she walked towards him. Polly's short dress had revealed more of her legs than she would have liked as she had got out of the Audi.

'Lookee here. What have we got? Mr Audi has his own bit of rough and what a bit of rough she is.' JJ continued to flail his knife about as though he was in some 'grime' gang video in LA.

'Okay, that's enough pal,' said Tom. 'Cut out the shit and let's all get going, or I'll…' Tom's voice petered out.

'Or you'll want?' JJ grabbed Tom's throat again and held the knife close. 'You be careful Audi boy. Now give me your fucking watch.'

The two young boys on their bikes scarpered. They had seen enough. Tom began to fiddle with the watch trying to get if off as he pushed the boy back.

'Come on arsehole, hand it over or perhaps your pretty girlfriend wants to pay me in kind. What you say pretty?' He looked at Polly. 'I bet you give a good blow job.' JJ grinned and nodded his head.

It all happened so quickly that neither Tom nor JJ were prepared for it. Polly marched towards JJ, who was trying to keep one eye on her, one eye on Tom, all while keeping hold of the knife.

'Leave him alone,' she called out. And without breaking stride Polly marched straight at JJ who, caught in confusion didn't know whether to challenge her or keep hold of her husband. In the end he did neither. It was a mistake. Polly was in full flow, bringing her foot back as she got close to Tom's assailant, kicking him so hard in his 'crown jewels', he let out an awful moan and went down as though he had been shot. The knife flew out of his hand. Polly wasn't finished. Bending down over him she pulled back her fist and cracked a punch on his nose as his head bounced off the concrete. Blood poured out over his face. She then aimed one more kick to his chest.

The guy was pole-axed and bleeding. His head had taken a frightful whack, his nose was covered in blood. He stayed on the floor and this time it was Tom's turn to stand on his throat, picking the knife up and throwing it away, as Polly lent over him.

'You want a blow job arsehole. Ask your sister for one you fucking inbred.' Polly was inches from his bloodied nose, but the boy could only groan. 'Don't speak about me like that you small pricked dick. Go back to your mummy and get her to wash that snot off your face and put some cold water on those things you call balls.'

She stood back up, looked at Tom. 'Come on, let's go.'

JJ tried to get up but was in discomfort. He eventually did so and limped off across the parking bay, swearing expletives and wiping his bloodied nose, which was likely broken. It had been quite a punch. A couple of other people from cars had now got out to see what was going on, they had heard the commotion but the show was over. Tom and Polly got back in the car, Polly drawing down the mirror from the sun visor to check her face.

'Jesus, Pol are you crazy? He had a knife.' Tom was staring at his wife. 'And where the hell did you learn to punch like that? Christ man, I should be cross with you. That could have been dangerous. Who knows what he might have done?'

Polly looked at him and was quite calm. 'But you're not cross are you? He wouldn't have used that knife. Be cross with me, but I'll get cross with you. And you just saw what happens when I'm cross. Anyhow, are you okay?'

'Am I okay? What about you? Yes, I'm fine, he was just full of bullshit. You didn't have to jump in, I had it under control.'

Tom started the car up and they headed out of the car park, Polly feeling her hand, which was sore from the punch. Not that she would let on.

'Do you think he'll go the police?' The radio was playing quietly in the background as they made their way round the ring road.

Tom smiled. 'Of course he won't. He's a dickhead, a loser. He was the one who was doing all the threatening, he got what he deserved. I'm just glad he got up to be honest, he hit his head hard on the concrete. Anyhow, how's he going to pass it off with his mates that some pretty bird in a short skirt smacked his lights out?'

She smiled back, although the adrenaline that had been flowing was beginning to ease and she had a headache. The rest of the journey home was quiet.

'The show was good.' Tom was getting dressed for bed.

'What show? The one in the theatre or the one in the car park?' Polly was already in bed. She smiled at him.

Neither was in the mood to read, so he switched his light out. He gave her a kiss on the forehead and looked at her. She had taken a couple of aspirins and was almost asleep. She looked so peaceful, it was hard to believe she could get so angry, so quickly. He smiled to himself as he remembered the look on the face of the lad she had punched.

He looked at her again.

'Polly Armstrong, you're completely mad. And I love you for it,' he whispered.

But she was already asleep.

FOUR

THE sun broke through the crack in the curtains of her bedroom window and Karen stirred.

She couldn't believe it, another good night's sleep. That's four in the last five nights. That hadn't happened for more years than she cared to remember. She was liking Norfolk, even if just for the fact she slept well. And she was enjoying her new home village of Oxton, just outside Norwich, it was a big sea change from London.

One look at her clock told her it was 8.30am. She remembered it was Sunday, so there had been no need to have set the alarm. She wasn't working at the pet shop today. It felt good to enjoy a lay-in and listen to the sounds of. Well the sounds of, nothing. Wasn't that one of the reasons of moving to the countryside? The nothingness, the stillness, the peace. It had taken some getting used to mind, no more cars roaring past at silly speeds, no more shouting in the street late at night, no more police sirens, no more parties and loud music from the neighbours next door.

From a two-up, two-down terrace in Woolwich, south London, to the peace and tranquillity of 'Nelson's County', Karen Harding was enjoying a change of lifestyle she had desperately been looking for. A change she had needed. Two failed marriages and one abusive relationship, life had been tough for the 33-year-old mum of one, her son, Lee, born when she was just 19. Holding down two, sometimes three jobs in London, her life had been a whirl of work and little play.

She was born in Greenwich to parents who both worked for the NHS. Their deaths, within six months of each other, when she was just 21, both from cancer, had left her depressed with little family around, as well as Lee to take care of. It hadn't helped that her sister Jane had emigrated to Australia with her husband Peter a few months after their dad passed. Jane and Peter now had two boys, Zac and Jake, Lee's cousins.

Life had not been easy in Greenwich and Karen and her sister grew up on tough housing estates. Not that they had been old enough to understand all that was going on around them.

Their parents had saved and worked hard to make a move to a three-bed detached, still in Greenwich, but in a more pleasant location. Manna from heaven for the whole family and it gave both girls a chance at a school which enjoyed better exam results. Karen had trained to be a hairdresser, while Jane went into the NHS, as a student nurse. Their parents never lived long enough to see how their careers would pan out.

The sisters had enjoyed a safe and happy childhood. Despite money being at a premium when they were young, holidays to Cornwall, Blackpool and Clacton-on-Sea during the long summer months were still enjoyed. They even all went abroad as a family a few times.

However, when Jane turned 18, she began holidaying with her friends on wild and whacky places like Ibiza, Gran Canaria, Majorca and anywhere else where there would be sun, sex, sand and alcohol. It wasn't long before Karen joined her, the first year with her sister. After that, Karen's summer breaks were spent abroad with her own fun, boozy crowd.

The only silver lining for the girls after the devastation of losing their parents was the money. The house in Greenwich was sold for £400,000 and the girls, who by then had both moved into rented digs, were handed a nest egg.

Looking out of the small cottage Karen was now renting in Norfolk, she remembered those teenage holidays. Yes, she had made mistakes. But she had seemed to make more than most. Why had it gone so badly wrong? Maybe she was too desperate, maybe she just wanted someone to love. Maybe she only wanted the best, not just for her, but for Lee. She should have shown better judgement when marriage number one broke down after only a year. What was she thinking off getting married to Mark two years after that shambles with Tony? Hapless Tony, a man only there to erase the memory of a boyfriend who had used her as a punch bag. It was not as if Tony deserved her walking out like that.

At least she'd always had Lee and, for a while, her parents' nest egg. But not now, not after that marriage with Mark was done and dusted – *'the cheating bastard'*. He had taken his half-share of their terrace house in Woolwich. Money wasn't everything, she was glad to be rid of him. But now she had to start again. It had been five months since she had kicked him out. Her former friend Tonya had called him 'Mr Smooth' after Karen had broken the news of his extra-marital affairs. 'I'm not surprised,' Tonya had told her. 'If he had been made of chocolate he would have eaten himself, Kaz. Best off without the arsehole.'

'Wish you had told me before I married him, Tonya,' Karen, who had now returned to her maiden name, Harding, after the split, had said.

When the house Mark and her had sold, she decided it was time to get out of London. Karen had created the insular world she was living in. She had helped create the mess she found herself in. It had been time for change. It had also been time for her to confront her secret, the secret she had been carrying all these years.

It had surprised Karen how little time it had taken to unravel her past. She had chased it once before, but to no avail. She had been so close. Now she had been chipping away at it. Her determination had accelerated and now she was within touching distance.

'You up mum. I would have brought you a cup of tea, but I don't know where the sugar is.' Lee jumped up on her bed, a heavy boy now he had turned 14-years-old.

'Morning darling, did you sleep well? Careful, you're squashing me.'

'Yeah great, slept good. It's so quiet around here, you can't hear 'nuffin''.

'You mean 'nothing'', his mum corrected.

'No, I mean 'nuffin'. You sound like my mate Dabber, at school. He said to me last week, 'you can take the boy out of London, but you can't take London out of the boy', after I said he was telling 'porkie pies'. He had never heard of it. He didn't know it was rhyming slang for 'lies'. That's when he said the London boy thing. Do we have any sugar or not?'

'We do darling, in the cupboard above the microwave. I know we haven't been here long, but I would have thought you might get to know where things were by now.'

He jumped off the bed and she smiled as he headed out of the bedroom and ran downstairs. Lee was the light of life, she was so proud of him. He deserved so much more than she had so far afforded and he was going to get it as well, she was determined of that. Lee was indeed a strong lad now. At school he was one of the biggest in his class, rugby was his game. He'd settled in well to his new surroundings.

Oh, how Karen so missed her sister Jane and her words of advice. Should she have gone over to Australia to join her? Should she still go? Lee wouldn't mind, he'd love it there. Maybe there was still time.

No, she was going to do what Jane had said she should have done all along. Something she had kept putting off. Why? She had no idea but now Karen had made the first move, getting a house and job in Norfolk. A baby step, but a huge step. She could hear Jane's words ringing in her ears.

'*Don't hide it sis. Confront the truth.*'

FIVE

THE village of Melsham, where Tom and Polly lived, was eight miles south of Norwich.

Chocolate box-style thatched cottages aplenty, typical of an English village that smacked of prosperity. Retired folk with successful careers behind them and young up-and-comers with budding careers in their infancy were the main inhabitants. It was a small village and most people knew each other. It had no primary school, but did have a convenience store, a fish & chip shop and most importantly, a pub – the Queen's Head.

Tom and Polly lived just off the village green in a rustic three-bed detached cottage. A tidy front and back garden with a few shrubs, Tom had bought the property after moving to Norfolk having spotted the opportunity to buy the surgery. Neither had green fingers, but they liked the place to look smart. The Audi TT was parked in the driveway alongside a Mercedes A Class, Polly's car. The trappings of a couple on their way up. They had lived there three years and loved it.

It was a carefree type of village, you didn't have to sit bolt upright in the middle of the night panicking you hadn't locked your car door. People's back doors were often left ajar. Tom and Polly had said they could see themselves living in the cottage, they called 'Greenside' for many years.

It wasn't often Tom's phone went off in his car on the way to work. He was an early starter and invariably in the surgery by 7.45am, especially on a Monday morning as he liked to take a quick look through the diary for the week ahead. It was just after

7.30am as he was heading into the city, having left Polly a cup of tea on her bedside cabinet. He was humming along to the Bee Gees 'Jive Talking' on the radio. His phone flashed up 'Craig'.

Tom answered. 'Hello mate, how are you? Fell out of bed? What do you want at this time of the morning? Please don't tell me one of your chickens has laid a bloody egg at last, Jody will be happy.'

Craig laughed as Tom continued. 'Or let me guess mate, Arsenal were so shit on Saturday and you are in such a bad way about it, you wanted to call me up and talk it over. And yes, before you ask, I did go. So, please tell me, and as uninterested as I am in poultry, you're calling about the chickens.'

'Ha, ha, hello pal,' said Craig still laughing. 'No, I've given up on them.'

'What the chickens, or Arsenal?' It was Tom's turn to laugh.

'Arsenal. I gave up on the chickens years ago. I watched the game on TV, but Jesus, Tom, we now have a defence most League One clubs would fancy having a go at and a strike force that couldn't score in a brothel. What has happened?'

'I know mate. Honestly, we were crap. That new guy up front, what's his name, Sulter, Salter, Shooter, whatever he's called. He's useless and we've paid £34m for him, how does that work? Imagine how much a player of your capabilities would have been worth in today's market?'

'Not wrong, mate. Shame I got no further than Hackney Marshes though, although to be fair Sulter does have a better hairstyle than I did when I played, which seems to be par for the course these days. Who needs to play like a tart, when you can look like one? And he's dating that bird from Love Island. Don't think I ever got close to dating someone like that, unless you could claim Sam Setchell as a trophy. She did once model for C&A. Trouble was, she slept about so much it was hardly a coup if you did score with her.'

'Who was Sam Setchell? I don't remember you ever talking about her.'

'Don't worry mate, most of the team have probably forgotten her name. The sex was a bit like that.' The two laughed.

Craig and Tom had met each other when Jody introduced

her 'new man' to the Armstrongs a year after Polly and Tom were married. Craig and Jody's meeting at a yoga retreat had always amused Tom.

'I bet they can get in some outrageous positions, all that yoga stuff. Wish I had a camera in their bedroom,' Tom had said to Polly, who had scolded him at the mere thought of the idea.

The emergence of Craig into Jody's life had been quite a thing, not just for Jody, but for Polly as well. You would have thought they were both set to date him, as the pair smiled and grilled the poor bloke in equal measure when the four met up for a meal and a show in London one weekend just before Christmas. The Lion King was hardly the thought-provoking musical the four of them would have undertaken in normal circumstances, but Jody having a new man was enough to get the two girls organising a weekend in the Capital so quickly, Tom had to miss an Arsenal home game.

'This is important.' Polly had laid the law down. 'Jody is excited and wants us to meet him. You can forget that stupid football team for once.' Craig, also an Arsenal fan, hadn't put up a fight.

'Jody says you work in shipping,' Polly had said to Craig, at the rather posh West End establishment Jody had booked for their meal ahead of the theatre date. A meal, with drinks that was going to cost the four of them little short of £300. 'You're paying', Tom had whispered under his breath to Pol as the four entered the lavish entrance. It was a fine meal and the conversation flowed, although for Craig it must have felt as though he was being interrogated.

'So, is it a big company, this shipping one you work for? What is its turnover? My friend likes to know she's dating a man with prospects. Don't you Jode? And as her friend, I like to know it to.'

Polly had been on her third glass of wine and it was starting to tell. Jody was all smiles and giggles, Craig didn't know what to say, so Tom had jumped in. 'Leave the bloke alone, *what's its turnover?* What sort of question is that?'

Tom had only met Craig an hour before, but was already feeling a tad sorry for him. Jody had almost spat out her drink with laughter at Pol's questioning that night, while Craig had looked amused, shocked and concerned in equal measure.

'Do you have a big mortgage on your house? Or are you mortgage-free?' Polly was in full flow. 'My friend doesn't like negative equity! Do you Jode, darling?'

Jody shook her head. 'Can't abide it.'

Poor Craig was a sitting duck, but Tom had to admit it was amusing stuff from his wife and even he couldn't hide a chuckle. She was so bad when like this and Jody was happy to let it roll, the pair were lapping it up and, although Tom tried to halt the bloodbath, he never really succeeded.

He had always remembered that night as Craig survived the grilling and by the end of the evening looked half-relaxed. He was nothing if not resilient and he'd even cracked a joke about men not having to pay the bill on a first date. Being half-Italian Craig claimed it was a tradition from where he came from, Camden Town.

It was 18 months later the happy couple became Mr and Mrs Baldini.

Back in the Audi as Tom continued his journey into work, he laughed out loud as Craig continued their conversation: 'I'm just calling to check you are still in one piece after the 'Battle of Maccie D' on Friday night. Polly called Jody yesterday, sounds like quite an evening.'

Craig clearly knew the story. There would have been no detail Polly would not have left out to Jody.

'Mate, you should have been there. Honestly, I've never seen anything like it. This bloke had a knife. Yeah he's a bit pissed but I must admit I was getting a bit worried because he had me by the throat for a time. But he wants my watch, that's all, the Tag, you know, the one I picked up in that auction. Anyhow, Pol flies out of the bloody car and kicks him in the nuts, full on. He went down like a sack of shit, mate. Made my eyes water listening to the noise he made. If that wasn't enough, she smacks him in the nose, I'm sure she broke it, and kicks him in the chest, follows it up with an expletive-ridden tirade. Unbelievable. You know what she can be like. People were getting out of their cars to see what the hell was going on. And Pol reckons she used to go to church.'

'Ha, ha, love it. Did you video it?'

'Course I didn't bloody video it, I hardly had time to video it. I was more concerned she wasn't going to kill the dude.'

Tom heard more laughing on the other end of the line.

'Yeah, I did hear,' Craig was pacing around his kitchen. 'Some girl you have there. I must admit I don't think Jody would have done the same, she'd have probably closed all the car doors, locked herself in, painted her nails and left me to deal with it, while trying to catch up on her Instagram page. She'd have scraped me off the bonnet and given me a rollicking for getting blood on the Z4.'

It was Tom's turn to laugh: 'I don't know, you do strange things at times like that. I'm still not quite sure if Pol was brave or mad. But, as I said, you know what she's like.'

'Well you better behave yourself pal. Wouldn't want to be in your shoes if you ever cheated on her. She'd slice you up, put you in a briefcase and throw you in the sea. In saying that, if it did ever come to that, you know, Pol killing you and walking out, she's welcome to come and stay at ours. Not right this minute though, at the moment five of the six bedrooms are being decorated. She'd have to share with me and Jody, which I wouldn't mind.'

'*Five of the six bedrooms,*' Tom mimicked. 'You tart. And as if Pol would sleep with you? On second thoughts, don't push her on it!'

Craig had always had a soft spot for Polly and the pair teased each other rotten. He often reminded her of that '*what's your companies' turnover*' question. How times had changed. Now it was Craig who would tease Polly about a '*ménage a trois*' when the four met up.

'So, is this just a social call at this time of the morning?' Tom was heading into the surgery car park. It was almost 7.45am, but he had a few minutes to chat to his friend. He knew Craig wouldn't call up at this time of the morning for nothing.

'Sort of, mate. I suppose you heard about the IVF not working out again?'

'Yes, I did and I'm sorry to hear.'

'Yeah, well Jody's obviously upset. We both are, but you know me. If it's not meant to be, it's not meant to be. Sorry to bother you with all this on a Monday morning.'

'No mate, that's fine, keep talking.'

'Well, I'm hoping to take Jody off to Vegas in a month or so, you know as a bit of a pick me up. We could both do with a break if I'm being honest. The thing is I don't suppose you and Pol want to come? It would only be like for four nights or something. Understand if not, seriously I won't mind, I haven't mentioned it to Jody yet, even about us going. But you're coming up in a couple of weeks aren't you? Perhaps we can talk about it then.'

'Leave that with me. I'll take a look in the diary. I'm sure Pol would be able to get time off and I'm my own boss, so that helps. Depends how many people want me to prod their molars and pick their incisors that week.'

'Cheers Tom, appreciate it mate, no hassle if not though. Anyhow, see you the week after next, should be fun. I'll look up the fixtures to see what games are on around here, plenty of choice. Oh, and one last thing before I go, keep that ninja chick of yours under control, will ya? We don't like violence up here in leafy Chester.'

'Ha, ha, will do. See ya pal. Speak soon.' The pair hung up.

Tom looked at his watch. It was nearly 8am as he pulled into the car park and got out of his car. He turned off the surgery alarm and went into the reception. Jill was just a few minutes behind him.

'Morning Jill. How are you?' Tom turned round as she walked in.

'I'm okay thanks,' Jill said quietly.

Her tone alerted Tom something wasn't right. Turning to look at her, it looked like she'd been crying.

'Hey, what's the matter? Is something wrong?'

'Oh, it's nothing. Nothing, please, don't worry about it, I'm fine.'

But she wasn't fine and Tom didn't like it. 'Are you sure? Because I can call up Susan to see if she can come in today.'

'It's Robert,' Jill said, taking her glasses off and cleaning them. 'That's all. We had a bit of a row last night, he went to the pub and, well, we had a row when he got home.'

Tom thought it may be best not to pursue the matter. The thought of Jill's husband and those hairy forearms was enough to keep him at arm's length and not get involved in their marital ups and downs.

'Well, are you sure?' Tom was concerned, he liked Jill a lot.

'Yes, I'm fine. It was nothing. I suppose if you must know I'm a bit hormonal as well. I'm at that time of my life if you know what I mean? Which I don't suppose you do at your age.' She half-smiled: 'I'm okay, I'll be fine.'

Tom went upstairs to prepare for his first patient of the day. Emily had arrived and had headed straight upstairs while he was talking to Jill.

Emily, like Jill, had always been a reliable member of staff. At 20 years old, she had her whole life ahead of her and was already enjoying it to the max from what Tom could tell. She made him cringe with her urban speak and ideas of a good night out. How long she would be with Tom he didn't know, dental assistants came and went.

'Morning Emily. Good weekend?' Tom hung up his coat on the back of the door.

'Wicked,' Emily replied in the type of speak he had become used to. 'Didn't get in till 5am on Sunday morning from the clubs. Great night, bit of a hangover yesterday. But had a great Sunday lunch out at the Feathers, near Washam-Green. You ever been there? You should take Polly, she would love it. She likes posh stuff, doesn't she?'

'Yep, she does. Don't think I have been there though. I'll have to give it a go.'

'Well, if you do, the Jagerbombs are ramming. Me and Chris had four each. They went down like really cool, I was a bit pissed again to be honest.'

'You had Jagerbombs, Sunday lunchtime? I thought they were last drinks of the night when you were already half cut? I must be getting old.'

Emily started preparing the work surfaces and getting some of the instruments ready and put a cup of water by the side of the patients' chair.

'Tom,' said Emily, her wry smile giving away she was after something.

'No, we are not having Jagerbombs for lunch.'

'I know. I'm not asking that. Just that if we are going to have a CD on can I make a request we don't have that rubbish you put on Friday afternoon. What was it? Fleetwood Mac, or whoever they are. It was awful.'

'Awful, awful,' Tom said, half smiling. 'That *rubbish*', as you call it, is by a super-group that won a Grammy for Album of the Year back in the '70s. And here you are millions of years later saying they were awful. You youngsters.'

Emily shrugged, super-group or not, she'd not heard of them. He flicked through his CD collection and plucked out a bit of Vivaldi. This would suffice for a Monday morning.

'Listen to this wonderful music. It's relaxing and so peaceful,' Tom pretended to be conducting an orchestra as Vivaldi started up.

'Oh no. Are you kidding me? This is even worse.' She put her hands over her ears.

'You concentrate on getting those instruments spick and span, I'll be the DJ. Anyhow, who's up first? If it's Mrs Jacobs or Mrs Smyth, they both love Vivaldi.'

'It's Mrs Smyth,' said Emily, who started to walk out of the surgery, turned and half-smiled.

'And I'll bet she hates Vivaldi, if you bothered to ask, I'm off to the loo.'

SIX

'ANDY, are you doing a bit of moonlighting on the quiet?'

Polly's boss did a double take. It was early. 'Sorry. Come again Pol?'

She smiled at him, not wanting him to take her comments the wrong way. 'I wanted to know, have you got another job? You know, is owning your own business not bringing in enough cash? Times are hard.' Still Andy looked confused.

'You'll have to run it by me again, we're not on the same wavelength.'

'Well Andrew,' Polly said, sarcasm in her voice, before raising her eyebrows and moving closer to him. 'I went with Tom to the theatre on Friday night and a guy who was the leading man in the show was the spitting image of you. I said to Tom, that's Andy. Looks just like him.

'I never knew you had such a good singing voice, the trousers were a bit tight, mind you and probably how you hit the high notes so well.'

Polly nudged him, Andy shrugged. It was still too early. 'I don't know what you're talking about. I was at the greyhounds on Friday night. Lost £50. Oh, and don't tell the wife, that's between you, me and the bookies at Yarmouth.'

It was the Monday morning meeting at AR Gym, Spa & Leisure and the management team, of which Polly was one, was gathering. Owner, Andy Reynolds, a gruff northerner who had bought the business six years ago, was waiting patiently as his team arrived for their get-together. For all his gruffness Andy possessed a good sense of humour and Polly had a good relationship with him.

Polly had been one of the first to arrive, hence the conversation. She had already helped herself to a cup of coffee, as had Andy. The rest of the team began to appear, James (finance), Kevin (gym manager) and Valerie (Andy's PA). Spa manager Tina was on holiday. It was just before 9am.

Andy stood up. 'Okay, everyone, listen up,' he said. The rest of the group were all seated around a table that was circular and cosy enough for them to gather around.

'I want to make this short and sweet.' He looked across at Valerie. 'Yes, I know Val, *so his wife says?*' I'll get the gag in.' Valerie, all teeth, boobs and lipstick, giggled as Andy directed his 'double entendre' in her direction. Polly smiled at Val.

'So, let's crack on,' he continued. 'James, as it's the start of the month, a quick update on figures and finances please. Make it good news, can't be doing with drab stuff this early on a Monday morning.'

James was mid-20s, but looked older, mainly due to his 1960s-style retro sideburns. He stood up, his three-piece light blue suit, dark blue shoes and bright orange cravat making him glow like a beacon, and just how he liked it. Andy was happy for his staff to dress casually, it was a gym after all, but James wouldn't dream of it. He liked a suit, he liked to make a statement. As far as he was concerned, in the workplace at least, casual was not cool. A brilliant financial whizz kid, he enjoyed looking dapper and liked to impress.

He also had a wicked sense of humour.

'Okay, boys and girls, here we have it'. James was up and running, his camp voice rising and falling as he handed out the latest financial news. He and his partner David had been an item for two years now. Polly had met David on many occasions. He also had a great sense of humour, she could see why the pair got on.

James' input was invariably entertaining. Polly liked it when Andy asked him to go first it always broke the ice.

'Last month we gained 33 new members and lost 12, where did they go folks, we have to ask? Losing 12 paying customers is careless.' James put his hands out, palms up, to express such shock as he locked eyes with Kevin, who didn't smile.

'Of the new 33, all were full-paying members, while guest passes, the rates that naughty Andy put up last month if you remember peeps, were up by 40% Now, that's more like it and means a good March all round.

'Costs are stable and although we are spending money on a new hot tub in the Spa that was factored in last quarter, it's a profitable four weeks and a profitable first quarter all told. Up 12% year on year. I say we all go to Papa Pete's for pizza and lemonade at lunchtime. Wahooooo!!!. What say you Andy?'

You would never believe James was a financial boffin if you saw or heard him in this type of flamboyant form. In fact, he was the opposite of everything you would consider of in a man who spent much of his time studying spread sheets and crunching numbers. But he was good, very good. Oxford University-trained, he had a master's in business finance and maths. He knew his stuff.

Although what had got into him this morning was a mystery. He was always full of beans, but was acting even perkier today.

'God, he's excitable,' Polly whispered to Valerie. 'Hope he's not pregnant!' Andy, overhearing, frowned at them both.

'So, overall as I say, a good month and it's been a good start to the year.' James was delighted with the figures. 'Who knows we might all get a mid-term bonus darlings, as well as that lemonade and pizza.'

'Okay, okay, thanks James, that's great. If I want cabaret, I'll ask for it and if I want someone to spend my money on bonuses and pizza, I'll also ask.' Andy stood up. 'But sounds good news all round, thank you James.'

James grinned and sat down, almost knocking over Kevin's coffee as he did so.

'Careful, dickhead,' he growled. 'Watch what you are doing.'

Kevin was the gym boss. Tanned, thick neck, mid-30s, he wore the shortest shorts you could imagine and had little sense of humour. Even Valerie gave him a wide berth. He had spent five years in the army before deciding to duck out. He then spent three years studying PE at University, had become a personal coach and gained his current job at the gym a year ago. He wasn't the most popular member of the team. He could be as aggressive in meetings as he was grunting when lifting weights, but James never shied away from him, neither did Polly.

'No need for that language,' James retorted. 'Who got out of your bed this morning? Just you?' The two faced off.

Andy butted in. 'Okay guys settle down. Kevin, you got anything to add about the gym? Anything we should know?'

'Nothing to report really boss,' he said. 'We've got a couple of new sets of dumb bells coming in on Thursday and a new exercise bike, one of the latest from Germany. Trial model, should be good. The personal coaching classes on Tuesday mornings have gone well and I'm having to limit numbers to 10, or I don't feel people are getting VFM. That's no problem though, I might look to put on another class on Wednesdays.'

'Keep me informed on that,' Andy replied. Kevin nodded.

James had not been put off by Kevin's lambasting. 'Oooh, how exciting that sounds. Can I try one of those dumb bell things when they come in? I like a good pump!' James proceeded to move his arms up and down in a weightlifting fashion, much to Polly and Valerie's amusement. Kevin's face never cracked.

'James, have you taken something this morning?' Andy said. 'You haven't dipped that cravat in meths have you?'

James shook his head, took his handkerchief out and loudly blew his nose. Kevin wasn't impressed.

Andy continued; 'Okay, Kevin, is that it? Right, Polly, over to you, what's happening in marketing?'

'Well, we've got the Norfolk Leisure Academy coming over to see us on Wednesday with some ideas for their show in August and I booked a few radio ads last week, in a contra deal, so it's not costing cash.' Polly had been pleased with that deal. Anything to get publicity but not spend money was a win-win in her eyes.

'They are putting their leaflets promoting their shows in our reception and we are sponsoring the 'Farming News' at 8.30am and 9.30am every morning for a month. A little jingle, I haven't heard it yet. They are sending it over to me tomorrow.'

Kevin laughed. Polly looked up.

'Something funny Kev,' Polly stared across the table at him.

He chuckled. 'No, not really. Just thought isn't sponsoring the Farming News a bit odd for a Gym and Spa? What, we trying

to attract cows, goats and sheep to our Jacuzzis? And what is the jingle? Some pigs grunting in a field. *'Oink, oink, come to AR Gym!'*
Kevin chuckled again. But he was the only one in the team doing so. He and Polly never had hit it off. He cocked a smile at Andy. He was always looking for a good reaction from his boss, but the smile wasn't reciprocated. Polly wasn't smiling either.

'That contra deal is worth two grand in radio advertising for us, in exchange for a few leaflets in our reception.' Polly glared at him.

'I'm sorry, but I can't understand why that is even remotely funny. It's a good deal for the gym. I sometimes think your brains must be in those tight shorts you're wearing? The bulge is so tiny, I hope your missus can tell when you're excited to see her naked.'

James burst into laughter. Val bit her lip trying hard not to laugh. Polly continued to stare at Kevin who looked down at his shorts, then back up at her. He wasn't happy but couldn't think of a retort.

'Okay, that will do. Thank you Polly. Anyone got anything else to add,' Andy was half-smiling at Polly's response, but felt it best if the meeting was wound up.

'Can we add toad in the hole to the spa menu. Oh, and carrot sticks?' James said with a cheeky grin. 'Asking for a friend.'

Andy stood up and picked up his folder. 'Meeting over'.

As they all left, Polly and Val had a quick chat about a forthcoming video call that was taking place that afternoon. Polly had forgotten to mention it in the meeting. Not that it was a big deal, a sales rep from a beauty company wanted to get her products in the spa and, with Tina off, Polly would be doing the initial negotiations.

'Is 2.30pm okay?' Valerie looked at Polly.

'Absolutely fine. No problem. I hope Kevin is not too pissed with me.' Polly bit her lip. 'I shouldn't have said that about his small bulge. Do you know his missus? I don't.'

Val shook her head. 'Me neither, poor cow. That was funny though. Kevin spends too much of his time acting mister macho and trying to play the hard man, which he's not very good at . And then he takes the piss out of what you are doing, bringing money into the business. Bloody cheek. You didn't see Andy's face did you? I did. He started to crack up, then decided, best not to. Anyhow, come in and see me in Andy's office at 2.15pm and we'll get the lady on the line, I think Andy wants to talk to her afterwards as well, but he won't be there for the main chat. See ya later.' The two girls went their own ways.

Polly had made a steady climb up the career ladder in marketing. After leaving university in London, she had headed south to Brighton and got a job in marketing with a local radio station. But after she'd met Tom, it didn't take long for her to find another marketing job at Andy's gym. She was happy there.

She decided to walk into the city centre at lunchtime, the sun was shining and although she occasionally had her lunch at her desk at work, she would spend more days of the week taking a stroll and getting a bit of exercise. Norwich was a pretty city she always felt. She picked up a sandwich and a packet of crisps and sat down on a bench outside a watchmaker repair shop. It was quiet for that time of the afternoon. She called up Jody.

'Hello my darling,' said Jody. 'How are you?'

'I'm alright darling. Main thing is, how are you? I thought about you all last night after our chat about the IVF. I hope you are okay.'

'I'm okay, don't worry. I'm fine.'

'You're one tough cookie, Jode. I do love you.'

'Well, you have to be tough, don't you? You know, it sort of sinks in after a while and being the third time it hasn't worked, it sadly sinks in quicker than it used to. It's not a physical thing, it's more how I feel in myself, you know mentally. But as I said last night, I'm just going to get on with it and live my life, no good feeling sorry for myself. As Craig always says, 'what will be, will be'. I hate that saying, but he's right. Anyhow, how are you 'Miss Fight Club'? I couldn't believe what you were telling me about hitting that bloke, you little aggressive cow you.'

Polly laughed. 'I'm know. I'm not proud of it, one of my knuckles on the hand I hit him with has turned quite blue and bruised. I daren't show Tom. He didn't know whether to laugh or cry at the time. If I start showing off my 'war wounds', he won't find it funny, up to now I've got away with a small ticking off but he still thinks I shouldn't have got involved.

'I don't know what is wrong with me. I had a go at Kevin, our gym manager, this morning during the team meeting. He took the piss out of a radio ad I'm involved with and with that I implied he had small balls, I'm taking on all-comers at the moment. I mean it's not as if it's my time of the month.'

It was Jody's turn to laugh. 'You sure you're not going through 'the change' early? I've never been scared of you, but I'm starting to worry now. You remember that time in that nightclub in Brighton when those girls called me a slag and you threatened them, all three of them? You were thrashing about like a windmill. Bloody hell, you were so drunk. Don't tell the Kevin story to Tom tonight, he'll begin taking up self-defence lessons. You'll start to scare the shit out of him.'

'Don't say that. I'm starting to worry I might have a gene in me that sets me off. Perhaps I'm going to become a serial killer or something in the future, and I'm not aware of it yet.'

Both girls laughed. They so enjoyed each other's company.

'Anyway my darling, how's business up there in posh, leafy Chester? You got yourself a part on *'Real Housewives of Cheshire'*, yet? Tom reckons you'd be a shoe-in should you get an audition.'

'Oh, does he now? Well you tell him that I'll audition for *'Housewives'* if he auditions for *'Britain's Got Talent'* as the nation's first-ever cross-dressing, gay dentist! I'd love to see him in a dress, got sexy legs, your man.'

'You can tell him yourself. We're coming up next week, I hope. Well, I definitely am and I'm sure Tom will be able to get away, so we can get up to you on Friday. It will be so nice to see each other. So, how is business?'

'It's okay. Today this guy comes in and asks if I have any old pair of ten-pin bowling shoes. Do you know the ones? Really popular back in the 60s. They are like red/white/black, no grip underneath so you could slide as you bowled the ball.

'Anyhow, he was, well is, a big 'Jam' fan, you know, that pop group. They were big in the '80s. I don't know any of their songs, but they used to wear shoes like the old bowling ones, so he reckons. So, guess what? He only bloody found two pairs of them at the back of the shop behind some scarves, he had them both, even though only one was his size. 80 quid! I was happy with that. I have no idea where I got them from originally. I think it was a house clearance a couple of years ago. Oh, hang on, I've got customers, so got to go darling, call me tomorrow. Love you.'

'See you Jode. Take care. Love you.'

Polly stood up and carried on walking. She smiled to herself, how lucky she was to have a friend like Jody. She was sure they would both have kids one day.

Tom was home early, in fact he got home five minutes sooner than Polly, whose afternoon video call had been put back an hour, went on for an hour, before Andy then wanted a debrief for 30 minutes.

'Fancy eating out tonight,' Tom said as Polly walked into the kitchen. Neither of them had got anything out for tea and while the cupboards were full, it was a nice evening. Just the sort of night to take a trip out to a pub.

'Yeah why not?' Polly was always happy not to have to cook if she didn't have to! 'How about a Maccie D?'

'You must be kidding.' Tom blew out his cheeks. 'We're staying away from any McDonalds for a while. I'm still worried they might have the CCTV footage of you the other night. I hope not, I've got a responsible job you know. If you get caught and that young brat JJ, whatever his name was, decides to take you to court, imagine if you are found guilty. I can see the headlines now.

DENTIST'S WIFE'S BIG MAC WHACK!

She laughed out loud. Tom could be such fun, even though she always teased him, saying he had the most boring job. His humour had been one of the redeeming features that drew him to her. Dentists were not the most obvious people you would think of with a sense of humour, staring in people's mouths all day and saying 'Open Wide' was hardly stand-up comedy. But her Tom was an exception. He had been brought up in a loving and fun household and his university life had been rewarding and at times risqué. He had been friends with a group of boys and girls who, like many at Uni, partied as hard as they studied. He knew a good time.

They were soon on their way to the Harlequin, just outside Hethersett, about 10 miles from their home. The menu was good, the ambiance very much so, it had been a favourite of theirs for years.

It was a nice way to end a Monday. They enjoyed their food, chatted about their day, Polly taking Jody's advice and not mentioning the *'Kevin balls incident'*.

'So are we going to look to go up to Chester soon?' She looked at him as they drove home.

'Well, yes, I suppose so, when are you thinking? Because next Friday, I could leave off early, by 4pm.'

'Yeah, let's do it, next Friday,' Polly looked pleadingly at her husband. 'I'll take the day off. I can drive.'

Back home they fell into bed and although both were tired and content after such a good meal, drinks and chat, Tom made the first move as he glided his hand up and down Polly's leg. She was never going to pull away. There was no seven-year itch in their marriage.

Afterwards, they slept like babies.

SEVEN

'COME in Mrs Harding and take a seat. Mr Trustbrook will be with you soon.'

Karen was shown into a waiting area by a woman she assumed was Mr Trustbrook's secretary. The woman hadn't introduced herself, just opened the door and closed it swiftly afterwards. The room was small, but had a large window. It had two wooden, dark chairs and a table with some magazines scattered haphazardly. She thought about taking a look at them, but couldn't imagine any magazines outside a Headmaster's office would be ones she would likely read.

The summons for Karen to attend the school Tuesday morning had come yesterday afternoon after Lee had returned home. She had ended her shift at the pet shop at lunchtime and was preparing tea when Lee came in. It soon became clear all wasn't well, the phone call just before 5pm confirmed such and Karen confronted him. Lee confessed all. Well, he confessed his side of the tale, she suspected it wasn't the whole story.

Mr Trustbrook opened his office door. 'Good morning, Mrs Harding, please come in. Take a seat.'

His office was three times the size of the room she had been seated in. Mr Trustbrook went and sat behind a large rectangular table with photos of people she assumed were family. There was a window each side of him and a couple of cups/trophies on top of a cabinet that was filled with books. She had never met Mr Trustbrook, which was hardly surprising as Lee had only been at Alde Valley a month. She guessed he was late 50s, his voice was deep when he spoke.

'I don't know if you are sure what this is all about, but I'll guess you have a good idea, have you spoken to Lee?' Mr Trustbrook didn't look her in the face as he spoke.

'I have,' she said, refraining from calling him 'sir', even though she felt as though she ought, being in a school environment! 'I think I know what happened, or perhaps I don't, you tell me. But, yes I have spoken to Lee.'

Mr Trustbrook sat back wearily and took up the story. There had been some sort of confrontation between Lee and a group of boys, some who were older, the result being a black eye for one boy and cuts and bruises for another, as well as a strongly-worded e-mail from one of the boy's parents. Lee, who had escaped with little or no damage, had allegedly inflicted the wound/s, if the story was true, which was likely, as two teachers who had been in the vicinity at the time and had broken the fight up, had also concurred.

Norfolk was hardly 'The Bronx' and Lee was sure to have come up against far tougher boys his age in London. So, Karen was surprised, and disappointed in equal measure, that her son had got involved in a fight.

'Has Lee told you why the fight started?' Mr Trustbrook said.

Karen started to speak, but it was clearly a rhetorical question as he continued. 'Well, we only have the word of the boy who seemed to come off worse, the one with the black eye. But according to him it all began after a joke about you, Mrs Harding. Whatever was said Lee took exception, although now it seems no-one is willing to recall what was actually said. Anyhow, the boys argued and now we have the result of that 'fracas', bruised faces, egos and one parent clambering for me to sort it out. I have spoken to the teacher who split the fight up. I am speaking to you now and will be speaking to the other boys and Lee, and any parents who want to have an input. It will be a thorough enquiry.'

She was about to say something, but Mr Trustbrook put up his hand up. 'Look. For now, I'm telling you what I was told and I am fully aware in my years of experience in this job that there are two sides to every story. All I need to hear from you is what Lee told you. Did you tell him you were coming this morning? Is he in school today?

'Yes, Lee does know I'm here,' Karen said, getting a word in at last. 'And yes, he's in class. All he told me, as you said, is that one boy said something about me, but he won't tell me what was said. A fight started and another lad weighed in to help his mate, and now we have what we have. It's all very sad to be honest, we only moved into the school a few months ago as you know. This is out of character, I'm so surprised.'

'I'm sure you will understand I will have to take this seriously, Mrs Harding. I just hope no parents want to take it any further and will let the school sort it out. If you know what I mean?'

Mr Trustbrook got back to his feet. This meeting was clearly at an end but he hadn't finished. 'The boy with the black eye could have been badly hurt, Mrs Harding, he went to hospital, I don't know if you know that. Boys will be boys, I understand, but fights of this nature are very rare here at Alde Valley. Certainly in my 11 years as Headmaster I can count the number, including this one, on one hand. Let me talk to the other parents and boys, I will speak to Lee later today. Hopefully it will all be sorted with little fuss.'

And with that she was ushered out of the door.

Lee bounded in from school just after 4pm. 'Hi mum, I'm home.' He went to go upstairs to play his X-Box. Not that he was a big 'gamer'. He was more into playing football and rugby. Being outside was more enjoyable for him than sitting cocooned in his bedroom. But every night after school he did enjoy an hour or so with his mates, in their own virtual worlds. Karen, like many parents, didn't try to understand the point of it. It was what kids did these days.

However, tonight the computer could wait.

'Don't go up there please, I need to talk to you,' Karen's voice was firm enough to get her son's attention. He stopped half-way up the stairs and turned around.

'I saw Mr Trustbrook today. About the fight,' she looked at him to gauge his reaction. He gave nothing away.

'One of the parents has complained. Mr Trustbrook is not sure if another one will as well. I know we have gone over this, but you need to be straight with me if you want me to help you.'

'I don't want any help with this,' Lee shrugged his shoulders. 'What are you going to do to help me? It's done isn't it? I gave Dodie a thump and Josh got a push and he went over. That's it. Nothing to say. What do you want me to do? What does everyone want me to say? They asked for it, I wasn't the only person who thought so, ask Jessica Adams. She was standing right next to me when it kicked off. She said she would have done the same.'

Karen loved her son deeply but knew this situation wasn't going to be easy. She had always taken his side, always defended him and she would again and again, but she knew he was clamming up about what was said.

'All I'm asking is you to tell me what Dodie said that made you kick off. Why is it such a big deal? You said Jessica Adams would have done the same, what did he say that was so bad? Have I got to ask Jessica? I need to know the full story because Dodie will have his say. And he might even make something up about what happened and get you in more trouble. I know he said something about me but I can't believe you hit him because he said your mum was fat.'

She was pleading with Lee to open up. He looked at her, this wasn't easy for him.

'Well, if you want to know. I'll tell you.' He had turned round, half-way up the stairs and was looking directly at his mum who was standing at the bottom.

'We were fooling about, you know messing about, talking a load of nothing really. I don't like Dodie and we keep away from each other. But for some reason he just came over and started to push me about. Taking the mickey about the rugby team because I was substituted in the game last week.

'I can cope with that. But then he just said, well, he just said about, well, about me not, sort of, you know… Oh, this is all crap and is doing my head in.'

Lee was struggling to get the words out. Karen moved a couple of steps up the stairs to get close to him. 'What Lee, what did he say?'

'So, he came out with it,' he was looking away from his mum. 'He asked me what it is like having no dad? Okay. Happy now? He turned to look at her.

'And that was it,' she looked surprised. 'You hit him because of that?'

'No, that was just the start. Then he went on and on because I didn't answer him. He started saying he was surprised no bloke was living with us because you were, you know, like pretty and he said he fancied you and he'd like to have a go with you if there was no-one, and all this shit. I was walking away, then he just muttered loud enough for me to hear. 'So, no dad? That makes you a London bastard then.' He laughed and that was it, I just turned, ran up to him and hit him. Josh came over and I pushed him in the face and he fell over like a girl. Dodie was holding his face and Josh was, well also holding his face. One of the teachers came over and that was that, so I walked off.'

She sensed tears welling up inside her. Lee continued to stare, he had nothing left to say. After what seemed like an age, but was no more than a few seconds, she put out her arms.

'Come here darling. Come here, I love you so much. I'm so sorry, I'm so sorry.'

There were tears running down her cheeks as she embraced him. She held him tight and wouldn't let go. He kept a straight face throughout, he didn't want to cry. He didn't know whether he was glad or not his mum now knew why the fight started. He'd been uncomfortable repeating what Dodie had said, but at least now she knew.

'I want you to know darling, you have no idea how proud I am of you,' Karen had dried her eyes and was holding Lee's cheeks in her hands. 'Not that I'm saying you should go round thumping people.' She smiled at him. 'But sticking up for me like that, well, I don't want you getting into trouble, but it shows you are more of a man than most, sticking up for your mum and not putting up with being spoken to like that. And I love you for it. Don't you ever act like that idiot Dodie and bad-mouth people, you are right to stick up for yourself, I love you.'

Lee was relieved with his mum's reaction.

He was old enough now to be aware of some of the men who had been in his mum's life, and his life, who had come and gone. He was getting to the age where he was starting to understand it hadn't been easy for her. He didn't know everything and he had never broached the subject to his mum of who his dad was. He knew she would tell him in good time.

'I will tell you about your father, I promise,' Karen said, still holding him. 'Please give me more time. Please forgive me for not telling you by now. I promise you, you will know everything, don't let those lads get to you, you're bigger than them.'

He kissed his mum on the cheek. They had a close bond. He trusted her, they were all each other had. He would fight any battle to protect her. And she would him.

Lee knew his mum would tell him when she was ready.

EIGHT

JODY was in the kitchen, pair of scissors in one hand, a string of sausages in the other. She wasn't expecting Craig home until 6.30. She would prepare a stir fry and include his favourite, Lincolnshire sausages.

'Alexa. Play music by The Jam.'

'*Music by The Jam from Spotify*', said the circular object sitting on the windowsill to the left of the Aga. And with that a rendition of '*Eton Rifles*' reverberated around the kitchen. Not that Jody knew the song.

She was pretty sure it wouldn't be her type of music and she wasn't wrong. She had heard of The Jam but couldn't name any of their records. After listening for a couple of minutes she'd heard enough. The understanding of why anyone would want to buy two pairs of shoes because it reminded them of music like this was beyond her. Still, £80 was £80, she wasn't complaining.

'Alexa, play Radio One'.

It was four days since her IVF had failed and Jody had contacted the clinic to tell them the news. As usual they were wonderful and caring in their response.

'If you want to come in and talk to anyone here, please do feel free,' the lady at the clinic had said. 'Don't worry about making appointments, just give us a call and come in and see us.'

But it never got any easier. The fact that after the first treatment Jody had fallen pregnant but lost the baby at 10 weeks was heart breaking enough. However, it had given them both hope that it would work again, and through to a full term next time, but that hadn't happened.

Poor Craig. He had been in control of very little throughout the cycles. He had hugged Jody so tightly last Thursday when he returned home and saw her red eyes, he had known immediately she had been crying and he knew why, she didn't have to say anything.

At least their weekend had been upbeat. They had enjoyed Sunday lunch at Jody's parents, who lived in Chesterfield. They hadn't told them they had gone for another cycle of IVF, so the conversation never went there. That night Jody had spoken to Polly on the phone, while Craig did some spreadsheets for his work, he was on the road part of the week ahead, near Carlisle.

Craig's car pulled up in the drive, his music still loud enough for Jody to hear when he turned the engine off. She smiled through the kitchen window as she watched him get out.

'Ah, Delia, Delia, pray tell me Delia, what have you cooked today?' He plonked a bottle of red wine on the kitchen table and a bunch of flowers in his wife's hand and gave her a kiss as he walked in. 'Let me guess, sausages, of the Lincoln variety!'

She laughed. 'I haven't even put them on yet, how did you know we were having sausages?'

'My love. You are nothing if not predictable. A wonderful wife and cook. A wonderful lover and seller of retro stuff that no-one else could sell or want. You've also left an empty packet of sausages on the side, just over there and I can see they say Lincolnshire!'

She laughed again. Despite all the pressure and hurt of IVF, Jody felt she had a rock in Craig.

'How are you feeling today?'

'I'm okay. I felt a bit tired this afternoon, so I closed the shop up at 4 but the city wasn't that busy anyway, although I had a good day, took nearly £400.'

'£400 in a day, that's superb. If you carry on like that, I'm heading closer to early retirement. Days on the golf course with Bob, months away in Spain with Tom. Can't wait.'

'What do you mean months away in Spain with Tom? What about me and Polly? You aren't going without us.'

He frowned. 'My dear if you think Tom and I are going to take our life in our hands with that mad woman, your friend, who is clearly liable to start a fight at any given opportunity, in any bar, in any city, in any country, in any phone box, any drive-through, you can think again.' He smiled. 'Boys need time on their own on occasions.

'Anyhow, Tom and I need to go out to Spain soon, to paint his apartment.'

'Paint his apartment.' Jody laughed. 'Since when? You two. The DIY twins. That'll be the day. I can't wait to tell Pol this. How are you intending to paint it, by numbers?'

He shook his head, although she had a point. DIY had never been one of Craig's hot topics. Tom was pretty hopeless at it as well. Indeed there was a hilarious story that did the rounds between the four of them of when Tom put up a shelf in his bathroom. It collapsed under the weight of two tubes of shower gel and some hand cream, cracking the bath below. Polly had been left unimpressed. 'A bloody £6.99 shelf ended up costing us £400 because we now need a new bath. That's no sex for him for a month.'

'Okay, okay, so we may not paint the *whole* apartment,' admitted Craig. 'We may just flick a feather duster over it and wash it, but we will have to go to check out that some of your favourite restaurants are all still open. You wouldn't want us to go over in the summer and find out that 'The Roadster' had been turned into a Tourist Advice Centre or a Barcelona FC Club Shop, now would you? It's you we are thinking of, not ourselves.'

'Baldini, you are a liar and a fibber and I love you. Now, go have a shower, dinner is in 20 minutes.'

Dinner had been a delight and Craig was trying to get Jody to sit down while he did the washing up, but she insisted on helping.

Their house was big and modern, had five bedrooms with a large garden and hot tub. Neither were gardeners and they had the luxury of being able to afford someone to come and prune the hedges and cut the grass every other week. They had a cleaner as well, who came in every Friday, spent the morning in the house. For £40 it was well worth the cost.

As they stood at the sink, he looked across at her. All they had ever wanted since they got married was to have a family of their own, but it wasn't happening. The frustration was compounded because neither of them had any reasons why it should not be the case. Nature just wasn't taking its course. They weren't getting any younger either, Jody was nearly 37 and her body clock was ticking. Craig was a year younger.

'What shall we do next?' Jody looked lovingly at her husband.

'I don't know, have you got the ice cream out? And do I see a little toffee cheesecake on the side over there?'

'Not dessert you plonker, IVF, do you want to talk about it? You don't have to.' Her voice was calm as she put her arm around him.

'All I want is a family, a baby with you. It's no good me saying I don't want to talk about it because I do. I'm just better talking about it than bottling it up. But sometimes I worry about you. This isn't just about me you know, I care about your feelings, darling.'

'I know you do, but you are the one putting your body through this. You are the one who is having to do so much. My role is pretty simple, in fact it's really over now. You know what I mean? I'll talk about it, of course I will.' They smiled at each other.

'I want to ask you something,' Jody said. 'It's something I am really not sure what you are going to think of, so please shout me down if it's a no.'

'What is it?' He looked concerned.

'How about we get a surrogate to carry our baby?'

'A surrogate?' That took the wind out of his sails. 'I'd never thought about that, but obviously you have. What makes you say that?'

'I don't know. I just think we are capable of producing a baby, it's just me perhaps not able to carry one. You are not saying no though are you? Because if you do, that's fine with me.'

Craig hesitated. 'Okay, look into it and see what it entails. I'm right alongside you and I'm not saying no, let me think about it.'

Later that night they watched a Netflix film, some American sniper thing that Craig was always saying was similar to one that was similar to one he had seen before. Quite why they kept watching them Jody could never understand.

When the film finished Jody, who had fallen asleep during the last 20 minutes, headed to bed as Craig got up to turn the television off. He was about to press the off button when a face appeared on screen. He froze as the TV reader spoke. *'A Liverpool man is starting a 25-year prison sentence for drugs offences after admitting a string of dealings in and around the Liverpool, Manchester and Cheshire area,'* the newsreader said.

'Stuart Archer, a former security guard, admitted the charges in December last year. He was sentenced today at Warrington Crown Court. Archer was the head of a mafia-style gang who operated in and around Merseyside and The Wirral, importing, dealing and distributing drugs. He had admitted more than 60 offences and police say their enquiries are still on-going. A police spokesman said they expected more arrests.

'In other news.....'

Craig continued to look at the man's picture on the TV.

His chest tightened.

NINE

'YOU are going to do what? Are you sure? That's a hell of a thing.'

Polly was returning Jody's call during her coffee break at work. Jody had left a voice message asking her to call back *'ASAP. I've got something to tell you'*.

'Surrogacy. Okay, well, that's great if that's what you and Craig are thinking of. But why have you thought about that? When did you decide? What does Craig think? Polly was firing questions, hardly drawing breath, having heard her friend's idea.

Both girls had known couples who had gone down the IVF route, but Polly knew of no-one who had gone down the surrogacy one, she wasn't sure Jody did, either. Polly thought surrogacy was one of those things you just read about in celebrity magazines, the sort of thing rich people did.

'Craig and I chatted about it last night. We are going to look into it.' But Jody didn't sound confident, Polly thought.

'I don't know if I can go through another IVF cycle, I don't know if I can take another upset. Craig has been wonderful. It's up to me, he keeps saying. Of course he will support me, we'll support each other. We are only starting out on the thought process of surrogacy though, I just wanted to speak to you, see what you think.'

'Well, it's up to you both. I'll support you, you know that. How are you thinking of doing it?'

'What do you mean?'

'Well, there are different ways of surrogacy aren't there? Or am I a bit behind the times?'

'Oh, I see. Well, a surrogate mother would carry my egg fertilised by Craig. That's about as far as we really discussed it to be honest, what we do next, if anything, I don't really know.'

'Who would you get to carry it?' Polly regretted the question the second she finished the sentence.

'I don't know, Pol.' Jody was slightly irritated with the bombardment. She had only wanted Polly's thoughts, not a Spanish Inquisition. 'We only started talking about it last night, I haven't even thought about who might carry it. Sorry, I don't mean to sound annoyed darling, but are there people who do it as a profession? Do we get someone we know? Am I right to keep going, keep wanting to start a family? Or should I just give it up and accept we will never have kids? This is starting to do my head in.'

Jody's voice was less certain now. She was wondering whether she should have taken stock of the situation instead of calling up Polly so quickly after her and Craig had discussed the matter. Then again, she was her best friend, they shared everything.

'If you want to go for it, you go girl,' Polly perked the conversation up. 'You are a strong couple, you are going to do this. You two keeping talking it through. You will make the right decision. If you want my opinion, I'll say whatever you do, both make sure you want to do it. I'm thinking of you so much, you are so brave, so determined. I love you.'

'I love you to Pol, and thanks, you're right.'

'Look, give us a call again tonight Jode. Sorry to cut you off. This is so important what we are talking about, but I'm running late for another one of Andy's bloody meetings and he's in a funny mood today, not funny ha, ha, either. I have never met anyone so obsessed with meetings as he is. Tom reckons he just fancies me and wants to keep meeting up. That's a laugh! So, you okay if I go?'

'Yeah, I'm fine. No, you get going, speak later. And if Andy does come on to you, remember one of your karate moves.' Jody laughed. Polly was glad the conversation had ended on a high.

'Don't say that. I told you the other night, I'm starting to get paranoid.'

You would have thought, bearing in mind the positive financial position AR Gym, Spa & Leisure found itself in, Andy would be in a good mood. He wasn't. Quite what side of the bed he got out of this morning, neither Polly nor James were sure, but he appeared more gruff than usual, not helped by the fact the Jacuzzi was again out of action and the company who repaired it were unable to come until Saturday morning, three days away, to fix it.

'Okay, Polly, James, thanks for coming, where's Val? Is she coming? Andy was abrupt and to the point. Polly didn't like meetings like this when he could be arsey.

'No, I saw her at lunchtime. She's arranging interviews for the assistant gym manager's position with Kevin,' Polly replied.

'Let's get on then. Okay, the reason I wanted to chat to you two is that I'm thinking of opening a vegan-style restaurant on site. Aside from our current one, I want a 'green area', where it's vegan and vegetarian food only. I wanted your thoughts Polly from a marketing perspective. How easy would it be to market? I wanted you here James for a bit of financial advice.'

'I say, how delicious.' James was dressed in white trousers and a green shirt, with a white handkerchief sticking out of the breast pocket. 'I love a bit of vegan. David is vegan, won't have processed sausages to save his life. I love a meat sausage, he won't entertain one.'

Polly wasn't sure if this was the time and place for any 'sausage' stories from James. Andy wasn't looking amused.

'Thanks James, I'm thrilled to hear about you and David's sausage preferences,' he said curtly. 'So, I'm guessing from that, you think it could be a good idea?'

'I do. Seriously, vegan is the in thing. Loads of people are finding goodness in it and especially young people, they are the ones who are really keen on vegan food. All that travelling around the world eating beans and green shoots is converting them. Saving the planet, no red meat, and all that. Personally, I love meat.' James raised his eyebrows at Polly and grinned. 'And I'm not a great lover of all those beans and lentils and stuff, only baked beans. I do love them. But David cooks vegan food like a top-notch Jamie Oliver and it does taste delicious. Even I now struggle to know a kidney bean from a butter bean.'

Polly smiled: 'How can you struggle to know that? Kidney

beans are red and butter beans are white.'

'Are they?' James looked surprised. 'Well, there you go, that just shows how good a cook David is because I can't tell the difference.'

'We are straying off the subject here,' said Andy who, as usual, was being tolerant with James.

He turned to Polly. 'Okay, Pol, marketing a vegan/vegetarian restaurant. Would it be easy? I mean, I don't know, would it put people off? Would they think we are all green? I know what Kevin is going to say, he's a steak and chips man. He'll say we are bowing to the minorities, but are we? Do you think people will go for it?'

'We're not bowing to minorities. James is right. Vegan and green food is the in thing, especially among young people, I think it's a great idea.' Polly could see the opportunities. 'Why not have a green restaurant? We can market ourselves as the Leisure Spa & Gym that has it all. Whether your taste is a sausage sandwich or bean and herb wrap, we cater for you. What's not easy to promote about that? We could have loads of ideas, loads of promotions, nothing not to like about the idea.'

Andy relaxed. He was beginning to enjoy the vibes of the meeting, in fact he was enjoying himself for the first time today. A day that had got off to a bad start after an early morning argument with his wife had seen him slam the front door with her words, *'are you ever going to decorate this bloody kitchen'*, still ringing in his ears.

He was glad he had Polly in his team, she was always so positive. In all the years she had been marketing manager within the business, he could only think of one occasion they had any sort of altercation, and that was when Andy laughed at an upcoming trip her and Tom were taking to Vietnam. 'Isn't that where they eat dogs?' He had laughed during a team meeting after Polly announced her holiday. A big animal lover, Polly hadn't found it funny. Indeed when he had pushed the subject further mimicking about a 'Collie on toast', that was it. Polly's eyes flashed. 'Excuse my language Andy and I hope you don't mind, but don't be a fucking moron,' she had said. And duly walked out!

Andy went to find her to apologise, but she wasn't having it. For him, it was clear his marketing manager had a great sense of humour, but only to a point. She wasn't a woman to be crossed.

For all James' frivolity, he too was a valued member of the team. When it came to the nitty-gritty of money, he was as good a financial man as you could wish for, and a 'yes-man' James was not.

'How much are you thinking of spending on building the restaurant?' James said. 'I assume that's why I'm here, unless you want to know my thoughts on vegan sausage rolls!'

'No, not fussed about you and vegan sausage rolls,' Andy replied. 'Initially thoughts are about £50K to build it and then I'll obviously need someone to run it. How are we cash-flow wise?'

'As I said earlier this week, we are in a good place and have enjoyed a good month. Year on year we are up and have a good cash surplus, about £44K at the moment. One of our bigger loans for the upgrade of the wet room only has four more months to run, we could tag the restaurant on the end of that for a few years. So long as business doesn't take a sudden downturn, it's your call, but I can't see any danger.'

That was good enough for Andy, who stood up, picked up his papers which he had placed on the table, but not looked at, and went to leave. He was always a man who was very good at looking busy, rarely did he appear to have a minute in the day to spare.

'Okay, you two, keep this conversation under wraps for now please,' he said.

'Bean or sweet chilli?' James grinned.

'Bean or sweet chilli what?' Andy looked blank.

'Bean or sweet chilli wrap,' James giggled. 'Which one do you want us to keep it under?'

Polly laughed. James smiled.

'Very good James,' Andy said sarcastically. 'For now, neither of you say anything to the rest of the staff. It's not a state secret, but I don't want the idea out there and then we have to shelve it.' And with that he walked out shaking his head, but smiling.

James and Polly were left looking at each other. She smiled.

'Bean or sweet chilli? You do make me laugh James.'

TEN

IT had been a busy day at the surgery.

Mrs Tynehurst and her young boys had been the first patients of the day, 8.30am. That way she managed to get them to school a few minutes late, but nothing untoward and then herself off to work. While her time in the chair was no more than a minute, she had a filling just a month ago, her boys, Ollie 10, and Sam, eight, were there longer. Not that they needed anything to be done, but Tom wanted to have a look at how their teeth were developing before giving them a quick brush and a few words on why it was best not to eat too many sweets, the signs were there.

'Open wide,' Tom said, as Emily passed him his dental mirror. Ollie went first. 'Let's see what we've got here. Been eating many sweets have you?'

The boys were cheeky lads and couldn't get their mouths open wide enough when Tom had asked! When they were each in the chair, they shook their heads vigorously at the mention of sweets. They must have hoped Tom believed them.

Ollie and Sam both had blond hair and were mad keen footballers.

'You still supporting Arsenal?' Ollie looked at Tom as the boys got their coats back on ready to leave. 'Why do you support them, they're useless?' It was Sam's turn to pipe up.

Mrs Tynehurst was about to reprimand the pair of them, but Tom enjoyed having a bit of fun. They were bright and sparky and took him back to the days when he and his best mate at school, Johnny Luckhurst, used to behave as kids. The pair were always getting into scrapes. One Halloween, they decided against treats and played only tricks on unsuspecting households, their party piece was placing Sellotape over people's door bells to make them stick and keep the bell ringing.

After doing 'the deed', the pair would run and hide and watch the reactions on the faces of the people opening the door as they wondered what on earth was going on and why no-one was about, as their bells continued to make a racket. It was harmless fun, until Johnny split his shin open as he dived over Mr Joseph's fence one year when they were both 11, Johnny could hardly walk and there was blood everywhere. Explaining it to Johnny's mum, who picked them up near the church after the boys found a telephone box to call home, was hopeless. They agreed on a story that the boys had been playing football and Tom had caught him with a tackle. It would have been fool-proof, but the lack of a football with the excuse that they had 'lost it', scuppered their story.

Back in the surgery, Tom looked at the Tynehurst boys. 'So, who do you two support, then?'

'Norwich City of course.' Sam piped up. 'We both do.'

Tom smiled. Many of his patients were Norwich fans.

'Norwich are no good.' He winked at Mrs Tynehurst as the boys took the bait.

'Yes, they are, yes, they are,' the boys protested. 'Better than Arsenal'.

'Let's get off to school shall we boys?' Their mum spoke up. They both gave Tom a high-five as they left.

Emily smiled at Tom. 'You are good with those boys. You should have kids.'

'Heavens no. There's still way too many pubs to visit, restaurants to eat at, countries to explore and fast cars to drive. Imagine all that coming to an end if Pol and I had kids, I don't think so.'

'Well, I'd love to have kids. I won't hang around too long, I mean can you imagine not having kids by the time you are 30?' Tom raised his eyebrows!

Jill was feeling and looking better and Tom was glad to see it. He had worried that night after she had told him about the row she'd had with Robert. It was none of his business but he felt protective towards her. He had no idea why. Maybe it was because he had seen his parents argue, not a great deal, but enough for him to remember. His childhood was, on the whole, fun, but his mum had been the home-loving water-carrier, his dad a hard worker and too often oblivious to the needs of the family unit. When his mum and dad did collide, it hadn't been nice.

'Morning Jill. Sorry I didn't catch you first thing, but I went straight upstairs. The little Tynehursts were in, as you saw.' He smiled at her. 'Everything alright with you and, well you know, Robert?'

'He's gone,' Jill said, catching Tom unawares.

'Gone? Who's gone?'

'Robert. He's gone, vanished, buggered off, scarpered. However you want to phrase it. And bloody glad I am too.' She looked up from her computer.

'The rat was seeing another woman. That's what the argument was about the other night. It's been going on for about six months and I had no idea. I caught him out because he had a bus ticket in his coat pocket, and I had never seen him on a bus for 20 years. He wouldn't know a bloody bus if it ran over him. But if catching a bus means the chance of a quick shag, then clearly he'll catch one. And that's what he has being doing.'

Tom didn't know what to say. Jill hadn't finished.

'I confronted him about the ticket and a few other little things that were stacking up lately, like his sudden love of having a bath, which was odd considering I'd only known him have about four baths in all our years together, smelly git. Anyhow, long story short, I told him to get lost and take his stinky clothes with him. He's obviously in love with this tart, whoever she is. So he's gone, I told him I'll see him in court.'

Tom looked blank. It was an interesting start to the morning. Polly would laugh her head off when he told her, she loved nothing more than a strong woman kicking a man up the backside.

Jill smiled. 'So there you go. Anything else?'

'Well, that's err, that's fine. So long as everything is okay, that's, well, great. I'm a bit surprised I must say, I always thought you and Robert were close. We all have odd rows.'

Jill took her hands off the keyboard and looked up at him. 'Robert is a hairy-arsed dick with his brains in his pants. I should have done this years ago, you have no idea what a lazy pain he is. And as for his bedroom habits? You don't want to know. Now, do you want a coffee?' And with that Jill went into the kitchen to put the kettle on.

Karen had the phone in her hand but was having second thoughts. They would be closing soon, if they weren't already.

Lee had been given a set of detentions by the school for his behaviour in the playground fight. Both the other boys and their parents had decided to drop the complaint and leave the punishments to Mr Trustbrook to sort out. He had done so, giving all the boys a good flea in their ears, before telling Lee he was to spend the next five Fridays after school in detention for an hour. Each detention would see him write out lines, lots of them.

She knew it could have been worse, although Lee didn't see it that way as rugby practice was on Fridays after school and he would miss it. That was something Mr Trustbrook was well aware of and that was exactly why he decided on the punishment. Mr Robin, the rugby master, could blow a gasket as much as he liked that one of his best players was missing training. In Mr Trustbook's world, discipline was more important for the development of a young man, than playing sport. That was his mantra. Sport and PE were low on his curriculum barometer.

Karen took another look at the number.

She would phone tomorrow.

ELEVEN

The Queen's Head at Melsham was a popular pub.

It had a good menu, not cheap and cheerful, but varied and most who ate there thought it good value. It also had a fine range of beers, especially cask ales, that attracted many folk from around the county, and it had an ambience that could be as serenely quiet and peaceful as it could be noisy and flirtatious.

The people of Melsham supported their pub. Jan and Paul Johnson, the owners, had been at the helm for more than three years and had not just transformed it into a thriving business, but made it into one the regulars of the village were proud of, while visitors appeared to enjoy the pub's fayre if the comments on their Facebook page were anything to go by.

The Queen's Head dated back to the 12th century and was said to be a stopping point for smugglers who had landed on the north Norfolk coast and were making their way down towards London with their booty. It had a rich history, although how many of the stories of highwaymen, smugglers and young boys, who were supposedly used as bait for the local constabulary to catch thieves in the 1800s, were true, was open to conjecture. But it was a good yarn.

'I'm going over the pub now,' said Tom. 'Some of the boys are having a game of darts and I said I'd be over. Take your time and come when you are ready.' Tom and Polly were one of a group of friends who met regularly on a Friday night at the Queen's Head. They had been doing so for a couple of years. Most were couples. At the end of a hectic week they all loved nothing more than a night out to relax and have a catch-up. For Tom and Polly it was just a 300-yard walk across the Green.

Numbers would vary. Their 'crowd' were aged between 28 and 39 and lived in the village. Most had jobs, some had children. No jokes were off limits, no dress taste was off limits. No egos were allowed. No-one should come down on a Friday if they weren't up for fun and have the piss taken out of them.

Some of the friends had closer relationships than others, while occasionally Jan and Paul would put on a karaoke or Open Mic night for a bit of fun. Last orders were at midnight, lock-ins were standard.

'I'll see you down there,' Polly called out. 'I've still got a couple of things to do.'

It was 8.30pm and some of the lads were meeting up for a game of darts. Not that Tom was any good. He had once joined a team at university but had only played one game after crashing his car on the way to his second match. He never played again, saying rather pathetically the association of the crash and darts was something he couldn't get over.

The pub was already busy when he walked in. Tom went over to a large circular table in the corner where he could already see Scottie and Ann, the Simmonds', Alison and Ben, the Smyth's, and Billy White, aka 'Milky', all seated.

'Open wide boys and girls, the doc is in.' Scottie had already had a couple of pints.

Tom went round shaking hands and fist-pumping the guys, while giving Ann and Alison a kiss. There was never the embarrassment of knowing or asking whose round it was, however many the numbers or however much you drank. Rules were simple. Each couple put £20 in the kitty. If you were on your own you put in a tenner. You wanted a drink, you took some money out and no-one abused it. Ben, a news journalist on the local paper, was 'kitty man'. How he had ever got the job, no-one was sure.

'Stick your money in there and get yourself a drink.' Ben was pointing to a large bowl in the middle of the table, the 'kitty pot'.

'Anyone else want a drink, while I'm up,' Tom said.

'I'll have another G&T,' said Ann, a mum of two hyper-active primary school boys, who were often seen with Scottie kicking a football on the village green, or throwing a rugby ball. No-one else wanted one.

Tom enjoyed his cask ale and the Queen's Head had a wonderful array. Cask ale was something he had got into at university. While most of his fellow students were knocking back lager, he was sampling a pint of 'Sheep's Nut', or 'Uncle Tom's Rock Ball Punch.'

He returned to the table with a pint of Adnams 'Broadside', as well as Ann's gin and tonic.

'So, are we busy?' Ben said looking at Tom. 'How's business in the world of 'Open Wide for 60 seconds then pay me £50'?'

'Very funny. I'm actually really busy,' said Tom.

'Everyone says they hate going to the dentist, but I can't seem to keep them away. I think it's the music I play in the surgery. People love it so much, they keep coming back for more. What is it about Vivaldi, or Fleetwood Mac? Plus the fact my receptionist has started giving away free lollipops to the kids. They love them of course but then have to come back for treatment in years to come because of all those worn cavities, keeps the old finances ticking over though. Alan Sugar would be impressed with my business acumen!'

'You don't give the kids lollipops, do you? You can't do that,' said Alison, who worked on the newspaper with Ben, as a sales executive. 'It's like giving people live hand grenades when they come out of the pictures after watching Rambo.'

'You've got to be proactive in this day and age,' Tom replied. 'You've got to keep them coming back'. He winked at Alison.

'Is Polly coming down later?' Alison looked at Tom. 'I wanted to ask her about joining her gym, she said she thought they may have a few offers on during May, and if so, I'd really like to sign up ASAP. I could do with a bit of gym work.'

'What do you want to join the gym for?' said Ben. 'You don't like all those weight machines and stuff. In fact you hate anything that involves a brisk walk, let alone any gym work. A walk to the pub being an exception, of course. Anyhow, if you are going to go, I'll join with you.'

'Who says I want to join to just go in the gym. It's the Jacuzzi, sauna and wet room I'm would like to go in, so you mind your own business, and no you are not joining with me. I need a bit of space at times, bad enough we work together. Plus, you never know who you might bump into in a wet room. Some hunky city boy with a six pack, looking for a bit of fun. How does that sound Ann?'

'Yes please,' Ann grinned and raised her eyebrows. Where are the membership forms? I'll text Pol to make sure she brings some with her.' The pair laughed.

'Why do they call it a wet room?' Milky was good at changing the tone of the conversation. 'Is it because it's wet? Or do you have to be wet to go in there, like sort of hosed down first, or had a swim or something?'

Everyone loved Milky. He was part of the group and the only single person in it, although he'd known a few girls, some he called girlfriends. He just couldn't seem to keep them. While many of the couples were only down the Queen's Head once a week, Milky was a regular, every night, rain or shine. *Four pints of lager and a packet of crisps please,'* was his regular night out.

He was a one-off and very much his own man. He was also one of the most popular people in the village, although to say he wasn't the sharpest tool in the box was an understatement, and while most of the Friday night crowd enjoyed professional, highly skilled jobs, Milky did not. He 'ducked and dived'. You wanted a fence putting up, or a room decorated, or a patio laid, or a bit of help behind the bar, Milky was your man. The entrepreneurial village idiot.

He lived next door to the pub and had a dog called Fourre, a greyhound he had rescued from a greyhound trust centre. It was called Fourre because, 'it's got four legs!'

'Is Pol coming down tonight? You didn't say.' Alison looked again at Tom.

'Yes, she is. She's probably caking herself with some new make-up stuff she has been flogged by a sales rep at the gym today. She struck quite a deal apparently and it came with a mass of free samples.'

'I do hope so,' said Milky. 'I'm going to thrash her at darts tonight.'

The door of the pub opened and Janie and Stuart Betts walked in. Stu was a firefighter, while Janie was, like Ann, a mum. A very new one, their baby Jacob had been born four months ago and this was only their second night out since.

'Hi everyone. We've got a babysitter. We've got a babysitter,' Janie was flinging her arms around as though she had just won the lottery. 'I'm gonna' get pissed. Now get me a bottle of cider, before mum calls to say Jacob has woken up and she can't get him back down.' Stu obliged his wife with her drink, while getting one for himself and plopping his £20 change into the kitty pot. As a firefighter he had a wicked sense of humour, it was the only way he and many of his colleagues made a job that could be stressful and upsetting, work for them. He had seen plenty of sights he wouldn't wish on his worst enemy. His humour could be dark.

'Hi friend, you okay?' Stu said shaking Tom's hand.

'Yeah, I'm fine mate. How are you? Hopefully you haven't been busy. Just a cat up a tree is all we want to hear about, not any bad stuff.'

'It's been pretty quiet to be honest. Although had a bit of a funny episode on Tuesday night mind you. I've simply got to tell you this. Come over here, Scottie, listen.' Scottie leant across as Stu began.

'We were called to what looked like a small fire on the side of the road just off the A11, near Thetford Forest. Anyhow, we get there, just one pump is needed. It's about 10.30pm by the time we put the fire out. It's no big deal and one of the boys goes off to take a leak. He comes back and says there are a load of cars in a clearing about 300 yards away. He's curious what it's all about, so runs over to take a closer look, only reckons he sees someone's arse up against a window and reckons it's a bloody dogging site!'

Tom and Scottie laughed. 'In the forest?' said Tom. 'Nice.'

'Anyhow,' Stu continues. 'One of the other boys who fancies himself as a bit of a lad, likes to play tricks, heads off towards the cars, gets about 20 yards away then crawls on all fours up to the nearest car and looks in. Apparently he's ready to pull a face and scare the shit out of the people in the car, but claps eyes on the girl, who turns around. It's his bloody sister! Can you believe it? His bloody sister is dogging. You couldn't make it up.'

'My God, that's unreal,' Scottie exclaimed. Tom half spits his drink out.

'Are you kidding us? No, bloody way.'

'Seriously,' Stu continued. 'It's true. She screams and all hell breaks loose. She jumps out of the car, shocked as shit, half naked and chases her brother a little way before stopping. She recognises him and shouts out his name, but he's not hanging around. He hurtles back to us and tells us to get started up and get of here. We ask what's happened. When he tells us, we all want to go and have a look, but he says, 'piss off', the screaming has alerted all the cars and everyone is on the move. They think we're the cops, can you imagine going dogging and your bloody brother turns up to watch you in action?'

The three roared.

'Apparently his sister is *'a bit of a girl'* according to him, if you know what I mean. In fairness she's with her boyfriend, dogging is something they obviously do, but this lad had no idea. Can you imagine the looks around the Sunday lunch table next time when they all sit down for 'meat and two veg'?

'That's a hell of a story,' Scottie laughed. 'Ben come over here. You will love this, print it in your paper or on that web site you have. That will put hits up.'

Stu relayed the story to Ben, who also laughed out loud when he heard the finale. The girls wanted to know what had happened. They all found it just as funny when Stu repeated it for a third time, but were left gobsmacked when Janie said she wouldn't mind doing a bit of dogging with Stu; 'It could be quite fun,' she said.

Stu didn't need a second invitation. 'Count me in baby. Just make sure you wear your extra high heels though,' he laughed. Ann wasn't so impressed and turned her nose up at the thought.

'You'd love it,' said Scottie. 'We'd make a great team me and you. Come on, we've been married six years now, why not a bit of fun? I wouldn't mind. We can go with Stu and Janie and put our cars next to each other. Better not take the Fiat 500 though, be hell of a squash.'

'You are joking,' said Ann, looking shocked. 'If you think I'm having people watch you shag me in the back of a Fiat 500, you've got another think coming Scott Simmonds. Anyhow, the time it takes you to do it these days, our car's MoT will have run out.'

The group laughed once more. Scottie nodded his head! 'In fairness, that's quite funny, my dear,' he said.

Milky listened in but didn't really understand what 'dogging' was. 'So, could I take Fourre to this dogging thing? Is it any type of dog can go? Can rescue dogs enter?'

There was more laughter, but before anyone could put Milky out of his misery, Ben got up and was throwing some darts. None of the players, only Tom, had ever played for a team, but they all liked to think they had great darting skills.

'Okay, who's in?' said Ben. Everyone? Alison, you playing?

'No, you boys play first, we'll get another drink in and play later,' Ann and Janie were also happy with that idea. The dogging debate was still in full flow.

'That must be one of the funniest stories I've heard in ages,' Janie said looking at her husband, who was about to get up to play darts. 'Why didn't you tell me earlier?'

'I didn't want to over-excite you my darling. Anyhow, that's enough of all that, you've marked your card and I heard what you said. We'll take the Range Rover and go tomorrow night, if we can get a babysitter again.' Janie gave her husband a thumbs up.

Polly was putting her shoes on. It was 9.25pm and she was ready to go to the pub. As usual she was looking glamorous, a short black skirt and red top. She put on her long black coat. She wore high heels. Just as she was leaving, the phone rang.

'Hello, Polly Armstrong,' Polly said. There was no reply.

'Hello, who is it? Hello, hello.' Still nothing.

Polly put the phone down. *'Another bloody sales call'*, she thought, *'at this time on a Friday night. Firms must be getting desperate.'*

Ten minutes later she marched into the pub where the hellos greeted her. She was hugely popular among the girls and you could see their faces light up when she walked in. She was also the only girl who could keep up with the boys drinking wise. But she could be the funniest person as well. She was certainly the most attractive, something that never went unnoticed by the rest of the blokes.

'You're punching so far above your weight Tom, it's bloody embarrassing,' Stu had once told him.

'She must have been so pissed when she met you,' Ben had said.

Indeed everyone agreed, Tom was one lucky fella. He didn't argue.

'So, Pol, what can we get you?' Ben had some darts in his hand, but was near the bar.

'Ah, a glass of wine please, Ben, dry white. The usual.'

'Large or very large,' he called out at the bar, as Jan waved over to Polly, mimicking with a pint glass in her hand. 'The usual Jan,' Polly laughed.

The darts was progressing well. They played 'round the clock', which meant you started with a double, then went, 1, 2, 3 up to 20, before finishing with a 25 and then bull. The final stages of the competition took an age to finish, with no-one able to get a 25, let alone a bull. It was early in the night and no-one was rushing.

'I'm seeing a girl,' Milky suddenly announced to Tom as they stood waiting for their throw.

'Are you? Do we know her? Hey guys, Milky is seeing a girl.'

The boys gathered round. They were all curious and pleased for him, in equal measure.

'She's nice, but I don't think you know her,' said Milky. 'She's Chantelle, works in the city, next to that Tesco Express place in the High Street. She asked me for my mobile number and called me last week, we're going out tomorrow night to the pictures, to see Peter Rabbit 2.'

Milky had enjoyed a few girl 'associates' over the years and the group were always keen to find out how his love life was getting on. He was 39 now, slim with glasses and dark curly hair, he wasn't ugly, but he was hardly George Clooney.

'Peter Rabbit 2,' exclaimed Tom. 'Isn't that a bit, sort of a bit young to take a woman to go and see?'

'Oh, she's not very old.' Milky replied, a comment that concerned Tom for a second. 'She's only about 28 or something.'

Tom was relieved to hear that. 'So, why does she want to see Peter Rabbit, if she's nearly 30?' Tom was baffled.

'She doesn't. That's what I want to see. She said, I was to choose the film.' Ben shrugged his shoulders. 'Why not Milky lad? Why not indeed?'

Meanwhile, Polly and the girls were chatting away about babies, work, the dogging story and Polly's recent 'fight night at the O.K. McDonalds drive through', which had made its way into village gossip after one of the cars in the parking bay that night, belonged to Mrs Curtis, who owned the fish and chip shop in the village.

It was just a coincidence the Curtis' would be at the takeaway at the same time as Tom and Polly. And although they didn't witness the whole scene, they were '99% *sure*' it was Polly leaning over pointing to a bloke on the floor. Their thoughts were confirmed when they recognised the Audi TT and then heard Polly's voice, obscenities and all! The Curtis' couldn't wait to tell the tale when the chippy opened in Melsham the next day.

'Are you bonkers? That was amazing to do though Pol. Didn't you think you could get hurt?' Alison was full of admiration when the story was re-told. Janie couldn't stop laughing through much of it.

'When I told Stu, he loved it,' Janie said. 'He asked me if I would have done the same. I told him to 'piss off'. He can fight his own battles and if he can't, he can sling his hook, or his firehose.'

'I don't know why I did it,' Polly said. 'It all happened so quickly. I've got a bit of a short fuse. I was just so pissed at seeing this guy grabbing Tom, I just went for it. Thinking about it now, it was a bit crazy and I did feel a bit bad because I kicked him so hard in the nuts. And I hadn't even had a drink.' She re-enacted the punch.

The drinks continued to flow as the chat got louder and the night wore on. The boys had finished the darts, with Milky being declared the winner after no-one had any success getting the 25 or bull. He had at least got the 25.

The music cranked up after 11pm and the singing started *with* 'Dancing Queen', by Abba getting most of the pub going.

It was almost 11.30pm and only the friends were left in the pub, and one elderly couple in the corner who were loving the entertainment the inebriated group, were putting on. With arms around each other and singing at the top of their voices, it was proving another fun night at the Queen's Head for all the friends.

Milky started up another game of 'round the clock' on the dart board. All the lads were having one last hurrah, but it was taking an age for anyone to make serious progress. Indeed most, including Tom, who was well worse the wear by this time, couldn't hit the board at all.

Last orders were called and Jan put on the song 'Happy Hour', by the Housemartins, a request from Janie, so she could do her party piece of copying the dance from the video that involved her doing a 'fly-kicking' move, that ended up with her in a sprawling heap on the floor.

Milky was the only one taking the darts seriously, Ben and Stu had given up, Tom was struggling to get three darts on the board.

'Come on, guys, let's finish the game off before we go,' pleaded Milky. But it wasn't going to happen. Last orders, and being too pissed to throw the darts, would beat them.

Polly was well gone by now. She'd had six large wines.

'What do you need to finish the game off Milky you sexy man.' Polly put her arms around his neck. He looked a shade embarrassed, but you couldn't embarrass Polly.

'Well, if you can hit the bull, we'll call it a night,' Milky said. 'And you'd be the winner.'

'And if I hit the bull, you've got to snog me.' Milky took a large slurp of lager.

Polly picked up the darts. But rather than stand at the board and throw them from there, she pushed Tom off his chair and stood on top of it. She was 20 feet away and eight foot in the air. She was throwing the darts from a long way out.

'No, don't,' said Tom. 'You won't even hit the wall, let alone the board, let alone the bull. Listen to me, you'll break something. Be careful.'

But it was too late, Tom would have been better talking to the bar stool. Polly was up and she was throwing. Sure enough, the first one didn't reach the board and dropped on the floor, there was a big groan.

'Go on girl, you can do it,' Alison shouted. 'Just be bloody careful up there,' pleaded Tom.

The second dart hit the outside of the board, but at least reached the board, there was much cheering. And then, with her last dart, Polly pulled her arm back and hurled it, fast and hard... Straight into the bull! It went like an arrow. The place erupted.

'Woooo, wooooo, woooo,' She jumped off the chair, fell on her knees, but got straight up and walked over to the board to check. It was in. She'd hit the bull.

Milky had to look twice. Three times. Tom was applauding, the rest of the group were shrieking It was brilliant. What an end to the evening.

'Come here Milky, you sexy beast,' Polly called out.

In all the excitement he had forgotten what Polly had said would happen if she hit the bull, as she flung her arms around him and kissed him full on the lips for a full 10 seconds. Jan and Paul were clapping like crazy behind the bar, everyone was laughing. When Polly pulled away Milky was staring into space.

'That's the best kiss, I've had, ever,' Polly teased. 'You are one mighty under-rated sex pot. I love you.'

'Wow!' It was all Milky could mouth.

After the excitement died down, they got their coats and began to leave.

'See ya Jan, see ya Paul,' the group staggered out of the pub, laughing out loud, although keeping the noise down as they hit the cold air, there were other houses about.

Everyone said their goodbyes and gave out more kisses as they embraced and went their own ways, Milky going in the wrong direction for a while, he was still disorientated after the kiss.

'Poor old Milky, what did you do that for?' Tom smiled and slipped her arm in his as they made their way across the Green.

'I made his night.'

'Made his night? The poor bloke didn't know what to do. I don't reckon he's been kissed like that in his life.'

'Oh, well, he has now. And if you are up for it, I'll make your night Mr Dentist man.'

'You can forget that. I'm feel well pissed. I think I'll just go to bed and get some sleep. I don't know what's got into you these days. If you aren't fighting men you wanting to shag them.'

'Excuse me, shag 'men'. I don't think so. Not men, just you,' She hugged her husband closer. 'Just you, my darling.'

'Well, you'll have to wait, you've had too much to drink as well. You got the key?'

Polly put the key in the door and Tom headed upstairs and collapsed on the bed. He didn't even bother to take his shoes off!

Polly wasn't far behind. She smiled at her husband who was

out for the count. She took his shoes, belt and trousers off and left the rest of his clothes on.

'I love you.' She kissed his forehead and lay beside him, before falling asleep herself.

TWELVE

There were a few hangovers in Melsham on Saturday morning. Tom didn't surface until 9.30am, while Polly was still asleep when he brought her a cup of tea. The digital clock said 10.07am.

'Here you are sleepy head. Sent with love from Milky.'

Polly turned over to see Tom looking at her. She half sat up and groaned. 'Oh, shit. I don't feel great, what time is it?'

'Just gone 10. I'm going to sit in the conservatory and have a cup of coffee. I don't feel too bad, slept like a log. You want anything else apart from the tea?'

'No thanks, and what do you mean, love from Milky? Oh, I see. That kiss. That was funny. I remember having to take half your clothes off because you collapsed into bed and went to sleep.'

'Well, I don't remember that. But I do remember Milky's face when you were snogging him. You're such a hussy. Poor old boy, you'd eat him alive.'

Tom smiled and headed off down the stairs and into the kitchen. He put the kettle on, called to 'Alexa' to play Heart FM and did what he always told himself not to do at the weekend, but always failed to take heed of, he turned his phone on.

The kettle boiled and he grabbed a sachet of latte. His phone went beep, not once, but twice as it fired up. One voicemail and two missed calls. The missed calls from Craig.

What would Craig want so early on a Saturday morning? The first call had been made at 8am. Oh, it could wait, he'll call him later. He was going to enjoy his coffee. He pressed 121 to access the voicemail. It was sent at 8.02am. Must be Craig. He was right.

'*Hello mate. I need you to call me ASAP. Sorry to call so early but I badly need a chat. And I mean badly.*'

Tom listened again. That was unlike his friend. Tom looked at his watch, sipped his coffee and noticed that Craig had called again at 8.44am. Must be serious. He called him.

Craig was sitting in his kitchen. Jody had gone to work. He looked at the caller. '*Good, it was Tom.*'

'Hi mate, how are you?'

'I'm fine, how are you? You called? Don't tell me you're heading off to Everton to watch Arsenal on Tuesday? You must be mad, we have a terrible record at Goodison, and before you ask, no I'm not coming up for it. Anyhow, what's up?'

'No mate, I'm not going to the football. I wish I was actually. Thanks for calling back.' There was a brief silence.

'Tom, I need to. I need to talk to you about something. This is massively private and I'm going to have to ask you not to speak to Polly about what I'm going to say. Can you talk now?'

'Yes, yes mate. I can talk. Polly is still in bed. What is it? What's happened?'

Tom was sitting upright. Craig had his attention, he had never heard his friend talk like this in the years they had known each other. He sounded worried, it certainly wasn't a wind-up. Or if it was, it was a good one.

'I best start at the beginning, because I'm not sure you are going to believe all this. But you have got to. You're the only person I'm telling, I could be in trouble, really deep shit.' Craig sounded worried.

'Jesus. You're serious aren't you? This isn't a wind-up?'

'Just please listen, this is no wind-up.

'About 18 months ago I got in a spot of bother. I didn't mention it to anyone because I hoped it would blow over and I thought it had. It all started when I went to a seminar in Liverpool on business, it was an overnight stay, Friday into Saturday. I can't remember the exact date, but I got pissed, the drink was free and everyone was having a good time, you know these business things.

'Anyhow, to cut a long story short, I got chatting to this bird from Liverpool. We were both stupid drunk, one thing led to another and. And well basically, we had sex. Pretty drunk crap sex.

Oh shit, I can't believe it thinking about it now.'

'Are you taking the piss, Craig?' Tom stood up and walked over to the window.

'No, Tom, I'm not.

'Anyhow we went our own ways and I thought no more of it. I was consumed with guilt about what would happen if Jody found out. Obviously she didn't and still doesn't know, I feel so shit for her and what I've done. But I knew if I told her that would be it, I'd be fucked. We were on our first IVF cycle at the time as well, I just couldn't, you know, I just couldn't bring myself to tell her.

'The girl I had sex with didn't seem bothered about anything at the time. I found her attractive but she was married, said she would just forget it all happened. Her marriage was a shambles. I thought that would be the end of it, I thought it was just a stupid, drunken night. One I'd never repeat, a bad lesson learned. But then I get a phone call about two months later.'

'Are you making this up, Craig? You better not be pissing me about because I'm starting to not find this funny. This a wind-up, right?'

'No, Tom, it's not. I promise you I'm not winding you up, please listen. So, I get this call from a bloke who says he knows what went on in that hotel room because Marie, the woman, had confessed to him. She was his bloody wife. It was no good me trying to get out of it, or say it wasn't me. He knew it was me, Marie had told him my name and company I worked for. He tracked me down, the room I was in, and all that crap.

'He said he wanted to meet up, I was shitting myself. He said I had a choice, either meet him or he would make sure my wife knew what happened. He'd done his homework. He knew Jody's name, the shop she owns, he even bloody well knew we were going through IVF. I was screwed, well and truly.

'He told me he wasn't going to hurt me. He just wanted to speak to me, I had no choice. We met up at a motorway café off the M60. He told me to park at the furthest end of the car park. He even knew I had a fucking Z4.'

'When was this?' Tom butted in.

'Just before Christmas last year. Anyhow, so we meet up and he starts talking. He talks about Marie as if she was a lump of shit and I soon realise that although they are married, they were living separate lives. He knows what happened that night, he also knows I'm in a different position to him because I'm happily married. His marriage is as good as over, he also says he has a tape, a DVD of me and Marie doing it that night, I had no reason not to believe him.

'His name is Stuart Archer and he also comes from Liverpool. Anyhow the long and short of it is, he's a drug dealer. A bloody big one at that. Not your spotty, low end smack head from the inner city, this bloke is the top man. He has the Rolex on, turns up in a Mercedes and talks eloquently, I've only gone and screwed a 'Mr Big's missus haven't I? And now he has me by the balls.'

Tom puffed his cheeks out and looked outside onto his garden. He was almost numb listening to it. This was Craig talking here, he had to remind himself. Craig, who was so smart, so sharp, so… normal.

'You really aren't making this up are you? Tom was worried and disgusted in equal measure. Craig didn't take kindly to his tone.

'No, I'm fucking not, man. Why would I make all this shit up?'

'I don't know to be honest, sorry mate. It just sounds like something out of a movie, not real life. Not your life. Surely you can see that?'

'Tom, I can see that. But I'm not kidding, I promise.'

'So, is that it then, mate?'

'No it isn't. Archer threatened me. Good and proper. He wanted me to run packages from Liverpool Docks across to Manchester. All I had to do was meet someone at an address on The Wirral and take them to another address in Manchester. He wanted me to do three runs and he supplied the van, gave me the dates, I would do the runs and after the third one, he said we would be quits.'

'Quits', repeated Tom.

'Yeah, quits. That was going to be it. He said I had his word, the word of a drug dealer mind you, that's smart isn't it? He said that once I had done the three runs that was it. All over, he would never contact me again and he would leave me in peace. He'd give me the sex tape. That was a year ago, almost exactly.'

'Shit. I can hardly believe this. I don't know what to say, and still Jody doesn't know?'

'Of course she doesn't know. I could never let her know, I could never tell her. You know what would happen. It would kill her. I've only told you this.

'So, I did the runs and in fairness Archer was true to his word. On the third run, he'd left a note in the van to say this was the final drop. It was over for me, I had his word. The tape was there. He finished the note, *'Fuck off and have a good life'*. If it wasn't so serious, it was almost comical.

'And I haven't heard from him since.'

'So, okay, you haven't heard from him since,' Tom said. 'So, why are you telling me now? Isn't it done? What's changed? You said that was a year ago.'

Craig was silent for a few seconds. 'Archer was banged up for 25 years last week for drug dealing. He admitted loads of charges apparently, it was on the news. The report also said the police were ongoing with their enquiries and expected to make further arrests.

'I have no idea if anything could lead to me, but at the end of the day, I'm not stupid. I never asked Archer what I was delivering in those packages, I just wanted to do as I was told and get the shit out of it, although I was pretty sure I wasn't delivering baby wipes.

'And now he's behind bars. I know I was delivering drugs. Okay, so it was a while ago, but Archer has just gone down. He might want to take others with him.'

'Really?' Tom sounded more than surprised. 'Why on earth would he be bothered with you? You said you were only doing it for three months, surely he is not going to be bothered about you. He's gone down for years. You were hardly a big noise, you sure you are not overthinking this?'

'No. I'm not overthinking this. There's something else, something much worse I haven't told you.'

'Haven't told me? Something worse? Christ, Craig. What else could there be?'

'Tom. It was me who helped put Archer behind bars.'

THIRTEEN

Sunday morning was rugby morning for Karen and Lee.

Had been for the last five years, since Lee had started playing in London for his local club. It was only 'touch' rugby at first and Karen always thought it fun to see the hundreds of children, from eight to about 10-years-old running around the rugby pitches of south London, using up bags of energy and enjoying the camaraderie the sport could bring. It was good discipline for them as well and also kept some of them away from their computers for a time. Lee had always been good at rugby, helped in his early years by him being twice the size of many of his peers.

Karen knew it wouldn't last of course. Young people all grew at different rates and it was likely many of Lee's friends, who were half his size at 10, would be bigger than him when they were all 18. However, back then Lee was picking up plenty of confidence at Kingstons U10s rugby team.

Mark had spent years taking Lee to rugby practice before him and Karen split. In fact Mark appeared to enjoy his trips to Rookery Park where Lee would practice with 'The Kings'. Bearing in mind he wasn't his son, Karen loved their 'bonding'.

Little did she realise that Mark had an ulterior motive to his love of Lee's rugby practice and cheesy chips. Her name was Sarah and it was all became clear a few months after Karen and Mark split.

It hadn't taken long for Karen to find a rugby club for Lee in Norfolk, and her son was now a member of South Walsham U15s, one of the county's best run clubs.

She had not made finding Lee a rugby club her first priority when moving into their new cottage, but she didn't wait long. Her son settling into his new area was important. So she had been glad when the coach of the Walsham team had e-mailed her back with all the details of practice days and times for the U15s. South Walsham placed a good deal of emphasis on youth and had a thriving youth set-up. It hadn't taken her son long to mix easily with his new team-mates and, after a couple of second team matches, in which he excelled, he was promoted to the U15s first XV.

Lee was still a good size for his age, but others around him were catching him up. While he had the aggression and physical strength, for someone so big he also had pace and could run fast at opponents. He was a fine player and although Karen didn't pretend to know much about rugby, she saw enough to see that her son was decent. He seemed to score plenty of tries. Karen knew he was highly thought of by the warmth of reception she got as a new mum within the group. Lee had clearly made an impression with most of the parents.

'Good player, your lad,' one dad had said to Karen after Lee made his first-team debut and scored a try. 'Strong, powerful, could go a long way,' another agreed.

This particular Sunday morning was a big event for Lee's team. It was the semi-final of the County Cup. South Walsham U15s were playing Slixworth U15s and Walsham were favourites. Indeed, Walsham hadn't lost a league game all season. They lost a couple of pre-season friendlies, including against Slixworth, but that was before Lee had arrived.

'Good luck darling,' she said as she dropped him off at the Walsham ground. It was 10am, kick-off was an hour later. She would sit in the car for a while, catch up with a few of her friends on Facebook and then go into the club house for a coffee. It was a ritual she had been doing for years, firstly in London after Mark left, and now in Norfolk.

Sitting in her car opposite the vast fields with four rugby pitches in front of her, the goalposts standing tall against the blue sky, on what was a lovely spring morning, Karen clicked onto her Facebook page and noticed her sister Jane had posted photos of her boys in the surf on the Gold Coast. It may have been the end of summer in Australia, but clearly the weather was still wonderful. She 'liked' all the photos and commented on the one of Jane and husband Peter with a couple of pints in their hands, with the boys, Zac and Jake, they must now be 13 and 14 she guessed, grinning in the background. She left a comment, *'Looks great Down Under as usual. You all looking good'*.

She knew her sister would like that as she continued to flick through her messages.

Tonya had posted photos of what looked like a crazy night in some club in London. She could just make out Tonya's face in most of them, although bottles of beer and even a couple of cocktail umbrellas seemed to get in the way of much of the 'selfies'. Tonya and Karen had grown up together in Woolwich. Karen smiled as she remembered a night out her and Tonya had enjoyed in the Capital many years ago.

The pair had gone to a kebab house at about three in the morning after a night out in Woolwich. The owner had handed them their kebabs and Tonya, so drunk, dropped hers on the floor in the shop. She could picture Tonya's face as if it were yesterday, as she demanded a refund shouting there was a hole in her pitta bread which had caused all the meat to fall out. Some big guy from one of the back rooms had escorted the pair of them out of the shop after Tonya threatened to call the police. She could remember the big guy's words…. *'You do that love, call the police and tell them you've got a hole in your kebab!'* Karen smiled to herself at the thought of that night. It was a shame the two no longer spoke. *It wasn't as if it had been Tonya's fault.*

Karen looked at the time on her phone. It was 10.30. She put it in her pocket and made her way to the club house. Once in she got herself a coffee and was soon chatting to some of the parents.

'Oh, good, Lee is playing then?' Max Tyrone's dad turned to greet Karen. He was a big man with a ruddy complexion. A businessman who commuted to London every day, his son played scrum-half.

'Yes, yes, he's here,' Karen said.

'Excellent', said another one of the parents. It was Jack Davis' father, his son was captain. 'Big game today. Hope, your lad had a good night's sleep. Be great if they could reach the final.'

Karen smiled.

The game was taking place on the far end pitch. Karen and the rest of the parents made their way across the field, walking round two pitches that already had lots of mini-rugby going on and lots of parents on the touchlines, cheering enthusiastically. As Karen got closer to Lee's game, she could see him jogging over to get in a huddle with the rest of his team-mates. He had the number 7 on his back and was not the tallest in the side, but was one of the biggest.

Walsham made a terrible start. From the kick-off the Walsham full-back fumbled it and Slixworth were soon picking up the pieces and charging at the Walsham defence. Slixworth got one try and then another. With two conversions it was 14-0 to the visitors. Lee had hardly got into the game and Karen now found herself, rather uncharacteristically, shouting for Walsham to 'come on'. She was really getting into it with the crowd on the touchlines bigger and more vociferous than normal. Not that the Walsham boys were responding and it was Slixworth who went into the half-time interval ahead.

It was too far a walk back to the club house at the break for most of the parents who instead waited on the touchline for the second half, the mums talking about the end of season Tour that was coming up, the dads dissecting what had been a poor first half by Walsham.

'Jack and Lee need to get into this game more,' Karen overheard Mr Davis say. 'It is a bloody semi-final, the boys do know that.'

'So, are you coming on the Tour, Karen?' said June, who was the mother of the full-back who had made such a hash in the opening minutes.

'I'm not sure to be honest,' Karen lied. She had no intentions of going. She couldn't stand most of the rugby mums, snooty lot. 'I'll have to see what time I can get off from my work. But hopefully Lee will be able to go. Just need someone to look after him if he comes on his own.

'Oh, don't worry about that, someone will look after him. Just be nice if you could come,' June replied. Karen smiled appreciatively.

Walsham came out in the second half a different team and Lee was immediately in the act, powering his way through flailing Slixworth tackles, passing the ball onto Joe Boulder, who raced through to score. Five minutes later, Joe scored again, his pace proving too hot for the Slixworth defence to handle. With both tries converted it was 14-14 and there was still half an hour to go.

It was all Walsham and Lee was at the forefront of all that was good in the team's play. Slixworth's players were looking downbeat and it was soon another try to Walsham, Jack Davis scoring. If that wasn't enough it was Lee's turn to score, not just one try, but two. He and his team-mates had enjoyed a terrific second half and the final score was 31-14 to Walsham. At the whistle, the Walsham players hugged each other and there were pats on the back all round from the coaching staff and parents to their boys. Slixworth were gracious in defeat and all the players enjoyed sausage and chips in the club house afterwards.

'Well done Lee, fine game, especially second half.' Mr Davis was going round to all the Walsham players and having a chat. Clearly, he thought it his duty as dad of the captain.

'Thanks,' is all Lee responded with. The game was done, there had been big celebrations in the dressing room, now it was time for food and phones.

Karen had given Lee a quick hug as he walked off the pitch. She didn't want to embarrass him with kisses.

It was 1pm before Lee got up to leave. He wasn't the first in his team to go, neither was he the last. The club house was still heaving with people. There must have still been 40 or 50 youngsters in the 'mini' sections picking up certificates and participation awards in front of enthusiastic parents.

'Let's go mum. 'I've said goodbye to most people,' Lee said, as he stretched his arms up high and then bent down to pick up his rugby bag. The pair of them made for the door.

'Lee, have you got a minute?' Lee turned around. The voice came from Mr Crowe, his U15 head coach. 'Mrs Harding, can I speak to you as well please?'

Karen looked at Lee and they both looked at Mr Crowe.

'Yes, no problem,' said Karen.

Mr Crowe put his hand out and led them into a room just off

the bar area where another man was sitting at a long table. Karen didn't recognise him.

'Thanks, this won't take a couple of moments,' said Mr Crowe, who was smiling. He continued. 'This is David Button, and he's a coach with England rugby. And he's come here because he wants to speak to you both.'

Mr Button looked at Lee and then Karen. He was a short, squat man, mid-40s, with thinning hair.

'Hi Lee, Mrs Harding. Thanks for your time. Look, I'll get straight to the point. We have been watching Lee for the last few months or so, in London and now up here in Norfolk. We have liked what we have seen. And we would like to offer him an England trial for his age group. It's in two weeks, in London. What do you say?'

Mr Crowe beamed. One of his players being asked to go for an England trial. Lee would be the first from South Walsham at this age group. He just hoped Lee would say yes. Lee looked at his mum, who just smiled and shrugged her shoulders as much as to say 'up to you'.

'I'd love to,' Lee said, his face breaking out in a smile.

'I'd absolutely love to.'

FOURTEEN

TOM'S head was all over the place.

The conversation with Craig was still fresh in his thoughts, but as he had promised, he wouldn't discuss it with Polly. He wouldn't discuss it with anyone.

The ramifications of what Craig had told him continued to spin through his mind. His mate could be in the shit, big time. And as for Jody not knowing any of it…. Wow! This was surreal. They had always been so close. If she found out she would leave him, no doubt about that.

He tried to imagine if the boot were on the other foot. He couldn't think how he would cope with the guilt. The truth always just a heartbeat away from coming out. How was Craig coping with such deceit? Tom was beginning to wonder if he knew his friend at all.

But, he'd promised to say nothing.

Driving into the office on Monday morning, Tom was listening to his usual radio station, humming to himself. He had a busy week ahead and he and Polly were preparing to go to Chester on Friday, so he had a lot of work cram in. The sun was shining.

Tom loved spring. It was his favourite season. It made him feel good. It made most people feel good, he always thought, summer on its way. So many of his friends went on about the different seasons in the UK, but spring was always Tom's number one.

He and Polly had gone for a long walk on Sunday along the coast. They had talked and chatted about life when they first met, life today, life in the future.

Polly had mentioned about them starting a family. She had done so before, a few years ago. But both their careers then were still in their infancy, and anyhow, neither felt quite ready to commit to children, well Tom didn't. Now, and with Jody struggling to start a family, Polly had started to think again if their conversation on the walk was anything to go by.

'Morning Jill,' how are you? Tom walked into the surgery and was surprised to find her already sitting at the reception desk. It was only 7.45am and she didn't have to be in until just after 8. He trusted her enough for her to have a key, just in case he was ever held up.

'Have you done something to your hair?' He looked at her. 'I'm no expert, so sorry if I'm wrong.'

Jill smiled: 'Didn't know you were into ladies' hair fashions? Yes, this is my new 'post-Robert' hair do. What do you think? It's my way of starting a new life without that hairy, disloyal, arse, who I hope has already caught some disease off his new girlfriend.

'I got my hair done on Saturday, and on Saturday night I went out with a few friends into the city and had a great time. Bumped into Emily, she was out with a group of girls as well. She looked a bit worse for wear. Then again, an hour or so later, so were we. We went back to Anne's flat. Do you know my friend Anne?' Tom shook his head.

'Anyhow, we went back to her flat and watched the 'Chippendales Live on Tour' DVD. It's a bit risqué, I didn't realise they almost got everything out. So, yes, in answer to your question, I have had my hair done, and I am jolly glad I have, welcome to my new life.' And with that she pulled a big grin.

She hadn't take a breath. Her new found single freedom was appearing to be just what the doctor ordered. Whether it would last would remain to be seen.

'I like it,' said Tom. 'And, well, great to hear you had a good Saturday night. Did you spot me in that Chippendales DVD?'

'I think I did actually. Weren't you the one with the very tiny thong?'

Tom winked and headed upstairs. 'So you did see me!'

In his surgery Tom was at peace with the world. He liked being alone for a few moments in his own room, a room full of instruments, basins and books, and of course his very own dentist's chair. All his own, all the result of his hard work. To others it may be boring, but to him it was a big part of his world. He didn't care what people thought, he was his own boss, in charge of the way his life was panning out. He'd done okay.

'Morning.' Emily walked in.

Tom looked twice. Did she also look different this morning? What was going on? Emily's hair was red! A very bright red!

'Like your hair, Em. It's very, um, bright.

'I see Jill has had hers done as well. Is it 'new hair day party' and I've lost my invitation? Because if so, I'll go get mine permed at lunchtime.

Emily laughed. 'Oh, yes, a perm would look good on you. No, I had it coloured yesterday at my friend's house. I like Jill's new style.

'Do you like red?' She smiled at him and flicked her head. 'Thought it might cheer me up a bit. Split up with my boyfriend, Tim, on Saturday night. Before you say anything, no, I don't give a shit.'

'Oh, sorry to hear that.'

'Don't be. I caught him round the back of the pub with some slag he knows. She was, you know, sort of, you know, doing things to him. I saw them in the act, so I told him to, well, told him what to do and slapped her round the face. I was a bit pissed and by the end of the night, very pissed. Well, we all were. I saw him later on in Ritzos, the nightclub, he tried to apologise and said what I'd seen wasn't happening. He must think I've never given a blow job.'

'Yes, thanks, I get the drift,' Tom butted in. This was all way too early on a Monday morning for this talk.

'Oh, sorry, yeah well, I can't be doing with idiots like him. Only known him three months anyhow. Bit of a wet blanket, crap in bed and a right boring job. He fixes street lights.

'So, I got my hair done. Glad you like it. Would rather men like you liked it, than dickheads like Tim.' And with that she went and hung her coat up.

It had been an odd start to the morning for Tom. He had only been in the surgery 15 minutes and had listened to two stories that had both ended with Jill and Emily changing their hairstyles.

It made his Friday night at the Queen's Head seem like a polite tea party.

Patricia Botten was their first patient of the day. She was 28, very attractive, single, but with a boyfriend who worked in London and owned a gym and leisure complex. Patricia was always asking after Polly – *'if she wants to come and work for John in London, Tom, tell her to call me.'*

'Morning Patricia, how are you.' Tom said.

'I'm good my darling. How are you and Polly?'

'We're great. Polly is her usual self, working hard, playing hard, if you know what I mean? How's John?'

'He's okay. The gym is busy. We're going on holiday to Brazil next month for a couple of weeks.'

'That sounds fun. Take a seat. Right, let's have a look. Had any problems? Open wide.'

Patricia didn't get a chance answer, she shook her head as she sat in the chair, Tom prodding through her teeth.

'Well, that all looks good. I'll give you a quick brush and polish, book up for six months.'

Brush and polish completed, Tom helped her with her coat. 'Enjoy Brazil and give my best to John. Don't forget to Samba as hard as you can.'

'Thanks my dear. I must admit we are looking forward to it. We haven't had a holiday now for two months!'

'Really, as long as that,' Tom said. Patricia didn't notice the sarcasm. She was too busy looking at Emily.

'Love your hair, darling, red suits you.'

Emily smiled broadly.

It was rare the gym had any serious complaints, but Andy knew he and his team would have to nip this one in the bud if there was not to be a real shit-storm over what Mrs Tankard claimed happened in the ladies changing rooms at the weekend.

Her story appeared genuine.

The 70-year-old, who had been a member of the gym and spa for three years, had been swimming and then had 20 minutes in the Jacuzzi, before heading back to get changed. On arriving back in the changing room and taking off her swimsuit, she noticed a man standing in the shower, naked! And he was whistling a tune that sounded *'like that one from Dad's Army'*. To say she was horrified was an understatement, she had immediately wrapped a towel around herself and run into reception hollowing for help. The whole spa area heard the commotion. Tina had been on duty and, after hearing Mrs Tankard shouting, had come running to see what was going on.

'He's naked. He's naked and in the woman's shower,' she had cried out. 'It's a disgrace, get him out of there, a flasher, a flasher, a pervert. Get him out, a whistling flasher at that.'

Tina had moved quickly and darted into the showers, with Kevin not far behind. He had heard the row from the gym and had come out to see what all the fuss was about. The pair went in and sure enough, there he still was, showering away, naked. Mr Peters, a gym member regular and a similar age to Mrs Tankard. What the hell was he doing in there? He was in the wrong changing room and his body was not a pretty sight. Mr Peters had been a member of the gym long enough to know which changing rooms were which. Tina left to find Mrs Tankard, while Kevin dealt with Mr Peters.

Poor, Mr Peters was all apologies. He was lost for words as Kevin sat him down in a room at the back of the reception. Mrs Tankard had gone home. Apparently Mr Peters had taken the wrong turning and gone into the ladies changing room, rather than the men's, he had no idea of his mistake until Kevin called him to get out of the showers. Quite why he had taken the wrong turning could not be established.

'I say, awfully sorry. What a bad show,' the former Army captain had said to Kevin. 'I can't even start to think what happened, I hope I haven't upset anyone, did anyone see me in there? Not much to see at my age, old chap but all a bit of an embarrassment isn't it? I don't know what to say, have never done it before, must have lost my bearings.'

It was clearly an innocent mistake. Mr Peters was hardly a sexual predator, but Mrs Tankard wanted a full public enquiry. Tina had apologised at the time and Mrs Tankard had seemingly accepted it was a mistake but, once home and having told her husband, John Tankard, who was a local councillor, what had happened, the stakes had risen. He'd phoned the gym demanding answers, Tina had taken the call. If the Tankards didn't get their full enquiry, Mr Tankard was, 'going to the papers'.

'Okay, Tina, we know the story, so what's the latest?' Andy was addressing that lunchtime's team meeting. He was not impressed by Mr Tankard's threats, but suspected if he was like the two councillors Andy knew, he could likely be vindictive enough to follow through with his newspaper threat.

'Well, I spoke to Mrs Tankard this morning and she and her husband have calmed down a bit,' said Tina, a tall ginger-haired woman in her late 30s, with a Geordie accent. 'She wants to know what we are going to do about it of course. We can make the signs bigger perhaps, although quite how Mr Peters ended up in the ladies is still a mystery, he must have come out of the men's first and then turned left into the ladies. But why? He's been a member here for years, no-one else has done that, have they?'

'Send him to Specsavers,' piped up James. 'That would solve everything if we can prove he can't see. Or read. We can't be held accountable for that, does he drive?'

'He can read.' Tina raised her eyebrows. 'I can't think what came over him to go into the ladies in the way he did. He said it was a mistake, I believe him. We need to convince the Tankards we are doing all we can to make sure it doesn't happen again.'

'Cancel the old fossil's membership.' Kevin was his usual diplomatic self. 'If he can't read, he'll do it again, but next time he'll do it when Mrs Ferguson is in there. And you know who her husband is, the bloody Police Commissioner'

'But he *can* read,' Tina was exasperated. 'James, why did you say he couldn't read? He can read.'

'And don't forget Kevin, 'old fossils' as you call them make up for 70% of our membership at the Spa. So, don't be ageist, you'll be old one day, sooner than you think if you spend too much time under that sun lamp.'

James giggled out loud.

'I don't use a bloody sun lamp. This isn't a fake tan you know. I went to Jamaica in the winter.'

'Did your wife go as well?' James smiled. 'Or Ja-mai-ca?' He gave Kevin a broad grin. 'Get it?'

Polly and Tina smiled, but Andy was getting irritated.

'Okay, get those signs made bigger and Polly I want you to contact Mrs Tankard and her husband and offer them free membership for six months, as an apology for what happened. Sweet talk them, perhaps get them in for a free spa day with lunch as well, on us. Just make sure they don't go to the papers.'

'I'll speak to them, they'll be okay. I'm sure.

'Just imagine if it had been James who had taken the wrong turning and ended up in the ladies.' Polly winked at James.

'No chance of that my darling, I always shower naked in the men's. I love a bare bum.'

Kevin shook his head. 'Are we finished here? I don't think I can listen to more of this crap.'

Andy nodded. 'Yep, let's get this all sorted and over with ASAP please. Last headline I want to read in the paper is, 'WOMAN STARTLED BY OLD MAN'S ARSE IN SPA CUBICLES!''

'Oooooh, I love that heading,' James laughed. 'You should have been an editor, Andy. Anyhow, I'm off, lots of facts and figures to study. Bottom's up, I say. But that's my world, I guess.' And with that he headed out, giggling again.

Polly, Tina and Val, who had been taking notes, smiled as he left, Kevin was muttering something to himself. Andy had already stomped out.

'What cheese is this on this tuna pasta bake?' Tom was prodding their dinner.

'Cheddar', said Polly 'Why?'

'It just doesn't taste the same. Sort of a bit strong, like a sort of, I don't know, Red Leicester, I didn't think I would notice on tuna pasta to be honest. But it does smell different. I have a good smelling nose.'

'It's cheddar, as we always have. You can cook it your bloody self if you don't like it. *I have a good smelling nose.*' The only thing you are good at smelling is when next door's cat has shit in your vegetable patch, you smell that alright.'

Tom shook his head. 'You can be so vulgar. What has next door's cat pooping in my vegetable patch got to do with this tuna pasta bake? Nothing! That's what.'

'I never said pooping, I said shitting.'

'We are trying to eat here.' Tom looked across at his wife, who was smiling. She loved being annoying. In a nice way.

'How was work today, anyway? How was camp man James?'

'Ah, he was his usual funny self,' Polly smiled. 'We had an incident in the women's changing rooms on Saturday. This old boy took a wrong turning and ended up in the women's showers and this lady came in and went nuts, the bloke was standing there naked, whistling the tune from 'Dad's Army' apparently. I've got to smooth it over. Anyhow, at the end of conversation we were all talking around the table about it and James says 'bottom's up — oops, that's my world', or something like that, as he leaves the meeting. He is funny.'

'I must admit, I'd like to meet this James one day,' said Tom. 'He sounds a bit of a laugh.'

'He is. He'd think my 'shit in your vegetable patch' quip was hilarious. Anyhow, how was your day?'

'Not too bad. Both Jill and Emily have new hair-dos, apparently Jill's is 'post-Robert'. And Emily split up with her partner on Saturday night, you don't want to know why.'

'Oh, I do. Tell me!' Polly stared at him.

'No, it's disgusting.'

'TELL ME!'

As much as Tom didn't want to go into details, he knew he couldn't win and told Polly why.

'You would never do that, would you?' Polly said after Tom had finished the story.

Tom looked at her: 'What give a bloke a blow job? I should bloody hope not.'

'Not another bloke, you idiot, let another woman do it to you, even if you were totally pissed?'

'What sort of thing is that to say? Of course I wouldn't. You do talk some rubbish, Pol. The only way I'd let another woman do it to me, is if you were doing the videoing of the pair of us.'

'TOM! That's horrible. And rude. And disgusting. And sort of pornographic. No-one is touching you, only me.'

'Sort of pornographic? What does that mean?'

'Oh, nothing, be quiet. Is the tuna pasta to your satisfaction

Mr cheese picky?'

Tom gave her a wink. Polly smiled.

'Actually, I was talking to Jody this morning and we were both saying how lucky we were to have husbands we can trust. There are so many arseholes out there, unfaithful blokes. We were saying we did strike it lucky, not that you two didn't do too badly of course, before you think the sun shines out of your backsides.'

Tom smiled. 'You haven't got to worry about me darling.'

FIFTEEN

CRAIG was still thinking of his phone conversation with Tom. *'That would have shocked his old pal'.*

In many ways he was glad he and Polly were coming up to Chester on Friday. The quicker he could talk to Tom again, the more he could tell him. In saying that, Craig was nervous about how Tom would react, how would he look at him when they shook hands? He had created an *'elephant in the room'.* Still, it had to be done.

It would certainly be a first for Craig, being nervous in front of Tom or Polly. Not since the first time all four had met in London all those years ago had ever been worried about meeting them.

Craig smiled to himself as he thought about that night the four had first struck up their friendship. It had been a fun night. Now, he'd gone and fucked it right up.

Craig had his own works parking space.

He was one of the directors of PJC Shipping, in Liverpool, a company that dealt with shipping companies from all over the world that used Liverpool Docks to land grain, timber and oil. His job had plenty of responsibility, Liverpool being one of the largest ports, by tonnage, in the UK. Craig had been there 10 years and enjoyed a good salary and a great package that included share options and private pension, money had never been an issue for him. He enjoyed his job and he and Jody enjoyed all the trappings that came with it. Along with Pete and Jason, the Benson brothers, Craig was a third director.

'Craigy, boy, how are ya? Jason was sitting in his office as Craig walked past. All three directors had their own offices. Jason was 39 and younger than Pete by 18 months, both were tall, with dark hair. Jason was married with a young son, Pete was divorced.

'I'm good my man, how are you?' Craig replied. 'Are you coming to Goodison tonight to see the mighty Arsenal? I've got the box and I think there is a spare ticket.'

PJC Shipping were a profitable company. They enjoyed a few 'creature comforts', one of them being executive boxes at both Goodison Park, Everton and Anfield, Liverpool. They were used to entertain clients. The directors took turns to host games. For the brothers, attending games was a 'no-brainer', as Jason was an Everton fan and Pete a Liverpool one, Craig, being an Arsenal nut, had to make do with the couple of occasions his team came up from London to see them in the flesh, or host a box when the brothers were away. The boxes cost plenty of money per season, but all three agreed it was well worth it, they'd had them for three years now. Clients invariably left a game having appreciated the hospitality. The boxes were good for business.

'Yep, I'm coming my man,' replied Jason. 'And I'm sorry to say, it's not looking pretty for you boys. I see a couple of your strikers are out tonight. Don't sulk if Arsenal get too battered will you? You going home first before going to the game?'

'Yeah, I think I will,' replied Craig. I'm knocking off at four and I'll go home, change and come back. Makes sense, I suppose I better wear my *'Henry 14'* shirt tonight!'

'Is Henry Cooper playing?' Jason was laughing. 'He'd probably do okay for you lot. When was the last time Arsenal actually scored?'

'Funny Jase, although you're not wrong, I wish Thierry Henry was up front for us these days. We were crap again on Saturday. Yep, we can't score for toffee.'

'Up the Toffees,' Jason jumped in, seeing a chance to promote his beloved Everton's nickname.

Craig smiled. 'Ha, ha, very good.'

He walked into his office and hung up his coat. It was pleasant outside, but not warm enough yet to leave the coat at home. Craig's personal assistant was Lisa, she was a scouser, married with three

children, all of High School age. She said it how it was and Craig
liked that. Lisa had been with the company four years and had
been his PA from the day she started, she knew how he ticked. He
sometimes said she seemed to know him as well as Jody. Lisa was
always prompt into work and today was no exception. As he sat
down, Lisa walked in.

'Morning. How are you?'

'I'm good thanks, and you?'

'I'm okay.' she replied. I'm looking forward to the game
tonight. I'm going 3-0.'

'What to Arsenal?' He raised his eyebrows. 'That's great, I'll
take that all day long.'

'Not Arsenal you muppet, Everton.' She tutted. 'And thanks
again for allowing me to bring Tim into the box, he's so excited. I
think he has only told the whole school he's watching it from an
executive box.'

Tim was Lisa's youngest lad, a big Everton fan. He was 12. The
three directors, who all had their own PAs, often invited them into
the football boxes on different occasions, all were keen fans, Lisa a
die-hard Evertonian. She wasn't invited to all the games, as clients
came first. But when she did get a chance to go, she grabbed it. The
fact Craig had told her yesterday that a client was unable to come,
'so bring Tim along if he wants to come', had made her day. And
Tim's.

'So, what's going on today, Lisa.'

'Oh, the usual stuff. There are a couple of companies wanting
to talk to us about our services, one from Cyprus, one from
Germany, all the details and numbers are there. Joseph Stannard
called about you attending his breakfast meeting next week. I said
you had put it in the diary, so you must be going.' Craig nodded.
'And one more thing, you haven't forgotten I'm off tomorrow,
have you?'

'Ah, glad you reminded me, I had actually, but now I haven't.
Thanks. Anything else?'

'Nope, that's it. Up the Toffees. And I'm wearing my Everton
scarf tonight, no formal dress code for me.' And with that Lisa,
smiled, turned and walked out.

Craig sat down and turned his computer on. Lisa had left six or seven letters on his desk to open. 'He was a big enough boy to be able to do that himself now', she had once said when Craig has asked her to open a couple of letters one morning. He flicked through them, the usual. A couple of invoices he would return to Lisa, a bit of junk mail.

Then he saw it. One with a *'Merseyside Police'* stamp on the envelope. Craig's heart skipped a beat. It was addressed to him.

Jody had three customers walk into her shop within minutes of her opening.

That was unusual, but she wasn't going to complain. Especially when the first man bought three shirts, all bright colours and very 1980s, for the princely sum of £30 each. A nice start to the day.

Customer No.2 didn't hang around long and left empty-handed, but her third customer was Mrs Bright, whose husband owned the fresh fish shop, just off Orchard Street. Jody wasn't sure she could ever own a fish shop, she couldn't bear the thought of smelling like haddock.

'There's a joke in there somewhere,' Craig had once said after Jody had said she couldn't do Mrs Bright's job, and 'smell like haddock'.

Yet, Mrs Bright was a nice person, if a tad sharp. She looked like she'd had a tough life, her skin wasn't the best and her hair always looked as though it could do with a good wash and comb. She was a lot older than Jody, but was often in the shop looking for different coloured bits and pieces, different styles, old-school fashions. Jody admired her for wanting to look a 'bit different' at her age, which is what many of her customers wanted to do. Her retro shop wasn't your 'run-of-the-mill' boutique.

'Hello Mrs Bright. How are you?' Jody held out her hand.

'I'm alright dear, sorry if I smell of fish, just come from the shop. Joe's dressing the crabs, so grabbing a minute or two to have a look around. I love this shop, don't suppose you have any hats? I'm going to a fancy dress party on Saturday night, thought I dress up as that blond girl from ABBA. You know the one?'

Jody did know the one but tried hard to imagine Mrs Bright, a 50+ and rather large lady looking like Agneta from the Swedish super group. Still, money was money and she would take Mrs

Bright's if she could find a hat to suit.

'Look at this,' Jody said, as she picked up a tall white frilly hat that could maybe be confused for one worn by one of the girls from ABBA, if you looked hard enough.

'Oh, that's wonderful,' Mrs Bright replied. 'Let me try it on, I have a white suit to wear, so if this fits. It does, it looks great. How much?'

'It's £25, but seeing as it's for a memorable fancy dress night, you can have it for £22.'

'I'll have it, thank you,' said Mrs Bright. And off she went.

More than £100 taken, and it wasn't yet 10am. Jody was pleased with the start to her day. And why not? On average the shop took £250 a day, just over £1k a week, profits had been good in recent years.

She went and made herself a coffee.

Craig stared at the envelope. *'Merseyside Police'*. Surely not, surely not? How, after all this time could he suddenly see a news report of Archer and then get a letter about his dealings with the man, all in the space of a few days? *After all he had done for that bloody police force.* It was absurd. It wasn't going to happen. He knew coppers who would back him up. Despite all that, Craig's hands were still sweating and his chest was thumping.

He opened it up, then laughed out loud.

The letter was confirmation that PJC Shipping had reserved a table at the Merseyside Police's Charity Fundraiser next month, 10 to a table, £500. Invoice attached. Why they had addressed the letter to him and not Pete or Jason? He didn't know, he didn't care.

He sat back in his chair, smiled to himself, shook his head and breathed out.

SIXTEEN

What a terrible night it had been for Craig's team. Everton thrashed Arsenal.

If it wasn't bad enough watching, it was made worse by Jason strutting around the executive box doing some kind of chicken impression, squawking out loud, each time Everton scored. Lisa and Tim were bouncing up and down like kids who had consumed too many sherbet dib dabs. And of course PJC Shipping's six guests were all Everton fans. It was a long and painful night for Craig.

'Craig, why did you bother coming?' James Bunter was one of the directors at Liverpool Docks and a regular guest in the box. 'I mean it's not as if Arsenal looked like scoring, let alone winning. Just as well they only come up this way a few times a year. That saves on your pain. Why don't you support a proper team? Have Arsenal been to Man Utd yet by the way?'

'Ha! Ha! Nice one James,' Jason joined in the banter. 'First game of the season wasn't it Craig? Lost 5-0! We don't have a box at Old Trafford, although if the entertainment is as good there as it has been here, might be worth a punt.'

'Well, thanks James for coming,' said Craig with a sarcastic grin. 'Always a bloody delight to have you in the box and so glad my team could help make your night. Now piss off, hope your car isn't blocked in the car park.' They both laughed and Craig patted James on the back as he walked out.

'Oh, by the way Craig, how's Jody?' James turned at the door. 'She's not daft enough to support Arsenal I hope, or have you indoctrinated her? Tell her to give me a call and I'll take her to watch some proper football.'

'She's fine mate. There's as much chance of her watching a game of football as there is me watching 'Housewives of Cheshire', or whatever it's called.'

'It's called 'The Real Housewives of Cheshire', Lisa pointed out. 'And I like it. Jody and I clearly have good tastes.'

'Thanks Lisa. I'm glad I invited you as well. You're welcome to go home whenever you like by the way, sort of now. Shame you are not in tomorrow. Then again, after tonight.'

'You wouldn't cope without me, my dear.'

Her son, Tim gave a 'high-five' to Craig as he and his mum left. 'Hope you enjoyed it Tim, or is that a stupid question?' Craig smiled. Lisa gave her boss a quick peck on the cheek.

The box had emptied. It was just Craig, Jason and a few nibbles on the table left.

'So, how are things mate? Jason had his arm on Craig's shoulder. 'All good? Well apart from the football, obviously.'

Craig frowned. 'Yes, all's well, why do you ask? The result wasn't good but I'm not suicidal you know. It is only football!'

'I know, I know. It's just you have seemed a bit tense at work of late, the last few weeks, I just wondered if all is well. I just get a feeling, something's not quite right. Tell me to piss off by all means, but we have been friends a long time, so, if there is anything, and you want to talk.'

'There's nothing Jason, honestly, if there was, I'd say so. No worries.'

The pair looked at each other and finished off their drinks. Jason put his arm around Craig as they walked to the car. 'It wasn't as bad as 4-0 if it's any comfort. You did have one shot in the second half.'

'Jase. It was that bad and you know it was. Let's not paper over the cracks. We're a fucking basket-case of a team at the moment.'

Jody was still up when he got in, she was watching a film, 'The Darkest Hour' about Winston Churchill's decision to sign a peace treaty with Hitler or continue the war.

'Hello dear, good film?' Craig lent over and kissed her on the cheek. 'A bit heavy for a Tuesday night, isn't it?'

'Yeah, I think you're right.' Jody was sipping a glass of wine. 'I didn't know it was going to be so intense, I wished I gone more for something like 'Notting Hill''.

'Well, 'The Darkest Hour' couldn't be less like 'Notting Hill' if you tried love, unless Hugh Grant reminds you of Winston Churchill. Which at some angles he could well do if you ask me.' Craig wasn't a Hugh Grant fan.

'I know. I just thought it might be good, and it sort of is. Just perhaps not my type of film, then again might as well watch it to the end now. Anyhow, how did they get on?'

'Arsenal were crap, lost 4-0 and I was in a box, full of Everton fans.'

'Is that good?'

'Is what good?'

'4-0, it doesn't sound good, was there any food?'

'Any food?' I didn't care about the food, we lost. Who cares about sweet chilli wraps and mustard pork pies when you are sitting watching your team get stuffed alongside a crowd of baying scousers who got great delight in taking the piss out of me all night.'

'Ah, you poor man. Well, I hope you are not all grumpy, it's only a game'.

If ever there was a comment about football to wind Craig, or Tom up for that matter, it was, *'It's only a game'*. It was far more than that, football could, and did, determine mood swings and emotions. It could ruin a Saturday, it could make a weekend. A football result had the ability to put a spring in your step. It could dampen your spirits. *'Only a game'!*

'No, I'm not grumpy, although if you go on much more I will be. And for your information, it's much more than *'only a game'*. So, if you say anymore, I'll get as grumpy as old Churchill over there looks, and he looks pretty miserable, like he's swallowed a bag of spanners.'

'Spoke to Polly tonight,' Jody said, changing the subject.

'You speak to Polly most nights.'

'She's looking forward to coming over for the weekend, and Tom is leaving the surgery early, they may be here by 8ish. So we need to book a table for dinner at somewhere in the town. Leave it to me, I'll arrange it this time, hopefully for the right date.'

'Very funny, Jode. Want a cuppa?' She shook her head. Craig put the kettle on anyway.

The last time they were set to go for a meal, it was with friends, Dan and Sarah Dennis. Craig had been left to book a table at Ainsley's in Chester. Jody didn't think for one moment that was something he could possibly get wrong. But he did. He booked Ainsley's all right, for the wrong night! When the four of them arrived on Saturday the 5th, all the tables were full and booked for the evening. Craig's booking was for Saturday the 12th.

Fortunately Dan and Sarah took it well, Jody didn't. In the end they grabbed four takeaway pizzas and headed back to Jody and Craig's place before drinking all of Craig's beer and wine and playing 'pin the tail on the donkey'.

'I'll do it. I won't cock it up again,' Craig smiled as he poured himself a cuppa.

'You aren't getting a chance lover boy to cock it up again. I'm booking it this time. Although, actually, no. I'll tell you what, I'll make a lasagne. Tom likes that. Have a few drinks here, then perhaps go to the pub.'

Craig sat with his arm around his wife as the pair watched the last 40 minutes of the film.

The subject of babies, surrogacy and IVF hadn't come up for a few days and Craig was relieved about that. The thoughts of Stuart Archer being banged up in prison and the cops looking into more of Archers' dealings continued to play on his mind and he was worried about the way he had reacted to the letter from Merseyside Police.

Life was spiralling a little bit and he wasn't liking it. He knew this would happen.

But he backed himself. He was a cocky sort.

SEVENTEEN

TOM'S surgery was always busy.

He was a good dentist and had built up a sound reputation. The trouble was, he didn't get much down time during the day, and the fact he had called up two patients to squeeze them in earlier this week, so he could get away on Friday, had put more pressure on Wednesday and Thursday's diary. Still, it would be worth it when he was sitting in Chester with Craig, pint in hand.

Apparently Jill had enjoyed a 'wonderful' Tuesday off. Coffee and cake with her friends and a visit to a pub in the countryside that evening with a new man who was, according to her, 'an old friend'.

'I've only been single less than a week, I'm not going out with him,' Jill responded to Emily's *'nudge, nudge, wink, wink'* retort after Jill had told her about the evening date with Bill.

'Honestly, Emily, who do you think I am? I've known Bill for 30 years. We went to high school together and we used to meet at the youth club. His sister, Elsa, was my best friend for a long time, before she went and nicked my boyfriend, James, not that I was happy about that. James and I had been together for a couple of years when we were 16 and I honestly thought we would marry, I was so much in love with him. But he packed me in and then went out with Elsa about two weeks after we finished.

'I thought it was all a bit sudden to be going out with my best friend and sure enough I found out he'd been phoning her at home and asking if she fancied going out for a drink while we were still together. Some friend Elsa was, her excuse at the time was, James and I had split up before they got together. I didn't believe her, I always reckoned he was two-timing me, the git. But I got my own back.'

'Got your own back?' Emily raised her eyebrows, as Jill continued.

'Although we didn't speak much after she started seeing James, we were all still in a group of about 12-16 who went out regularly. So we sort of covered up our dislike of each other by avoiding too much conversation when we all met up. I could have stayed away from the group because of him still being there, but then I wouldn't have gone out much, they were all my friends.'

Jill was looking at the computer and talking to Emily at the same time.

'Anyhow, one night I had enough. The two of them were kissing and laughing in the corner of the pub, we were all about 19 I suppose. I had a bit too much to drink and was getting the hump looking at what they were up to. I knew another boy in the pub, Sam, who was a right laugh and a good mate. He wasn't with our group, but was with a load of lads who I knew. Sam liked me, I went over to him and asked if he would do me a favour. In return I said we could have a snog behind the pub, and a bit of a fumble. I knew he would be up for that!'

Emily laughed out loud. 'A bit of a fumble!'

Jill looked up. 'Oh, yes, those were the days. Anyway, I asked him to go over to Elsa and James, he didn't know either of them, and make out he knew James and how he was annoyed James had two-timed his sister, Barbara, and was going out with someone else. Sam would then point to Elsa and say, 'and I suppose this is the bird you have been two-timing her with.'

'You are kidding me,' Emily was engrossed. 'You asked him to do that?'

'Yeah. And Sam did. He comes over after I've sat down and starts giving James, who was a bit of a weed, a mouthful about two-timing his sister. He then points at Elsa and says, 'and I suppose this is the tart?'

'Well, all hell breaks loose, Elsa fell for it, she was so angry. She picked up her drink and tipped it over James, called him names and stormed out of the pub. James pleaded his innocence, saying he didn't know anyone called Barbara. It all happened so quickly and was hilarious, Sam walked off and James went after Elsa, but she'd gone.

'It took two weeks for her to believe James that it wasn't true. Although they got back together, she never really trusted him again. After about two months, they split up for good, serves them right.'

Emily shook her head. 'You are one bad girl, Jill. I wouldn't like to cross you.'

Jill smiled. 'And that night, after James' 'fumble' with his words, there was another 'fumble' at the back of the pub with me and Sam, oh, to be young again.'

Emily laughed out loud. 'I don't know what to say.'

'What to say about what?' Tom walked into the reception.

Both girls looked at each other. 'Have I missed something funny? Come on, don't leave me out of this one. 'What to say about what?''

'You don't want to know,' Emily said. 'All I'll say is, don't cross Jill, or you might get more than you bargained for.'

'Or you might get exactly what you bargained for,' Jill said, with a wry smile!

Tom looked confused. 'Okay, keep the joke to yourself, I'll stay on the outside. Clearly wouldn't want to be on the wrong end of Jill's wrath from the sound of things.'

Jill shook her head.

It was a cloudy morning and there were hints of rain in the air. Tom had driven into the office and had thought about giving Craig a quick call on the drive in. Then again, as they were meeting up on Friday, it could wait. After reading the local paper for a few minutes upstairs, he had come down to see the girls, and butted in on their 'joke', now it was time for work.

Jonny Gordon was a good pal of Tom's. A former professional rugby player, he had played much of his rugby in France, after going over to Toulouse at the age of 24, before returning to England three years ago to coach in Norfolk. Tom found him easy to listen to and enjoyed his stories. Jonny had played with some of France's top players and although he had never played international rugby, he had played in the French top league for five seasons and had only retired 18 months ago. It was only when his wife, Anna, who originated from Norfolk, had fallen pregnant and wanted to return to the UK to bring up their child, did he quit the French rugby scene.

At 6ft. 7ins. Jonny dwarfed even Tom, who could never imagine trying to stop Jonny in full flight on the rugby pitch. He wasn't just tall, he was built like a brick out-house and, while fatherhood had maybe softened him emotionally, physically, Jonny was still a man mountain. It was just before lunchtime when he walked upstairs and into the surgery.

'Good morning Tom. How are we?' Jonny had a big smile and an even bigger handshake.

Tom greeted him like a lost brother, with a big hug. The two had formed quite a bond considering they rarely saw each other, although Tom and Polly had attended the christening of Jamie, Jonny and Anna's only child. It had been a grand occasion for a christening, at a posh hotel in the Norfolk countryside. That was almost two years ago now and the pair had exchanged phone numbers and kept in contact.

'Come on, get in this chair and open wide.'

Tom was sure he was unlikely to find much wrong with Jonny's teeth. He had an almost perfect set, even if one of his front incisors had been punched out during a game some years ago. Whoever had done the repair had done a good job.

'So, how's this old dentist lark,' Jonny smiled. 'Still making a fortune?'

'Well, so long as people continue to play rugby and drink fizzy drinks, there will always be teeth to fix and fill. I don't know, people don't seem to listen, sugar isn't good for you, and then again rugby can be pretty dangerous.'

Jonny laughed. 'Are you saying eating sweets is as dangerous as playing rugby, my good man? Because if you are, I'd have never eaten all that sherbet back when I was a kid.

'Anyhow. You got kids yet? Can't believe that pretty Polly wife of yours doesn't want them. Or, have I put my foot in it. Shit, I do this all the time. Anna tells me I'm such an arse.'

'No, we haven't got any kids yet,' Tom said, patting his friend on the back. 'It's our choice at the moment, but watch this space.'

'Well, I'll keep listening out.'

Tom changed the subject. 'How's the rugby coaching going?'

'It's going great mate, I'm over at South Walsham at the moment. Coaching the first team and helping with the kids. We're doing okay and we have some great young talent coming through, you should come over and watch a game some time. The firsts play on Saturdays. We are always looking for match-day sponsors, you would get an invite to the vice-president's lunch, just give me a call if you fancy it. Not many games left now.'

Tom thought for a second. 'Actually, that sounds a plan, I'm serious. Polly is always saying I should get the surgery's name out there a bit more when she has her marketing head on. I have lots of patients, but could always do with more, sponsoring a game could be a laugh. Especially if there's drinking involved, Polly would love that.'

'Don't you worry Tom lad, there's plenty of drinking involved for sponsors. This is rugby we're talking about. I'll drop you some details, I'll see you soon, hopefully.' And with that he shook Tom's hand and headed out of the surgery.

'Don't forget six months,' Tom shouted to him as he was walking down the stairs. 'For another appointment'.

'Will do mate.'

Tom made a few notes about Jonny's teeth, Emily had gone out of the surgery to make a coffee and Tom pondered the idea about sponsoring a game at Walsham, it was something he had never thought about. I suppose he would get a mention in the programme and maybe a mention on the day via the PA. He didn't really know what to expect or what it would cost. If the price was right, he'd leave Polly to sort out the logistics and requirements.

She'd get him a good deal.

It was rare Tom went to the Queen's Head midweek, but seeing as he and Polly were up in Chester on Friday night, he decided to pop over for a quick half or three.

Polly hadn't wanted to go, so he went alone. He had no idea who would be in there. If there was no-one, he was happy to enjoy a couple of pints on his own, perhaps a packet of peanuts.

He walked across the village green. It was a cool Wednesday evening and the wind had got up. He and Polly had enjoyed sausage casserole for tea.

As he entered the pub, Tom could see there were not many people in. Paul was behind the bar, Jan had the night off. The darts team, who Tom had thought may be playing, were instead away from home in a league match. But, despite the lack of people, the Queen's Head had a warm glow to it, Paul and Jan always kept it bright and this April evening with the weather cool, Paul had lit the open fire.

There were two couples in the restaurant but only Milky was sitting in the corner of the bar, reading a paper. He looked up at the same time Paul greeted Tom.

'Evening Tom, how are things?' Paul had a pint glass in his hand ready to pour a pint. 'Nippy tonight. I've put the fire on, first time this month. Didn't Polly get a call to play for the darts team after her heroics here on Friday? Paul laughed. 'What a throw that was to hit the bull.'

'No, she didn't. To be honest, I'm not sure if last Friday's episode is anything to judge her on as regards her darts prowess. She only throws a mean dart after about five vats of wine! She'd be far too expensive to take out for league matches.'

It was Paul's turn to laugh, 'the usual?' Tom nodded.

Milky was tucking into a steak and kidney pie, baked beans and potatoes as Tom approached him, pint in hand. He had asked if Milky wanted a 'top up', but he had shaken his head, which was unusual, Milky rarely refused a drink.

'You okay?' Tom went to sit down alongside him. 'Okay if I join you, or are you deep into that steak and kidney pie?' Tom smiled, but sensed something wasn't right, Milky was easy to read.

'Of course you can sit down,' Milky said, moving his chair over to allow Tom to pull his closer. 'No, I'm fine, just had a bit of bad news this week about Chantelle. She's, well she's ended it. We're no more.' He shrugged his shoulders. 'She said we're not compatible. I said I didn't know what compatible meant. She said, 'well, there you go, see what I mean?' Which I don't. If you see what I mean? So, I assume it's over.'

'She doesn't think your relationship will work is what she was trying to say, mate.' Tom tried to put it as nicely as possible. 'I'm sorry, when did you split up?'

'On Sunday night, after Countryfile.' Milky took another

mouthful of his dinner. 'Well, I called her after Countryfile. I always watch that, never miss it. She had called me earlier in the afternoon and said she wanted to talk, I didn't know about what, but I assumed it was about everything and nothing. Perhaps I should have called her back sooner, but I like Countryfile.

'I'm a bit sad to be honest, because I liked her as well. She cooked me a nice chicken tusalla last week as well.'

'You mean chicken tikka masala,' Tom said.

'Yeah, one of them. And we both like heavy rock music, and spiders. I thought we had lots in common. And she had nice boobs.' He winked at Tom.

'That's no way to talk about a lady,' Tom nudged him. 'I thought you were sorry it was all over.'

'Well I am in some ways sad. But only some ways.'

Milky dug his fork into one of his potatoes and took another mouthful. Tom wasn't sure what to make of his demeanour, one minute he had appeared subdued, the next, at the thought of Chantelle's chest, he had perked up!

'So, how long have you been in here tonight?'

'Oh, I came in straight from finishing a little job I have at Mrs Robbins' house. I'm building her a greenhouse. Been in here about an hour I suppose.'

'Well, although there is no more Chantelle, at least you still have a smile on your face,' said Tom.

'Plenty of fish in the sea. I thought when I walked in you looked a bit down, hopefully the break-up hasn't affected your drinking capacity. You want another?'

'Yeah. I think I will this time.' Milky supped up.

'I was a bit confused when you came in to be honest, I was just reading a text from Chantelle, she sent it 10 minutes ago. It said she was wondering if she had made a mistake ending our relationship. Don't know why she was now saying that, she wanted it over. I can't be doing with all that type of hassle, Tom.'

'No, you can't. That's playing about with your mind. And mind games are enough to do anyone's head in. I wouldn't do with it either, if you want my advice.'

'Oh, I'm not worried about mind games.' Milky finished his pint.

'I haven't got enough up top to worry about that. Anyhow, I'm seeing Denise tomorrow night, we're going for a pizza. I met her at Mrs Robbins when I was doing the greenhouse. She was there doing some housework. I once went out with her sister many years ago, lovely bum has Denise. She's just split up from her husband. Did you say you were getting another pint?'

Tom smiled and supped up his beer, before going to go to the bar to get them both another drink.

The grass didn't grow long under Milky's feet!

EIGHTEEN

MR and Mrs Tankard accepted Polly's offer of free membership for a year, Polly deciding to up it from Andy's initial idea of six months.

They also accepted a full apology and were pleased to hear that the signs for 'MEN'S CHANGING' and 'LADIES CHANGING' were to be made much bigger. They also accepted that Mr Peters had made an innocent mistake, Polly telling them both he had been given a warning that if it happened again, his membership would be cancelled.

Polly's news about the 'Tankard settlement' got Thursday morning's team meeting at the gym off to a good start and Andy was especially pleased to hear the news. The last thing he had wanted was the media all over a story about a man in the woman's changing rooms at his establishment. And while Polly was always telling him that all publicity was good publicity, he hadn't been convinced.

The whole team was assembled in the office, although Kevin was a bit on the drag.

'Bloody traffic on the ring road,' he mumbled as he walked through the door two minutes late. 'Apologies everyone.'

'Apology accepted,' James shot back. Kevin stared.

'I came in on my Brompton today,' James continued 'It was a lovely ride, you can't beat a lovely ride, Kevin. You ought to get a Brompton, soft on the bum.'

Kevin wanted to say something, but decided as he had arrived late, it would be best simply to sit down.

'Okay, folks, well thanks for that Polly about the Tankards. Good work,' Andy said. He then relayed the story to the late-arriving Kevin that all had ended well on that front.

The sun was pouring through the room and Valerie got up to adjust the blinds as Andy continued. 'Okay,' he said. 'Now, I've got some news about an idea I have been floating around in my head for a while about us having a 'green area' with the central hub of it all, a green restaurant.

'James and I have done some preliminary work on costings and we are confident we can afford it. And I have spoken to Polly about marketing.' He looked at Polly, who nodded her agreement.

'So, now it's time to open it up to you Tina and Kevin about your thoughts. A 'green area', a green restaurant, green food, what do you think? It would be as well as our current restaurant, it would be an addition.'

Kevin shrugged his shoulders. 'Don't worry me, I can't stand all that green muck, but I know plenty of people who do seem to like it. Can't really fathom out what's so great about bean shoots and noodles. I'll tell you something though, you aint' gonna dead-lift 300 pounds living on a diet of rabbit food. I would suggest we don't over-promote the restaurant in the gym area, most of the guys who work out eat steak and raw eggs.'

Polly tutted. 'Don't be daft, it's been proved you don't need steak and raw eggs to build up muscle and strength. It's all about diet today. Years ago people were eating steaks for fun, but you don't build muscle up that way. Plant-based foods are the way forward. We should very much promote it in the gym, that's the first place I would promote it.'

'Listen to you the weights expert over there,' Kevin's sarcasm befitting a man who hated being questioned by a woman.

'Why don't you come into the gym one day and speak to some of my guys and offer them a bean sprout or chick pea soup and see what they say. I dare say most of the millennials who work out in the gym eat plant food, but they are hardly next year's World's Strongest Man contestants. Most of them are more interested in safe spaces, iPhones and grass, and not the edible variety.' Kevin looked around the room for appreciation of his little joke.

'That's a stupid argument,' Polly hit back. 'This is the 21st

century, not 1970. Diet has moved on. Science has moved on. I thought people who kept themselves fit knew this stuff. And guess what? People today don't use sunbeds as much, either, it's not good on the skin you know. You'll catch up with that fact soon, Kevin.'

Kevin opened his mouth and was about to respond, but Andy jumped in.

'Okay, okay, you two. All I want is your thoughts on the project and, while I know you aren't a fan of vegans, vegetarians, bean sprouts or rice, at least give me your thoughts Kevin, from a business angle.'

Kevin looked at Andy. 'Suppose it might work,' he begrudgingly conceded.

'I think's it's a great idea,' piped up Tina with gusto. 'It will be a big hit. Green food and diet is huge these days. My friends' children are at Uni and they live off green food, burgers and chips are okay as a treat, but are very much yesterday's food. When are we thinking of building it and where?'

'At the far end of the swimming pool and off to the side, to the right, about 20 metres from the Jacuzzi,' Andy said. 'There's space there for a small restaurant area and about four tables with say four chairs around each table. It's at the other end of the gym to our main restaurant and obviously it won't be as big. We are hoping to crack on with it next month or so when the loan arrives, which should be soon, shouldn't it James?'

'It should be soon,' said James, who was dressed in an all-white suit with a red handkerchief sticking out of the top breast pocket. He looked dapper. 'I'm speaking to John at the bank tomorrow, but it's pretty well a done deal. It's just a case of when we want the money.'

'That's great,' said Andy.

'You selling ice creams today all that white clobber you have on? Looks very smart, I'll have a '99 with double flake. Where's your van? Parked outside?' Kevin smiled. He could never resist a pop at James.

'Did you say a '99 or a '69 darling? James retorted. 'Anyhow, I'd get you a choc ice if you came to my van. You know, brown on the outside, white on the inside, a bit like you! By the way, always remember not to frown too much when tanning, gives you white stripes across your forehead.' James giggled. Valerie started to laugh then thought best not to.

'How many more times, this isn't a sunbed tan,' Kevin protested.

Again, Andy had to intervene to get the conversation back on track.

'Okay, people that will do then, unless anyone has any other business?' he said. 'We are all on board with the green restaurant then?' Everyone nodded. 'I'll let you know of developments, hopefully it will prove a winner. I have high hopes.'

The meeting ended and Polly was walking down the corridor towards her office when her mobile went off, she went to answer it, but it quickly rang off. She looked at the screen, it said 'unknown'. No sooner had she slipped it back in her pocket than it rang again. Again it said 'unknown', but this time she answered it before it rung off.

'Hello, Polly Armstrong,' she said

'Hello. Who is this?'

'Hello Polly. Nice legs'. It was a ladies' voice. Or at least it sounded like a lady. Then, as quickly as the words had been said, the caller rang off.

Polly stood still and looked at her phone, then tried to call the number back. There was no reply. She went into Valerie's office and told her what had happened and to see if she knew a way of finding out a number that was 'unknown'. Val didn't.

'So, what did she say?' Valerie was looking at the phone.

Polly told her but Val looked blank. 'Well, what was the point of that? 'Nice legs' How bizarre! Are you sure it was a woman, or a man with a high voice?'

'Don't Val,' said Polly, trying not to make light of it. 'I hate stuff like this. I know. It sounded like a woman, I don't mind when people say nothing, perhaps they hear your voice and think they have the wrong number, but to say 'nice legs' is a bit more sort of odd, don't you think?'

Val could sense the call had bothered Polly, which was unusual. She wasn't the type of girl to worry.

'Has something else happened that's bothering you?' Val

asked. 'It's unlike you to seem so concerned over something that was probably nothing. And let's be honest, you have got a cracking pair of legs.'

The comment made them both smile.

'I know I shouldn't worry, it's nothing. Perhaps it's my time of the month coming up. But thanks anyhow. You walking into the city lunchtime? I'll walk with you.'

'No, I'm not. I'm meeting my mum. She wants to treat me to coffee and cake, she's catching the train in from Lowestoft.'

'Ooh, sounds fun,' replied Polly, who gave a little wave with her hand as she left Valerie and walked towards her own office.

Polly checked through her e-mails. The deal with the radio station was all set to go ahead next week. She was excited about that and a couple of 'ditties' for the promo trailer would be sent over to her tomorrow or Monday. She would have to ask Kevin to join her to listen to them, seeing as he had been a big fan of the idea of the gym sponsoring the Farming News!

Her mobile rang. Polly stared at it... 'Unknown'. *'Oh, not again'.*

'Hello, Polly Armstrong, can I help you? Look what do you want?'

'Hi Polly.' It was the same caller again. And it was a female. *'Tom's little secret'.* The phone went dead. Again Polly called the number back, no reply.

She sat in her office and looked at the phone. It wasn't often things bothered her, but for some reason this did. Who the hell was it? She was sure it was the same voice. She'd have to tell Tom when she got home tonight.

He would say it was nothing.

NINETEEN

THEY had been in the car three hours and were still 30 minutes from the ground.

Roads out of Norfolk were never the best, that's one thing Karen had already learned during her short time in the county.

To get to London by road, something she knew plenty about having gone backwards and forwards from Woolwich on numerous occasions before moving to Oxton, could be a nightmare, especially if the traffic was heavy, which this afternoon, it was.

Lee's England rugby trial, the first of two he was to have over the coming weeks, was taking place in Barnet, at the home of Saracens Rugby Football Club. The fact the trial date had come through so quickly, just a few days after the Slixworth game, and the fact it was being held at Saracens, had meant Lee had concentrated little on his schoolwork as he tried to take in such exciting news. Many of his friends were awestruck at him playing at the home of one of the country's biggest rugby clubs. He hadn't been able to wait for Thursday to come along, but it was here now, and he and his mum would be there soon.

'We aren't going to be late mum, are we?' Lee had taken his eyes off the game he was playing on the phone.

'No dear. We won't be early mind you, but it did say be there at 7pm and the sat nav says we'll be there at 6.50.' She hoped her answer would satisfy him, she knew they were cutting it fine.

'How long will it take for you to get ready once we get there? All you stuff is in the back of the car.'

'About two seconds. You did pack my new gum shield didn't you?'

'Yes. Along with the other five gum shields you already have in that filthy bag of yours. I hope you wash it before putting it in your mouth. It looks disgusting.'

'Why would you wash it?' Lee pulled a face. He went back to his phone.

Karen pulled up outside the ground at 6.57pm. It was cutting it fine, but they weren't late, she could see lots of boys milling around in the car park and some were funnelling into what she assumed must be the changing rooms.

Lee dived out of the car and opened the boot to rescue his kit bag, he shot off in the direction of the rest of the boys. It wouldn't take him long to get ready.

'Good luck darling,' Karen shouted as he slammed the boot shut. But he was gone.

She was glad to sit back and close her eyes for a while after the drive. It had taken longer than the two-and-a-half hours her sat nav had told her it would take, and it had been a bit stressful as the time had ticked closer to 7. Just as well she left at 3.45pm. She would never have forgiven herself had Lee missed his first trial. She turned the radio on and closed her eyes.

When she opened them, she looked at her phone, it was 7.45pm. The car park was now almost full and she could see the floodlights were on as they beamed across the fields and into the car park. She wasn't sure whether she was allowed to go and watch what was going on. This wasn't South Walsham U15s training, this was England training. Karen decided to get out of the car and go have a look around. The ground was imposing and was clearly on a different level to any rugby ground she had been to with Lee in the past.

She walked around the car park once and then doubled back on herself as she seemed to be walking away from the floodlights and there was no sign of any entrance. It was a cold night and she had put a scarf on, as well as a thick coat. She was surprised at the lack of people around considering the amount of cars in the car park, they must all be inside. Karen noticed two men walking away from her towards what she assumed must be the entrance, they turned left and vanished out of sight 50 yards or so ahead of her. She decided to follow and, as Karen turned the corner, was confronted by two huge glass doors. It looked like the reception entrance.

She walked through the doors and on her right a voice spoke up. 'Hello, can I help? It was a middle-aged woman, with slightly grey hair. She was standing behind a counter with a Perspex window between herself and Karen.

'I'm a bit lost to be honest,' Karen said. 'My son is here for the trials and I was wondering if I could watch? But if not, no problem, is there somewhere I could get a coffee?'

Two questions in one were soon answered by the lady who pointed to a door directly in front of Karen.

'There's a bar area in there which does teas and coffees and where you can see a bit of what is going on with the trials. You are not allowed near the pitch, so you have to keep behind the glass, but it's warm in there. Go take a seat.' The lady smiled, Karen appreciated her helpfulness and was soon pushing open the door she had been pointed towards.

Inside was a vast area and there must have been 50 or 60 people standing around, or sitting down, many holding glasses, mugs and cups. She walked to the bar and ordered a coffee, the young man behind it was as polite and smiley as the lady in reception.

The room had lots of chairs and tables and what Karen assumed must be a large dance floor. There were cups, jerseys and trophies on the walls and the room looked out onto the rugby pitches through a mass of glass panelling that most people were behind watching the action on the pitches.

There was no way to get pitch side to watch any closer. Not that she wanted to. She had always let Lee get on with his rugby. She had never interfered before and she wouldn't start now just because this was an England trial. Her place was to support him and listen. Not that he'd likely listen to her on anything to do with rugby.

'Mum, what do you know about it?', he had once said to her after she had told him how well she thought he had played after a school match in London one evening. 'I was crap, okay? We lost and the coach is furious. Please don't tell me I played well if you don't know what you're talking about. Which you don't!' She never commented again.

Karen looked at her watch, it was 8pm and she sat down behind the glass at a space in the corner to watch what was going on. She found it hard to spot Lee among the mass of players, although she did think she spotted him once, but then again was he wearing his old Woolwich top, or a South Walsham one? She didn't know what he had chosen, he packed his own playing kit. There must have been 40-50 boys involved in the trial and although she was behind glass, she could hear plenty of shouting.

'Is you son playing?' A lady with dark wavy hair who looked a similar age to Karen, came alongside to chat. 'Mine is, then again, I suppose everyone here has someone playing. Exciting isn't it – for the boys, I mean. England trials. Been a long journey down from Bradford though. Sorry, I'm Isabelle.'

Karen looked at Isabelle and smiled as the two shook hands. 'I'm Karen. That is a long way to come. We've come from Norfolk and that was far enough. Yes, it is exciting. My son has been talking about it non-stop all week, pretty sure he has done little work at school. I don't mind so long as these trials aren't too often, I would like him to pass his exams to be honest. The chances of him being a professional rugby player are, well, I don't actually know how good they are, I'm not really into rugby that much, I'm just the taxi driver.'

Isabelle smiled and nodded her head. 'Well, I let William have his dreams. My husband used to play rugby, he's standing over there,' she pointed. 'Not at a professional level mind you. He has already told William it's a hard profession to get into, but you never know, someone has to play for England.'

'Well, indeed,' Karen replied. 'Someone does. Not sure if my Lee is good enough, but honestly I don't know because, as I said, I don't know enough about it.'

'Maybe you don't. A bit like me. But the men like to think they know it all don't they? I bet Lee's dad is like my Bryan, like to think they know it all.' Isabelle laughed. Karen smiled.

'Well, I best go stand with hubbie and ask him what's going on. I'm sure he'll know, or if he doesn't he'll make it up! See you about. Maybe when the boys both play for England, how much fun would that be?' And off she went with a big smile on her face.

Karen let Isabelle's words sink in.

It wasn't the first time mention of Lee's dad had cropped up in conversation during her and Lee's 14 years together, and it wouldn't be the last.

Karen looked around. There weren't many women in the vast hall. Any that were there were with men, likely their husbands or partners, plenty of men appeared to be on their own. How many women were on their own? Not many.

Karen finished her drink and ventured over to one of the windows on the other side of the room and looked out across the fields. She thought she spotted Lee again. How proud she was of him having rugby trials for England, how his dad should see this.

Lee threw open the car door and chucked his rugby kit in the back before plonking himself in the front next to his mum. It was almost 9.30, the trial had finished 15 minutes ago and Karen had headed straight to the car when she saw all the boys starting to walk in off the pitch. She passed Isabelle on the way out, saying goodbye.

Karen assumed he had enjoyed a quick shower as his hair was wet, he was also in a bubbly mood.

'How did it go darling? I was watching a bit behind the glass in the club house but I couldn't see much.'

'It was great mum. I did well. At least I think I did well. No, I know I did well. One of the coaches came up to me afterwards and wanted to know my name and where I played rugby, he said I had done well. He said don't get too cocky or over-confident, keep playing my game and listen, listen, listen to the coaches.'

Karen was thrilled. Lee wasn't a boy who blew his own trumpet. 'That's great. Well done, fancy a thick shake on the way out of here, if I can find a McDonalds?' She didn't have the chance to get the sentence out before Lee was high-fiving her. 'Let's go for it mum. I'm starving.

'Can I have a Big Mac as well?'

It was almost 1am when Karen pulled into the driveway of their cottage in Oxton. The journey home had been uneventful, even more so after Lee fell asleep 20 minutes after finishing his food and drink.

Lee woke up when the engine turned off. He was sluggish as

he came round and it took him a few minutes to gather his senses.

'Bring your kit bag, darling,' she said as she put the key in the front door. 'Go straight to bed.'

Karen went into the house first. Lee did as he was told, yawned as he walked up the stairs, and was soon collapsed in his bed. It wouldn't be a long sleep, as he had to be up at 7am to catch the bus to school the next day. Karen wasn't happy about that, but the importance for her son to have rugby trials for England outweighed one tired day at school.

She kissed him on the forehead, went downstairs to close up and then went back upstairs to get ready for bed. She put her phone on the side cabinet, plugged in the charger, looked at it again, bit her lip and wondered.

'No', she thought.'

She won't be up at this time of night.'

TWENTY

Stuart Archer had run risks. Big risks.

He'd been drug dealing for more than 15 years. Getting caught was not something he'd ever thought about. You couldn't think like that. If he had done so, he would never have built the empire he had. But caught he was and a long stretch in Strangeways was upon him. To say he was not looking forward to it was an understatement, to say he was pissed in the way he had been caught was an even bigger understatement.

Archer had been stitched up, he knew that. But by who, he wasn't sure. His operation had been so tight-knit, so professional, how the hell had the cops infiltrated him? Here he was, sitting in a prison cell at 50 years of age. He could have done without this shit, especially as he had been planning to 'retire' from the game in the next year or two, a quiet, relaxing, sun-kissed life awaited, not your usual crap on the Costa del Sol with the other plebs. Archer had proper plans, real plans, living on an island in the Caribbean. Maybe his own island, and Marie would be no-where in sight. He would have paid her off, or worse if she didn't co-operate. She'd promised she would, though. Marie was hard-nosed and thick-skinned, she'd had to put up with much during their near 20-year marriage, but now they had gone their own ways.

The 'sting' that had caught him had been the classic set-up. Get a copper to infiltrate the gang. Make recordings, take notes. They wanted Archer, they wanted 'Mr Big', and they had got him. He could picture the bloke now, all white teeth and shiny shoes, he should have seen through it. Archer sat in his cell wondering how he hadn't worked the bastard out. He was usually so good at detecting that sort of thing, he hadn't expected the other gang members to suss out who the 'new guy' was. That was his job, they trusted his opinions. He had always known what was right for the business. Who to bring on board who to ship out. Archer had got this one wrong though, badly wrong.

Archer's gang had scarpered far and wide after his arrest. Most now likely thousands of miles away in countries the UK had no extradition warrant for, if they had any sense, that is. He couldn't blame them, the cops wanted him and him only. As far as they were concerned, his minions could go whistle. He'd lost nearly all the people he could trust. Not that he trusted many in the first place. At least Tony Statton was still about.

Statton hadn't been involved in any of Archer's operations for the past eight years, as the importing and dealing had ramped up. He was a foot soldier from the early days. Back then there was just Archer, Statton, Charlie Cantwell and a couple of young lads from Liverpool. Making a grand a week was seen as life-changing, then. Two years ago, Archer's 10-strong gang were making £300k a month. Statton had missed out on the big bucks, but had still made a packet.

He had left Archer's side after landing a job down south. Although, back then, he could earn more with Archer in a month than he could in his new job at Southampton in a year, a new woman, marriage and 'love sickness' had taken over Statton's world. He had told Archer he wanted out. He was a true trusty and Archer granted it. They'd kept in touch through the grapevine.

It had taken Statton six days to act on Archer's phone call, and six hours to drive north to HM Prison Manchester, more commonly known as Strangeways, north of the city centre. It was a foreboding-looking place. The ventilation tower and imposing design enough to make anyone look twice as you walked up to it. Statton had driven past it enough times when he lived just outside the city. He remembered being told the prison walls are rumoured to be 16 feet thick, and plenty of notorious criminals had been housed there. It had also been notable for a series of riots in 1990. Statton remembered them, he also remembered his old man telling him how the place was, 'a shit heap'. His dad had spent a year in Strangeways back in the '80s for drug offences. It was another reason Statton had wanted out of Archer's operations.

So, anyone other than Archer calling him up and asking him to come and talk to him face to face in Strangeways would have seen Statton stay firmly in Southampton with a list of excuses as long as his arm. But they went back a long way. School kids, early drinking buddies, early girlfriend sharing. Blood brothers, Early drug dealers. The families had also been friends, loyalty came first, second and third in the world of the Archers and Stattons.

Statton knew Archer had been arrested two days after it happened. Even though he was no longer a 'noise' in the criminal underworld, Statton had enough sources with fingers on the pulse. After the arrest, he followed the case on the internet, he knew Archer would be in for a long stretch if he was found guilty.

After spending more than 30 minutes in security at Strangeways, Statton emerged into a large room with about 20 tables with two chairs at each. He could see Archer sitting at a table in the corner. They may not have met for a couple of years, but neither had changed much, Archer looked a bit thinner, Statton thought. And certainly more than his 50 years of age, he was a year older than Statton.

'Alright Tony?' Archer got up from his chair and shook Statton's hand.

'I'm alright pal. How are you getting on in here?' He held Archer's stare for a good ten seconds, before they both sat down.

'Not great to be honest. It's fucking shit. Was sharing a cell with another drug dealer who thinks he is running the Mafia. He has no idea, mid-20s. In for possession and a few drugs. He'll get out in two and be back within a year for about 20. How's Alice? And the boys?'

'Yes, mate, they're fine. Alice is working for the NHS and both boys are at secondary school. They both want to go to Uni. Luckily I can somehow afford all that easily enough.' Statton winked. 'Still a bit left in the old pot, although it's going faster than I would like.'

Archer smiled. 'Spend it mate, don't let the pigs get hold of any.'

'And Marie,' Statton said. 'She okay?'

'Fuck me. No idea mate. I haven't seen her since the day of

my arrest about six months ago. She's probably in Monte Carlo spending all my bloody cash. But you know what? Can't blame her, I treated her like shit but she's a loyal girl, a really loyal girl, she deserves whatever comes her way. Our marriage was over years ago, but we stuck together. Our relationship always gave me an alibi, but that's all gone tits up, hasn't it?'

They both looked at each other. Statton shrugged his shoulders at Archer's last comment. He was right, it had all gone tits up.

Statton knew he hadn't been called up to Manchester to discuss his and Archer's family affairs. He'd been wondering for a few days what this was all about, Archer wouldn't discuss it on the phone.

He leant over to speak to Statton.

'Listen. I've been stitched up, Tony. That's why I'm in here and I'm pissed about it. Very pissed. The thought there are people out there who have set me up fills me with fury, you understand, don't you mate?' Statton nodded.

'The rest of the boys who fled the gang? Well, I've had a few calls made and I'm confident none of them had anything to do with that bastard copper who infiltrated our group. That's how we got done. Did you know that? A copper in our midst, how the fuck did I miss that?'

'I had heard, mate.'

'None of the boys knew him. They trusted the bastard because I trusted the bastard. It was my mistake. Anyway, I'm not after the copper, I'm after the bastard who helped get the copper in. Who tipped the cops off? Who is the fucking grass in all this? Because someone did it, someone must have. I've already had lots of time to think in here and I want you to do something for me, I have a name.'

Red flags flew through Statton's mind, *'I have a name'*. He didn't give anything away to Archer, he would hear him out.

'About 18 months ago I got some dirt on a guy in Chester, a Craig Baldini,' Archer moved closer to Statton as he began to speak.

'This Baldini fella shagged my Marie at some works do, nearly two years ago. He was happily married. I couldn't have cared too much about him and Marie. We were history by then. But I used it to my advantage, he was shit scared I'd tell his missus, I had a DVD, I had lots of DVDs. Having dirt on someone never hurts, does it?' Archer half-smiled.

'Anyhow, I meet up with him. Tell him what I know, tell him about the DVD and I get him to do some 'runs' for me, or those DVDs could end up where he didn't' want them to end up. You know what I mean?' Statton nodded. 'He was only running small stuff, bit of dope here and there.

'Anyhow, after about three runs, I tell him to fuck off and that's that. Trouble is, I think the cops visited him, this is where I'm not sure. I did keep an eye on him, but nothing seemed out of turn. But I want him checked out. There's 50K in it for you if you can help me out here.' Statton began to shake his head. Archer read the signs.

'Look, before you say anything, I just want him checked out, Tony. Nothing more. I know you don't want to get involved in this shit, you're all loved up down south, happy families.'

Statton remained poker-faced.

'I just want to know what this Baldini bloke is up to. He works for some shipping company in Liverpool. It's just a hunch because I don't know him well enough. I had Baldini by the balls, maybe I was too smart, and perhaps I should have just left it. It was too easy to blackmail him. Maybe I blackmailed the wrong guy, I don't know. Just check him out for us pal and then if you think so, I'll get Charlie's boys to pay him a visit. You remember Charlie?'

Statton nodded and looked at his friend. He didn't know what to say. Having rebuilt a life in Southampton, working as a sales rep for a plumbing company, the last thing he now wanted was to get involved in this sort of stuff again. Then again 50K was a tidy amount and he wasn't being asked to do anything other than check the guy out. No violence, no intimidation, no questions just use his hunches. Charlie could do any messy work.

'Look mate, let me give it a thought,' Statton said. 'I'm not saying no, but let me get my head around it. I'm pretty sure I'm in Stu, but, well, you know how my life is now? Give me a few days.'

'I will mate, I will. But just a few days, I need closure on all this. I need to know who stuck me in here. I've got at least 15 years ahead of me mate and I'll go fucking mad in here if I don't find out who tucked me up, that's just the way I am, you know that. Call me. Soon.'

Archer stood up and Statton followed. They still had 20 minutes to talk if they wanted. But the talking was over. They shook hands and Archer turned and walked out, accompanied by a prison guard.

As he walked out of the prison Statton turned back and looked at the front of Strangeways' huge imposing structure. What was he doing here? What was he getting himself into?

As he headed into the city centre to get something to eat, Statton's mind was racing. He had to keep this from Alice, she would go crazy if she knew what he was thinking of doing to help an old friend. Not that she knew who Archer was. But he really didn't have to do this. Then again what would have happened if the boot had been on the other foot, and it was he who had made the call to Archer? It was he who was desperate and needed closure? It was he who was in prison?

He knew the answer to that.

Archer would have been there for him all day long.

TWENTY ONE

'OPEN wide, Mrs Churchyard.'

Tom was seeing his final patient of Friday afternoon and it was only 3.30pm. Jill had done him proud re-jigging a few appointments, although the incentive for her to leave off early meant it had been no hardship.

Tom was in the good books. Polly had taken Friday off from the gym and packed up the Audi the night before. It meant a lay-in for her, while Tom had been under strict instructions about getting off as soon as possible to head to Chester.

'Excellent, let me just give you a quick polish, but everything seems in order,' Tom said, as Mrs Churchyard rinsed her mouth out and smiled warmly at him. Five minutes later, she was heading out the door, Tom leaving Emily to tidy up a few bits and bobs, before going downstairs to let Jill know he would be leaving when Polly arrived, leaving her to lock up.

The reception door flew open and in strode Polly, all smiles, dressed in a light blue skirt and white blouse, with light blue shoes. As usual, she looked a picture.

'Hi Pol,' Jill said. 'You look gorgeous as usual, wish I was 20 years younger, even then I couldn't dress like that.' She pointed to Polly's clothes. 'Looking forward to your weekend?'

'Hi. Yep, I am. We haven't been up to Chester for a few months and it's always great to catch up with my friend Jody. Is he on time? He had better be, I did tell him I'd be catching the 2.45 bus in. I didn't think he would dare not be on time after what happened last time he was late. Or the time before that.' Polly winked at Jill.

'He's almost done I think. His last patient has just gone, so I don't reckon he'll be long. How are you anyway?'

Polly smiled. 'Oh, I'm fine. Work is okay, the weather in Chester looks rubbish though, but hey, me and Jode will probably get a bit drunk tonight, and tomorrow night. What a time to be alive.'

It was Jill's turn to smile. She had always liked Polly. When she had become Tom's receptionist, Polly had sent her a bunch of flowers with a lovely note wishing her well. Polly had also put in the note that if Tom ever gave her 'any crap', she was to let her know, she would deal with him! That had made Jill laugh. Thankfully she had never had to call on Polly's services.

'I hope you don't mind me mentioning, but I hear you and Robert are having a bit of a break. Tom did tell me. I hope you are all okay with it?'

'A bit of a break? Make that a permanent one, he's history. I don't know if Tom told you the whole story. Robert has being seeing some tart for months now.'

'I'm sorry, no Tom didn't elaborate.' Polly went over to hold her hand. 'You know what men are like, so good for you, I say. I always told Tom, if you can't keep it in your trousers and I find out, I swear to God, I'll cut the bugger off.'

Both girls laughed, just as Tom entered the reception.

'Oops, talk of the devil,' Polly grinned at Jill.

'Oh yeah. What are you two talking about?' Tom said suspiciously. He put down a couple of folders on Jill's desk. 'In saying that, I don't think I want to know, you alright love?'

'We were just talking about you darling, not to you,' Polly moved to give him a kiss on the cheek.

'Not surprised. I seem to keep coming in on the back end of conversations just lately, missing the punch line time after time. Happened the other day with Jill and Emily. I hope it's not just me all the fun is being poked at, I'm a sensitive chap. You know us dentists can be fragile creatures.'

'Rubbish,' Polly laughed as she smiled at him. 'Anyhow, if you want to know what I said, we were talking about men 'playing away from home'. You know, having affairs, and I was just telling Jill that if you ever did that, I'd cut it off! Probably in the middle of the night while you were snoring.'

Tom looked to the sky, then looked at Jill, who was trying not to laugh. 'You're unbelievable. Jill doesn't need to know that.'

'You're quite right, I don't need to know, but it helps if I do. If you ever came into the surgery speaking in a high-pitched voice and walking with your legs crossed one morning, then I'll know what you've been up to, you naughty boy.'

'You make my bloody eyes water.' said Tom. He looked at Polly. 'Right, are we almost ready?'

Emily joined the three of them in reception, she was happy to leave off early. She was going to go home and get a few hours kip before painting the town red tonight with some of her girlfriends.

'Hello Emily, are you well?,' Polly smiled at the young assistant, who looked her up and down, before firing back a curt response.

'I'm alright. See ya. Tom, I've done everything, see you on Monday.' And with that she hurried out of the office.

'Blimey, that was short and sweet,' said Polly. 'Is she always as polite?'

Tom shrugged his shoulders. 'She's been fine chatting away with me today, but she can be a bit off sometimes, don't take it personally.'

'Take it personally, off her? I don't think so.' Polly was annoyed by her husband's response, especially in front of Jill.

Tom ignored Polly's tone. 'Anyhow, you all okay with locking up, Jill? I'll take a look upstairs and then we'll be off.'

'Make it quick then, get going. This lovely wife of yours is waiting and it's Friday afternoon traffic. It won't be great, have a good weekend.' She got up to tidy the files behind her as Polly waited at the front door.

Tom had a quick check upstairs before flying back down as they headed out into the car park and into the Audi. They were off and it was only 3.50pm. It would still be five hours at least, Tom reckoned, but at least Jody would have some food ready when they got there and they would still be able to get out and into Chester for a few drinks, a good way to end the week.

'What time do you reckon we'll get there?' said Polly.

'Oh, don't start, we've only been going 20 minutes. That's the sort of thing kids say on a car journey — 'how much further have we *got to go, dad?' a*fter they've just left the house.' She punched him gently on the arm. 'Just answer the question.'

'You can see, the sat nav says 8.25, but I'll reckon nearer 9.15. That's okay though, just make sure Jody is cooking something and we'll let her know the exact time we will be there when we are about an hour away.

The pair chatted about their day and Polly relaxed in her seat. The Audi was a two-seater, but both of them loved it. She had put their overnight bags in the boot before Tom had gone to work that morning. It was a car that went fast and although Tom wasn't a 'boy racer', he did like having a fast car.

He was even still 'boyish' enough to accelerate away from other cars at traffic lights, much to Polly's annoyance, but she knew it was a car he had always dreamed of owning. And while it wasn't brand new, it caught the eye of many as it went by, especially after Tom's mate, who owned a garage, converted his exhaust system, so it made more noise on acceleration.

'I hope Craig and Jody are okay,' Polly said as the pair took the toll road around Birmingham. The sat nav now said it would be 8.50pm when they arrived.

'What makes you say that?' Tom flicked her a glance. 'Has she said something to you?'

'No, well not really. It's just that with the IVF failing and all that, Jody also said Craig had been a bit distant lately, you know, a bit quiet. I phoned her this morning, she reckoned he'd been a bit huffy.'

Tom wasn't sure what to say. Craig had told him in confidence about Archer, the drugs, the runs, the one-night stand, there was no way he would tell Polly. And anyhow, Craig's moods might be nothing to do with all that, although Tom had wondered how on earth he was living with it.

'I'm sure everything is fine. You know what Jody can be like, a bit dramatic. IVF can affect men just as much as women, so I've read! No, seriously, it must be just as difficult for Craig, not that he says anything to me of course, but you know what I mean.'

His answer seemed to satisfy Polly.

They were off the toll road, which had been nice and clear, and heading up the M6 towards Chester. Polly had put her head back for 30 minutes or so and had a snooze. When she came round she smiled at Tom as he looked across at her. She stretched out her hand and put it on his arm.

'We nearly there yet, dad?' He laughed and shook his head.

'Stop that silly voice. God, could you imagine kids in this car? Kids and you, what a bloody nightmare that would be!'

'I can't imagine it,' Pol said sarcastically. 'For a start the Audi's only got two seats.'

'You know what I mean, if we had a bigger car. We are about an hour away, so get ready to call Jody and tell her to get her finger out in the kitchen because the Armstrongs are 'incoming and bloody hungry!''

Polly smiled. The radio was playing Radio One, a station Tom enjoyed listening to. Polly wasn't the greatest lover of it, but she accepted it. It was infinitely better than listening to the cricket on some crackling station that he seemed to also love.

Polly relaxed and thought about the phone calls she'd received. She put them to the back of her mind, just some crank who was trying to be funny. If they continued, she'd tell Tom, but for now it was a weekend away, and they didn't have many of them. She wasn't going to spoil it.

'Talking of kids, when are we having some?'

Polly loved watching Tom squirm when she brought up topics she knew he wouldn't want to discuss. Then again, she had been thinking about it for a few months, and while there had been other opportunities to talk to him about it, she had always thought Tom would duck out of answering the question, or at least look to hold it over for another day. He had no escape now. He would have to broach the subject. He couldn't tell her he was tired, or had to tend to the wild garden bed. Or go to the pub. It was just him and her in the car, with an hour to go. An opportune time for baby talk.

'Oh no, not now, Pol. It's not something we should discuss right here, is it?'

'Yes,' Polly said, staring across at him, putting her hand on his leg as she did so and moving it up and down.

He was trying not to give in. But she could be so damn sexy when she wanted, even in the confines of an Audi TT, heading up the M6. Polly continued to edge her hand up to Tom's groin, leant across and blew in his ear.

'I'm trying to bloody drive here,' Tom protested in a pathetic manner. He was quite enjoying it.

'I know it's not a great time, but when is a great time? Come on, seriously. What do you think?' She had taken her hand off Tom's leg and was looking at him.

'No,' said Tom. 'I'm not talking about it now, there are better times than this and you're deliberately being provocative by touching my groin. I might get excited.' He winked at her.

'Get you excited?' You sound like a 14-year-old. Oh, come on, you know you want kids, we're not getting any younger, we should be thinking about it. And don't tell me we agreed not to have kids, because having them was one of the things we used to talk about a lot. Remember? When we used to sit outside your mum's house after Sunday evening lunch and I would unzip your flies, just to watch your face as you were scared your mum might come out.'

'That's enough, what's wrong with you?' Tom was trying hard to be serious. But he couldn't be. 'Why do you have to stoop to these levels?'

'Because you fancy me like shit, that's why!' Polly moved closer to his face and kissed him before sitting back and lifting her skirt up to show off her tanned legs.

'And you can put them away.' Tom was again trying not to smile. In the end he put his hand on her thighs. He couldn't resist.

'See, you can't help yourself,' Polly smiled, then pulled her skirt back down.

'We'll see,' Tom said. 'We can have a chat over the weekend.'

'Nope. I think we'll have a chat right now.' Polly had turned in her seat and was looking directly at him. 'Because I love you and I want your babies, we can talk now. You won't find time over the weekend. Don't fib to me.'

Tom knew he was beat. He looked across at his wife, who was smiling and staring at him in equal measure, she was right and he knew it. They weren't getting any younger and they had both always wanted children. The fact Jody and Craig had been struggling with IVF had even made Tom think, not that he let on. Maybe it was time expensive holidays, pubs, late nights, getting drunk, meals out, fast cars and all the other trimmings of their

D.I.N.K.Y. lifestyle came to an end.

'Okay, I'm not saying yes right now, but, well. But okay, you're right and you know it because you have that smart-arse look on your face. We'll talk, I promise. Let's get this weekend out of the way first shall we? Call Jody because we are not far away now'

'Knew you loved me,' Polly touched his leg again. 'Wouldn't it be great to have children?'

'I said, I'm not talking about it now, not while I'm driving.'

'Oh, dear. I'm sorry. Driving and talking, life can be so complicated for you men. Okay, but you said we can talk later,' She pulled a grin as Tom stared ahead. 'Yes, I said, later.'

Polly slid back in her seat, put her feet up on the dashboard, pulled her skirt up high above her knees, turned the music up and looked ahead.

'Knew I'd win.' Tom shook his head.

'Oh, and by the way. I stopped taking the pill three weeks ago!'

TWENTY TWO

THERE was much shrieking and screaming as Jody and Polly hugged, hugged and hugged again on the doorstep.

Tom and Polly had arrived at Craig and Jody's plush house just on the outskirts of Chester at just after 9.15pm. It had been a long drive but the warmth of the greeting made it worthwhile. The house was set on a hill with a long stone driveway and two greyhound statues each side of the front door. The front garden was modest with a couple of small trees in the corners and there was ample parking for three or four cars. Tom parked the Audi next to the Z4 – *boys and their toys!*

They all made their way into the large hallway, Jody and Polly still entwined and chatting, as Craig and Tom turned right into the kitchen.

'What are you drinking old chap,' Craig said. 'Great to see you.'

'A beer sounds great, thanks,' said Tom, picking up the local paper and taking a look at the headline about a man who had been bitten by his pet snake in his own home late one evening.... 'SNAKE BITE FRIGHT NIGHT', was the heading. It made him smile.

'How are things with you, Craig? All good?'

Craig smiled at Tom, raised his eyes slightly and said; 'Yes, they are fine. Looking forward to having a chat. And a bit of football tomorrow afternoon. Might go to see Chester City play, they're at home.'

'I had wondered who you had lined up,' said Tom. 'The good thing for us both is that Arsenal are at home and we're 250 miles away and, after Tuesday night's effort at Everton, I would be happy if they were 650 miles away.'

'I know. I went, remember?' Craig raised his eyebrows.

The two took their beer and walked outside into the back garden where the girls were already seated at the patio table, a tall heater keeping them warm on what was a now a chilly night, everyone keeping their coats on for the time being.

'And our drinks are where?' Jody looked at her husband. 'Have you left them in the kitchen? Or did you just get you and Tom one?'

'I'd suggest you say you have left them in the kitchen,' Polly jumped in.

Craig didn't sit down. He smiled at them both. 'Yes, ladies. Don't panic. I was just coming out to ask, what would you like?'

'Prosecco is in the fridge and please excuse my husband's rudeness, Polly. He is still sulking from me not allowing him sex this morning.'

'Oh dear. Really Craig? Who's been a naughty boy? Hope it wasn't because your performances are falling below the required standard.' Jody laughed with Polly.

'Ha! Ha! Very good my dear, I didn't want sex anyway. I was in a rush.'

'*Not true,*' Jody mouthed to Polly while shaking her head.

'A bottle of Prosecco between you, or one each?'

'You know the answer to that,' Jody replied. 'Just the one for now, but make sure there's one ready in the fridge for when we have finished that.' She smiled at Polly.

Craig went off to get the drinks. It left Tom with the girls.

'How are you then, my sexy man?' Jody put her hand on his knee. 'Everything okay?'

'Everything is fine, thank you. And you are looking as gorgeous as ever. I said to Pol on the way up in the car, if I ever came back to this planet and you were the only female on it, I would happily mate with you.'

Jody laughed. Tom beamed at his little joke.

'No he didn't, Jode,' said Polly. 'On the way up he said do you reckon Jody would be up for a threesome this weekend? I said you would, it would just depend if he minded Craig shagging his wife

138

while he watched.'

The girls laughed out loud, Tom nodded his head. 'Oh, very good, very good. I didn't say that Jode.'

It was Polly's turn to mouth to her friend, *'he did!'* They both laughed again.

Craig returned with a bottle of Prosecco and a couple of glasses. 'Obviously missed a joke, have I? Tom shook his head.

'No, just Pol being her usual witty self, talking about threesomes, she's so bad sometimes, don't know why I married her. Her dad always said I was too good for her.'

'No, he did not,' Polly jumped in. 'The reason you married me is because I'm good in bed.' Craig spurted out a mouthful of beer. Again Tom was left shaking his head.

'Good girl Pol,' said Jody.

The girls took sips of their drinks before Jody went into the kitchen and brought out a lasagne, with garlic bread, a favourite of everyone's.

'Right, help yourselves and if you want anything else like sauces, everything is on the kitchen table.'

The four tucked in. Craig and Jody had waited for their friends to arrive before eating, so all were ravenous and for a few moments there was silence around the table. Craig and Jody's garden was big and stretched at least 300 yards, it was square and, apart from a large shed in the top right of the garden, it was full of shrubs and trees. The pair also kept chickens, Jody's 'babies', as she liked to call them.

'This lasagne is great, Jode. Oh, by the way, how are the chickens?' Tom broke the silence as they ate. 'You still have some?'

'They are all fine thank you. And before you ask, yes they do lay eggs.'

'Not bloody many, they don't,' Craig piped up. 'I don't know why we have them. Last week they laid two eggs between them. It cost about £10 in feed, it would be cheaper to just buy 24 eggs at Waitrose.'

'Why don't you eat them?' said Tom.

'We do eat them,' said Jody. 'Don't take any notice of Craig, they laid four the week before and they were delicious, I had them poached.'

'I don't mean eat the eggs, I mean the chickens!' Tom caught Craig's eye as he said it. They both grinned.

'Tom! Don't say that, that's horrible.' Polly said. 'Chickens are family, aren't they Jode? I'd like chickens one day.'

Jody was about to say something but Tom got their first. 'Family? How can chickens be family? You don't eat members of your family.'

'And we're not eating them either,' said Jody. 'I'd kick Craig out of the house and make him go find food before eating our chickens!'

'What?' Craig looked most indignant. 'What have I got to do with it? I didn't say we were to eat the chickens.'

The four enjoyed the craic. It was good to be back together. It had been a while but the chemistry had never vanished. Craig got up to get him and Tom another beer, while the girls began 'talking shop'.

'How's the gym, Pol? Is Kevin still being a dickhead?'

'Of course. I think it's all that testosterone he and his gym buddies build up during the day makes him big and brave. He's okay, he just needs putting in his place once in a while. And you? How's the shop?'

'Going okay, to be honest.' Jody had finished her plate and was pouring them both another glass of Prosecco. 'Had a really good week this week, no idea why. It seems things are picking up a bit and now the days are getting longer, people come out more. Retro stuff seems popular at the moment.'

Craig and Tom had taken themselves off down the garden. Jody had put up lots of lights down a pathway that split it in two and while the pair couldn't see all the shrubbery and plants, there was enough to look at.

'Nice garden this,' Tom said. 'Must be about three times the size of ours. Don't know how you keep up with it all, mate, I don't think I could. Cutting the grass alone must take hours. You got one of those little tractor mowers?'

'Yep, certainly have, a beauty. Oh, and a gardener! That helps.'

Tom laughed. 'You cheeky bugger. Have you really? And there was me wondering how the hell you did it. Now I know. Good idea though, a gardener. English, Polish, or Romanian?'

'The lawnmower is English, the gardener is Polish,' Craig smiled! 'Don't cost a fortune and he's a hard worker, gave him a couple of eggs the other week, made his day.'

The pair carried on their walk, talking work. Tom was ready for Craig to resume their conversation about Stuart Archer. But he didn't know if he could stomach it after such a long day, thankfully for Tom, Craig never mentioned it.

They reached the bottom of the garden and Craig produced a pack of small cigars, his guilty secret. He had promised Jody he would pack up when they got married.

'Cigar, old friend,' he handed one to Tom, who took it. Tom used to be 15-a-day back in his early 20s, but he'd managed to kick the habit, although an odd cigar was something he enjoyed.

The pair sat puffing away and enjoying their beer.

'Fancy walking across to the Maple Leaf?' Craig took a drag and puffed cigar smoke out as he looked at Tom. 'Karaoke night tonight and it will be in full swing by the time we get there. Could be a bit of fun, unless you're knackered.'

'No, I'm fine. If the girls want to go, I'm up for it.'

They finished their cigars and headed back up the garden, flicking the butts over Craig's hedge and onto a pathway on the other side. The girls were polishing off the last dregs of the Prosecco and the idea of going to the Maple Leaf hit the spot.

'Shall we do a song together if it's karaoke?' Polly took Tom's arm as they stood in the hall waiting to go across to the pub.

'I'd rather not. The last time we did a karaoke together, do you remember, down at Brighton at John's birthday party? You were giving it so much Tina Turner you fell back into the speaker and blew the disco lights out. Pissed as usual.'

'Oh, God yeah. We had only just met as well, I'm surprised you still wanted to see me after that, it was so embarrassing. Wasn't John the one who got married, then came out as gay and ran off with a young boy from Iceland?'

'Wow! What a great story,' Craig said, as he joined the pair of them in the hallway. 'Is that true?'

'Yes,' said Tom, smiling. 'Left a note on the table telling his wife to get the Argus newspaper that day and look at the births, marriages and deaths page. He'd put a notice in there thanking his wife for their eight months of marriage, but he was leaving, with Ricki from Iceland. Although I don't think he actually put the name Ricki. But he did the rest. What a way to announce leaving your wife.'

'That's a horrible thing to do,' said Jody. 'Why didn't he have the balls to tell her he was leaving to her face?'

'In fairness to him, he did have a good reason for leaving,' Tom said.

'Only two weeks previous he'd caught her in bed with the physio, who had been there because she had something wrong with her back. John was a bit timid and she, I think her name was Alison, or Andrea, took advantage of that. Anyhow, when John catches them, she gets out of the bed and the pair of them, her and the physio, tie him to a chair and make him watch them shagging. Then they take him downstairs and Alison or Andrea, whatever her name is, makes all three of them something to eat. How weird is that?

'You making that up?' Jody looked horrified. 'That's disgusting. If I caught Craig in bed with another woman, I'd slice his testicles off! Make me watch, indeed.'

'I'm not making it up, it's true.'

'That's not true is it?' said Polly. 'That's not nice. I said the same though Jody. If I caught Tom at it, I'd cut his todger off.'

'This is a lovely conversation, can't we go to the pub please?' Craig said, pushing the door open. 'I like all this, what if Tom or I did something, what about you two? I suppose you two are both holier than though? Wouldn't look at another man, wouldn't dream of sleeping with another man.'

'If you caught me in bed with someone else,' said Polly looking at Tom and trying to pull a serious face, despite already having had three glasses of Prosecco, 'first, he would have to be pretty special. And second, if he was so good I'd would wink and say, come on Tom, you can join in. You wouldn't be able to resist, not with this body.' Polly slinked her hands down her hips.

Craig laughed; 'Quite right. Who could resist those hips?'

'Oh, yes and what do you mean by that Craig Baldini?' Jody stared at him. 'I thought you valued your crown jewels. Clearly not. We're wasting drinking time here, now come on. Let's go karaoke.'

The four headed to the pub.

Craig's earlier confession had Tom feeling uneasy. While the 'drugs run' was something Tom could try to put to one side, his one-night stand with some woman he hardly knew muddied the waters. The mimicking and joking about threesomes and other partners had always been fun among the four of them.

But now, Tom wasn't so comfortable, Craig had messed it all up.

The Maple Leaf was heaving.

It usually was on a Friday night, but with Chester Races having been on that day and the karaoke proving popular, it was especially busy as plenty of racing fans had flooded into the city. It was standing room only.

Tom and Craig made their way to the bar as the four walked in, Polly catching the eye of more than one drinker as she swept into the pub all flowing hair and that exquisite short skirt and her low cleavage. The main bar area was spacious and wide, and there was plenty of standing room, tables and chairs were up both sides and there was a step up to a wider area as you walked further into the pub. The karaoke was situated at the far end. Jody and Polly decided to stand next to a large pillar near a fruit machine that no-one was playing, typically not until the girls decided to stand next to it.

'Excuse me love,' said a middle-aged man, as he moved in to play the machine. He was talking to Polly and he barged into her as he tried to get past. He stunk of BO.

'Sorry,' said Polly. 'Did you say something?'

'Yeah, I said excuse me love, I want to play the machine.'

The man had a pint of beer in one hand and a rolled-up cigarette, which he was obviously going to smoke later, in the other. Polly stared at him. She hated being spoken to like that, it made her blood boil. Jody could read the signs.

'Leave it Pol. Let the man play his little fruit machine.' The girls stepped aside.

Tom and Craig returned with the drinks to where the girls were standing, which was now a few yards away from the fruit machine. A woman on the karaoke was killing Tina Turner's *'Simply the Best'* and you had to shout to hear yourself think, let alone talk.

'It's lively in here,' Polly said. 'I love it, a real good vibe. We going on the karaoke, Jody?'

'What shall we sing?' Jody asked. 'How about *'Livin' on a Prayer'* by Bon Jovi? Or *'Delilah'*? I love that, Tom Jones, and we're near Wales, so that would get a great reception, so long as we don't destroy it.'

'*Delilah'*, that's the one,' Polly agreed. 'Just need about two more glasses of Prosecco and I'm ready to go. What's the time?'

'10.30,' said Craig. 'Pub is open till midnight. You don't want to be in such a state as that woman singing Tina Turner. God man, she's terrible.'

'So, we're going to watch Chester City tomorrow then?' Tom turned to his friend. What league are they in?'

'I think it's either the National League or National League North,' Craig replied. 'Should be a bit of fun, they are enjoying a decent season.'

'Who are they playing?'

'Great question, I have no idea. I think it might be King's Lynn. I just know they are at home.'

'King's Lynn, what sort of my local team?'

The two continued to talk football, before Polly and Jody's request for *'Delilah'* was granted by a hip-looking DJ who gave a 'big-up' introduction to the pair of them as they went up to great cheers and a few wolf whistles.

'Okay, folks, let's all join in, we know this one,' the DJ said. 'It's Delilah. My, My, My, how we love this one.'

Tom and Craig looked at each other and shook their heads. They knew what was coming and it wasn't going to be a quiet, understated version of the Tom Jones classic. The girls would have this place rocking.

'Are you ready for this? Tom looked at Craig. 'You know it could get messy. They must have had a bottle each by now.' The boys laughed.

By the time the final chorus of *'Delilah'* was being sung, Jody was waving her arms from side to side, while Polly was on one knee and singing in the faces of a young couple in front of her. They were joining in. It was great fun and the DJ was quick to praise the pair of them as they headed from the stage and back to Tom and Craig to raucous cheers.

'Overall, that was pretty awful, but I'm clearly in the minority,' Tom laughed. 'You can't argue with the crowd, and the crowd seemed to love it.'

'We were bloody good, weren't we?' Jody was on a high. She looked at both of them. 'I know we were, so it's no good you two saying different, either of you. Had them in the palm of our hands. Now get us another drink, I can feel an ABBA classic coming up next. What say you, Pol?'

Polly nodded and headed off to the loo, pushing her way past what was now a packed pub on the way. She was a bit unsteady on her feet and just a few yards from the toilets when a bloke, younger than her, stood in her path. Polly went to go around him, but he moved across to block her. He was holding a pint of lager.

'You were good up there darling, on that stage. Loved that,' he said. 'You here on your own? If so, fancy a drink, or something else?'

Polly looked at him. She'd been in this situation before many times, men would often try it on. But most would just fling a comment her way or flash a wink, not block her path like he was doing. He was handsome, she thought. Black hair and blue eyes, bit unusual. And while she was feeling a bit worse for wear, he was clearly pissed.

'Just move out of the way,' Polly said. 'I'm with someone, so don't spoil your night.'

'Spoil my night. You won't spoil my night, but I could make yours, gorgeous. Come on, just a drink. You're not with someone I know, you're just saying that. You look too high maintenance to be a settled babe, you need someone like me. A little bit of rough.'

The man was with a couple of mates. 'Hey, Kyle, that's enough, don't speak to the lady like that,' said one of them, who had overheard the conversation. He came across and put his hand across Kyle's chest.

'Fuck off Tammy, she likes me.'

Polly looked at Tammy and then looked at Kyle.

The crack that came next was Polly's fist on the point of the Kyle's nose, a martial art move she had never forgotten from all those lessons as a teenager. Short back lift and accuracy. The man went sprawling backwards, his pint flying to the ground. Polly moved forward and leant over him.

'Don't fuck with me... Kyle... you shithouse.' Polly looked behind her, but Jody, Craig and Tom were at least 30 yards away. They were in conversation and hadn't seen her hit the man. Then she looked at Tammy. 'I'd clean him up if I were you.' Tammy shook his head. 'Shit man,' he exclaimed.

The other blokes who had been with Kyle came over to see what was going on. Tammy explained to them what had happened, Kyle was sitting up, shaking his head and trying to speak, blood running down his shirt, while a few others in the pub looked over to see what had happened. Thankfully a guy on the karaoke had the pub transfixed with his take of Robbie Williams' 'Angel'. Not many, apart from those close by, had noticed Polly's punch.

After Tammy explained what had happened, Kyle's mates were sympathetic to her, asking if she was alright.

'I'm fine,' Polly said. 'Just make sure your mate gets that broken nose fixed.' She headed off to the loo.

Kyle was helped up and a combination of the shock of the punch, as well as the amount of drink he had consumed, saw him wander off towards the exit in silence, his mates in tow. Two security guards came from the front of the pub to see what had happened. The injured bloke's mates spoke to the guards, telling them Polly had defended herself. The security guards shepherded Kyle and his mates out of the pub, Tom and Craig looked across as they went past them.

'What happened to him?' Tom said.

'No idea. Got a good crack from the looks of things, perhaps someone was trying to stop him doing 'I'm Too Sexy for My Shirt'. Seems a bit strong a reaction mind you. His shirt is now covered in blood. They laughed.

Polly re-joined them and smiled at Jody.

'I needed that wee, are we having another drink before we go? Either get us another drink, or me and Jody will do ABBA.'

'I'll get them in,' Craig said. 'Don't think I can stand another song from you two, don't know if the pub can, either. Give us a hand, Tom.'

The boys went to the bar and Jody smiled at Polly, she noticed Polly's knuckles were cut.

'What's happened? How did you do that? That looks nasty, bloody hell Pol, it wasn't something to do with that guy who was just helped out of the pub, was it?'

Polly half-smiled. 'What man helped out of the pub? No, I caught it on the door as I pushed it open, fell forward a bit, it's nothing.'

Jody didn't believe her. Polly could be defensive when she wanted to. Jody knew when to push it and when not to, and anyhow, they were having a fun night out as the boys returned with a final drink. The four left the Maple Leaf just after midnight, crossed the road, and crashed straight into bed.

Tony Statton had seen the punch. It was quite something, and not what he had expected, especially from a girl. A girl who had been standing with Craig Baldini.

Statton's trip to the north-west had been good, but he would return home to Southampton tomorrow. While he still hadn't let Archer know whether he was going to help him out or not, Statton had decided to make tentative enquiries about Baldini the day after he left Strangeways. Just to see if it was a job he could do, or wanted to do. It was worth 50K, it hadn't been hard to pin Baldini down and find out where he lived.

Statton had watched as the Baldinis had gone shopping on Friday afternoon and he'd watched them return to their nice house, what a happy couple they seemed. He staked things out for a few hours and was about to head off home for the night when the Audi TT had turned up. He was curious, who the occupants were, seeing as they drove into the Baldini's property. So he hung around for another hour before the four people, including the Baldinis, headed into the Maple Leaf. It was easy for him to take a closer look at Craig Baldini in a pub, especially one so busy. Job done.

Statton had only been 10 feet away from the punch that floored the guy. He had seen enough as soon as the bloke hit the deck. He didn't want to be around if the police were called and wanted statements. He had made a sharp exit.

But he would be back.

TWENTY THREE

CRAIG and Tom paid their money and walked through the turnstiles of Chester City Football Club.

'We'll have to get under cover or we're going to get bloody drenched watching it here,' said Craig.

'Does it always rain up north?' Tom replied as he followed Craig towards the stand on the far side of the ground that was under cover. Craig nodded. 'There are going to be some right dodgy sliding tackles going on out there, I reckon,' Tom continued. 'The groundsman is going to have his work cut out after this one is over repairing all the divots.'

Chester were playing, as Craig had thought, King's Lynn, which was beyond ironic for Tom, as Lynn was only 20 miles from where he and Polly lived. Not that he watched them much.

Tom paid for both of them. 'My treat. For all the Prosecco, Pol is downing at your house this weekend.'

'Thanks pal, but no need to do that. We knew Pol was coming, so I took out one of those 'pay-day' loans to cover the Prosecco. Shall we get a pint? We don't want to wait till half-time. Let's grab one, I'll get them.'

Tom needed no second invitation and although both were still feeling the effects of last night's karaoke and drinking at the Leaf, their heads were coming round, aided by a hearty cooked breakfast Jody had prepared earlier that morning.

'What you having?'

'Carlsberg please mate.'

'Good shout, I'll make that two, I think,' Craig headed to the bar, which was surprisingly busy for such a miserable day.

He ordered the beers and the two went back pitch side. Chester's stadium was well appointed. The club had seen better days on the pitch, however, it now found itself battling in the lower leagues and a hoped-for return to former glories. The stadium was neat and trim, with many blue seats and covered stands. Tom and Craig walked round to find a place to sit.

'Have you seen Chester play this season?' Tom looked at Craig, who was cursing spilling his pint after tripping on a step.

'No, not this season, I came here about three years ago with a couple of mates. One of them was sponsoring the game, it was good fun actually, and we were treated like royalty. But, as you know, I go to Everton or Liverpool on occasions and on the other Saturdays when I'm free, Jody and I often go out for the day. I like football, don't get me wrong, but it's nice to have a Saturday off, go to a pub, have a meal, come home and crash out, get a takeaway in the evening, glass or three of wine.

Then watch Match of the Day.' Craig winked!

Tom smiled, he knew the feeling. He would go to Arsenal, but Polly liked them to spend some time together on Saturdays when Arsenal were away, Saturday was, after all, her only day off.

Both sets of players walked out onto the pitch, the rain still thundering down, and a hardy group of Lynn fans behind the opposite end goal began chanting their team's name. Tom was impressed with their loyalty, it was a long drive from Norfolk to get to Chester, as he knew, to support their side and they were turning round and going straight home at the finish, no doubt. That's one long day.

As the game kicked off tackles flew in on the wet surface and the pitch was cutting up. It was going to be a muddy affair. Sure enough it didn't take long for a goal to arrive, and it was Lynn who got it, much to the joy of their small throng behind the goal.

'Fair play, he took that well,' Craig said. 'That ball was coming over his head. He's played well so far, that No 11.'

Tom agreed and one-nil to King's Lynn was how it stayed until half-time.

The pair went for a drink at the same bar they had got a pint before the game. It was even busier at half-time, but Tom emerged with two plastic glasses and a couple of Mars Bars.

'No pies I'm afraid,' Tom said, looking disappointed.

'Apparently we can get one on the other side of the ground but we're not walking across in this weather, so, it's a bar of chocolate. Thought Lynn just about deserve the lead. You say they are in the play-off positions? I'm not surprised, they are well organised.'

Craig nodded. 'I don't think the scoring is over.'

The two supped their pints. But at least they were still dry, although the rain showed no sign of abating. Tom checked his phone. 'Arsenal were leading Burnley 1-0, much to the delight of both of them.

'Long way to go. Let's not get our hopes up.' Craig said with caution.

He then nipped to the toilet, but came back a couple of minutes later.

'I'm sorry I had to burden you with that story the other day about Stuart Archer, Tom, but I had to tell someone, I hope you don't mind and I hope you don't think shit of me. I know I've fucked up, I should have addressed this years ago. As I said, I thought it would go away.'

Tom looked at his friend. He was going to be brutally honest, he had given it a lot of thought since Craig had told him. Too much thought. In many ways, he had wished Craig hadn't confided in him.

'Mate, I can't say I'm impressed with what you did with that woman, Marie.'

'But we are friends and have been for a long time now, so I'm not judging you. What happened, happened, I don't know if I could have coped with that guilt all these years, the one-night-stand, I mean. The drugs thing? Well, what will be, will be, I suppose. The only thing I don't really get about all that is why you think Archer will suddenly squeal about you? I mean you said you only did a few runs. With all due respect you are hardly Mr Big. If he's been running his operation for years, why would your short time involved be of any importance? He won't remember you? You said he left you a note about buggering off and it's all over, now you are saying you have a horrible feeling it might all raise its head again. Why?'

The second half had kicked off and all around Tom and Craig, Chester fans were getting excited. The home side had clearly been given a rocket at half-time because they had started the half with vigour.

Wave after wave of Chester attacks had come in on the Lynn goal in the opening minutes of the half and the fans were in a raucous state, a state that reached fever pitch when Chester were awarded a penalty. It was duly despatched, leaving Craig and Tom to 'high-five' and applaud loudly, Chester's equaliser.

Craig turned to Tom. 'We'll watch the rest of the game and I'll tell you something else you need to know about Archer and all this on the way home. Tell me to piss off if you don't want to know. I'll understand.'

'I won't tell you to do that, mate.'

Chester were now in control of the game and with 20 minutes to go, they scored again, a fine header from a corner. It looked as though the home team were going to pick up all three points until, right at the death, King's Lynn broke clear and the No.11, who had been their stand-out player, slotted home at the far post for the equaliser. The Lynn fans, who had been singing a rendition of, '*I Can't Stand the Rain*', minutes earlier, were delirious with joy, one jumping over the small barrier to join in with his team's celebrations, before being ushered back by a steward.

Tom and Craig shook their heads. They were Chester City fans for the day and could feel the pain of the home supporters, even more so when the referee blew the whistle just two minutes after the re-start. It finished 2-2.

They walked back to the car, the rain still teeming down. They had driven to the ground in Craig's Z4. He had parked it away from the ground, but only a couple of streets away and it was a 10-minute walk. They wouldn't get too wet. The good news for both of them was, Arsenal had won 2-0. And Tom had missed it! He wasn't surprised. The last time Arsenal won at home, he and Polly were at a wedding, back in December.

'At least the Gooners are back up and running,' Craig said. 'Burnley don't have a great record at our place mind you. Still, a win's a win.'

'You're not wrong mate. And I've missed a win again. I'm a

jinx I reckon, come on get this bloody BMW's doors open.'

The pair got in and Craig started it up. He loved his Z4 and gave it a few revs.

'That's a hell of a noise. 'You're such a boy racer.' Tom laughed.

'Look who's talking?' Craig shot back.

As they headed off, it didn't take long for Craig to open up about Archer. He wanted to talk and Tom listened, like the friend he was.

'So,' said Craig, looking across at his friend. 'Going back to Archer. There is a really good reason why I'm bothered about him, and it's not because of his wife and that one-night-stand. It's worse than that.'

Tom looked across at Craig. 'Worse? Worse than shagging his missus? Jesus, Craig.'

'I know mate, but hear me out. Basically, after I finished the runs for him, the cops got wind of what I'd done. They knew, they bloody knew. Someone had taken a photo of me getting out of the van with the packages and taking them to the house. The house was raided, the packages were there, it didn't take the cops long to put two and two together. I'd delivered drugs. You think Archer had me, now the fucking police had me.

'Okay, so Archer could have done worse than just make me do some runs for him, but at the end of the day he didn't. That's all he wanted me to do. He didn't love his wife, he wasn't that bothered about me and her. He was probably shagging around himself. He just wanted me to do those runs and then piss off, but the police, that was different.

'They called on me at work one Friday afternoon, about a month after I had done the final run for Archer. They were plain clothes, got me in the car park as I left off, so there was no big scene. They had photos of me, the packages, what was in the packages, me delivering those exact same packages, told me I was under arrest. It was shit, man.'

Tom was hanging on Craig's every word.

'The only bit of luck at the time was that Jody was away with one of her friends in Newcastle that weekend. So, while I'm down the nick, she's not around, I'm held overnight and released the next day. I got my solicitor in. He said if I plead guilty, I'll do maybe four years, so two with good behaviour, but that's crap Tom. I'd have been finished.'

'Shit man, I never realised all this,' Tom interrupted. 'Fuck. Why didn't you tell me all this the other day? How the hell have you coped? So, why aren't you in jail? Was there a trial? Obviously not.'

'There was a trial.' Craig looked across at him. 'But not mine, Archer's. There was no trial for me because I was given a 'get out of jail' card, not a great one, mind you.'

'Get out of jail free! How did that work?'

'Well, basically, the cops said they would drop all charges and I could go free.' Craig looked across at Tom as the pair sat at a set of traffic lights.

'As long as I told them all I knew about Archer's operation, and I was to help them infiltrate his gang. I was nothing to the cops. I was small fry, but I could help land the 'big fish'. It wasn't as hard as it sounded, to tell them what I had seen and heard. I knew a few of the people Archer spoke to, a few names, because he mentioned them to me during our conversations. I had Archer's private mobile number, I knew where he picked up drugs and dropped them. I hardly knew the works, but I knew enough for the police to get a foot in, the rest was up to them once they were in.

'And they did it. They got in and much of what I told them had helped. It never occurred to me at the time what it might all mean, I was just glad, for me anyhow, it was all over. Or so I thought.'

He looked again at Tom.

'You said you'd read up on Archer's trial on-line. Well, if you read it closely, it tells of how his gang was infiltrated by the police. Archer was grassed up/stitched up, however you want to put it, and that allowed the cops to get in. It was fucking me who did it. It was me who stitched Archer up, Tom. I grassed him to the cops.

'I told you on the phone the other day I was worried about what Archer might say. But I couldn't have been further from the truth. It's not what he might say that bothers me, but what he might do. Or get someone else to do, if he finds out I was the one who grassed him up. You think Archer is going to let it rest? Going to let the person who helped put him in prison just wander about free and happy? I would love to think so, but I doubt it.

'He'll want to know who it was. I don't know why I thought I could just do what I did and vanish into the sunset.

'And now I'm scared Tom, fucking scared.'

The girls decided a trip to the Trafford Centre, in Manchester, would be a good way to spend Saturday afternoon. The inclement weather meant a bit of 'retail therapy' would likely brighten their day, especially as Jody was after some new boots and Polly was never one to say no to new dresses or skirts.

Polly took the Audi and the girls were soon on their way, leaving just before Craig and Tom had headed off to Chester for the football. The four had enjoyed Jody's 'fry-up' brunch after none of them surfaced much before 11am. It was just what they all needed.

'Have you been to the Trafford Centre?' Jody said as the pair headed out of Chester.

'I don't think I have. Does it have a Primark?'

Jody looked at her, not quite working out if she was serious or not. Polly had very good taste and wasn't afraid to splash out, but she was also quite cute with her money and could spot a bargain, Primark was probably right up her street.

'Don't know if it does. Got a Fat Face though. And last time I was there they had a Radley, London. Great handbags, if you need another for your collection.'

'Oooh. I like Fat Face. I shop online with them a lot and a girl can always do with another handbag as well, 20 is never enough.' Polly laughed.

The girls continued their drive through the dreary Lancashire rain, their pace of conversation never easing up.

'So, do you mind me asking, what's the latest on the idea of surrogacy? Last time we spoke you were thinking about it.'

'I don't know Pol, to be honest. Craig has been a bit quiet of late when it has come to speaking about babies. I mentioned a surrogate mum to him again the other night and he sort of laughed it off with stuff like, 'do I have to have sex with the woman first?' He's only joking around and sort of pulled a face after he said it. But it was his way of deflecting from talking about it. One thing that bothers me to be honest is, who would be the surrogate mother? I wouldn't know where to start. Don't suppose you fancy it?' Polly smiled, saying nothing.

'In theory there's nothing wrong with me or Craig. But I don't think I could live with going through another cycle and losing one again, I certainly don't know if Craig could. He is trying to be all brave about it, but he's hurt inside, I know he is. And, as I said, he's really gone into his shell lately, I put it down to me talking about kids too much. Perhaps I should just give him space.'

Polly didn't know what to say to support her friend. She had cried with her on many occasions over recent years as the disappointment of the failed IVFs continued. But Polly had no experience of having children. She'd only really started wanting them of late. Wanting them was still a long way from having them, or just being pregnant. She was at the start of her baby journey, or so she hoped. Jody was way down the line.

'Have you thought of fostering?'

'No. I don't know if Craig would want to go down that route, I think he would love a 'mini Craig or mini Jody'. I'm not sure he would embrace someone else's child, even though I know it's a really worthwhile thing to do. We haven't spoken about it.

'Anyhow, enough about me, what about you and Tom? Have you convinced him he needs to start pulling his finger out, or whatever he needs to pull out, and start a family?'

Polly laughed. 'No, I haven't' yet. But I have given him a bit of a shock. In the car on the way up here I told him I'd stopped taking the pill three weeks ago, so it was no good him not thinking about starting a family anymore.'

'Are you serious? Have you really stopped taking it? You cheeky cow, what the hell did Tom say? Jody was open-mouthed. Only Pol could pull a stunt like that.

'He didn't say much really, I didn't give him a chance. We were only about 10 minutes from your house when I told him, so we weren't going to have time to debate it. And I turned the music up loud to let him know I wasn't interested in talking. Which is just as well. Because I actually stopped taking it three months ago. He'd go ape if he knew that, not that I'm pregnant, well, I don't think I am.'

Jody laughed out loud, this was classic Polly.

'I love you. You are so funny, three months. I bet you do get pregnant, and soon. I'll be so chuffed for you if you do.'

Polly smiled and rubbed Jody's arm. She knew her 'bestie' really meant that, despite all the difficulties she was going through.

The girls got to the Trafford Centre at 2.30pm and left just after 5. Both of their credit cards had taken a bit of a dent by the time they left, with Jody finding a pair of boots at £130, half price, while Polly's two new short skirts and handbag came to a cool £200.

'Your Audi boot is not very big,' Jody said. 'Hope we can get the bloody bags in it. I'm not heading all the way back to Chester with bags around my feet and on my head, that's the only trouble with these sporty cars.'

'They'll get in Jode.'

When they got home, Craig and Tom were already sinking into their second beer. It would be a quieter night, than the night before, with Jody cooking up a grand chicken dish, as well as a wonderful apple crumble, Tom's favourite. They would drink wine, beer and joke around until midnight before tiredness crept in.

The night in the Maple Leaf was catching the four of them up.

They weren't getting any younger.

TWENTY FOUR

JONNY Gordon wasn't a man to wait around. His invite for Tom to sponsor a South Walsham 1st XV rugby game came via a text on Sunday night.

Tom and Polly had left Chester at lunchtime that same day after another Jody breakfast 'special'. The four had embraced and hugged, kissed, shook hands and waved goodbye for 10 minutes before the Audi sped off towards Norwich. It had been a nice weekend, even if the weather had been awful.

'I thought Jody looked well,' Tom said as they made their way down the M6. 'I was worried all that had been going on with the IVF may have upset her, but she seemed in good form. Was she okay when you two went shopping?'

'Yeah, she was great, not sure about how they both feel about babies at the moment. Don't say anything, but they have talked about surrogacy.'

'What, you mean have a surrogate mother carry the child?' Tom sounded more than surprised. 'I suppose it is possible because Craig is clearly fertilising the eggs. It's just Jody is losing them, or at least I guess that's what's happening.'

'Ooh, listen to you. Get Mr IVF man sitting there, all knowledge about test tube babies are we?' Polly poked her husband. 'I didn't know you knew so much about it all, I've always thought you would struggle to tell your sperm count from your test tube.'

'Ha, ha, very funny. I'm being serious, and for your information, I'm more than just a dentist boffin, I studied more than just molars and root fillings at Uni.'

'Yeah, but you didn't study the reproduction system in women,' Polly laughed. 'I know you Tom Armstrong, you would faint at the mere thought of conducting a smear test. Let alone be in the same room when one was taking place.'

'Okay, that's enough. Why do you stoop to such levels? I should really smack your arse.'

'Promises, promises.' Polly grinned. 'Anyhow, talking of surrogate mums, I told Jode I would happily be hers if she needed one. And I was serious.'

'No, you're bloody not. It's the sort of thing you two would concoct together.'

'Absolutely it is my darling, and I even told Jody that Craig could have a free practice run with me if he wanted, Jody said it seemed only fair.'

'Piss off, that's enough, you are so rude you two. I hope you didn't discuss that, although you probably did, and don't give Craig wind of the fact he'd be allowed a test run. I know what his answer to that would be.'

'As if I'd let him, my darling. I only have eyes for you, and only you.' Polly was staring at him, her eyes wide.

'Look, you'll put me off my driving. Now behave.'

'I'll put you off even more if you want,' Polly said as she put her hand on his knee.

'Stop it, Pol. Or I'll call the police.'

'Call the police? I'd like to hear you say what you're calling them for.'

Polly took her hand away and sat back, smiling. It wasn't long before she dropped off to sleep for an hour as Tom drove them home, getting back just before 5pm. When he got in and looked at his phone, he saw the text from Jonny.

'Hi Tom, Big Man the Dentist. Great to catch up the other day. Fancy sponsoring the Walsham rugger game this Saturday, as we spoke about? We are at home to Luton. Look, I've got you a deal because we have three sponsors, so it's £100. Sit down meal beforehand, advert in programme, mentions on the PA and online. Polly can come. Let us know ASAP as we have to get things moving/progs printed, etc. Cheers pal, JG'

Tom looked at the text and tried to think what he was doing

on Saturday. Nothing, he thought. He had better check with Polly. But it sounded fun.

The pair took their suitcases upstairs and began unpacking in the bedroom.

'Pol, what we doing this Saturday? Jonny Gordon wants me to sponsor a rugby match at Walsham. He came in the surgery last week and mentioned it. I don't think they have many matches left, so I'd have to do one soon, he suggested Saturday.'

'We aren't doing anything, as far as I know,' Polly said.

'So, I'll tell him we'll do it then.'

'We?' What's all this 'we'? I assume that doesn't include me.'

'Yes it does. It's a meal and a few drinks, then the rugby, be good fun, you'd like it.'

'Are you kidding me? Since when have I liked bloody rugby?' Polly had her hands on her hips and was half-laughing. 'I don't even know what happens at rugby, I can think of 100 things I would rather do on a Saturday afternoon than watch bloody rugby. Take Jill with you, she likes rugby.'

'How do you know Jill likes rugby? Anyhow I'm not taking Jill, she's not my wife. Come on, I'll ply you with wine before the match and you can go to sleep in the car during the game if you want.'

'No, I'm not going. I refuse.'

'What do you mean, refuse. I'm not asking you to go into space, or shag the milkman, just come with me to the rugby. You will come!'

'Oh, will I, now? And who is going to make me?'

'I will. Or I'll… I'll stop all sex for a month.'

Polly laughed out loud and went over to put her arms around Tom. 'Oh, will you now darling? What, are you going to take yourself off down the shed and have a little fumble among your old magazines, like a little dirty old man? Or sit up late and watch Babe Station?'

Tom shook his head. 'You are just so bad. I don't have them anymore, as you know. You threw them out years ago. And I don't watch Babe Station, either, well not often.'

Polly raised her eyebrows. 'How often?'

Polly kept Tom's arms around her and kissed him, and kissed

him again. He smiled. She so loved him. If Tom wanted to sponsor the game, she'd support him, of course she would, even if she hated rugby.

'Okay, I'll come,' Polly said. 'But on one condition, and you must say yes!'

'Oh, no. What must I say yes to?'

'Come on, say it, or I won't come.'

'Honestly, you are like a five-year-old, Pol. Okay, I'll say 'yes'. Now what is it?'

'Knew you would. Well, the yes is that, 'yes' you will throw out all the condoms in the 'just in case I've forgotten to take the pill' drawer. Because those days are gone honey bunch. We're going for it, and if it takes 10 times a night, then 10 times a night it is.' And with that she gave Tom a smacker on the lips before running downstairs to put the kettle on.

Tom was left smiling to himself.

He followed her down ten minutes later and dropped Jonny a text to say he would be happy to sponsor the match, Jonny was quick to reply with a 'thumbs-up' emoji, then telling him he would be in touch later in the week to confirm times.

'How did we cope before texts and mobile phones?' Tom said as Polly went out of the front door to the Audi to pick up more bags. She didn't answer.

As he went into the kitchen, Tom heard Polly's phone 'bleep'. He wasn't usually one to look at her phone, although Pol never asked him not to. But seeing as he had put his down next to hers, he glanced at the text, he could make out the first line.

'Tell me you know, Polly?...' is all it said.

Tom looked at the number the text had come from but it was 'unknown'. He found that strange. 'Tell me you know, Polly?' What did that mean? He knew not to pry his wife over personal things like texts.

However, Tom was curious. He knew he probably had the wrong end of the stick and it all meant nothing. Still, he decided he'd say something. He went into the living room and turned the TV on. He looked at the TV guide, Countryfile was on at 7. He smiled and thought of Milky, he was bound to be watching.

Polly walked in.

'Your phone went off, sounded like a text.'

Polly didn't say anything, but turned back to go into the kitchen. Tom got up and followed her, pretending to go to the sink to wash his hands, all the time keeping one eye on his wife as she read her phone.

Polly read the text, clicked into it to read it in full. *'Tell me you know, Polly?…'* was all it said.

Tom was watching. She clicked the phone shut and walked back into the dining room.

He followed her. 'Who was that from?'

'No-one,' said Polly unconvincingly.

'No-one? Is that Mr No-one or Mrs No-one?'

'It's none of your business, no-one. No-one you know, anyhow. Why are you so interested? I can't remember the last time I quizzed you about who a text you received was from.'

Tom was shocked.

'Alright darling, no problem, calm down.'

'Don't *'no problem'* me, Tom. If you want to have a look at the text, you are welcome, but you won't know who it is from, it's someone at the gym, okay? Fuckin' hell, what's the matter with you? Take a look if you want. Sorry if you think I'm keeping secrets from you. I'm going for a bath.'

Polly picked the phone back up and pushed it towards him. Tom turned away. 'Don't be daft, I'm not that bothered.' She brushed past him and took it upstairs with her, he heard the bathroom door slam.

Tom was left stunned. Only minutes before they had been laughing and joking in the bedroom. What the hell just happened?

Polly turned the bath taps on, she could do with a soak and relax. That text had been the last thing she had wanted after what had been a fun weekend. Who the hell was it? What did they want? It was starting to get to her and she knew it. She rarely flew at Tom like she had just done and she hated herself for speaking to him in that manner. He didn't deserve that.

Polly undressed and looked in the mirror. She had such a figure. Whoever sent her the text would soon get bored, she wouldn't reply to it and she didn't have a clue what it meant. *'Tell me you know, Polly?'* She mustn't give whoever it was any oxygen.

She lay in the bath and thought of the weekend she had just enjoyed. It had been fun to catch up with Jody and Craig. The four had laughed a lot, although she had to admit Craig had seemed a bit distant at times.

She would chat to Tom to find out if Craig had said anything. Find out if something was wrong.

That's if Tom would accept her apology, first of course.

She knew the answer to that.

TWENTY FIVE

TONY Statton posted the letter to Strangeways as soon as he got home on Sunday.

He wouldn't usually send a letter in the post, but felt he would rather contact Archer this way to begin with. He could have phoned, but putting something in writing would make Archer feel better, he was sure of that, a coded letter from one of his former trustees. They could chat on the phone later.

Statton had to be careful. Archer's mail was bound to be read by the prison security staff and he didn't know a way to bypass that procedure. It didn't matter, all he wanted was for Archer to know the 'job' he had tasked him with was a goer.

Hi Stu,

Just writing to let you know I saw that guy we talked about and yes, that doesn't seem a problem. He's keen to help and so am I. It's one we can do. So we'll start on the house next week. He reckons the price of 50 will be fine. I'll be in touch, let you know how it's coming along. Look good when it's done. Give us a call when you get a chance. I'll go over the plans.

Tony.

He put the letter in the envelope, re-reading it three or four times to make sure he wasn't giving anything away that could be construed as suspicious. He wondered if he should have left the 50 bit in, then again what could anyone make of that? He mustn't get paranoid.

'Who's that for?' said Alice.

His wife had seen him stick the envelope down and put a

stamp on as she had walked into the kitchen. Statton picked it up quickly and put it in his pocket, he didn't want her to see the address.

Alice was younger than her husband, by almost 10 years. She was petite and attractive and the two children she had presented him with were the lights of Tony's life. It was Alice who had been the reason he had taken himself out of Archer's gang. It had been a big decision at the time because the money was rolling in, he was living a rich bachelor's life. Archer's drug empire was beginning to take off, but he had fallen for Alice, hook, line and sinker. They met at a pub in Warrington. Alice was with friends on a hen night out, he was there drinking with pals.

The two groups got chatting, the pair getting along like a house on fire. Phone numbers were exchanged and Statton was soon on his way south to meet up with her and, the rest is history.

But, it had meant him having to leave Archer's gang, not an easy task and a gang Alice never knew anything about, then and now. Statton had plenty of money, cash and deposits, while Alice already had a house in Southampton. It was only a two-bed terrace, but after Statton sold his place in Warrington and arrived in Hampshire with plenty of liquidity, they bought a large farmhouse on the outskirts of the city, outright. They had lived there ever since. Alice still worked in the NHS, while Statton was a delivery driver, few questioned how they had afforded such a property. Alice had believed her husband to be when he said he had been left money by a late uncle.

'So, who is it for?' Alice repeated the question. 'The letter.'

'Oh, I'm just sending it to a pal up north, he wanted me to send a photocopy of an invoice of something. So, I've done that, it's nothing.'

Statton got up and went into the dining room. The last thing he wanted Alice to want to see it with the address on it, Strangeways. Not that she would question it. Alice knew not to over question her husband, they shared everything, but he ran the show. She accepted her husband's explanation, picked up some washing and went to hang it out on the line. Statton puffed out his cheeks.

He decided to post the letter now, before he made another schoolboy error. He knew there was a letter box just down the road, so he took a stroll, enjoying the late evening sun after what had been a wet weekend. As he plopped it in the letter box he realised there was no going back.

Statton had watched Baldini over the weekend, he now needed to think of a way of finding out if it was definitely him who had snitched on his pal.

He smiled to himself as he turned away from the letter box. 50K, that would be nice.

He would call in some favours.

TWENTY SIX

POLLY was in a good mood as the team sat down at the gym for their Monday morning meeting.

Tom and her had made up after she had shouted at him over that text and she was trying to forget all about it. It was someone playing silly buggers and she wasn't going to let it get to her. Feeling sorry for herself, wasn't something Polly did. Anyhow, they had made up their little tiff in the best way possible, in the bedroom.

Andy was already seated at the table when Polly walked in.

'Morning Pol. All good?'

'Yes, really good Andy. Am I the first one here again? Gosh, shows how keen I am!' She winked.

Valerie and Tina were the next to arrive, both smiling with hellos, as they headed straight for the coffee machine, Tina looked radiant and had a terrific tan. The weekend weather in Norwich had clearly been better than it had in Chester.

'You got a sunbed, Tina?' Polly was looking at her up and down. 'Just, you look so lovely and tanned, or is your garden the best suntrap in Norfolk and you're keeping it to yourself. I was in Chester at the weekend and it rained almost all the time, clearly I missed the good weather.'

Tina laughed. 'Well, actually, I do have a sunbed and a garden that attracts the sun. But I'll be honest, yes I did have time on the old sunbed on Saturday. Hubbie went and played golf with his mates, so I grabbed a few extra hours on it. He doesn't like me spending too much time under it, but if the cat's away.' Tina raised her eyebrows, Polly smiled back.

'Well, I think you look great, we thought about having one once. Well, I thought about it. I mentioned it to Tom and he said, hot tub or sun bed? Which was a no-brainer. You can't hold a glass of Prosecco while lying under a sunbed. Then again, never did get the hot tub, either – yet.'

It was Valerie's turn to laugh. 'That's a great point.'

Kevin and James walked in. It was 9.15am and Andy was keen to start.

'Well, guys and girls, I have some news,' Andy said, in a cheery manner. 'Some exciting news.'

James almost spat his coffee out, it didn't take much to get his juices flowing. 'Oh, I say. Please tell me you have booked the Chippendales for a water party and fluffy dressing gown night in the spa. Champagne and tapas, £30 a ticket. Free for staff and one guest, I can't wait.' He turned to Polly. 'My dressing gown is made of Mohair, that's hair from the Angora goat, don't you know?'

They all laughed, apart from Kevin and Andy, as James stood up and did a twirl, doing an impression of someone wearing a fluffy dressing gown.

'If the bloody Chippendales are coming here, I'm on day off, or week off, however long they are staying,' Kevin was his usual miserable self. 'Just keep them away from the gym, we don't want them anywhere near there.'

'Why keep them from the gym? They are more toned than me and you put together,' said James, as he lifted his shirtsleeve up to show off his biceps to Kevin, who was becoming irritated.

'Get away,' Kevin grizzled as he pushed James' arm. 'What a world we live in today, I'd have been happier living with cavemen, rather than some of the excuses we have for the male race today. Pathetic creatures some of them.'

'I hope you are not referring to me,' James said, trying to look offended, but enjoying his little cabaret. 'Each to their own Kevin, as far as I'm concerned. This is a modern world, would you rather live in the 1600s?

'Yeah, probably would actually. And if the 'pathetic creatures' cap fits. Or the dressing gown for that matter, you wear it'. Kevin nodded and grinned.

Polly smiled to herself. Kevin loved to think he had been

funny, even when he wasn't. Lord help his wife, the long winter nights in their house must just fly by.

'Okay, listen up, that's enough,' Andy said.

'We are having a visit next week from some of the players from Norwich City Football Club. They are going to use our gym and the pool, it's a bit of self-promotion that Pol has set up. We spend a bit of money with them, programme advertising, etc., and Polly has asked if a few of their players can come over here to give us a bit of exposure, the papers will be here and the radio. They will be speaking to the players and some of us as well, it's next Wednesday. I think that is great news and is a real chance for us to push the gym and spa and hopefully get more customers, well done Pol, for that. Great stuff.'

'Oh, really well done Pol,' Kevin said with a hint of sarcasm. 'Are they coming before or after the Farming Today ditty on the radio?' He smiled at Polly.

'Piss off you bore.' She smiled sarcastically at Kevin.

'Thank you Pol,' Andy jumped in quick before things got out of hand.

'Kevin, for your information the Farming Today jingle has already prompted interest in the gym from potential new customers,' Andy continued. 'So, give it a rest mate, will you please?'

'What, are farmers joining us?' Kevin laughed out loud. 'I haven't noticed any tractors in the car park.'

Polly was about to let him have both barrels, but James nipped in this time. 'You are rude, Kevin. Sometimes I think your mouth opens before your brain computes, then again, I'm not sure your brain computes ever.' And with that he blew him a kiss!

'Now, come on, you lot, for goodness sake,' Andy said. 'Stop all this bickering, grow up. This is supposed to be a staff meeting. We are doing well as a business and the footballers' visit is just another example of how we can bring more people in. As I said, that's great work from Pol and I hope it will be a good day, I want to make sure we are all in next Wednesday ready for a photo opportunity.'

Tina looked across at Polly and mouthed *good girl* to her. Polly smiled back.

Andy continued. 'That was all I wanted to say, anyone got

anything else they want to add.'

James stood up. 'The loan for the 'green area' will be with us on Wednesday week. I had word from the bank late on Friday. That means we will be able to start planning what we want to do as soon as we want to do it, I suggest we crack on as soon as possible, but that's above my pay grade to make that decision.'

'Good, James,' Andy said. 'You and I will have a meeting later today, anything else?'

'We are trialling new products in the spa as from tomorrow,' Tina announced. 'The rep left them with us on Friday and we will have a look at them today and see which ones we want to use. They look quite good. For now, he has left us a bundle of them for free, if we want to go ahead with any of them, we will get together with you Andy, and decide how many we want to purchase.'

'Oooh, can I come and try some,' Polly said. 'Are they cruelty-free though? Need to be in this day and age.'

'They are. Come over lunchtime,' Tina added, glad of Polly's interest. 'And some of them are for topping up your tan, so you should come and have a look as well Kevin, you might find something for the 'older man's hairy chest.'

James burst out laughing. Kevin shook his head. He liked Tina more than Polly, so he wasn't going to reply with any derogatory comments to her.

'Okay, anything else?' Andy was winding the meeting up. 'As I said, we are in a good place right now with the business and I know the 'green area' will be a big plus, and don't forget, no-one is to book next Wednesday off.'

They all hurriedly left, Tina and Polly continuing their conversation about the new products as they headed towards the spa.

'I love to try new products, don't you?' Polly said as the pair linked arms and walked round the poolside.

'Especially freebies!' said Tina. They both laughed.

Tom was enjoying his packed lunch as he sat in his surgery. Emily had gone home. She was taking the afternoon off to visit her gran.

Polly always packed him a good spread and today was no different. Tuna baguette, crisps, one of those corner yoghurts she knew he loved, a carton of orange juice. Pretty healthy, he thought, his cholesterol wouldn't be taking too big a hit today.

It had been a busy morning, as Monday's often seemed to be. Mrs Cartlidge's root canal filling had gone well, as had Mr Anson's filling. He had allowed 30 minutes for each of them, a good decision. Apart from them, most people were check-ups and polishes.

He sat down and read *The Times*. The sports coverage on a Monday was always good value. And seeing as he hadn't been at the Emirates to see Arsenal win on Saturday, it was pleasing to read a report that hailed their performance as *'robust'* and *'impressive'*.

Polly had been apologetic for her swearing at him last night, not that he needed an apology. He loved her to bits, and anyhow, if she apologised every time she swore, she'd be apologising all day.

Yet, he knew that text had ruffled her and even though they made love later that evening, he couldn't forget the way she had reacted to him in the manner she had.

Tom put down his paper and picked up his baguette, took a bite and thought again about what Craig had told him. His mate's revelations were concerning and Tom had kept thinking about it. If Archer did find out it was Craig who had stitched him up and helped put him in prison, what next? Was Archer capable of finding out who did it? Tom suspected he likely was. This guy was a gang leader, he would, and probably did, have eyes everywhere, even while in jail, Craig seemed to think that to.

All this because Craig couldn't keep it in his trousers. What a prat! In some ways his friend had it coming and he deserved it. Tom shook his head. *What a web of lies we weave.*

He continued to eat his lunch and read the paper. Jill had gone into the city for a bite to eat and she had locked the front door, all was quiet.

The silence was broken as the phone rang from downstairs. Tom didn't know if he could be bothered to interrupt his lunchbreak. Then again it could be important, it could be a patient with an urgent request, or a new patient wanting to join.

He walked downstairs, running the last two steps, just in case it rang off. He got there in time.

'Armstrong's Surgery. Tom speaking. Can I help?'

There was silence at the other end for a few seconds and then… 'Hi. Um, yes, hi. I'd like to book an appointment, as soon as possible. I have a toothache and I could do with it being looked at, if you could fit me in,' the woman's voice said. 'Please.'

'Okay, are you a patient already at the surgery?'

'Um, no, I'm not a patient. Does that mean you can't see me? Or can I become a patient? How does it work?'

'Okay, well look. I'll just check the diary. Hang on a minute.' Tom put the phone down and looked around.

He spent a couple of seconds trying to find the diary on the desk. Jill was very efficient and Tom always felt she knew where everything was, but likely no-one else, her desk could resemble a bit of a pickle, fortunately he found the diary.

'Okay, well I can get you in tomorrow morning, but it would have to be early, say 8am, if that's any help,' Tom said as he went to write the woman's name down in the diary. 'We can sign you up for our surgery dental scheme if you like, my receptionist will help you. Or you can pay a one-off fee for the treatment. It's up to you.'

'I'll come in tomorrow,' the voice on the other end of the line said. 'Thank you.'

'Okay, that's fine. Who is calling? I'll put your name in the diary for 8am tomorrow,' Tom said.

'It's Karen, Karen Harding.'

'Okay, Mrs Harding, see you tomorrow.' The line went dead before Tom had finished his sentence. That was odd, he thought, whoever it was hung up pretty quick.

'Mrs Harding'. Tom remembered hearing that name recently, but he couldn't think when. He shrugged his shoulders, made a mental note to let Jill know to contact Susan this afternoon, to tell her they had an early 8am appointment tomorrow, so could she be in ASAP? Tom would be there anyhow.

With that he went upstairs and finished his lunch and took a look at the Premiership table, Arsenal were up to fifth.

Karen put the receiver down sharpish.

Her heart was beating ten to the dozen. Oh, wow, it was him she had spoken to. She hadn't expected that, she'd expected the receptionist. So, what now? Last time she had booked an appointment, she hadn't gone through with it.

That was not going to happen again.

TWENTY SEVEN

TOM walked in just after 6pm, Polly was in the kitchen cooking dinner.

'That smells good. 'What is it?'

'What is it? If it smells that good you will know what it is.' Polly turned and kissed him.

'Why do men say that sort of thing? *That smells good*', but they don't know what it is. Honestly, I'd rather you said nothing than something as daft as that. Sometimes Tom Armstrong I think you do it on purpose, act stupid. If I didn't know you better, I'd think that was the case.' Polly brushed past him. 'Spaghetti bolognaise. Love you really!'

Tom smiled. Polly had clearly enjoyed a better day, he could tell from her demeanour.

'You will never guess what?' Polly continued to stir the bolognaise. 'Norwich City are only sending players to our gym next week for a bit of promotional work. I organised it and Andy had it confirmed over the weekend, isn't that great news? Andy announced it at the meeting this morning. He told us all he had some exciting news, James thought the Chippendales were coming. Shall I get autographs for you?'

Tom laughed as he hung his coat up on hooks on the wall in the utility room. 'I don't think so. I don't think I know any of their players, or Chippendales for that matter.'

Polly frowned as Tom walked back into the kitchen. 'I hope you are not belittling my successful attempt at getting footballers to our gym? This is a big coup for us, you know, great publicity.'

'No, no, I'm not belittling it one bit. I may not know them, but plenty of people will. I mean they are the biggest club, well, the biggest club in Norwich!' Tom laughed and at the same time hugged Polly.

'Ha, ha, ha,' Polly said, pulling away from him. 'Well, I don't see many Arsenal players coming to your surgery to support you, bearing in mind you bung the club £800, or whatever it is, for a stupid season ticket. Perhaps they should refund your money, seeing as you are always moaning about them not giving you value for it.'

'Ah, that's different,' Tom said, as he started to go through the post that was scattered on the kitchen table. 'You see, my £800 is money well spent. For a start think how many times a year I am out of the house on a Saturday, so you can go shopping? And just think of the amount of times a year you hold it against me and use my season ticket as a guilt trip, so you can get you own way? It's all in your favour, my darling. I'm going for a shower.'

Polly smiled and watched him go upstairs as she continued cooking.

A few moments later, she was laying the table when a text came through on her phone. She went back into the kitchen to look at it, likely Jody. But it wasn't.

She looked at it again. She had no choice but to click into it. She didn't want to, it was from the 'unknown' number again; 'Your hubby's sexy voice. Sooooo sexy voice', it said.

She could feel the blood drain from her face. What the hell was going on? Who was this? She felt sick and suddenly had no appetite, it was all getting too much. Calls to the home phone and her mobile, now two texts in two days. She would have to speak to Tom and she would have to speak to him now. Tom would know what to do.

Polly stirred the dinner, but her night had been turned on its head yet again and she felt like shit. Tom came down the stairs with a towel wrapped around him.

'Right, darling, I'm famished, is it ready?' He walked into the kitchen, all smiles. 'I might put a sprinkling of cheese on top of it, do you want some?'

Tom went to the fridge to get the Parmesan out. He looked at

Polly, who was still stirring the bolognaise, she hadn't answered him.

'Pol, are you listening to me? Do you want any of this Parmesan?'

She looked up. 'Yes, yes, sorry. Um, no, I don't want any cheese with it, I'll have it ready in about five minutes. You've got time to get changed if you want?'

He closed the fridge door and brushed past Polly, giving her a kiss on the head as he did so. He went back upstairs to get properly dressed. He decided he wouldn't put on a white t-shirt, seeing as they were having bolognaise, it had the potential to be a recipe for a disaster.

He decided to put on a blue shirt and a casual pair of trousers, came downstairs and sat at the dining room table. He cracked open a bottle of wine, a nice Sauvignon Blanc. Polly walked in with the food already on the plates, the Parmesan was on the table.

'This looks great,' Tom said as he poured out the wine and delved for the Parmesan. 'After dinner, perhaps we can have 'dessert' upstairs again later. That was fun last night.' Polly smiled. But it was fake, her mood had changed and Tom could sense it.

'What's wrong?' Tom put down the wine and looked at her. 'Are you okay?'

Without warning, Polly put her hands to her face and burst into tears as she leaned her elbows on the table. Tom struggled to comprehend what was happening, it caught him totally unawares. 'What on earth is wrong?' He got up from the table and went across to put his arm around his wife. 'Hell Pol, what's happened? Why are you crying? A few moments ago you were fine, what has brought this on?'

She pushed her food away, Tom hadn't seen her like this for years. Polly shed tears, but not like this.

'Come on love.' Tom was beginning to get desperate, and scared of what his wife was going to say. 'Talk to me darling.'

She looked up at him and took a breath, while rubbing her eyes. Tom was staring at her, still staggered by it all.

She choked back the tears: 'The last few weeks, I've been getting calls on the phone at home and on my mobile and when I answer them there is no-one on the other end, or they are there, but don't answer. I call back, there is no answer and this week I've been getting texts with messages I don't understand, all from an unknown number. I ignored the calls, thinking it was just, like, scam stuff. But the texts have got to me, I call the number, no answer. There was one last night, that's why I flew at you when you kept asking me who it was from. It said something like, *'tell me you know, Polly?'* And then I've had another one tonight, just now, while you were up having a shower, it just said something about *'hubby's sexy voice'.'*

Polly looked at him and shrugged her shoulders. If ever she needed his calm manner, now was the time, he was sure to come up with words to sooth, she hadn't wanted to cry, but it had just come out. Tom kept his arm around her.

'How many of these calls and texts have you had?' He kissed her on the head. 'Come on, wipe those tears away.'

'A few calls, I think three, a couple of texts. The calls came first and more recently the texts. They're the ones that are not nice, because now they are mentioning you.'

'And you have no idea who they have come from?'

'No, the number is always unknown and I don't know if you can block numbers that are unknown. Or how you can do it? I just hoped whoever, was just going to go away.'

'Was any voice you heard a man or woman?'

Polly had regained a little composure. 'I think it was a woman on the landline call, the Friday night before we went down the pub the other week. I really can't be sure. But it's the texts that are getting more frequent, and whoever, knows my name. The phone calls were so quick.'

She looked at Tom, who smiled at her. 'Don't worry. I'll take a look at them. Look, you know this is nothing, don't you? Just some weirdo has found your number somehow. They don't even know who you are, they just have the number and you have probably picked it up and said 'Polly Armstrong', so that's where they have got your name from, these things go on all the time. Try and forget it, but from now on, you must share stuff like this with me, you've had a few of these calls and said nothing, you must tell me if you are worried. I'll have a word with Mike, he knows his phone tech stuff and he might know a way of blocking unknown calls and texts.'

'Mike who?' Polly said as she took a sip of her wine, her tears had now stopped.

'Mike Gremshall, he owns a telecoms shop opposite me. You don't know him, I'll speak to him. He may be able to help. Right, now start to enjoy this bolognaise will you before it gets cold. I'm not having my beautiful wife slave for hours over a hot stove to produce this outstanding piece of cookery cuisine, and then not eat it. Have another litre of wine as well, you'll feel better.' Tom raised his eyebrows and smiled. Polly stuck her tongue out.

This is why she loved him so much, he never made a drama. Tom was so always in control. She knew he would have been shocked to see her cry, it wasn't something she did. Polly considered herself a tough cookie, her tears had even caught her by surprise. But Tom was right, it likely was just a crank, who had found out her name because she had answered with her name.

The pair of them were still eating and chatting away when Polly's mobile phone rang. She flashed a look at Tom, the phone was in the kitchen.

'Go and answer it. Go on.'

Polly got up and went into the kitchen, Tom was all ears as he heard her pick up the phone. He was hoping against hope it wasn't another call to spook his wife, he hadn't enjoyed seeing Polly cry like that. She picked up the phone.

'Oh, hi Jody, how are you?' Tom was relieved. 'Yeah, I've got time to talk.'

He smiled to himself, he may as well eat his spag bol up.

Polly wouldn't be returning to the table any time soon.

TWENTY EIGHT

KAREN set her alarm for 6.15am.

She would drive into Norwich, leaving at 7.15, and leave her car in a car park and be at the dentist's surgery for 8.

All she had to do was get Lee up and ready. He caught the school bus and was quite capable of sorting himself out, she would leave his packed lunch on the kitchen table, but wake him before she left, just in case he overslept.

She had a quick shower, got dressed and put on her make-up before going downstairs to grab some breakfast. It was almost 7. She didn't eat much and was feeling nervous, this was going to be a big day. After all these years, how would she react to seeing him? How would he react to seeing her?

'Lee, darling, get up now can you?' Karen whispered in his ear as he lay snoozing in bed. She needed him up and about. He grunted something and appeared to stir.

She went downstairs and began gathering her things. She was concerned she was making a fuss of all this, bearing in mind she would be home by 9.30. No, she wasn't making a fuss, this was important.

Lee got out of bed, came downstairs and sat at the kitchen table.

'I'm off to the dentist, so get yourself off to school.' Karen picked up her handbag and gave him a kiss on the head. 'Your packed lunch is on the table, make sure you pack your sports shoes. You said you had running or something today, I'll see you tonight.'

Lee said something as he poured his milk over his Corn Flakes.

He had an hour before he had to leave the house and catch the bus, he was a sensible lad and knew his responsibilities.

She got into her car, a yellow Citroen C1, and headed off into Norwich. It was a drive of no more than 20 minutes at this time of the morning, the butterflies in her stomach were whirring as she wondered what she was going to say to him. To start with, how was she going to convince him she even had toothache?

But she had to be strong. It was time to meet Tom Armstrong again.

Tom took Polly up a cup of tea in bed and was surprised to get a drink so early.

'Where are you going?' She looked across at the small clock on her sideboard. It's only 6.30.'

'Where do you think?' He smiled as he put her cup down. 'I'm going to work, I have an 8am emergency appointment, some lady has toothache and I said I would take a look. See, that's the sort of nice Mr Dentist man I am.'

'Oh, you never told me that, I was looking forward to a cuddle and now you are up and about and are going, just jump back in here for a minute.' Polly pulled back the covers, revealing her legs.

'No, Pol. Anyhow didn't you hear the shower? I can't be jumping in bed with you now.'

Polly was still half asleep. She smiled at her husband and turned over. Tom got dressed and looked at his watch, it was 6.35 and he would start to make his way into the surgery.

He leant over and kissed her. Polly had gone back to sleep. He picked his briefcase up and headed for the door.

He turned his phoned on as he got in his car. He'd missed a call, what at this time? Jonny Gordon had left a voicemail.

'Hello mate, sorry to call so early. I'm always up with the larks and doing a quick 5K before breakfast. Ha! Ha! Anyhow, this Saturday, 2pm start for the rugger match. Be at the ground at 12.30pm if you can for a spot of lunch and e-mail me over your details of what you want your business promoted as… You know, something like, 'I'm a dentist and it's money for old rope', that sort of thing (Jonny laughed). *No, just give us your address, etc., and what you want to say, new customers always welcome, etc. And don't forget to bring that firecracker Pol along please.*

She's the only reason I asked you to sponsor the game. Ha, ha, only joking mate, see you Saturday.'

Tom smiled as he continued his drive in. Jonny was a laugh, he and Polly would have a fun day on Saturday, even if Pol didn't like rugby she would join in the banter and could hold her own with Jonny and his rugby friends.

He pulled into the car park, parked up and went into the surgery, turning off the surgery alarm as he did so. Susan had told Jill she would be in just before 8. Tom had 20 minutes before his patient arrived. He went upstairs and prepared for the day, already half hoping this Karen Harding's toothache was nothing more than an abscess that she could have antibiotics for.

As Tom was sorting his instruments out, Emily came running up the stairs, he had told her the day before to come in early.

'Morning, thanks for coming in earlier, Em. You didn't have to come in until 8 you know, I did say 8.'

'Oh, that's alright,' said Emily as she took off her scarf and woolly hat, hanging it up on the coat stand in the corner of the surgery room. 'I was up early today anyhow and had to go home first to get my stuff on before coming here.'

'Go home first?' Tom turned to look at her. 'Where were you staying last night, if that's not a personal question?'

'Oh, I stayed at a mate's house, just by the river, near the city centre. She had a bra, panties and cup-cake party last night. No alcohol, just a good film for us all to watch, there were about five of us, we watched 'The Devil Wears Prada', I reckon it's the fourth time I'd seen it, but still.'

'What on earth is a bra, panties and cup-cake party? I suppose it is what it says on the tin. I've never heard of such a thing, is it just women who go?'

'Of course it's just women? What men do you know wear bra and panties? It's a right laugh.' Emily put her hand on Tom's arm and stroked it, smiling at him as she spoke, she was fond of her boss, not that he noticed.

'Basically, you turn up and change into your bra, panties and have a dressing gown on if you want, but you don't have to. And everyone has to bring cup-cakes, but no alcohol, that's the only proviso. It's fun, you should let Pol have one. I bet she looks good in bra and panties. Even better stuffing cup-cakes!'

'Don't give her any ideas, she doesn't need any excuse for a party, cup-cakes, bras or alcohol.'

Emily smiled.... *'No, I bet she doesn't need any fucking excuse,'* she thought.

'Do we have any notes on Mrs Harding?' Emily looked up at Tom. 'I can't say I've ever met her.'

Tom shook his head.

'No, she's a new patient, so, let's treat her as if you know her. You never know, she might come back.'

Karen parked up in one of the town centre car parks and bought a ticket. She didn't think she would need any longer than two hours, her heart was racing as she approached 'Armstrong's Dental Surgery'.

She had been to the surgery before, many times. She had never gone in and had never spent much time hanging around, she had just wanted to see where he worked.

The door was open, Karen walked in and saw a lady taking her coat off and hanging it up on a pedestal behind her. Karen made a shuffling with her feet, so as to attract attention to herself, the lady turned around.

'Good morning,' said Susan who, despite only working a day a week in the surgery, took her job seriously and was well organised. Susan was 41 and married with one girl, who was at university in Southampton.

'You must be Mrs Harding.' Susan smiled at Karen, who nodded her head.

'I know you are not on the scheme, so could you quickly fill in this form, before going up and perhaps we can talk about the scheme when you come down, see if you want to join.'

Karen was presented with a tablet that she had to put her name and address in, job details, any children? Did she smoke? Etc.

After filling it in and signing it, she sat back down. By now she was shaking with nerves and she started to breath slowly, as she had been taught many years ago by her sister Jane when they were growing up together. Jane had been keen on yoga and the importance of keeping calm. Karen was trying to remember all the things her sister had told her. Oh, how she wished Jane was next to her now.

Footsteps came down from the floor above. Tom walked into the reception area.

TWENTY NINE

'MRS Harding, I'm Tom, how are you? I'm assuming it is Mrs Harding.' Tom smiled and shook Karen's hand.

'You are the only patient booked in for 8am, unless you are my 8.35 and very early.' He smiled again.

She shook his hand and looked into his eyes. It was him. No doubt, she was sure even before she had come into the surgery. She had spied on him enough, even followed him into the city one lunchtime, Karen had even been to his house and seen him with his pretty wife.

'Hi, I'm Mrs Harding, Karen.'

Tom looked at her, registering nothing. She looked at him, but it was clear he didn't know who she was.

'Well, come upstairs,' Tom said as he led the way up towards the surgery.

She followed him, took her coat off as she entered the surgery and sat in the chair. She was as nervous as hell, had it really been 14 years since the pair had last spoken, where had the time gone?

Karen saw Emily standing in the corner as she made her way in, the pair didn't exchange glances.

'So, you have toothache, Karen,' Tom said as he put on some gloves and picked up his instruments. 'Whereabouts?'

'Bottom left, one of the big teeth,' she lied. This was where she was worried everything was going to unravel. 'Although it's been a bit better this morning, I hope I'm not wasting your time.'

'I'm sure you're not, let me have a look. 'Open wide.'

Tom poked and prodded around the area of complaint, but

Karen didn't flinch. She was enjoying the smell of his after shave, his closeness to her. He tapped her teeth, prodded and poked more, but still there was little reaction. Tom started to wonder if there was any pain at all because he certainly couldn't see any damage to any of her teeth in the area she had been pointing at. In general Karen's teeth were in rude health.

'Okay, well, I can't see much wrong here with your teeth.' Tom looked at Emily and shrugged. He put his instruments down. 'Take a rinse out.'

'I don't want to do anything if I can't see anything. Are you okay this morning with the pain? I can give you a prescription for antibiotics just in case it is an abscess, which it could be if it's been giving you grief for a few days.'

Karen had rinsed out and was laying with her head back again. She nodded in agreement with what she was being told to her, before sitting up in the chair. She looked again at Tom, that dashing black hair and those strong blue eyes, how could she forget?

'Sorry, I'm so sorry to be wasting your time,' she stuttered. 'Perhaps it doesn't hurt as much as I thought.'

'You're not wasting my time, it's better to get these things checked out. I mean what's the point of me being here if people don't come to me when they have tooth pain, I would suggest we make an appointment for next week and take another look. If there is still a problem, I'll take an x-ray, you are not on the scheme are you? So, have a chat with Susan downstairs and we can put you on it if you like, and your son. I see you have a son according to your notes. Does he have a dentist? Anyhow, there will be no charge this time, but likely a small one next time if nothing needs doing, is that all okay?'

Karen took a deep breath.

'You don't know who I am, do you?' She surprised herself at the confidence in her voice.

Tom was filling some notes in, he turned around and looked at her. 'Um, pardon, no, I don't think I do, do I? Should I know who you are?'

Emily looked up from cleaning some instruments.

Karen continued, keeping her voice calm. 'You do know me, and I know you, actually you seriously have no idea how much we know each other, but not now. Now is not the time for this, I'll be in touch and we will talk. We have a lot to talk about, so be ready, Tom. Please, be ready.'

Before Tom could reply, Karen had got out of the chair, leant across to collect her coat, gone out of the door and ran down the stairs and out of the surgery, Tom was left holding his pen and looking stunned.

He looked at Emily. 'What was that all about?' Emily shrugged her shoulders.

For a few uncomfortable moments neither of them said anything. *'You have no idea how much we know each other..... I'll be in touch'.*

Emily broke the silence.

'Did you know her then? Because that was weird if you don't, she seemed to know you. I don't think she even had a toothache, she just wanted to come in and say that. Aren't some people strange?'

Tom didn't reply. He replayed the words through his mind, he had to admit the whole episode had left him stunned. Karen hadn't even taken the prescription for the toothache, it was as though, Emily was right, she didn't have anything wrong with her teeth.

He went downstairs to speak to Susan.

'That Mrs Harding who was just here, can I look more closely at the form she filled in? I don't suppose she stopped to make another appointment?'

'No, she didn't, her form is here on the tablet,' Susan replied as she handed Tom the small screen. 'I haven't had time to process it yet, or even looked closely myself at it to be honest, I assume that was her running out of the surgery was it? She hasn't paid anything, was she supposed to pay, or make another appointment? I didn't get a chance to stop her.'

Tom didn't answer, he put Karen's name into the tablet and sat down on one of the chairs in the reception area. At least she had put her name in correctly, or so he assumed. He looked at the address she had given. 'Bletchley Hall, Crosswaite House, Lowestoft'.

'Where the hell was that, Bletchley Hall?' He suspected the address and mobile number she had filled out didn't exist as he

grabbed hold of the surgery phone and called the mobile number. Sure enough it was unobtainable. He shook his head, *'what the hell was that all about?'*

'If Mrs Harding calls back, please get me, I need to talk to her,' Tom said. He handed the tablet back to Susan. 'That mobile number she has left is unobtainable and I bet that address doesn't exist.'

'Okay, will do,' said Susan putting the tablet down on the desk. She looked up at Tom. 'Are you okay? You look like you have seen a ghost, is something wrong?'

He shook his head. 'I don't know, but I need to talk to her if she does call, thanks. Send up my 8.35 when they come in will you please?'

He went back upstairs, Emily was pottering about, cleaning instruments and refilling the rinse water.

'Um, Emily, I need you not to say anything about what just happened. Not even to Jill or Susan. Please, do you understand? I don't quite know what that was all about and I need to find out. So, keep it to yourself, you know surgery rules on stuff like that, patient confidentiality. I don't want to find out you have told anyone, is that okay? Thank you.'

Emily nodded. And as Tom turned away, smiled.

Mrs Blanchard and her two teenage girls came into the surgery just before lunch. The girls were teasing Tom as to why the surgery didn't have a Facebook page. The girls had been coming to the surgery since Tom first opened. They were now 13 and 14 and had plenty to say for themselves, although they never had anything wrong with their teeth.

'Why isn't your dentist surgery on Facebook?' said one of the girls, as Tom was looking into their mother's mouth, he had already looked at both girls' teeth.

'I don't really do Facebook,' Tom replied, as he told Mrs Blanchard to 'rinse out'. 'I call it Faceache! A bit like toothache!'

The girls laughed. 'Don't do Facebook?' the other sister replied. 'How can you live? Do you do 'tik-tok'?

Tom half smiled. 'The only tik-tok I know of is the sound of my uncle's grandfather clock. That goes tik-tok. And bongs 11 times at 11 o clock!'

The girls laughed, Emily shook her head.

At lunchtime, Tom took a stroll into the city centre, he wanted to clear his head. He hadn't had that much time to go over what Karen had said to him in any detail and it was playing on his mind and had done so all morning. What an outburst, it appeared calculated. But where the hell did she know him from?

He wracked his brains. Karen was no-one he had met since he had arrived in Norwich, he was sure of it, his memory wasn't that bad, he knew who he had met since coming to the city. Okay, he was hardly the social animal of Norfolk, Polly met loads more people than he did, but he would have remembered Karen, wouldn't he? Then again, did he go to school with her many years ago? University? Now, there was a thought. He had met so many people at university, there was every chance Karen was one of those people, but why didn't she just say they had been to Uni together? That would hardly have been a state secret, and why was she going 'to be in touch'?

Where else? Where else could they have met?

Pubs, clubs, holidays, he thought. Holidays here in the UK, holidays abroad; Holidays abroad, he thought hard, he couldn't be sure. He had enjoyed two or three holidays with his mates during their final years at university during his late teens, early 20s. There was one in Gran Canaria, one in Ayia Napa, Cyprus, and there had been a great holiday in Crete. He thought of the fun he and his mates had enjoyed, beer, sun and girls on all of the holidays, oh, yes lots of girls.

He smiled as he remembered the numerous wet t-shirt competitions, honestly some of those girls. And then there were the few he slept with, well more than a few. He had been single, then, no strings, no promises, just fun, most of the sex pretty appalling as usually he and the girl were drunk. Just getting each other's clothes off often proved a feat.

He thought again, Cyprus, Gran Canaria, he met loads of girls there. Then it dawned, or at least he thought it did. Crete. 'Shit', he said to himself. 'No, surely not…. Karen. Karen from London. Karen in Crete, was her name Karen Harding?'

He had been walking some distance now, but stopped and

sat down on a bench just outside a coffee shop, he needed time to think. Karen, yes, Karen. Was that the Karen he had met in Crete in his surgery earlier this morning?

Come on, he met loads of girls on those holidays, but he had slept with a Karen, he remembered her now. She had a very pretty mate as well, but he couldn't remember her name. But yes, he remembered a Karen, they had spent quite a few nights together in Crete, was that her?

No, he was imagining all this, why on earth would a girl who he had met on holiday all those years ago come into his surgery? Why didn't she just introduce herself?

'Hi, Tom, I'm Karen. We shagged in Crete years ago. How are you? By the way, my tooth aches!'

If nothing else, that would have made Emily's day!

He was going mad, he blamed Craig, it was his shock bloody revelations about Marie and the drugs run that was turning Tom into an anxious mess. If he wasn't thinking Craig was about to be killed by a drugs mafia, he was now starting to believe girls from previous life were popping up in his surgery.

He got up and carried on his walk around the city.

If he didn't have clients in the afternoon, he would have taken himself off for a beer to chill out.

Polly and Tina were comparing more of the new spa products when James walked in.

'Hi girls,' he said, closing the door behind him with incredible force. 'I need a favour.'

'Oh, no you don't,' Polly said. 'My Tom is mine and you can keep your grubby hands off him.' Polly looked at Tina and laughed. James smiled.

'Polly Armstrong, don't be so vulgar,' James said as he came up to the girls and sat down in a chair next to them. 'I'm a taken man. Anyhow, David and I are off to Thailand next month, did you know? That's the reason I'm here, I was wondering if you had any potions or products that would be good sun screens. David is ever so fair, I could get all the usual stuff from the supermarkets, but I thought I'd ask you. Price isn't an issue, doesn't matter how much, I just thought I would like something different, but with a good track record, perhaps something vegan, you know with none of those chemicals in it.

'David is a terrible worrier, he won't put deodorant under his arms because he thinks it will give him cancer, I do struggle with him sometimes because he pongs. But he is such a lovely man, I forgive him. Well, I love him!'

Polly and Tina smiled again, James talked so fast.

'You have come to the right people,' Tina said, standing up and going over to a box in the corner of the room. Her trial products. 'I have some new sun creams here and you are welcome to take some, a couple of factor 15s and a factor 50. If David is really fair, he would need a 50, I imagine.'

'Oh, he does,' James said. 'Sometimes I can't get him to come away from the beach bar because it's so hot and he burns so quickly. Then again he loves nothing more than a Pornstar, that's why he's always at the bar. A Pornstar Martini.'

Polly looked at him, then looked at Tina. 'What on earth is that, a Pornstar Martini? Are you making that up? It's not a drink is it?'

James looked bemused. 'Have you never heard of a Pornstar Martini?' He flicked his hair back. 'It's lovely, passionfruit and vanilla vodka, with a shot of Prosecco on the side, David loves them! You'd love them Polly.'

'I bet I would, I'm going to order one down at the Queen's Head next time I'm in, that will get Tom going when I ask him to get me a Pornstar.'

James laughed out loud. 'You must say Pornstar Martini, you can't just say Pornstar. You'll get barred.'

Tina smiled and bent down to grab some of the sun creams they had been talking about, she handed James three of them.

'These are all factor 15, the rep is bringing 50s and 30s in next week,' she said. 'Come and get some more, is that okay for now? When do you go?'

'Not for another three weeks,' James said as he got up and duly dropped one of the sun creams on the floor. He picked it up. 'Brilliant, thanks, anyhow, got to dash, I have a meeting with Andy and Kevin about new gym equipment, I don't suppose you have any perfume do you? I'll spray some all over me just to annoy

Kevin, he wants to think I'm a tart, that's fine. I'll smell like one.'

Polly was up for that, anything to annoy Kevin. 'Here you go.' She pulled out some Chanel from her handbag. 'Have a couple of squirts of this and then get close to Kevin, blow him another kiss, he'll love it!'

'Um, smells nice,' James said, before squirting himself three times over his neck. 'I shouldn't bring my social life habits into work, but Kevin just seems to ask for it, anyhow, bye girls.'

And with that he was off.

Polly smiled at Tina. 'Well, I better be going as well.' She got up to leave. 'Oh, there goes my phone, I better take this, see you soon.'

Polly went outside and got her phone out of her bag but just as she was about to answer it, the call went dead. It had only rung twice, she looked at who it was from, but the number was unknown. Oh, no, not again.

As she went to put it back in her bag the phone bleeped, it said voicemail. She felt a knot in her stomach.

Apprehensively, she pressed 121.

'You have one new message. Message received at 1.45pm....'

'Babe! I love you. My sexy little wife.'

Polly smiled, she never got bored of hearing Tom's voice.

THIRTY

KAREN was back home by 9.30am.

She had run straight to the car park. Anyone watching would have thought she was being chased. She had said her piece to Tom and wanted to get out of the surgery, there was more to come. If she had done little this morning, at least she had left him with something to think about, and for now that was good enough.

She took off her coat and put the kettle on. She was working at the Pet Shop that afternoon and would have to leave by 11 which meant she had time for something to eat, breakfast having been skipped.

Tom had looked completely bemused, he hadn't recognised her. In some ways that hurt.

Was she surprised though? No, typical man. It had just been sex for him, nothing else. Why remember a face when all you needed to remember is a pair of tits? Men all over.

That wasn't the situation for her though. Her life had always been complicated, but now she felt things were starting to move in her favour. Seeing Tom had been a big plus, saying what she had said had also been a plus. What would happen now would be up to her, she was in the driving seat. The next move would be hers, and the next move after that. For the first time she was in control.

Just as she sat down to enjoy her cup of tea, the postman pushed some letters through the letterbox. She stood back up and went to pick them up off the mat, one a Tesco statement, one a bank statement and one addressed to Lee.

That was interesting. Lee didn't get many letters addressed to him. Then she saw the watermark, it was from England Rugby. Her heart skipped a beat. Oh, gosh, was it news of his trial? It was sure to be, she had forgotten all about it, she so hoped it would be good news. Karen desperately wanted to open the letter herself, but she couldn't do that. She would have to wait until Lee came home. She would plan for the worse, which was often her default position.

In saying that Lee had been in a positive mood after the trial, there was no reason the letter should be bad news. She kept her fingers crossed, Karen wanted nothing more than for her son to continue his rise up the rugby ladder.

She got get dressed and put on her Pet Shop attire, which comprised of a pair of blue trousers and a blue shirt with the logo of the shop emblazoned. Cat walk candy she certainly was not in her work clothes. Still, it paid a reasonable wage, she liked working with animals, even if it were only the likes of rabbits and guinea pigs.

Just as she was about to go out of the door, her mobile bleeped, it was a text. She saw who it was from and opened it up, smiling to herself as she read it.

'You are one sassy girl Karen Harding'…. It made her smile.

Stuart Archer didn't get many letters.

The ones he did get had always been read by prison security staff and he hated that. So, he'd told members of his family not to bother, loyalty was his number one rule and other people reading his letters smacked of arrogance as far as he was concerned.

Archer had been in Strangeways almost seven months and wasn't enjoying the ride. He had many more years to go, he would survive. He had as many friends on the inside, as the outside, who would make sure a gang leader like him would be okay, he knew he didn't have to worry about any surprise attacks in the showers, or three or four blokes coming into his cell to beat him up. Archer's business in the criminal world had been drugs and, while it wasn't everyone's cup of tea, it wasn't something that was frowned upon in prison. Indeed some inside had been clients of his. He was no paedophile or rapist, the sex offenders were always the highest risk in prison.

So, it was a slight surprise for him to receive a letter, he opened it carefully, not that he needed to bother. It had already been read by goodness knows how many nosey prison officers, he could see that. He smiled, it was from Tony and Tony's message was cryptic, but Archer could read between the lines. It was good news, he knew he could trust Tony.

Archer had a new cell mate after the small-time dealer he had been spending time with was moved on. His name was Tommy Tobayson, an armed robber from London. He was a tough guy, built like a brick outhouse. He came from the East End and was doing 25 years for a robbery that went badly wrong. A security guard ended up paralysed after a gunshot shredded his spinal cord. Tobayson had fired the shot. That was 10 years ago now. He still had at least six left.

'You look happy bro,' Tobayson said as he walked into the cell, he had been in the gym, where he spent much of his time. At 46 years old he may have been just a few years younger than Archer, but he looked 20 years his junior. Archer was always impressed with Tobayson's commitment to keeping his body and his mind fit, he would have to start to do the same. The pair had got on well from day one.

'Yeah, I suppose I am a bit perky,' Archer looked up at his 6ft. 4in. cell mate and put down the letter.

'Just had a note from a trustee outside who will do a job for me. A good job, I'm sure. Got stitched up you see, that's one of the reasons I'm in here, and I don't like people stitching me up, stitching anyone up come to think of it.' Tobayson nodded his agreement.

'So, I need to find out who it was and my man on the outside is just the sort of guy who will find out for me.'

'Sounds good,' Tobayson replied. 'Never had that problem myself, everything's my own doing for being in here.'

'Don't get me wrong Tommy, I'm in here 'cause I was fucking caught, got no complaints. But someone snitched on me and that's why I'm here. Whoever that was needs finding, or I'm never going to rest easy.'

'What will you do if you find out who it is?' His cell mate sat on his bed. 'You still got that much clout on the outside?'

'You bet I have.' Archer laid back on his bed and picked up a book. 'And I have the cash to back it up. If I find out who it is, well, let's say I will have my revenge.'

Lee wasn't often home before his mum.

School had been boring, although Mr White, his history teacher had singled him out for special praise after his World War II essay had seen him get 77%, an excellent mark, and one of Lee's best-ever in the subject. He had already decided he would study it at GCSE.

He had let himself in, chucked his rucksack on the settee and headed straight to the fridge. Ah, lovely, it was Tuesday and mum had done the weekend shopping, so there was still plenty of snacks, yoghurts and drinks to choose from. He picked up a couple of those red cheese ball things, a yoghurt and poured himself some orange juice, he looked in the cupboard just beside the cooker and grabbed some crisps, prawn cocktail.

He was about to head into the dining room to switch on the TV and play a bit of FIFA on the X-Box, when he noticed the letter with his name on the kitchen table just beside the door. He had walked right past it on the way to the fridge.

He didn't get many letters. He studied it for a second before ripping it open, it was just a single sheet and as soon as he unfolded it he could see who it was from, England Rugby.

His eyes read quickly through the text, trying to take in as much as he could and get to the salient points as quickly as possible, the smile on his face broadened the more he read.

Dear Lee,

Thank you for attending the recent England U15 rugby trials at Barnet. I'm delighted to say you have been selected in the final 22 for our upcoming games against Wales and Scotland U15, which are taking place at the end of this month.

More details will follow in the coming weeks. Again, many congratulations and we look forward to seeing you again shortly.

It was signed by Mr Button, the man who had spoken to Lee at South Walsham a couple of weeks ago.

He read it again to make sure he hadn't got it wrong. He had been selected for England. Wow! There must have been 50 players at that trial and he was down to the last 22. He put the letter back down on the kitchen table after looking at it for a third time. He smiled to himself.

'Mum will be so proud.'

THIRTY ONE

NEITHER Jody nor Craig had slept well, tossing and turning, fidgeting, both of them with heads spinning with thoughts. It had been a long night.

Eventually they had got some sleep, but not much. The alarm had gone off at 7am and Craig was first up, he went down to make Jody a cup of tea and came back up a few moments later, she was still fast asleep.

He looked at her laying there. She looked so peaceful. '*Shit! What had he done?*'

He had to remain strong, why should Archer, or any of his cronies, come looking for him? Archer was inside and the rest of them, if they had any sense, would surely be long gone, Spain, Italy, Timbuktu.

Last night, Jody had wanted to know if everything was okay, again. It was his own fault. He had been less chatty over the last few days and weeks, even when Polly and Tom had come to stay over the weekend, he had found it difficult to laugh and joke quite as much as the other three. He had done his best and there had been plenty of laughter, but Craig just knew he wasn't his old self.

He liked to think he had batted Jody's concerns away, but he knew he hadn't. They had watched a film in virtual silence, polishing off a bottle of Merlot between them. He had tried to make light of the silence with some half-witty line about '*look at us sitting here saying nothing staring at this film… Hope this isn't how it will be in retirement….*' Jody had smiled at his attempted humour.

Craig jumped in the shower and came out five minutes later

to find Jody sitting up in bed drinking her tea. She smiled, the sort of smile that says *'are we okay?'* It hurt Craig to see her like this, all she had been through to try and help them start a family, all she had been through with the hurt of the IVF failing. To make matters worse, he had secrets. *'Fuck, he didn't deserve her.'*

'Morning sleepy head,' Craig said. 'I don't think we slept that well last night.'

'No, I slept awful, was it as bad for you?' Craig nodded.

'Look, tonight, let's go out for a meal.' Craig kissed Jody on the head. 'That pub in Nantwich you like, the one with the sexy barman who reminds you of Justin Bieber.'

He grinned at her. She smiled back. 'That would be nice, a meal with you and the Bieber, perfect.'

Craig lent over, his hair dripping, and let his towel fall from his waist as he stood naked. He moved close to Jody who put her hand out to touch him. Craig was quickly aroused. The clock said 7.20, but time was irrelevant, they made love, right there.

'You do love me, don't you?' Jody was laying alongside him, looking up at the ceiling.

'Of course I love you.' Craig put his arm around her. 'I love you very much, I know I've been a bit quiet of late, but I hate seeing you unhappy. All we want is a family and the hurt that it's causing you, hurts me just as much, men do have feelings, I know that sounds odd.'

'I know you do, it's just, oh, it's just, I wonder sometimes if everything is okay between us. It is, isn't it? I'd love nothing more than to be able to give you a baby, sometimes I feel, I don't know, inadequate.'

'That's rubbish.' Craig sat up. 'I didn't marry you to have a family, I married you for you, sometimes I think it's me who doesn't' deserve you.' He smiled. 'Listen to us, all feeling sorry for ourselves.'

'Come on, we've just had great sex, I've made you a cup of tea. I can see you have laid out those sexy pink knickers you are going to wear for work today, so I'll be able to pull them straight off when you come home.'

'Is that all you will think about at work today, my pink knickers? I don't know Craig Baldini, you are so rude. Polly always said she never knew how we ever got together, I'm too prim and proper for you.'

'Polly said that?' Craig raised his eyebrows. 'That's good coming from her. Miss goody-two shoes herself, she's either sticking her chest out knowing full well everyone can't help but stare at her boobs, or she's punching people's lights out! Bang!' Craig mimicked a punch.

Jody laughed. 'I wouldn't be without her. She's so funny.'

He got out of bed, it was going to be a rush to work now, not that he cared. 'I suppose I better get back in the shower, two showers in one day, that's more than Robinson Crusoe had in a lifetime.'

'Robinson Crusoe?' Jody looked confused. 'Where did that come from?'

'Don't underestimate my literary knowledge my dear. Crusoe was shipwrecked on an island and met a person called Friday. He called him Man Friday, well, today is Tuesday.' And with that he winked at Jody and walked back into the shower. Jody just shook her head. *'What on earth did that mean?'*

It made her smile. That was more the Craig she knew.

Craig arrived at work a little after 9. Jason and Peter were already in as he breezed past their offices, putting his hand up to greet them as he did so.

He had only just taken his coat off when Lisa knocked on the door and marched in, Craig could tell she had her efficient head on!

'Morning, am I alright to come in?' she said in her cheery Scouse accent.

'Well, it looks like you already are in, make yourself at home why don't you? I'm surprised you haven't made yourself a cup of coffee here in my office.'

Lisa raised her eyebrows: 'Well, I've actually been in the office since 8.30, unlike some, so I've got plenty done and I need a few signatures off you and before you say you are the boss so you can come in when you like, go when you like and do what you like, just remember without me, your life would be twice as hard, if not impossible here in this office. And you would be a disorganised mess. So, unless you have had to take your cat to the vets, which I know isn't the case because I know you don't have a cat, I'm not interested in why you were not here when I started this morning because there is nothing in the diary work-wise, so if the truth is known, you have just come in when you fancied. Anyhow, sign these.'

Craig smiled. 'Crikey, you're in feisty form this morning. Anyhow, do you really want to know why I'm late?' He winked! 'A little morning pleasure, don't you know.'

'Don't start that sort of smutty talk with me,' Lisa replied. 'Just because I'm old enough not to take offence to any of your fluffy little innuendos, I'm still big enough and certainly old enough to give you a clip around the ear, boss or no boss. And I don't care who sees me do it. Now, are you going to sign these or not?'

Craig smiled as he began signing the forms the other two directors had already put their signatures to.

'Oh, by the way, Lisa.'

'What now? I'm busy today and I'm having my hair done at 5, so I'm going to be prompt leaving off.'

'No, that's fine, you rush off, don't worry, I just wondered if you wanted to go to the Everton game on Saturday, against Liverpool I think it is.'

She spun round.

'Seriously? Yes please.' Her mood suddenly forgiving. 'I didn't think we would have any spare tickets. You are so good to me.'

'Oh, that's right, change your tune now haven't we? A second ago you were going to clip me around the ear and not be bothered who saw it, now, I'm too good to you.' Craig grinned as he looked up from his desk.

'Your fickleness knows no bounds Lisa Gooding. Yep, there is a spare ticket in the box and James and Peter are more than happy for you to go, most of the guests are their clients anyhow, probably Liverpool fans, so don't go causing any fights.'

'Thanks. I won't.' Lisa blew him a kiss as she walked out.

Craig poured himself a coffee and sat down. He turned his computer on noticed the FTSE was down four per cent this morning, bloody China and America arguing again, he thought of his pension pot.

Not that he really gave a shit.

Archer had put the call in that night to Statton after receiving his letter, despite saying to himself he would leave it a few days. He wanted to get things moving and he hardly had that much to think about while he was sitting day after day in his cell.

The call had been swift and to the point, Statton was going to start making more serious enquiries about Baldini. There was already much Statton knew about him and he had seen him in a pub on Friday night, but now it was time to up the ante and delve deeper.

Archer had promised Statton 25K of the 50 would be in his bank account the next morning, sure enough it was, Statton quickly moved it out and split it up. Receiving that amount of money all at once could raise suspicions, he didn't want that, he also didn't want to waste time. Statton wanted nothing more than to get in and get out of this situation as soon as possible and leave Archer and whoever to 'finish the job off', if that is what was required.

He would head north next week.

THIRTY TWO

SHE had always enjoyed her work at the Pet Shop.

The fact Karen loved animals helped, although at 'Pets for the City' there was not a huge array, rabbits, guinea pigs, gerbils, fish, if you could count fish as a pet. However, she liked it there. It suited her lifestyle, with flexible hours.

She had been in work most of the day when Roger Tomkins collared her in the small canteen that doubled up as a storage area for rabbit food. Mr Tomkins was the store manager, a kindly man in his 50s and all the staff liked him.

'I don't suppose you could work on Saturday could you please?' He spoke in his usual polite manner. 'I would appreciate it. Not for the whole day, just in the morning?'

'Of course.' Karen was pouring hot water from the kettle into a cup of instant coffee. 'I'm going to the rugby in the afternoon because Lee wants to watch the first team and I said I'd drop him off, as long as I'm away by 1. Do you want a coffee?'

'Perfect,' replied Mr Tomkins. 'And no, I don't want a coffee, thanks anyway.'

Mr Tomkins liked Karen, she hadn't been there long, but had never let him down since she had started. Then again he liked all his staff, he considered himself a lucky store manager. His small workforce of 15 were hard-working and loyal, he liked to think he ran a happy ship.

She looked at her watch, it was just after 4pm and Karen left off at 5. It was her job to check on the rabbits at the end of each day, making sure they were comfortable, fed and watered for the night. She would laugh with some of the other girls in the shop, they would call the rabbits 'Roger', after Mr Tomkins.

As she began walking around the hutches her mobile phone rang. She took a look. It was Lee.

'How are you darling? 'Is everything alright?'

'Yes, everything's fine mum. You okay? I've got some news.' She sensed excitement in his voice.

'Oh, yes, what is it?' She tried not to sound too excited.

'Well, you know the rugby trial?' Lee sounded upbeat. 'I've only gone and got in the squad, the final 22 for games against, um, I can't remember now, Wales is one of the teams. I can't remember the other, but how cool is that? I'm in the England squad.'

Karen could hear the joy in her son's voice, it was a lovely moment. The pair had been through so much together, there hadn't been enough moments like this. She could hardly contain her delight, but she had to keep quiet, she didn't want to disturb the rabbits or make a scene in the shop.

'Wahooooooo!' she said quietly down the phone, but loud enough for Lee to hear how happy she was. 'Well done, I'm so proud of you. You did say you thought you had done well, don't throw that letter away will you? I want to have a look at it when I get in and we'll take a photo of it and send it to your auntie Jane. She'll be thrilled. What do you think darling?'

'Its great news.' Lee sounded chuffed. Karen hadn't heard him like this for a long time. 'It's only the last 22, so I'm not actually in the starting team, but I might be. I thought I did well but you never know. Anyhow, got to go, the boys are waiting for me on FIFA, what's for dinner by the way?'

'Tuna pasta bake, dear. Or perhaps we'll go out and celebrate with a pizza. That sound good? You go and play on the computer, and well done, so proud of you, love you.' And with that Karen finished the call.

She couldn't stop smiling.

'You look happy.' Mr Tomkins had crept up on her. Karen was standing next to one of the hutches with rabbit food in hand. 'Happy in your work.'

Karen turned to look at him. 'I'm just taking in a bit of news, that's all. From Lee, my son. He just called me and I was day-dreaming a bit to be honest.'

'Good news I hope?' Mr Tompkins smiled.

'Oh yes, it is good news, very good news. He had rugby trials for England a couple of weeks ago and he's had a letter through to say he's been selected for the final 22, for games against Wales and someone else, he couldn't remember.' Karen smiled as she put food in the rabbit's bowl. 'Typical boy, playing for England but can't remember who against.'

Mr Tomkins smiled broadly. Despite him and his wife not having any children, he was always interested in his staff's family matters.

'Well, that's super news,' he beamed and gave Karen a little peck on the cheek. 'Absolutely super. You must be so proud? And rightly so, to be picked to play for England, I assume that's at his age group, not for the full England first team?' Mr Tomkins laughed at his own joke. 'A great achievement.'

'It's for the U15s,' Karen said, laughing herself. 'He's so chuffed, I think I'll take him out for a pizza tonight, he'll love that.'

Mr Tomkins smiled once more, he put his hand in his pocket and pulled out his wallet. He got out a £20 note and went to put it in Karen's hand.

'What a great idea. You do that, take him for that pizza, my treat,' he said as he went to push the note Karen's way. 'A great day for him and proud mum t'boot.'

'No, no, you can't do that.' Karen pushed his hand away. 'That's very kind of you, but you can't.'

'But, I can, and more's the point I would like to. As I said, my treat, it's not every day we have one of our staff's children get picked to play for England. Now, take it please and go and enjoy the pizza with Lee. My treat, my pleasure.' And with that he stuffed the note into Karen's hand, smiled and walked off.

'And don't forget to have coleslaw with it,' he added.

Karen looked at the money. In any other circumstance she would refuse it. But Mr Tomkins was a good human being and he would be offended if she made a fuss, she put the note in her purse. Pepperoni was Lee's favourite topping.

Polly and Tom got home almost exactly the same time, which was unusual in itself.

She had only been in a few minutes before he walked in, briefcase in hand, bunch of flowers in the other.

'Are they for me?' Polly grinned. 'If so, thanks baby, shall we go upstairs and do it right now? Twice if you're feeling brave.'

Polly kissed him on the lips as she took the flowers off him.

'Yes, the flowers are for you.' Tom handed them over and put his phone on the kitchen table. 'But we don't have to go upstairs to celebrate the fact I've bought them. It's not a bribe for sex, just my little gesture to my lovely wife.'

Polly got a vase out of the cupboard and filled it with water. She turned and winked at Tom. 'Well, it's up to you. If you can resist, fair play.'

He went and put the kettle on. 'You're in a good mood? You had another good day at the gym? Or is being surrounded by 'camp' James making you hungrier for 'real men'.

'Ah, that's not nice. James is a real man, I like him. I like him a lot. And I find him attractive at times. He just doesn't find me very attractive.' Tom got the t-bags out of the cupboard.

She put the flowers on the dining room table and came back into the kitchen, putting her arms around his neck.

'Come on, upstairs. My treat.'

'No, Pol'. But Tom's eyes gave away his smile, she was such a pain when she was like this. 'Not right now, I've just come in from work, I'm going to have a shower.' Polly raised her eyebrows.

'For goodness sake behave. What is wrong with you? After the shower I'll take you out for dinner. Save you having to cook, I'll even drive, so you can enjoy a drink, now I can't be fairer than that.'

'Ah, that sounds lovely, but can't we have dessert before we go out for a main course? You know the sort of dessert I'm talking about?'

'Honestly. I think it's you who needs a shower, a cold one. Now come on, let's get ready and go out for dinner, we can do the sex stuff anytime.'

'Oh, can we now? I might not fancy you next time.' Polly pecked him on the cheek and went into the garden. She had noticed it had started raining and she had left a couple of cushions on the patio set. Tom watched her go, he smiled to himself. She looked good.

He went upstairs to have his shower, as he sat on the edge of his bed taking his clothes off, his mind went back to Karen Harding and the episode in his surgery that morning. Surely she wasn't really some fling from a past holiday, as he had thought. And if she was, why was she bothering him now? All those odd things she said.

He decided to forget it. He'd likely never hear from her, or see her again.

As he stepped into the shower, the warm water felt good, it had been an early start to the day and a long day. As the water trickled over his body, he felt relaxed and breathed deeply. He needed this, indeed, he was so relaxed he didn't notice the bathroom door opening. As he cleared the soap from his eyes and turned himself around in the cubicle he saw Polly walk in, naked, smiling. She stood there for a few seconds and raised her eyebrows.

'You can't get away from me that easily, Mr Armstrong,' she said as she stepped into the shower. 'Ooooh, What a surprise. I've only been in here five seconds and I can already see you are pleased to see me.'

They kissed passionately and looked at each together, before Polly put her hands on Tom's chest, moving them down slowly, before dropping to her knees, still looking up at him.

The lower she went, the more she smiled, the more he smiled, as the water dripped down on her face.

THIRTY THREE

MR Hornchurch was a new patient and Tom was going to give him 20 minutes of his time to check his teeth from top to bottom.

It meant an earlier 7.45am start this Thursday morning and Tom had told Jill and Emily not to rush in. There would be no procedures with Mr Hornchurch, this first consultation was simply to check things over.

'Morning Mr Hornchurch,' Tom greeted him as he opened the surgery reception door. 'How are you this morning? Thanks for coming in so early, let's head upstairs.'

'Call me Colin, can't stand all this formal rubbish, I wasn't christened Mr Hornchurch. And I'll call you Tom, if that's okay with you?'

Colin was late 60s, an abrupt man who Tom sensed wouldn't take much crap off anyone. Colin was dressed in a suit and had a tie on and a fetching pair of red braces, this was also a man who liked to make an impression.

'Bloody weather is awful again,' Colin said as he followed Tom upstairs. 'The wife and I go to France for a couple of months every year, take the old motorhome. Can't stand the French particularly, but their weather down south is certainly better than drivel we have to put up with in this country. Some people say the weather in Britain is wonderful, different seasons, different temperatures and all that. Can't see it, just seems to rain to me most of the time and if we do get two weeks of sun we have a bloody drought. Shall I take a seat?'

Tom guided him into the chair at last managing to get a word in. 'Have you had regular treatments on your teeth?'

'My dear boy of course I have. We moved here from Richmond, in Yorkshire, a year ago. I was in the Army, the wife was a solicitor, both retired now, chap. Love it around here, didn't think Norfolk could be as nice as Yorkshire, but it's done pretty well in our eyes. Bit flat, compared to 'God's own county', obviously, but it's peaceful where we are. Folks are nice, if a bit reserved.

'I've been looking around for a dentist, found some chap near Gorleston, but that was too far to travel and he was rude to the wife once, so she said, anyhow. Well, not so much rude, but she's a bit touchy when it comes to her height. Martha's only 5ft. you see. This dentist bloke told her he would have to put her seat up to the maximum setting so he could get the light shining in her mouth, apparently he laughed as he said it. She took that as a bit of an insult, and that was that! She can be absurd at times, but she's the boss in our house.'

Tom found that hard to believe.

'Okay, well, let me take a shufty in the gods to start with and then we will take a trip downstairs, I'll have a good look.'

'What are you talking about?' Colin shuffled in his chair. 'Shufty in the what? Is that mumbo jumbo talk? You're not one of those new age dentist people, are you?'

'No, don't worry, I'm not a new age anything. Open wide.' Tom smiled.

Colin's teeth, apart from needing a clean, were in good condition, as were his gums.

'Do you smoke, Colin?'

'Used to, quite a bit old chap when I was in the Army, I have just the odd one here and there now. A cigar or two when I'm watching the rugby, but that's about it. Don't smoke at home, the boss doesn't allow that, is everything okay?'

'Yep, everything seems fine. You like rugby you say?'

'Love it, dear boy.' Colin sat up in the chair. 'Love it. Man's game, not like that namby-pamby football those pathetic blokes play, diving around all over the place.

'Always been rugby and rugby league. We used to make a weekend of it back when we were up north and take in some rugby league matches, Keighley, Widness, Warrington. Loved going to them all, Martha to. Great sport. I'm involved at South Walsham now you know, rugby union. You heard of them? Decent club, on the committee and all that. Like to keep involved, keeps your brain active.' He tapped one of his temples.

Tom's ears pricked up. 'South Walsham?' Are you now? That's a coincidence because I'm sponsoring their match on Saturday, well, I'm one of a few sponsors I think. The first team are playing Luton aren't they? My friend Jonny Gordon, he's at the club, asked me if I wanted to get involved, I said yes.'

'Bloody hell.' Colin's face lit up. 'What a coincidence indeed, good man. Jonny Gordon, now there's a good chap, loves his Guinness. Yes, we are playing Luton and you are one of the sponsors, you say? Well, I'll be damned. If you're coming for the pre-match meal, we can sit together and have a beer or three, you can meet Martha.'

Colin got out of the chair just as Emily headed up the stairs and walked into the surgery. She looked a bit flustered, her bright red hair all over the place, it was wet and windy outside. Tom assumed she didn't possess an umbrella.

'Morning,' she said as she hurried in. 'Sorry. I'm a bit late.' Then looking at Colin, her demeanour changed as her eyes caught his.

'Emily, my dear girl, fancy seeing you here,' Colin said as he started to ease himself up out of the chair. 'This is your place of work then, nice to see you.'

'Mr Hornchurch, how are you? What a surprise. I didn't know you came here, I haven't' seen you here before.'

Tom looked at Emily and then back at Colin.

'You two know each other?' Tom tried not to sound shocked.

'Of course we do,' Colin said, now standing up. 'Emily works at the rugby club on match days, serving behind the bar. Been with us six months or so now, fine worker, aren't you girl? Not sure if she's a big rugby fan mind you.' Colin looked at Tom, smiled at her and coughed. 'But she pours a bloody decent pint.'

Tom looked at Emily. 'I didn't know you worked at the rugby club, what at South Walsham? You never told me you liked rugby Em.'

'I don't work every Saturday,' Emily said rather sheepishly.

'And I'm not a great rugby fan, gives me a little extra, you know. Not that I'm not happy here but, well you know, a little bit more cash doesn't hurt, I assume you don't mind?'

'Mind? Of course he doesn't mind, do you Tom?' Colin said abruptly. 'Work hard, play hard, was always my motto, I admire people who take on extra work. I hope you're working this Saturday, Emily, got some special guests.'

'I am working Saturday. Who are the special guests?'

'God man, do you lot not talk to each other in this room about what you're up to?' Colin shook his head. 'It's Tom here, he's sponsoring the match. So when you serve him, don't pour any beer over his suit. Well, I've got to be off now, send me some forms for this scheme you run here and I'll join up. Me and the wife, I suppose I can pay direct debit. Is there a payment for today?'

'No, there's none for today.' Tom had secured two more patients. 'Yes, you can pay direct debit and that's fine for Martha to join, it would be good if she could book in and see me soon though, so I can give her a quick check-up.

'You can book a four monthly appointment with my receptionist downstairs and ask her to send you the forms, or she may have some downstairs. She will be in now, see if you can get Martha in before then though.'

Colin shook hands with Tom and Emily. 'See you both on Saturday, then.' He took his coat and hat and headed down the stairs.

Emily looked at Tom. 'Well, that was a surprise,' she said as she started to clear up and prepare for the next patient. 'To see Mr Hornchurch. He's a big noise at the club, in more ways than one. As I said, I hope you don't mind me working at the rugby club?'

'Of course I don't mind. Good for you. I'm sorry I can't pay you more than I do, although I am going to be looking at you and Jill's wages in the next month or so, perhaps I can find a little extra, especially if we continue to get more patients.'

He smiled at Emily. Tom liked her, although he never felt he had really got to know her, even though she had been with him for almost a year. The age gap may only have been about 13 years, but it felt more 33 at times, what with her urban language and odd social habits.

'Why are you sponsoring the rugby?' Emily said. 'I haven't seen you at South Walsham before.'

'I haven't actually been to South Walsham before. But a mate of mine, Jonny Gordon, is pretty persuasive. Actually he was in here the other day, I'm surprised you didn't recognise him, he was the big guy. He's a regular at South Walsham.'

Emily had to think on her feet. Of course she had recognised Jonny, she had seen him at the rugby club on more than one occasion, but he clearly hadn't recognised her, unlike Mr Hornchurch.

'Do you know what? I thought I recognised him. But I have only seen him once or twice at the club, now you mention it,' Emily lied. 'I wasn't sure. I've seen Mr Hornchurch loads of times.'

At least Tom now knew of her bit of moonlighting, but he was cool about it. That's why she thought so much of him, he was a good boss. She enjoyed her work, there were worse ways to spend her days than with a guy like Tom. *She really liked Tom.*

Originally from Birmingham, Emily had moved to Norwich to study nursing at one of the local colleges. Her parents had helped finance the rent on her apartment. But the nursing course had been a disaster and she had quit after just three months, finding jobs in retail and hospitality. She had ticked over for a year before the job at Tom's surgery came up. She had been there ever since.

Thursday morning sped by and at lunchtime, Emily went into the city. She needed to get some kitchen rolls and bleach for her apartment, mundane chores she hated doing. Her apartment was not the tidiest and wasn't helped by having a lodger who was equally untidy. But at least Gwen and she got on well.

As she walked, Emily thought about the weekend ahead. I suppose it would be fun seeing Tom at the rugby. She had never seen him out socially and while she would be working, it would be a different environment for the two to chat, if they were able to of course. She really hoped Polly wouldn't be there.

That wasn't likely to happen. But if it did, that would be nice. It would be perfect.

THIRTY FOUR

FRIDAY morning, and it was another early start for Tom.

He wanted to get done and home for dinner. He and Polly were going down the Queen's Head that night. They didn't want to still be eating dinner late, and it would be wasting good drinking time.

When he arrived, Emily was outside the surgery door waiting, which was slightly odd as he was 20 minutes early himself. She smiled as he approached.

'You okay? Couldn't you sleep?'

'I'm okay,' she said, taking her hands out of pockets as she did so. 'It is just that Gwen had a bit of a party last night in the apartment and I told her I needed to get up early to go to work, so I asked if it could finish about 1ish? But she didn't take any notice. I knew I should have put my foot down. I went to bed at midnight, they didn't turn the music off till about 4. She only had a few friends over but they were making a bit of noise. I told them to quieten down and we had a bit of a row. When I woke up at 7 they were all asleep, so I made as much noise as I could, rang the doorbell on the way out and made about five phone calls to the land line on the way into work. That'll teach them!'

'They'll know it was you. They'll track down your number.' Tom raised his eyebrows.

'No, they won't. I can withhold my number, I know how to do that. Serves them right.'

Tom opened the door and Emily walked in first. He had never realised his young assistant could be so vindictive.

'Do you want a coffee?' Emily went into the canteen.

'Yes please, that would be good. Black, no sugar, although don't know why I'm saying that, you know that.'

Emily smiled and headed into the kitchen, which was in the next room to the surgery. She felt good getting her boss a coffee. Just him and her. Jill would be in soon, but she had Tom to herself for a few moments.

'Are you looking forward to the rugby tomorrow?' Emily passed Tom his mug. He took a sip. She pulled up a chair close to him.

'Yes, I suppose I am, I haven't been to a rugby game for years. I'm more football as you know. But it will be good and Arsenal are playing on Sunday, so it would only mean me and Pol maybe going shopping. Instead we can enjoy the rugger.'

'Is Polly definitely coming?'

Tom puffed out his cheeks. 'Yes, I'll admit I've had to twist her arm a bit, but she will enjoy it when she's there. Don't think she has ever been to a rugby match, I imagine she will likely bring a book with her. Can't see a game of rugby retaining Pol's interest for more than 10 seconds. Right, let's crack on, is that Jill I heard come in?'

Emily attempted a smile and started to organise the surgical instruments.

'Morning, morning.' Jill shouted up the stairs as she walked into the surgery. 'How are we all? Hello, hello. Am I the only one in? Did someone leave the door open overnight? Is anyone there?'

Jill was in a lively mood, although in fairness she was rarely quiet. Tom went down to meet her, Emily followed.

'Morning, you're in fine fettle,' Tom said as he walked into reception. 'Have you won the lottery or something?'

'I'm fine,' she replied with a smile. Then looking at Emily. 'Who said you can't teach an old dog new tricks, hey?' And with that she winked at her.

Tom and Emily looked bemused.

'What do you mean by that?' Emily's eyes widened.

Jill couldn't wait to spill the beans. 'Well, last night I had my friend Eve over and we invited a couple of guys we had met at yoga to the flat, remember me telling you I was taking up yoga?'

They didn't remember, but went along with it.

'Anyway, they came over. We all had a few drinks and played a bit of poker, not any poker mind you, strip poker.'

'Oh no.' Tom screwed his face up. 'Are you serious? Too much information, please don't tell me there's more?'

'I hope there is.' Emily jumped in.

Jill smiled. 'Oh, there's more. So, we all play strip poker and guess who was left with all the money and all their clothes on?'

'You', said Emily.

'No, not me. Eve, I was butt naked. Eve was so disappointed she'd won, she took all her clothes off anyhow. Honestly, it was such a fun night, there was no hanky-panky or anything, we just fooled around and got drunk and the blokes left at about midnight. Have you ever played strip poker, Tom?'

Tom was trying hard not to picture the scene in Jill's flat. 'I can honestly say of all the card games in the world I have dabbled in, strip poker isn't one of them,' he said.

'I haven't played it either, but I'm going to suggest it to my friends.' Emily laughed.

Tom didn't know what to say, the pictures in his mind were far too graphic. He tried to shut them out, Jill and her middle-aged friends playing strip poker. What a sight that conjured up. Emily was still laughing, Jill seemed like a new woman since she had split up from Robert.

'What has happened to you lately?' Emily was smiling broadly. 'I like the new Jill, but I hope you are not mixing with the wrong crowd.'

'Don't worry. I can handle myself, it's just the drink I sometimes have trouble with! Booting Bob out was the best thing I ever did. Wrong crowd? We are all over 50 dear.'

Tom found it all most awkward. 'Well, as I said, never played strip poker, and doubt I ever will. Not sure Pol would like it either, to be honest.'

'Oh, I bet she would,' Jill replied, as she got behind her desk and began to start her computer up. 'Best be careful with that beautiful wife of yours though, if I were you. If she suggested playing strip poker, she would have most of the country wanting to join, just in case she lost. She is gorgeous is our Pol, isn't she Emily?'

Emily shrugged her shoulders.

'Okay, I think that will do,' said Tom looking at Jill. 'What exciting lives you two both lead. Emily's lodger had a late night party, you've played strip poker and you both had your hair done the other week. Makes my dinner out with Pol the other night seem tame.' Then Tom remembered their shower before they went out last night. *Maybe not!*

'Right, who have we got up first?' Tom leant over the desk. 'And are we fully booked today.'

'Miss Bright is in first and we are pretty booked all day and we've had a cancellation at 11, Mr Hartwell called yesterday. He has flu but apart from that most of the day it's just check-ups, apart from Miss Bright actually. You are doing a root canal for her. She'll be in soon, she's always early.'

Right on cue, Tracey Bright walked into the surgery just as Tom was going upstairs. Emily was following behind.

Tracey Bright was 41 and single. She was a member of the gym where Polly worked. She had spoken to Polly on numerous occasions and had got to know of Tom's surgery through that. Well spoken, and well off, she had been divorced twice and lived in a huge mansion on the north Norfolk coast. *'A man-eater'*, Polly had once described her to Tom. *'She'd eat you alive.'*

'Morning Tom,' Tracey said as she walked in, her long green jacket looking chic on what was another drab Norfolk morning. Emily looked her up and down, she'd met Tracey Bright before in the surgery and first impressions were she hadn't liked her.

Tracey had also caused a bit of tension between her and Tom one time, and Emily had never forgotten it. Emily had dropped an instrument during a procedure Tracey was having. She'd had to go and get a new one, while Tracey sat there mouth open. Tom had flown at her... *'Come on Emily, sort yourself out, please'*, he had said. It was unlike him, although he was under pressure at the time. When it was all over Tracey had swilled out her mouth and looked at Emily. *You're clumsy aren't you?'* she had said in her snotty tone. Emily never forgot things like that.

'Morning, Tracey, how are you? We have a root canal filling to do, I believe.' He looked at Emily. 'Is that right Emily?'

'Yes, that's right,' said Emily, who was looking at the notes and hoping it would hurt.

'Please go easy on me, darling,' Tracey replied as she slipped her coat off, handing it to Emily to hang up as though she was her maid. 'You know I hate needles.'

Tom turned his music on, a little bit of Roxy Music. Emily was glad it wasn't turned up too loud. She wanted to hear Tracey Bright scream if the needle hurt, or at least watch her flinch.

'We'll be okay. Now, open wide.'

It took a few minutes for the anaesthetic to work and Tracey's mouth to go numb before Tom could begin. Root canals were never his favourite procedure. They could be messy with a bit too much blood around and, where Tracey's root canal was required, top left, it could be awkward.

Emily stood patiently beside him watching him go to work, passing him the instruments as instructed. This was the serious bit of their job together and she liked the intensity of the moment.

Emily smiled to herself as she stared at Tracey's mouth. *'She didn't look so posh now'.* Gob wide open, looking helpless, blood swilling around, oh, how she wished she could take a photo on her phone and put it on her Instagram page. Or better still send it to Tracey with the caption *'fucking state of you'* emblazoned across it. That would teach her for talking to her like shit that time.

Ten minutes later, Tracey was sitting up in the chair and swilling her mouth out. Tom was happy with the way the filling had gone, but he told her he wanted to see her again in a month just to check all was okay.

'I hate it when my mouth feels like this.' Tracey got out of the chair, trying to talk properly despite the numbness.

She looked at Emily. 'Pass me my coat?'

Emily picked up the coat but dropped it just as she handed it to her.

'Oh, sorry, I thought you had it,' Emily said. 'Let me pick it up for you.'

'Don't worry, I'll get it,' Tracey said looking directly at her. 'Weren't you the clumsy one who dropped something last time I was here? You should give the girl catching practice, Tom, darling. She clearly needs it, see you soon.' And before Tom or Emily had time to say anything, Tracey was halfway down the stairs.

'Snotty bitch.'

'Thank you Emily. Remember she pays our wages. It takes all sorts, go on and make us another coffee. And try not to drop that on the way back like you did that coat.'

Tom winked at her, she smiled back.

Goose bumps.

THIRTY FIVE

'RESIST? Of course he couldn't bloody resist.'

Polly was talking to Jody on the phone. She had called up her friend during the pair's lunchbreak.

'Look Pol, I've had a long day. Look Pol, we're going out for a meal soon. Stop it Pol.' It was pathetic. But what do you expect from a man? In saying that, it's a long time since we had sex in the shower, you tried it lately?'

'Can't say I have,' Jody replied as she sipped a green tea. 'I'm not sure how Craig would act if I came on to him like that at the moment, he's still a bit quiet, you know, although he's been a bit better the last few nights. We even had sex the other morning before he went to work. He had to have two showers, but I wasn't in any of them. I'm not sure everything is right at work, he won't tell me. If I ask, he'll just tell me everything is fine.'

'But, ask him. I would Tom. If I thought something wasn't right, I'd bloody well ask and ask until I got it out of him, it's your life as well. If you don't think things are right, get it out of him. It might be nothing and you are starting to worry about just that, nothing.'

'You're right.' Jody got up to tip the rest of her tea down the sink.

'I'll see how he is over the weekend, we're going to Jason and Wendy's for a fancy dress party tomorrow night. That should be fun and I'm going as Maid Marian, you know, from Robin Hood. Craig is going as a Minion. We tried his costume on last night and he looks a right berk. He's not happy, but he'll wear it. He might be a bit grumpy but he'll still do as I say, I'll send you a picture. What you doing this weekend?'

'Off to the pub tonight and, oh yes, I've got a thriller of a day tomorrow. Tom has only gone and sponsored a rugby match. Apparently, we're both going, there's a meal beforehand and then we watch the game.'

'Oh dear, how awful,' Jody said, her face cringing. 'A rugby match? Can't you feign a sickie? Tell him your period has started, we can't have pretty you standing watching all those sweaty men grunt and groan. And what if it rains? Your hair.' The pair laughed.

'I know, that's what I told Tom, all those hunky men to watch. Come to think of it, sounds like fun. Perhaps I'll get to go into the dressing room afterwards to present the man-of-the-match.'

'Now you're talking, didn't think of that, perhaps it will be a laugh. Wear your short skirt and show off those legs. Never know, might get Tom jealous and you can take him in the showers with the rugby boys. Oh, I forgot, you've had enough showers for one week you dirty cow.' They both laughed again.

'Love you Jody,' Pol said, as she looked at her watch, lunchbreak was almost over. 'Look I've got to go, so have a great time tomorrow night and we'll catch up on Sunday. Having a bit of a quiet Sunday, I think. Love to the Minion. And remember, if things aren't right, get it out of him.'

Jody smiled at the other end of the line. 'Bye Pol darling, love you to.'

Statton picked up the phone. This was a big gamble, but one he was prepared to take. A 25K gamble he was prepared to take. He was going to revisit his past in the hope of securing a tidy sum of cash for his future.

He still had the number in a contacts book he had held onto after leaving Archer's gang. It was another example of Archer having complicit trust in his friend. Archer had put together a contacts book and each member of the gang received one when they joined. It was only eight pages, but bound in red leather, a bit like Mao's Little Red Book.

If you ever wanted to leave, or were told to leave the gang, Archer insisted the contacts book would be the first thing you would return. That and the gun.

In all the years Statton was part of Archer's set up, only Rusty Fitzroy failed to return the book or gun. There was good reason. He'd messed up a drugs deal after blabbing his mouth off in a pub one night after having too many drinks, it was a big no-no. A schoolboy error. Fitzroy's loose words were overheard by a member of another gang and passed on up the chain and the deal went dead leaving Archer to explain to a group of very wealthy, very unpleasant and very pissed off individuals, what had gone wrong. Archer was given more than just a slap on the wrist, his reputation had been damaged.

So, Fitzroy's contacts book was taken back after his confession, his gun used to put a bullet in his own head, before he was buried 60ft deep on a building site in Manchester, the gun crushed at Worders' Scrap Yard, just outside Ellesmere Port. How did Statton know? He was the one who had taken the gun there. Big money gains, big money stakes, it was a world Statton had been in for years. He had the memories, many good, many unpleasant. At least he still had his contacts book.

He dialled the number, would it still be in use? Long shot. It rang for what seemed like an eternity and Statton almost hung up, before suddenly.

'Hello, who's this?' Statton recognised the voice straightaway.

'Hello Billy? It's Tony, Tony Statton, long time, no speak.'

'Jesus, Tony Statton, what the fuck are you doing calling me up? How are you, you old bugger? Keeping your head above water and on the right side of the law at last, I've been told. Down south somewhere. Is it Portsmouth, Southampton, somewhere like that? Am I right? Bloody hell, I didn't think I'd ever hear from you again, please don't tell me this is just a social call, because there is no way in the world this is just a social call, is it Tony? Not on this number.'

Billy Wade was still as sharp, smart, and clearly in the know, as he was back in the day when he proved to be one of Liverpool's most prolific bent coppers. A top dog in the CID on Merseyside, Wade, who was now nearing 65, had been Archer's 'insider'. A man who had made a small fortune by keeping the drugs baron and his gang one step ahead of the police.

He'd been cute as well, getting out well before a sniff of

suspicion ever came his way. The only people in Archer's gang who knew of the part Wade played were Archer and Statton, no-one else had a clue and certainly no-one in the police knew of his indiscretions, or if they did, they had never seen the light of day.

Wade had taken voluntary redundancy three years ago from the Force, after his wife was diagnosed with breast cancer. He was given sympathy and cakes at the time. If only the coppers who signed his leaving card knew the half of how he had betrayed them.

Around the same time Archer was starting to look for a way out. He had hoped it would only take a few more years, but in the meantime he had wished Wade happy retirement with a £50K goodbye 'gift', they hadn't spoken since.

Wade was still 'working' for Archer when Statton had decided to call it a day. The three got on well. Statton and Wade had laughed over a few drinks at Archer's house one Sunday lunchtime that if Statton ever croaked about 'that bent copper from Merseyside', Wade would have him kneecapped. Statton knew he had meant it.

'It's no social call Billy boy,' Statton said. 'Why the fuck would I call you up after all these years to have a social chat? It's not your birthday is it? In saying that, how's life treating you?'

'Life's okay mate, all pretty chilled.' Wade was walking round his kitchen with his dressing gown on. It was almost lunchtime, but he was a man of leisure these days.

'Sarah has shaken off the cancer, thank goodness, but it took a few years before the all clear. We've got a place on the Algarve and spend about six months there. Wish I was there now. Don't miss work that's for sure.'

'Glad to hear about Sarah, and you still have this number and that phone? I wasn't expecting you to still have it, I thought you may have tipped it over the side on one of your world cruises. Or don't you like the water?'

Wade laughed. 'I've always kept this phone for some reason, and charged up. Don't ask me why, because if I had any sense, I would have had it melted down and crushed years ago. But, I don't know, perhaps I'm sentimental, perhaps I've always been waiting for a call. A call like this, so, cut to the chase my friend.'

Wade's past was as murky as Statton's and Archer's. The only difference between the three of them was that Archer was doing time. *There but for the grace of God.*

'Okay, Billy. I will cut to the chase. Obviously you know Stuart is in jail and he isn't coming out any time soon. The thing is he thinks. No, he knows, he was stitched up, grassed up. He's sure someone put him in there, a snitch, and he wants to know who it was. He has an inkling, but nothing definite.'

Wade was listening intently.

'He's asked me to do some digging, so I've come to you for some help. Look, I don't want you to get yourself in any shit. Like me, you're out of it now and want it to stay that way, but come on, we both know Stuart has been decent to us. He never dropped us, or anyone in it, however high the stakes got. All he wants is a bit of closure on the bastard who snitched him up. Can you help? Make a few enquires, I can pop you 5K if you can just get me a name, I'll do the rest. After that you can melt the bloody phone if you like.' Statton gave a small chuckle, hoping a relaxed end to his request would do the trick.

There was silence on the other end.

'So, after all these years, you call me up and want me to get involved in all that crap again?' Billy walked into his living room.

'Are you fucking crazy? Why would I want to do that? I've put my head above the parapet plenty of times for you guys and I know when to stick. I appreciate your call and loyalty to Archer but I'm not twisting again, I'm out of it now.'

'Hold on, Billy, don't put the phone down. Please,' Statton begged. 'Please, hear me out.'

'Look, I wouldn't do this for anyone only Stuart, I would rather not be in this position one little bit, either. When he called me up I thought what you're thinking now, *'fuck, I don't need this'*. But he's in prison for another 15 at least I reckon, just think of what we all went through together, all the laughs, all the risks, highs, lows. But Stu never went against his word, he never let us down. Look at the lives we are enjoying now and he's got Jack Shit. He allowed us out when we wanted out, okay, honour among thieves, it may have been. But I'm not just going to let him rot in prison, the agony of deceit eating him up inside. He wants closure on why he's in there, that's all. I feel I owe him. Come on pal. Just a name, that's all I'm looking for.'

Again, there was silence. Statton could hear Billy breathing into the phone. Cogs churning.

'I want 15K. Just for a name, mind you, if I can get one,' Billy shot back, before continuing. 'Listen to me and fucking listen well, I said, if I get one. Do you understand? I've cut ties with everyone bar one or two guys I used to work with and I don't need this shit. But okay, I hear what you're saying. Give me a week and if you haven't heard from me, I have no name. But you have to trust me, I'll be making some calls, okay? I appreciate how Archer feels. I'll make the calls, but I don't want you telling him I'm involved or am helping out and I don't want old times to resurface on my timeline. You understand that don't you? I'll text you a name from this number and bank details. I'll trust you to pay the money in. All I need from you is a reply to say you've got it, then this fucking phone is really going to see its last days. I don't want you calling me up again. And no, you can't have my new number.'

Statton smiled to himself. He knew Wade would delve and delve deep, he may have been a bent cooper. But he was a *'good'* bent copper and he had always been driven by money, another 15K would top up his old pension pot nicely.

'Cheers, Billy. Look, I appreciate it okay? 15K. Have a good life my friend....'

But before Statton could finish his sentence, the line went dead.

THIRTY SIX

OPEN Mic night down at the Queen's Head was the third Friday in every month.

It was a chance for Elton John or Robbie Williams wannabees to murder the living daylights out of their pop heroes' hits, not through a karaoke but unaided. It was also a chance for up-and-coming hopefuls to play their preferred music, strum their guitars and even perform songs they had written themselves.

For Polly, Tom, Milky and the Friday night crowd it was an excuse to get pissed, have some rubbish chat and catch up on the world. Of Tom and Polly's regular crowd only Milky took part in 'Open Mic'. He would bring along his guitar and sing a tune or two.

Alison and Ben were the first to arrive at the pub. It was a warm Friday. They were wearing light jackets and the pair grabbed a large circular table in the corner, a good enough distance from the Open Mic, so they could hear themselves speak as the evening wore on. As well as choosing a table with plenty of space for the rest of the friends.

'Were you in on that meeting this afternoon?' Alison said, turning to Ben. The two of them stood at the bar waiting to get served.

'Yeah, it was pretty negative. Much of it was about the latest web stats. As usual those with the biggest voices made the most noise, even if what they were talking was utter bollocks.

'I don't know how long I can stand working there to be honest Al. Newspaper sales are down, web figures maybe up, but you and

I know the web won't pay our wages forever, unless we all take a 10K pay cut.'

'The ad department didn't hit target again this quarter, either,' Alison said as Jan came over to take their drinks order. 'Motors is up, but that is all, even digital is down.'

'Hi guys. Oh, you look a bit miserable, come on, no tiffs down the pub on Friday nights.' Polly walked in and marched up to Ben and Alison, handing out kisses to both. As usual Polly was looking striking.

'Ah, no, we're fine. You look great, as usual,' Alison replied. 'You want a drink? We were just moaning about work, nothing new in that. Don't worry, no tiffs and we are still madly in love, aren't we Ben?'

Ben shrugged, as much to say, *'are we?'* Before getting a kick in the shin from Polly. 'Yes, we are, aren't we, Ben? I think is the answer,' Polly stared hard at him, then smiled.

Ben grinned. 'Of course we're in love. Love is all around in our house. Even Bongo was singing as we came out of the door tonight, wasn't he Al?'

'You don't still have that parrot, do you? I thought Al said she was going to feed it tuna so it would snuff it.'

Ben looked at his wife. 'Did you? When did you do that?'

Alison nudged Polly and smiled. 'I didn't say that, as if I would, look at Pol's face, as if she's telling the truth.'

They laughed as Tom joined the three of them, kissing Alison and shaking Ben's hand.

'You been having a quick 'fat one' outside? I can smell cannabis from here,' Ben joked. 'Polly's been here ages.'

'As if I would.' Tom put his arm around his wife. 'No, just had to go straight to the loo if you want the real reason, not as exciting as smoking a 'fat one', as you put it. Not quite sure why I didn't go for a pee at home, it's only five minutes' walk away. Oh, yes, I do know why, Polly was still in the bathroom and had been for about six hours getting her face ready and the downstairs loo is not working because we're having it decorated. But Pol looks good on that six hours, don't' you think Al?'

Polly scowled at her husband, who flicked her a wink.

'But it was worth it,' Alison replied, as she touched Polly on the arm. 'She looks gorgeous, as usual, too good for you.' She blew Tom a kiss.

'Jesus, we've started early tonight,' said Ben. 'And we haven't got all the drinks in yet. Prosecco, Pol?'

Polly nodded, went and sat down with Alison, while Ben and Tom called Jan over to order the Prosecco and a pint for Tom.

'So, how's work, mate?' Tom fiddled around in his jeans for his wallet. 'I assume we have got a kitty going by the way.' Ben nodded.

'Not great to be honest, paper sales are down and advertising is so hard to come by. The office is like a morgue. Businesses have their own web sites and social media stuff, so why do they want to come to us? All a bit depressing to be honest.'

'Sorry to hear that mate, although I must admit I got a copy of your paper on Tuesday and it wasn't that great content-wise. Only five sports pages, and it's a quid now, I didn't realise that.'

'Oh, yeah, it's been a quid for a while, but you can go online and read all our stuff for nothing. What a business model that is!'

Ben and Tom got the drinks and joined the girls at the table.

'How's the old surgery, anyhow?' said Ben, taking a sip of his drink. 'I should have gone into something like that, people are always going to want their teeth fixed.'

'It's going well, staring into people's gobs every day can get a bit boring mind you. Talking of your job again, don't you think papers will always be around, surely they will?'

Ben sort of nodded. 'Maybe'.

'Polly was telling me you're thinking of getting a dog.' Alison turned to Tom, who frowned. 'No, we're not.'

'A little one,' Polly looked at Alison. 'A little Westie perhaps. Tom will give in.'

'Don't have a dog, pal, a parrot is bad enough,' said Ben. 'I like the old thing, but it's a bloody tie. We were going to go to the Dales next weekend, get an Airbnb, but we can't get anyone to look after the bloody parrot. What a state is that to get into at our age? Then Al says, we'll take Bongo with us, can you imagine that? Take the bloody parrot with us.'

'We're not getting a dog,' Tom said, but Polly wasn't listening.

'That's a lovely idea Al,' Polly said, all smiles. 'Take Bongo. She will love it.'

'She', said Al. 'It's a he, not a she.'

'You can take the parrot, can't you?' Polly looked at Ben.

'You can't take a frickin' parrot in your car on holiday with you,' Tom laughed. 'I'd be right pissed off if someone turned up at an Airbnb I was renting out, with a parrot in tow, that's mad.'

Polly wasn't having it. 'Don't be such a misery, people love their pets. We are going to have a dog, and a cat. And people should be allowed to take a parrot to an Airbnb.'

'Take a parrot, take a parrot, where?' Stu and Janie joined them at the table as Stuart fired the question.

Stu and Janie hugged and kissed everyone, before sitting down to catch up with the conversation before chucking in their £20 into the kitty and duly picking it up again to get drinks in.

'Ben was saying a parrot was a tie because you couldn't take it on holiday with you,' said Polly. 'Al and Ben were thinking of going to the Dales but can't because no-one will look after Bongo.

'Who's Bongo?' said Janie.

'Their parrot', Polly replied. 'You must remember Bongo'.

'Feed it chocolate biscuits, it would be a natural death, but quick and painless.' Stu was no animal lover. Janie slapped her husband on the arm. Ben laughed, Alison didn't.

'That's not nice, ignore him, Al.' Janie glared at her husband. 'We'll look after him.'

'Will you? Seriously?'

'No, we won't,' Stu replied quickly. But Janie stepped in. 'Ignore him. If we can, we'll look after him, let me know the dates.'

'You're a sweetie, Janie,' Al hugged her friend. 'Bongo's no trouble.' Stu shook his head and got up to get the drinks.

Open Mic night was beginning to take off. A young girl, who did the rounds of the local pubs wherever there was Open Mic, began singing. She was about 20 and had a lovely voice, while a man, who looked as though he could have been her boyfriend, friend or brother, was playing the guitar alongside her. They made a nice couple and her choice of songs were pleasant, including a bit of Karen Carpenter and Carley Simon, followed by a track she had written herself.

'She's good,' Janie said to Polly. 'I'd love to be able to sing like that.' Polly nodded in agreement.

'I was out your way the other night, Tom,' Stuart said as he leaned across the table. 'Yeah, there was a shed fire about a mile from Melsham. Can't remember the exact place, bloody tiny little roads to get to it. Anything coming the other way, the pumper would have had to stop and reverse back half a mile.'

'I heard about that fire,' Tom said. 'Read it in the paper, it was old man Cooper's place. Well, not his place as such, an outbuilding. Likely a few local kids, most of the ones out that way are a bit feral, a bit in-bred. Reminds me of that joke, 'what's the difference between a cheese and onion sandwich and young kids from near Melsham? Nothing, they're both in bread!'

Stu and Tom laughed. Polly looked up to try and find out what she'd missed.

'What was that?' Polly looked pleadingly at her husband.

'Nothing, dear, just a joke, you wouldn't get it.' Tom nudged Stu and raised his glass with his friend in a sarcastic gesture. Polly clocked it. She fake smiled at them both. *'Tom would regret that remark. Not get it, hey?'*

'I've got a joke everyone. Listen to this.' Polly stood up to take centre stage. Tom looked up. *'Shit, what was she up to?'*

'Listen,' Pol said, speaking just loud enough for the friends to hear, and any eavesdroppers if they wished. 'Quiz question. Who, sitting around this table right now, said, *'no Pol, don't Pol, I said no Pol, not now Pol, not in the shower Pol, that's enough, oh, fuck it, go on then. Keep going down on me?'*

Tom shook his head in disbelief as Janie roared with laughter. Alison laughed. They both looked at Tom, while Polly smiled at her husband, then sarcastically whispered in his ear; *'Sorry, Tom darling. Only a joke. You wouldn't get it.'*

Alison clinked glasses with Polly as Janie high-fived her. 'A blow job, in the shower? We'll have to try that Stu.'

'Good idea love, I'll bring my fire hose!'

Scottie and Ann arrived, exchanging the pleasantries.

'You ever done it in the shower, Ann?' Janie was still laughing.

'Done what in the shower?'

'You know... sex in the shower. Polly was just relaying a little tale to us about naughty boy Tom, over there.'

'Well done Pol, see what you've started.' Tom tried to look annoyed. 'We do have marriage secrets you know, our lives don't have to be played out in public. This is now going to be the topic of conversation for the next hour.'

'Rest of the night, I reckon,' said Stu. 'I want to know more, come on Pol, few more details would be good.' Polly went to say something, but Tom stepped in.

'No you don't Stu. My darling wife has said way too much as it is.' Polly raised her glass to Stu, *'tell you more later'*.

'Don't think we have done it in the shower, have we Scott? Ann looked quizzically at her husband. 'Although I remember in Majorca that huge bathroom and huge bath. I think we did it in the bath?'

'The bath? Wow that takes some doing. Bloody hell Stu, we've got some catching up to do, you up for trying that as well, my darling?' Janie was loving the conversation.

'Told you dear, I'm up for anything, me. Fancy coming over Pol to join in the fun in our bath?' Stu winked at Tom.

'What to put the bubbles in?' Polly took another sip of her drink. 'I'm not going all that way just to put the bubbles in. If the bubbles are in, I'm in, bet you'd like that Stu. Or are you, like most men, all mouth and no trousers?' Stu's eyes nearly popped out of his head! Janie was in hysterics.

'Alright you lot, that's enough, who wants another drink?' Tom stood up. 'I've got a headache just thinking about all this.'

An elderly gentleman had got up to go on the Open Mic. He was singing a cappella. When he started most people in the pub turned around almost immediately. His voice was deep, but with a lovely tone and his rendition of Elvis Presley's *'An American Trilogy'* was spellbinding, it had the whole pub on their feet applauding at the finish.

'Thank you, thank you,' the man said. 'Do you want another? I don't want to be greedy up here.'

Most in the pub cried out 'yes', so the man carried on, this time with the Bee Gees' hit, *'How Deep is Your Love'*.

At the end people were on their feet applauding once more as the man went back to the bar, got himself another half and went and sat back in the corner.

'That was beautiful,' said Alison. 'Who is he? I haven't seen him before.'

'I've never seen him in here before either,' said Ann. 'But you're right, what a voice.'

Scott leant over and spoke to Tom. 'I was going to ask you something, Tom. I was wondering if there had been a robbery at your dentist the other morning.'

Tom looked surprised. Polly, overhearing, looked up. 'A robbery, no, why do you say that?'

'Well, I was in town, I think it was Tuesday, could have been Wednesday, time just is all over the place these days. I was walking past your place, was going to call in but I thought you would be busy. Anyhow, this woman comes flying out of your surgery door and nearly bowls me over. It was about 8.30 in the morning. She ran up the road like a bloody gazelle, I wouldn't have thought anything about it but there was no-one around that time of the morning, thought maybe she had either nicked something in your surgery, or you had given her a pretty rotten filling and she couldn't escape quickly enough. Do your patients usually leave your surgery in such a hurry?'

Tom shook his head. Ann and Janie were talking but the rest of the group, including Polly, were listening for his answer. The fact Tom appeared to look uneasy didn't go unnoticed by Polly.

'Um, no, I didn't see anything, I'm not sure what you mean. Are you sure it was my surgery?

'I was probably upstairs. I'll ask my receptionist if she saw anything. I did have a patient in early on Tuesday but I don't remember the procedure being that painful.' Tom tried to smile.

'Who was it?' Polly was too sharp not to notice Tom's withering answer. 'Who was it? Who ran out?'

'Honestly, I don't know,' came Tom's stiff reply. 'I didn't know anyone did run out of the surgery. I think Scott may have crossed wires.' Scott shrugged. 'Yeah, perhaps I have.'

'Don't worry, Scott, I'll call Jill or Emily. Or Susan. They'll tell me and I'll be able to tell you next week.' Polly smiled at her husband. 'Doesn't worry me, just thought I'd ask.' Scott turned to talk to Stuart.

How the hell had the conversation drifted into this? Tom was not happy. What were the odds of one of his friends coming past his dentist just as Karen Harding flew out of the surgery? Bloody hell.

'Don't worry,' Polly took hold of her husband's hand. 'It's no big deal is it? Oh look, here comes Milky.'

Tom was glad to see Milky walk in as the conversation got away from Karen Harding leaving the surgery.

'Evening everybody.' Milky was grinning. 'Here's my money for the kitty, who wants another drink?'

Tom, Polly and Janie were all takers, while Stu hummed and hawed before saying no. Milky went to the bar, Ben accompanied him.

'Milky looks well,' Alison said, looking at Polly. 'He's all smiles and he's even got a different pair of trousers on.'

'I hope he's not going to do a turn on the Open Mic.' Stu pulled a face at Tom. 'Remember his *Bat out of Hell* rendition a few months ago? Blimey, I thought he was going to blow a gasket, and do you remember that poor woman who was walking across to get to the bar? He put his arm out and danced with her for a few seconds, I'll bet she's never been back since.'

Milky came and sat down, clutching his pint and chucking a few packets of crisps into the middle of the table.

'How's life then Milky?' said Stu as he reached to get a packet of salt and vinegar crisps. 'Treating you good? You still with Chantelle? It was Chantelle, wasn't it?'

'Yep, it was Chantelle, but it's Denise now. I've been seeing her a couple of weeks, took her for a kebab the other night.'

'A kebab?' said Alison, wide-eyed. 'You are a romantic old schemer, did she enjoy that?'

'Yeah, I think so. We both like our kebabs, heavy on the chilli. We've got so much in common, me and her. And she collects beer bottles.'

'Beer bottles?' Alison sounded even more surprised, while Tom patted Milky on the shoulder. 'If you've got a girl who likes kebabs, heavy on the chilli, and collects beer bottles, that's a girl you should try to keep hold off. I imagine she likes a drink as well?'

'Yeah, she loves a drink, she's coming down here in a little while. I told her where we meet up.'

'Oh, that will be lovely,' Polly said enthusiastically. 'We'll all be on our best behaviour. Won't you Stu?'

Stu smiled and shrugged his shoulders. 'Depends how many drinks I've had.'

Milky smiled at Polly. He was her No.1 fan, *if only she knew.*

As the drinks flowed, so Janie and Polly talked about doing a turn on Open Mic. This wasn't karaoke though and neither of them could sing that well if not accompanied by music.

With time ticking on and most people seemingly having had their turn on the Open Mic, landlord Paul cranked up the music on the pub's speakers, put on some sing-along songs and left the microphone on so people could join in from that, a sort of karaoke without the words to assist.

'I suppose you ladies are going to do a song?' Paul had come over to Tom's group to collect glasses, and was looking at Polly, Alison, Janie and Ann. 'What do you want me to put on?'

'*Simply The Best*', by Tina Turner,' Polly said. 'Come on girls, up for it?'

There were still 30 or 40 people in the pub as it turned 10.30pm. As usual, Polly needed little encouragement to get up and perform. Alison, Ann and Janie had enjoyed enough drinks not to be too bothered either. As the four blasted out the Tina Turner classic, Tom and the boys laughing and clapping along, none of them noticed Denise walk into the pub.

Denise was mid-40s. A little plump but with a happy-looking face, she saw Milky in the corner and approached the table.

'Hi. How are you?' Milky's face beamed as he saw his new girlfriend. She had timed it well, the girls had just finished on the microphone and were coming back to the table. He introduced Denise to everyone.

'You look lovely,' Polly said. 'What do you want to drink? Go on Milky, get your lady a drink.'

Denise looked a bit nervous and with good reason. The friends were now all a bit the worse the wear for drink. They could also be pretty intimidating as a group, all staring at her. Denise, who had arrived by taxi and was staying with Milky for the night, was cold sober.

'I'll have a snakebite.' She looked at Milky. 'Pint.'

'A snakebite, shit, I haven't had one of them since Uni days,'

Ben said. 'That's a proper drink.'

Denise smiled as Janie began the interrogation. 'So, what do you do?'

'I'm a housekeeper at a few houses in Norwich,' Denise replied nervously. 'I go in each house for a day once a week and tidy up. Okay money, not great, but it's a job.'

'Where did you meet Milky?' Alison said, slurring a tad.

'He was doing a few jobs for one of the people I housekeep for. We started chatting and went for a kebab that night. Funny, we were going for a pizza but the pizza shop was shut so Milky said let's go for a kebab. He's such a great bloke.' Denise blushed.

All the girls agreed what a good bloke Milky was as he came back with her snakebite and another pint for himself. He went back for more drinks that Stu and Ben had asked for.

'We could do with a housekeeper, couldn't we Tom?' Polly turned to her husband. 'Would you be able to fit in another house to do?'

'Do we?' said Tom. 'Since when?'

'Since about a minute ago darling.' Polly smiled at Denise.

'Well, I would be able to do another house but not for a little while because me and Milky have got a few things to sort out in the next month or so. We are a bit busy to be honest.... We're getting married.'

Tom spat out his beer, as Ann and Alison both gasped, 'what?'

'Bloody hell, Milky, you never mentioned that.' Stu thumped his beer down on the table as Milky returned from the bar.

Polly was overjoyed. 'A wedding, a wedding, a wedding. When? When? When is this? New hats, new hats, new hats everyone.'

Milky nodded at Stu but looked slightly embarrassed as Denise held his hand. 'We're starting to organise it next week. It will be just a small gathering at the registry office, I'm just waiting for my divorce papers to come through!'

Denise was still married.

'Well, that will be wonderful when it all happens,' Alison said. 'I hope we will be invited Milky?'

'You will. And Fourre the dog will also be there. We'll have the reception down here, I reckon, it's up to Denise.'

She nodded. 'Of course we can have it down here.' And she

smiled at him lovingly. 'I know you love this place.'

'Well, I think big congratulations are in order' Stuart stood up. 'Let's all chuck in another tenner boys, not you Milky, treat's on us, and let's get a couple of bottles of plonk to celebrate.'

When the bubbly came over, Paul had chucked in a third bottle to say congrats to the happy couple from him and Jan. They all stood and raised a glass to Milky and Denise. Then Polly went over to Paul. 'Put *'Congratulations'*, by Cliff Richard on the speakers will you please? We're going to have a sing-song.'

As *'Congratulations'* rang out over the sound system and Paul cranked the volume up, Polly grabbed the microphone and all of the friends huddled behind it singing and pointing to Milky and Denise... *'Congratulations and celebrations....'* The rest of the pub joined in, dancing and waving their arms. Milky and Denise were taken aback by all the fuss, but you could see they were chuffed.

The night finished with the elderly man with the soothing voice coming back on the Mic, after a little persuasion from Polly, to sing *'How Deep is Your Love'* once more, as Milky and Denise danced on the floor, hugging each other tight.

As they did so, Polly and Tom cuddled up. 'Ah, isn't that lovely to see,' she said. 'I'm so glad they're happy. I love you Tom Armstrong. I love you so much. Remember our wedding day? No-one is ever going to come between us.'

Tom smiled and hugged his wife. 'Never.'

THIRTY SEVEN

TOM was standing over the hob fiddling around with two eggs that were bobbing around in the boiling water.

It was Saturday morning and both he and Polly had decided to have an easy breakfast. They were set for lunch at the rugby later that day.

'Pol, do you want soldiers with your dippy eggs?'

'Yes please. And two eggs as well.'

Tom tutted. He would now have to reorganise his 'dippy egg strategy'! He had it all planned, until Pol had now gone and said she wanted two eggs. He currently had two eggs on the go and two slices of bread and butter already done, should he give both to Polly and start again for himself? Or should he give them both one egg and soldiers now and make Polly another one when she's finished?

In the end he decided the best policy would be for them to enjoy one each now. He'd make Polly another when he'd finished. He would take her a glass of orange juice and cup of tea, which would buy him a bit of time while he was eating his egg. Then he'd do her another. Life skills!

'Here we go,' Tom said, as he took the egg, juice and tea up to her and pecked her on the forehead. 'Did you sleep well?'

'Yes, thanks. That was another fun night wasn't it? And Milky and Denise. A wedding. I do hope they haven't jumped into it a bit quick.'

'A bit quick?' Tom put the juice down on the small side cabinet on Polly's side of the bed. 'Of course they've jumped into it a bit quick, he only met her two weeks ago. Still, you never know. They may end up together for 50 years, have 10 kids and be as happy as a pig in shit for the rest of their lives. I've long given up trying to understand people and how things will turn out. Look at Jill.'

'What, Jill in the surgery, what about her?'

'Well, you know she's split from Robert?' Tom took a seat on the bed next to Polly. 'Now she's living the life of a hell-raising teenager. Do you know what she did the other night? Played strip poker with her mate and two blokes from her yoga club, can you believe that?'

Polly laughed. 'Really? That sounds brilliant, more power to her, I say. I think I'd quite like strip poker, perhaps with three men and me. You can be the croupier. Anyhow, what time do we have to be at this bloody rugby?'

'Don't you 'bloody rugby' me after making me the croupier in your strip poker game,' he laughed.

Polly grabbed him and kissed him full on the lips. 'Love you,' she whispered.

He pulled back and stood up. 'You'll enjoy the rugby, it's a sit down meal at 1.30pm. The game starts at 3, I'll drive if you want so you can have a drink and see the game through a haze of alcohol.'

'No, I don't want to drink. I've still got a bit of a thick head from last night. Now, can I eat this egg please?'

Tom went downstairs, he'd forgotten that his egg was sitting there waiting to be eaten. It was a bit cold, but he finished it off and put a second one on for Polly. An hour later the two of them were showered.

'What do you wear for rugby?' Polly was holding up a pair of jeans. 'And what's the weather going to be like today? Is it a posh do?'

'It's going to be nice this afternoon,' Tom said as he slipped a shirt on. 'Take a jumper or cardigan. Dress is smart, casual. Put a coat in the car just in case it does get cold.'

Tom was watching the news. It was hurricane season in the US and there were frightening pictures of one hurricane sweeping through Texas, flattening everything in its path. He'd been to Texas once before, for a dentist's seminar, that was a long time ago now, but he remembered what a great time he had. It was the portions of food he couldn't get over. They all seemed double the size of ones in the UK.

The sports news followed. Arsenal were playing tomorrow, he would be there. Polly came down the stairs looking, as usual, stunning. She was wearing a light blue blouse, jeans and had a white jumper draped over her shoulders, she'd put waves in her hair.

'Hey girl, you look good. Right, I'm just going to go up and get finished, we'll leave in about 15 minutes.'

He went upstairs and put a tie on, with a casual jacket. He splashed on a bit of after shave and looked at himself in the mirror... *'Not bad old boy, not too bad'*, he grinned to himself.

They got into the Audi and looked at each other and smiled. They'd have a good afternoon, even if the rugby turned out to be rubbish.

Karen was in the garden first thing. She enjoyed sitting on a chair, cup of coffee in hand, listening to the birds and looking at the high white clouds.

It was an overcast morning, she had to get to work shortly and then get home to take Lee to the rugby. He was still in bed.

It would give her the afternoon to do a bit of housework before going to pick him up later. She enjoyed Saturdays, even if she did occasionally have to work. It was Saturday nights she enjoyed most, with Lee. They would get a Chinese meal from the shop in the next village, have a couple of drinks, Lee some Coca-Cola, her a couple of glasses of her favourite wine. Then it was Netflix time. He would choose the film, they would cuddle up on the sofa and watch. How many more years it would last for, she didn't know. He was 14 now. She'd enjoy it while it lasted. Saturday nights was a ritual the pair had been enjoying for years.

She came back indoors and made some toast before scribbling a note and leaving it on the kitchen table.

Lee,

I'll be back at 1.30 to take you to the rugger. Have something to eat before we go. And if you can do the washing up please.

Love Mum xxxx

Lee was still asleep. She went upstairs, had a shower and got dressed, then headed off to work. She hoped Mr Tomkins would be in this morning, Karen wanted to thank him for the lovely meal she had enjoyed with Lee, pizza, coleslaw, et al.

She started up the car and headed for work.

Tom and Polly pulled up in the car park at South Walsham rugby club just before 12.30pm.

The sun was now beginning to shine despite the appearance of white wispy clouds. They headed towards what looked like the entrance to the clubhouse and opened the double doors.

'Is this the way in?' said Polly, looking one way, then the other. 'Have you been here before?'

Tom shook his head. 'We want the directors' suite, apparently, ah, what's that say?'

Tom was pointing to an arrow that was pointing upstairs, *'Directors' Suite'*, it said. The pair started walking up the stairs.

Just as they got to the top, Jonny Gordon came bursting through a set of double doors.

'Pol, Tom, how are you?' he said planting his arms around Polly and shaking Tom's hand furiously. 'Great to see you both, so glad you could come. You just got here? Look, I was going to go for a pee, but that can wait a second. Come with me in here and meet some people, this is where we are eating, and watching, the game if you want.'

Before Tom could get much more than a 'great to see you, Jonny', in, he and Polly were being led into the suite. As they went through the doors the room opened up into a very large room. There were four long tables with seating for about 15 each side and there was a top table with seating for what looked like 12 or 14 people. All the tables were nicely made up, not too fancy, wine was on all the tables.

To the left, as Tom and Polly walked in, was a long bar, to the right it was all windows, with a balcony looking over the pitches.

'Well, Polly, you look as gorgeous as ever,' Jonny said. 'Tom, you're a lucky man, you little rooster. I hope he's looking after you Pol.'

Polly smiled. She liked Jonny. She also got on well with his wife Anna, she wondered if she was here, but didn't have to wait long to find out.

'Anna, look who's arrived?' Jonny led Tom and Polly towards a very sun-tanned, dark-haired lady, who was sipping wine alongside another man.

'Excuse me, Paul,' Jonny said to the man Anna was talking to. 'This is Tom and Polly, who are part sponsors of today's match? You two know Anna of course.'

'Hi Pol,' Anna said.

Anna had a radiant smile and gave Polly a hug. 'You look great. And Tom, our wonderful dentist.' She gave him a hug. 'It's great you could come today. Jonny told me you were doing so. I've been looking forward to seeing you again. It must be six months.'

Paul was the club's press officer, but made his excuses to leave, the four of them continuing to chat before Jonny excused himself to go to the loo, promising he would be back. But not before getting Tom and Polly a drink.

'So, how's little Jamie? Polly was glad she had remembered Anna and Jonny's only child's name. 'Gosh, he must be nearly 18 months now.'

'He's great thanks, yes, 18 months in July. Blimey, where has the time gone? He's great fun, a real treat, starting to sleep better now, which is nice. My parents are looking after him this afternoon. They often do on match days here, as Jonny likes me to come. To drive him home more the like. And you guys, how are you?'

'We're all good,' said Tom, who just as he said it caught the sight of Emily out of the corner of his eye. She was behind the bar pouring a pint for a rather rotund gentleman.

'Still working hard on the old dentist front as you know, and Polly is doing pretty well at the gym, aren't you Pol?'

Polly smiled. She let Tom's condescending comment pass... *doing pretty well.* 'Yes, the gym is going well, lots going on. Not sure about this rugby stuff though Anna, I've never been to a rugby match.'

Anna laughed. 'Oh, don't worry, I'm not a great fan, lots of grunting and groaning, but the pre-match meal is always good and the social side of rugby is great.'

Jonny returned and called out to the rotund man who Emily had been serving and who had turned away from the bar and was staring at the laid-out tables.

'Victor, have you got a moment?' Jonny called the man over. Victor made his way over to them, he looked as though he had already had a couple or three.

'Victor, this is Tom and Polly. Tom is from the dentist surgery I told you about, he is one of today's sponsors and this is his wife Polly. This is Victor Hassing, our president.' Jonny looked pleased with his introduction.

'I say, Tom and Polly, what a belting pleasure it is meeting you.' Victor was old school, early 70s, although his drinking had also put a few years on him. 'I believe this is the first time you have sponsored us, thank you both. Meeting new people is fascinating and a great thrill.'

Victor took Polly's hand and gave it a kiss. 'Could I say my darling, you look wonderful. I do hope you are sitting next to me on the top table.'

Polly smiled. 'Thank you Victor, I hope so to. I'll let you tell me all about scrums and whatever else they do on a rugby pitch, because I haven't a clue.'

Victor and Tom both laughed, Jonny went over to meet more people. He was clearly social secretary on match days. Anna continued to talk to Polly, as Tom spoke to Victor.

'So, any kids yet then Pol?' said Anna. 'I hope you don't mind me asking.'

'No, not yet. Maybe we will start to try soon.'

'Don't leave it too late, they are tiring. I'm 32 and I must admit it can be knackering at times. Anyway, ignore me. Look, I've got to go and say hello to someone over there, Jonny is waving, see you again shortly.' Anna gave Polly a kiss.

Victor had also made his excuses and gone to speak to another elderly gent, who was in a yellow and black tie. Tom and Polly looked around, there must have been nearly 100 people in the room by now and there was a real buzz.

'Quite nice here, isn't it?' Tom said gazing about. 'Fancy another drink?'

Polly looked at her empty wine glass. 'You driving then?'

'What happened to your thick head from last night, Mrs Armstrong?' Tom smiled. 'I thought you were going to just have the one.'

'I feel better now.' Polly hugged him closer. 'Come on, get me all squiggly and you can have your wicked way with me when we get home.'

Tom turned and put their glasses on the bar, Emily came over.

'Hi Tom.' Emily was smartly dressed in her South Walsham RFC t-shirt and black trousers. 'You alright? I see you have met Victor, and Colin Hornchurch is over there. Go and say hello to him as well, he'll want to meet you.'

Polly came up behind Tom. 'Hello Emily, I didn't know you worked here. Tom, you didn't tell me Emily worked here.'

'Well, she does, I only found out the other day, didn't I Em? She's been here about six months doing the odd Saturday shift.'

Emily half-smiled. Polly, typically, looked amazing. She was the most stunning woman in the room. Yes, Emily was jealous, she wasn't going to talk much to Tom today.

'You guys want a drink, then?' Emily wiped down the bar.

'Yes please,' said Tom. 'A pint of lager shandy and a red wine. Make it a large wine, please.'

She went away and got the drinks.

'I'm going to ask Emily about that woman running out of your surgery the other day,' said Polly. 'You know, the one Scottie reckons he saw.'

Tom flashed a look. 'Don't do that here. Emily is working today. This isn't the place to talk to her about the surgery. Anyhow, I don't think she will know what you are talking about.'

She looked at her husband, she would do as he asked. But why did she not believe him?

Lee had made a sandwich and was ready to go when Karen pulled up in the driveway. She got out of the car and came into the house, it was 1.45pm, she had time to quickly grab an orange juice and bit of fruit.

'Come on mum, don't be long,' he said pulling his coat on. 'I want to get to the game. Mr Crowe dropped me a text to say he wanted me to be there at 2.25, he wanted me to go to the directors' suite for some reason.'

'Really, what for?' Karen was intrigued. 'You're not playing are you?'

'Hardly mum, it's a first XV game. They are men, I'm 14. I'm not going to be playing with the men. I know you don't know much about rugby, but I can't believe you don't understand, I don't play with the men.'

She smiled. Of course she knew he wouldn't be playing in the first team. She liked to keep her son at arm's length when it came to rugby. The more she made out she knew little, or nothing about it, which in fairness was the case, the more he could go and enjoy it.

Karen drank her juice, ate a banana and called up to Lee to come downstairs, they were ready to go. He came down with a shirt and tie on. Karen nearly fell off the bottom step.

'What have you got that on for? You are only going to the rugby.'

'Mr Crowe told me to put the club tie on. So, I've put the club tie on.' Lee was looking down at it. 'I don't know what it's about, but he texted me again today to say don't forget the tie.'

Karen was confused. What was going on? Why was Lee being asked to go into the directors' suite? She decided she wouldn't just drop him off, but sneak in behind him and see what was going on.

The pair jumped into her car and headed for the club.

Polly was seated next to Victor, much to the delight of the president, who couldn't keep his eyes off her. Tom sat next to Polly and had Martha Hornchurch on the other side of him.

The meal was three-course and nice and simple. Soup, followed by lamb cutlets, potatoes and peas, or a vegetarian option, cheesecake for desert. Polly and Tom enjoyed it.

'So, have you watched any rugby, Polly, my dear?' Victor said as he went to put a mouthful of lamb into his mouth.

'Well, I must be honest, this is my first game and I hope it won't be my last.'

'I hope that too,' he replied, giving her a smile. 'As I said to you both, new sponsors are always welcome, especially with such attractive wives. I'd love my wife to come along, but she refuses, never have got her here. On another subject, what do you think of women playing rugby? Not keen on it myself, I don't think a woman's place is on the rugby pitch, do you?'

Polly was on her third glass of wine and Tom overheard the question Panic set in. '*Oh no, don't suggest any 'place' that is best for women.*' Tom was about to interrupt, but it was too late.

'And where do you suggest a woman's place is best served, Victor?' Polly touched his arm gently and stared into his face, her stunning blue eyes piercing Victor's armour.

'Well, well, I don't really know. I wouldn't dare say the kitchen my dear, that's not very, what do you call it? Politically correct, I believe is the term.'

Tom turned his head to talk to Martha, he didn't want to hear the rest of this.

'Well, isn't that strange, Victor? Because Tom once said to me when he came home from work one night, it was nice to see me in the kitchen.'

'Did he now?' Victor smiled. Nice to meet a woman who understood him, so he thought!

'Yes, he did.' Polly moved closer and whispered. 'So, do you know what I did Victor?' He shook his head. 'Well, I picked up the cooking pans, one had mince in it, one had green beans and one had potatoes and I tipped the whole lot on the floor in front of him and told him if he ever made an arrogant, chauvinistic comment like that again, I'd punch him in the testicles…. Please excuse me, I've just got to nip to the loo.'

Victor didn't know what to say, he'd never heard such talk from a lady. Polly, meanwhile, had got up from the table and left. Tom leant across to speak to him. 'Are you okay Victor? You and Polly seem to be getting on like a house on fire.'

'Um, yes, I, I, I think we are,' Victor said. 'I think we are.'

Lee arrived at the club just before 2.20 and hurried out of the car and headed towards the club entrance. Karen turned the engine off. 'I'm just nipping to the loo before I go,' she lied. 'You go ahead, I'll pick you up at about 5.'

Lee put his thumb up to say goodbye and on entering the clubhouse, headed up to the suite where he was to wait outside until Mr Crowe came out to get him.

Back in the main hall and at the top table, Jonny came over to Tom. 'Hi mate, how are you getting on? You enjoying the meal?

Game starts in 30 minutes, but I have a quick favour to ask.'

Tom looked at him. 'Fire away.'

'Well, we've got an award to make to a young lad who has just been selected for England U15s. He's a South Walsham player and we wanted to recognise his achievements, so, we've had a little certificate made up and framed. Would you do the honours? I'll call him in and do the speech. As one of our sponsors today, will you just present him with the certificate? Is that cool?'

'That's fine. When we doing it?'

'In about five minutes, mate.'

Mr Crowe came out of the directors' suite and found Lee standing patiently outside.

'Hello Lee. Glad you've got your tie on. I expect you are wondering what this is all about?' Lee nodded.

'Well, we just wanted to say a big well done on getting in the England squad and we are going to present a little something to you to say congrats, is that okay?' Lee nodded again. He was more than happy with that. He half worried he'd done something wrong.

'We'll go in the suite in a minute and there will be a little speech and then someone will present you with your award, give a big smile, we'll take a picture for the papers and then go and enjoy the game. I'll keep the award behind the bar if you want until you go home. Or you can pick it up tomorrow, you are playing tomorrow?'

'Oh, yes. I'm playing tomorrow,' Lee said.

Meanwhile, Karen had made her way to the bottom of the stairs. She could see Lee above her, he couldn't see her she made sure of that. He was talking to Mr Crowe, before being led into the suite. With that, she made her way up the stairs and slowly opened the suite doors.

She could see Lee standing at the bar, halfway down, opposite the top table, alongside Mr Crowe. Karen walked in and slid herself at the end of the bar, near the toilets. There were three waitresses standing around, she stood with them. No-one knew she was there, except Emily, who'd clocked her.

Jonny stood up to speak.

'Ladies and gentlemen, boys and girls, partners, mistresses, friends, lovers, welcome to South Walsham Rugby Club for today's clash with Luton.' There were a few laughs.

'Can I first welcome the president of Luton Rugby Club, Mr Keith Walmer and his directors, here with us this afternoon? We hope you enjoyed the fayre we have put on here and we hope you will enjoy the game, not too much of course. Playing away can be fun, as I'm sure a few of you know. But playing away and winning is simply not the thing, here at South Walsham. As my late granny used to say, 'it is better to have loved and lost, than never to have loved at all.' I would suggest to our friends from Luton today, it's just better to have lost.'

More laughter filled the room. From her vantage point in the corner of the room, Karen thought whoever was talking was quite funny. She glanced at Emily, but noticed she was watching the speeches. Then something caught her eye. No, was that Tom Armstrong sitting there? Surely not. She couldn't' be 100 per cent sure because she was at the back of the room and the top table was at least 30 yards away, plus the fact the guy doing the speeches kept walking in front of the top table.

'Before we retire for further drinks and then the game,' Jonny continued. 'We have a little presentation to make. One of our younger players here at South Walsham has done us and himself very proud, he has only gone and been picked for England U15s. We are so proud of him.'

Jonny smiled across at Lee. Karen was wide-eyed. '*So this is why he had to wear a tie.*'

'Therefore, we would like to ask young Lee Harding to come up to the top table where one of our sponsors of today, Mr Tom Armstrong, who runs a dentist practice in Norwich, little plug there Tom for you, will present the award. And perhaps Tom's lovely wife, Polly would come in on the photo as well.'

The room filled with long applause.

'Come on everyone, a future England player perhaps,' Jonny continued. He was in full flow. 'Learning his trade here at South Walsham.'

Karen's jaw dropped. 'Jesus,' she said to herself. She looked at Lee striding forward, she looked at Tom and Polly coming round from the top table to meet him. She glanced at Emily but didn't catch her eye, this was surreal.

'Well done Lee,' Tom said, as he stretched out his hand.

'Well done,' said Polly, as she too stretched out her hand.

'Thank you very much,' Lee replied as he stood in the middle of the pair of them, with Tom putting his arm around him, while the club photographer took photos.

Karen was struggling to take it in. Tom was presenting an award to her son. She watched as he engaged in conversation with Lee and then put his arm around him again and joked something. Karen was almost in a trance. She didn't want Lee to notice she was there, she turned, shot out of the door and ran down the stairs.

She was running away from Tom Armstrong for the second time in a week. It would be the last.

She got out her phone and sent a text.

THIRTY EIGHT

'BITCH'

Polly looked at her phone and felt sick.

They had enjoyed a lovely afternoon watching South Walsham beat Luton. Not that Polly had really known much of what was going on. By the time she was on her fifth glass of wine, the rugby was going by in a blur.

Tom and Jonny had stood cheering throughout. Polly was all smiles and jokes with some of the other players as they came up to the directors' suite after the game to mingle with the guests and sponsors.

They had left at six and got home half-an-hour later. It was then Polly had checked her phone which had been on silent for much of the day, and there it was... 'BITCH'... from the unknown number. She wanted to cry. She was standing in the kitchen, phone in hand as Tom went upstairs to go to the loo, he came bounding down from the toilet and went into the living room to turn the TV on.

'Well, that was fun,' he shouted through to Polly. 'I think we'll sponsor a game again next season, what do you reckon? Bloody hell, some of those rugby boys enjoyed chatting to you, I was going to go over to a few of them and tell them to behave themselves, ogling all over you like that.

'What you say? Shall we do it again next year? Pol?'

Tom poked his head in the kitchen. 'Did you hear me, love? I said, shall we do it again next season? Sponsor a game.'

He looked at her but didn't have to say anything as his eyes flicked towards the phone Polly was holding up, the screen facing him, he looked, got closer and looked again.

'When did you get that?' he said, quietly.

'Don't know when it was sent. This afternoon, it wasn't there this morning. I'm getting really pissed off with this, Tom. It's starting to get to me, you know that don't you? I need help here. I thought you had a mate who could look at my phone. I mean it, it's starting to hurt. I don't know why someone has it in for me like this, but now they are saying stuff like this. I can cope face to face with people, but I can't cope with this.'

She looked at him, her eyes welling up. He hugged her.

'Come on,' he said, kissing her on the head. 'We've had a great day. We mustn't let this get to us, it's nobody, a total nobody. You know it is, we'll sort it. We'll change your phone, get you a new number, get rid of all this shit, I promise. Just some sad bastard, they will get bored.'

She looked at him, but wasn't reassured. She released herself from his grasp. 'I hope so because I don't know how long I can put up with this anymore.' Polly shook her head. 'I'm going to have a shower.'

Polly went upstairs and Tom was left with her phone.

Who the hell was doing this?

Karen had gone home after Lee's presentation, but returned to the rugby club at 5pm to pick him up. Sure enough he was waiting in the car park, framed certificate in hand, he jumped in beside her.

'So, did Walsham win?' Karen said.

'Yep, thrashed them,' Lee replied. '44-7, real easy, they weren't very good. Even big Alan got a try and he never gets a try.'

'Wow, sounds fun, were many of your mates there?'

'Yep, there was about eight of us, Brendan and Steven went to the football. Boring gits. But Gully was there and he never usually comes and he's playing tomorrow for us.'

He smiled and looked at his certificate as his mum saw him doing so. It was a good size and had his name in big script writing emblazoned in the middle with the South Walsham club crest at the bottom.

'What's that?' she said.

'It's mine.' Lee showed it to her. 'I got presented with it, to congratulate me on being picked for England. One of the sponsors presented it to me, they took a photo and said it might go in the newspaper. Some bloke presented it, the woman he was with was a bit of alright.'

'Oh, was she now?' Karen raised her eyes. 'Did they say anything to you?'

'Um, no, not really, well, apart from well done. And something about my parents being proud of me, playing for England and all that, I told him you were.' He gave her a big smile.

'You know I am, we'll put it up on your bedroom wall.'

Lee turned the music up and sung along to some rap song that Karen could not stand as they drove off. They stopped off at their favourite Chinese to pick up their usual Saturday night treat and headed off home.

She put the plates in the oven to warm up as soon as they got in and sorted out a bottle of wine for herself, while Lee found himself some Coca-Cola.

'Lee, get a film sorted. And don't make it a violent one, something nice we can enjoy for a change.'

She came in with the food and the pair sat down. 'I hope this is a nice film. I've had enough of blood and guts in recent weeks, and zombies!'

She smiled at him, he smiled back. She was so proud of him and so proud of what he had achieved. She thought about what had happened today, it was almost beyond belief. They had their dinners on their laps. She put her glass of wine on the floor, beside the rest of the bottle, her phone bleeped.

'Mum, turn that thing off. You tell me to turn mine off when we are watching a film.'

'Sorry, darling. I will.'

Karen bent down to look at her phone. She looked at the message on her screen and smiled, before firing a text back... *'I know. Thanks babe. Sorry we couldn't talk'*

She turned her phone off.

THIRTY NINE

CRAIG hadn't been keen on going to the party dressed as a Minion!

'Come on, I look absurd in this and you know it,' he said to Jody.

Then again, it was his own fault. When Jody had asked if he wanted to go as a Minion, he was too busy watching the football on the TV. 'Yeah, whatever you think,' had been his response. Now, he wished he'd paid more attention, the sight of himself in the mirror dressed in a little yellow outfit with blue trousers and a large set of spectacles was not a good one. Funny, yes. He just hoped other people at the party were going to the same extremes to look as stupid.

'Did you know my darling, according to Google, Minions are characterised by their childlike behaviour.' Jody was reading her phone and watching, as Craig attached the oversized set of spectacles, a similar size to a cut-down Pringles packet, to his face. She burst out laughing. 'Should suit you down to the ground.'

She cuddled up to him. 'You look so sexy, darling. Everyone is going to love you in that, I can't wait to hear what Pete and Jason say. Perhaps they are coming as Minions as well. All three directors dressed as Minions, what fun that would be! You could have your own Minion water party in Jason's swimming pool.'

'I look a complete dick.' Craig looked in the mirror in the living room.' You know it, I know it, and everyone will know it. Most people going won't know what a bloody Minion is, I bet.' Jody laughed again. 'Of course they will.'

'They won't. Everyone else will be dressed up as the Queen,

Boris Johnson, or bloody Robbie bloody Williams, and I go there as a Minion. What a basket case I look. And look at these blue pants. How much tighter can they get? Look at my tackle sticking out.'

'People will at least think you have made an effort, my darling, and no-one will be staring at your tackle, apart from me. I must admit there is something sexy about the way you look though, I don't think I've ever made love to a Minion.'

Craig walked out of the room and started to go upstairs to clean his teeth. He stopped on the bottom step. 'I can't imagine you *have* shagged a Minion, Jode. I can't imagine Minion shag Minions. Anyway, aren't these supposed to be children's characters? We shouldn't be talking about them like this. And don't suggest to anyone else at the party about shagging Minions, I don't want whatshisname's wife getting all excited, if she's there. You know, that woman who is married to Guy, from the car warehouse, the one who gets easily pissed.'

You mean Kate? No, she won't be there, her and Guy have split up, she ran off with their window cleaner.'

'Their window cleaner, that's a bit random isn't it? When did this happen?'

'About two months ago. Lisa told me when I called the office the other day. We were just chatting. Anyhow, turns out when he was cleaning her windows, she was leaving one of the latches loose on her bathroom window. Splash! He was nipping in for a quickee.'

'What? You serious? Who told you that?'

'I told you. Lisa, but it was her Avon lady who told her. The talk of the street for a while apparently, so she said. Anyhow, the pair of them have moved to Blackpool, he's got another cleaning round there.'

Craig shook his head. 'Blimey, hopefully it's Blackpool Tower he's cleaning. That will keep him busy and keep his todger in his trousers.'

She followed Craig upstairs to finish getting dressed. The Maid Marian outfit that she had bought home from her shop was light and wispy, and very pretty. It had a pink headscarf, pink light blouse over a green tunic and a pair of tight shorts, almost like 'hot pants'. She had bought it from a customer a few months ago and it had sat in her shop ever since. After she had tried it on, she had liked it, and it saved her having to spend a fortune on a new, or hired outfit.

The fancy dress party was being held at Jason and Wendy's house.

Of the three directors of PJC Shipping, Jason had the biggest residence. Seven bedrooms and two acres of garden, it was situated in a small village near Ellesmere Port, not too far for the pair of them to catch a taxi.

'Bloody hell, Craig, it is Craig isn't it? And the beautiful Jody. I say, what an outfit, my man. Oh, before I go any further, don't mention the football to Pete.' Jason smiled as he greeted them. Jason was the first person they bumped into as they went through the front doors, a security guard ticking off guests from a list that looked to have at least 100 names on it.

'Seriously nice attire old chap,' he added. 'I didn't think Smurfs were still all the rage are they old boy? Obviously I'm wrong, I stand corrected, great costume though Craig. And Jody, gorgeous as ever.'

'I'm not a Smurf, I'm a Minion. Smurfs are blue, with blue faces. Do I look like a Smurf?

'He's a Minion,' said Jody, trying not to laugh.

'Sorry, what's a Minion?'

'Piss off, you know what a Minion is.' Craig pushed past him. Jody smiled as she kissed Jason on the cheek, whispering. 'Don't be naughty. It's taken me all night to get him into it, now behave and tell him he looks great. Or I will get him to mention the football to Pete.'

'For you Jode. But I'll let him stew for now.'

'No. You say no more Jason.' She kissed him again and smiled.

Wendy was in the dining room. It was a large room with a big chandelier hanging high and was clearly where most of the indoor party was going to take place. There was a pianist playing in the corner and on the other side of the dining room, a band were putting together their set.

'Hi,' said Jody as she walked over to her, the pair had always got on well. Jody liked the fact that, despite the wealth, Wendy had always remained down to earth. 'How are you my darling, Wendy? Gosh, you look radiant, Princess Leia, one of my favourites.'

'Ah, thanks.' Wendy did a quick twirl. 'You look very sexy. Maid Marian in those green pants, how did you get into them? My backside would look like the rear end of a bus if I tried, you do have a good figure, girl.'

Lisa came bounding up to Craig all smiles. She was dressed as Cilla Black. Everton had beaten Liverpool 2-0 that afternoon and she been there, thanks to his offer of a place in the box.

'Hi, it is Craig, isn't it?' Lisa laughed, giving him a light punch on the arm. 'For a second I really did think you were Bob the Builder.'

'Ha! Ha! Ha! I assume you are not serious? I'm not Bob the Builder, I'm a Minion. Are you taking the piss? The look on her face told him otherwise.

'What's a Minion?'

'It doesn't matter. Are you supposed to be Cilla Black, Lady Gaga or Katy Perry?'

'The cheek, Craig Baldini. As if Katy Perry or Gaga have ginger hair. Don't have a go at me just because I thought you looked like Bob the Builder, anyhow, how are you? And what a game it was. You'd have loved it, there were a 'lorra lorra' quiet Liverpudlians in the box!' She laughed at her Cilla impression. It made Craig smile.

'I bet you enjoyed that? I hope you behaved yourself, I can't imagine there were many Evertonians in there with you.'

'No, just David Simpson, from the Storage Company. You know that big one on the Wirral. He's an Evertonian. God, we had a right ball, and a 'lorra, lorra' laughs. We scored twice in two minutes just after half-time, the rest of the box had only just got back from their half-time drinks. Only me and David saw the first goal, thanks again for the invite, Bob. Speak later, got to say hello to my friend Toni over there.'

Lisa walked off towards a tall, thin lady, who was dressed as a candle, blowing him a kiss as she did so.

As he looked around, glass of bubbly in hand, Craig spotted Jody chatting to Postman Pat, aka Tom Cummings, who was Head of Delivery Services, at PJC Shipping. As he stood watching, he saw his wife laugh and flick her hair back. She was very beautiful.

He was such a shit...

He took off his Minion spectacles and went over to the bar, near where Pete was standing.

'Jason and Wendy always know how to put on a party,' Pete said to Craig as he saddled up beside him. 'Are you sure he's not paying himself more than us two, it seems strange that one director has a house the size of a castle, while we live in mere mini mansions. And he's got two swimming pools. I've only got one. What about you?'

'I don't have any. Just a large bath.' Craig grinned.

Pete was dressed as Captain Hook. He had his hook leaned on the bar, he looked Craig up and down. 'What the fuck have you come as, Humpty Dumpty?'

'Don't ask, I'm a Minion, from those Despicable Me films.'

'Really?' Pete looked confused. 'Can't say I've ever seen them, what does your Jody think, you coming as a Mini?'

'Minion,' Craig said, taking a sip of his drink. 'She ordered the outfit, so she obviously thinks it's good. But she seems to be the only one who does, most people don't even know what a Minion is, I should have taken more interest when she ordered the bloody thing and come as Peter Pan. Or Prince Harry. Or Bob the Bloody Builder.'

'Prince Harry would have been a good one,' Pete said. 'Still, at least you are unique. There's only one Million about tonight, I certainly haven't seen another.

Craig didn't bother to correct him. 'So, what happened to your beloved Liverpool, today?'

Pete scoffed. 'Don't mention it. It was a typical derby game, we go for half-time drinks and by the time we get back into the box, bloody Everton are one-up. By the time we sat down, it's two. Lisa was having a right ball, as you can imagine. She can be a gobby little cow. Still, she's a good sort. Anyhow, I don't want to talk about it how did the Gunners get on, didn't see their result?'

'Playing tomorrow.'

Jody appeared from around the corner and joined the pair of them, she kissed Peter on the cheek. 'How is my favourite director?' She knew he had soft spot for her.

'Oh, you look gorgeous, as usual. Let me guess, you're one of those dancers from Pans People?'

Craig burst out laughing. 'At last, someone other than me. Pans People. That's a good one Pete. She's Lady Marian, can't you tell?'

'Maid Marian,' corrected Jody. 'Robin Hood's bit of stuff.'

'Oh, yes of course, I see it now,' said Peter. 'I wish I was Robin Hood, rather than this Hook idiot, I wouldn't mind you as my bit of rough.'

'I said 'stuff', not 'rough'. How much have you had to drink? But you never know, you play your cards right, Captain. But no more drinks, I don't want you too pissed, you never know where that hook might go.'

Pete smiled. 'Oh, well, it will have to be another time, I've had too much already, although I'd try, and try bloody hard girl, I can assure you.'

Craig and Jody both laughed. Pete always got a bit flirty after a few drinks. He was single again. At the Christmas party last year he had asked Lisa to marry him. Thankfully Lisa was just as pissed as him. But apparently she said 'yes', although neither remembered. When on Monday morning everyone in the office started whistling 'Here Comes the Bride' when Lisa walked in, she was taken aback. Pete had come out to see what was going on, it was left to Craig to re-tell the story out on the floor in front of everyone.

'I know you would try, Captain,' Jody smiled. 'You're like Craig, he's always trying. And if he manages it once, he'll try again. But after all these years of marriage he's only managed it twice.... twice... if you see what I mean, but I love him to bits, don't I darling?'

'Ha! Ha!' Craig smiled.

Jody walked away, deliberately wiggling her bum as she did so. It made Pete smile.

He raised his glass. 'Nice arse your wife.'

FORTY

IT wasn't often Tom bought a copy of the local paper.

But after his chat with Ben on Friday night it had made him realise that behind his stubbornness not to spend money on a paper were people's jobs. How would he feel if everyone decided to boycott going to the dentist because it hurt too much? And anyhow, more importantly, Jonny had texted him to tell him to get the local rag that day as his picture was in it.

And there it was. Tom and Polly presenting Lee Harding with his certificate. It was a good picture as well, wrapped around the report of South Walsham's big win over Luton. He looked at it again, young Lee was almost as tall as him, and much taller than Polly. She always took a good photo.

He smiled as he read the caption and looked at the match report. Perhaps he would give this paper one more shot, the only downside was the lack of Premier League reports, although Arsenal's 0-0 draw with Leicester would not have warranted more than a couple of paragraphs.

Polly had cooked them both a roast on Sunday, coupled with a bottle of Pinot Grigio, it had gone down well. They had talked no more about the 'BITCH' text she had received. Tom would speak to Mike about getting her a new number. Polly had been determined not to have her phone on at all on Sunday, she called Jody up on the landline Sunday night. Apparently Craig had got so drunk at the fancy dress party, he had gone to bed still dressed as a Minion.

'So, you see, she has now had sex with a Minion,' Polly had joyfully told Tom after putting the phone down to her friend. 'They

255

did it first thing in the morning, how much fun is that? I'll have to dress you up as a pilot, like Tom Cruise in Top Gun.'

It had been a busy Monday morning and Tom was glad to get a bit of fresh air as he walked into the city. Two fillings and three check-ups had seen him and Emily on the go from early on. The pair had chatted about the rugby on Saturday, she was glad he had enjoyed it.

It was 1pm and the morning had flown past, he hadn't even had a cup of coffee. So, with the next appointment not until 2.30pm, he had told Emily to get some lunch, he had gone to get some himself.

Sitting in one of the parks, just off the city centre, Tom had enjoyed a good walk. He had stopped at Greggs for a sausage roll and coffee and was sitting on a bench, flicking through the paper. His phone rang.

'Hello, Tom Armstrong.'

'Hello Tom. It's Karen, Karen Harding.'

Tom put his coffee down.

'Hi, Karen, what can I do for you? How did you get my mobile number?'

He had thought about their conversation in the surgery and her running away like she did. Although it was almost a week ago, something about the whole episode hadn't sat well with him.

'Don't worry how I got your number.' Karen sounded agitated. 'That was the easy part, now we need to talk and we need to talk soon. Face to face.'

'Face to face? Hang on. What's this all about? Is it something I said in the surgery? Why did you just run off? And why do we need to talk?'

'I'll tell you when we meet up, how about this time tomorrow? I'll meet you in Eaton Park. You know where that is? There's a cycle racing track there, I'll be near there, 1pm okay?'

Tom thought quickly. He knew Eaton Park and yes, he could be there at 1pm but he'd rather talk now. 'What is it that you can't tell me here and now? What the hell is this all about?'

'You'll find out, just be there. 1pm tomorrow at the park.' The line went dead.

Billy Wade, like Statton, wasn't keen on dredging up the past.

He didn't really want to get involved in Archer's revenge on the man who had put him in prison. But, like Statton, he knew how he would feel if the shoe was on the other foot. The three of them had been good pals, he had succumbed to Statton's request and now he was searching for a man who could put a name in the frame. He only had two options, Dan Swan and Roger Awning, both current coppers on Merseyside and both coppers who knew Billy well, although Awning was less likely to speak. He and Wade had a falling out a few months before Wade left the Force, Swan on the other hand might help.

He owed Wade after a young lad had been hurt outside a Liverpool nightclub about six years ago. Swan, who was Wade's partner at the time, had given the lad a slap after he resisted arrest for spitting at him. But the boy, so pissed, had fallen and banged his head and was in a coma for two weeks before making a full recovery. Swan was shitting himself during that time, hoping the boy would recover, Wade had given him his back. No-one, only Wade, had seen Swan slap the boy. Everyone assumed the lad had fallen over. Wade never back-tracked on the story even when questions started to be asked and it was clear some further up the ranks were suspicious.

Not that it mattered in the end, the boy recovered and got a bit of community service. He never remembered anything about that night. But Swan had never forgotten how close it could all have come to a serious charge had Wade coughed.

'Dan, Billy Wade, how the hell are you?'

'Bloody hell, Billy bloody Wade. I'm fine mate. What do you want?'

Dan Swan was 40 and still single, he enjoyed playing the field and enjoyed his 'Dan the Man' title among his peers, especially the single women cops. He still held high hopes of promotion through the ranks. The days of him and Wade patrolling the streets of Toxteth as constables were behind him. He was CID now, he loved his job and had a clean slate. His only indiscretion had been the slap that night outside the nightclub, but that was all in the past. He'd never forgotten what his former partner had done for him during that time. Billy had phoned him at work, at Merseyside Police.

'Mate, I need a favour,' said Billy. 'Just a small one, I want a name. I can bung you a few quid or you can just go and find it for me, it's no big drama. If you can't, you can't, but I would seriously appreciate it pal.'

'Oh, yeah. Go on then.' Swan had a tinge of concern in his voice.

Wade continued. 'That drug baron, Stu Archer, you know the one? He has just been put away, got about 25 years, I think. Anyhow, for the case to get to Crown, he was grassed up, someone in his own bloody organisation did it. I need to know who that someone is. It's important, trust me, I wouldn't call if not.'

'Fuck me, that's a big ask.' Swan walked out of his office and began pacing in the hallway outside. 'How the hell am I supposed to get that? I know of the Archer case. I didn't know he was grassed up though. Forget the money, I'm not interested in that, but what do you want to know for?'

'Look. I can't say, other than to tell you, I need a name and you are my number one hope. All I need is for you to see what you can find out, someone will know. Who was on the case? Likely a few of your buddies there. The only way Archer went down is because someone helped us to get a copper into Archer's gang. Who was it who helped us? Just a name.'

Swan looked up and down the corridor, then looked at his phone. This was not going to be easy. Accessing information on the computer would be a big 'no-no', it could be tracked back.

'Okay, Billy, here's what I'll do. I'm working now, but I'll make a few soundings. I do know some of the boys on that case, but I'm going to have to be careful. One young lad, lippy and full of himself was close to it, we get on well.

'The lad is on CID with us now. Leave it with me. You on this number? Listen, I'll call you ASAP. No promises though, you know that.'

'Cheers Dan. And ASAP'.

Billy hung up the call.

FORTY ONE

THEY was sitting in the living room and looking at the photograph of the rugby presentation.

'Fancy, we're in the paper.'

Tom had brought it home that night, he knew Polly would like to see how good she looked.

'It's a good one of you,' she said as she looked at the photo. 'That makes a nice change, you don't often take a good picture.' She smiled at him. 'By the way, what had that lad done again?'

'The boy we presented the certificate to has been picked to play for England,' Tom said. 'Which is quite impressive, don't you think? Can you imagine having a son or daughter who gets picked to play for their country? His parents must be proud, he seemed a nice kid as well.'

'We had better keep this paper then.' Polly folded it up and put it on the chair. 'Who knows? When he plays for England they might win a big cup or something big and we will be able to say we know him. What's his name again?'

Tom looked at the caption. 'Um, hang on, let me read this, Lee... Lee Harding. So, if a Lee Harding ever plays for England and they win the World Cup, we can say we know him. In fact I'll say it was my influence on giving him that certificate that pushed him towards glory.' He laughed as Polly got up to go into the kitchen.

But before he did so, the name dawned on him.

Lee Harding. Karen Harding. No. Just a coincidence, it had to be a coincidence. He half-smiled to himself at the absurdity of it. What's the odds of meeting two Hardings in the space of a week?

In saying that, Harding was not an unusual surname.

'Yes, or no?' Polly had her hands on her hips as she stood at the living room door. 'Shall we or not?'

'Pardon?' What did you say?' Tom was day dreaming, the name Harding reverberating around his head.

'Are you listening to me? Bloody hell, sitting there staring into space.'

'I'm okay and please don't keep swearing Pol. I was just thinking, you know, stuff, you know who Arsenal play on Saturday. That sort of stuff. What did you say?'

'Oooo! What fun you are Mr Excitement. Your life is so full on, who Arsenal play Saturday! Can it get any more thrilling?'

He looked up at her and gathered his thoughts. 'Stop the crap Pol.'

She shook her head. 'You weren't listening. I said, shall we go to Vegas with Jody and Craig, yes or no? I know you are aware of it because Jody said Craig spoke to you about it, they are thinking of booking in June and they are going to want to know in the next week or so, I think they are looking at about the 11th.'

Tom shrugged his shoulders. 'Craig said it was going to be a surprise, which it obviously isn't if you all know. Well, if you want to go, I'm in. Never been to Vegas.'

'Well, I don't actually know why I'm asking because we're going, I told Jody we are going. I knew you would say yes.' Polly headed into the kitchen.

He got up and followed her. 'So, why did you ask? I may as well not be here. Just organise my life for me.'

'Well, I might as well. Keep gawping into space, have you got something on your mind? Don't keep things from me Tom Armstrong, I'll get them out of you.'

He looked at her and smiled. He did have a lot on his mind but she didn't need to know. He needed to sharpen up. 'I'm fine love, I'm fine. Sorry, I'm just a bit tired, it was a hectic day and a few big procedures are always a bit stressful, ignore me.' He went across and kissed his wife on the cheek.

Polly began to get the dinner.

Sitting down on the sofa, Tom picked up the TV remote and turned the television on. He picked up the paper and looked at the photograph once more.

He read the caption again.

He didn't sleep well, his mind was racing. This woman, Karen Harding. What did she want? Her running out of the surgery in the way she did, after saying what she did, meant it likely she had news he didn't want to hear, for that reason Tom was becoming more fretful of meeting up with her.

He took Polly a cup of tea in bed and jumped in beside her, giving her a cuddle as he did so. It was only 6.30am and he had turned the alarm off, he'd been awake since 5.

'What time is it?' Polly looked across at her cup of tea. It felt a bit early for tea, not that she was complaining.

'6.30. I didn't sleep that great, so I got you a cuppa, I'm having a shower. I've got to go into work a bit early again today.'

She was still half asleep and wasn't woken by the sound of the shower going off. Tom let the water run over his body, he felt lethargic due to lack of sleep and his day hadn't even started yet. It wasn't a good sign, hopefully by tonight things would feel different.

He got dressed and went downstairs, he didn't feel like much breakfast, which was unlike him. One yoghurt, an orange and banana later he went back upstairs and kissed Polly on the forehead. She was sitting up now, reading a book, she smiled back.

'Are you okay?' Polly put the book down. 'You look tired. We'll have an early night tonight. Try and get home early, I'm getting my hair done this afternoon, Andy has let me have a few hours off. We have the footballers coming in tomorrow and I want to look my best.'

'You always look your best darling. You're beautiful, have a good day, I'm off.' He kissed her on the cheek.

Tom got in his car and started it up, he didn't notice Polly at the window above looking down on her husband as he drove away, she loved him so much, but something wasn't right.

'Open wide,' Tom said, as he stood over Luke Calper, who was a patient he had known for many years. A plumber, Luke had once fixed a water leak in the toilets at the surgery. He was also rather keen on Emily and the pair often bumped into each other when out in the city at weekends. Luke was, according to Emily, always asking her about boyfriends. Did she have any? That sort of thing. 'Don't know why he keeps asking me that, must be keen on me,' she had once said to Tom. 'He's quite cute, though.'

'All looking good in the gods,' Tom said. 'Let's have a quick shufty downstairs as well. Yep, all looks fine, I'll give you a quick brush and polish.'

Emily was standing over Luke just in case Tom needed any assistance. She smiled at him, Luke was a couple of years older than her.

'You going into Norwich this weekend, Em?' Luke said. 'If so, we can meet up, perhaps. We'll be in Maritzos on Friday, a few of us. We can talk about, well, talk about teeth to start off with. You can show me yours, seeing as you've seen mine!' He laughed.

She smiled. 'I'm not sure what I'm doing, but I expect I'll see you if I do go out. It would be nice to talk to you earlier in the evening when you are not so pissed. I don't imagine you even remember speaking to me the other Saturday at Chuffys, do you?'

'Of course I do?' He looked indignant. 'I'm not always drunk, and at least I don't dance on tables.' The two grinned as Tom continued to fill out the details of Luke's treatment he had just given him.

'That wasn't my fault. Your mate Dan dared me, I'll do anything for a Jagerbomb.'

'So I could tell, and obviously cider, that you followed it up with?'

Emily smiled again at Luke, she was a bit bashful. He had a kind face and was the sort of boy she would like to get to know... *but he wasn't old enough for her.*

Tom broke up the conversation.

'Well, enough of your weekend frivolities, you two. How about I polish these teeth?'

'Yeah, sorry Tom, go for it!'

Five minutes later Luke got up and left the surgery, going downstairs to book another appointment for six months. Tom looked at Emily. 'He likes you.'

'Yeah, he's okay. He's fun to meet up with, but he can get so drunk, he's a bit of a boy, if you know what I mean. I like the more experienced man. I've had too many boys for boyfriends.'

'Oh, I don't know, he seems like a nice lad, it's good to keep young, don't wish your life away. I wish I was your age again.'

'Oh, yeah, that sounds interesting. Tell me more.'

'Not now. Polly might walk in and I don't want her to hear of my single years before I met her. Not that she was Mrs goody two-shoes either. Enjoy being young, that's my advice.'

He looked at his watch, it was noon and his next appointment was in 10 minutes. It gave him a chance to nip over the road to see Mike Gremshall, the phone tech guy. Tom had texted him yesterday to say Polly wanted a new number, but she was happy to keep her old phone. He had explained about the crank calls, it was just that he hadn't heard back from Mike, which was unusual.

'Hi, Tom, how are you?' said Mike, as Tom walked in. Mike had the shop long before Tom had bought the surgery. 'What's this about Polly and crank calls? Not very nice, anyhow, yes of course we can help set her up with a new number. Get her to call me tomorrow and I'll sort.'

'Cheers Mike. 'I nipped over because I hadn't heard from you after I sent the text about what time can I come over, but obviously you got it.'

'Sorry, I thought I'd replied, you must think I'm a right idiot. And I'm supposed to be a phone guy as well, all rather embarrassing.'

Tom smiled. 'I must admit I did think it odd, anyhow, no worries, I'll get Polly to call you.'

Karen decided she would make an effort to look good for her meeting with him.

A little flowery short dress, show her legs off. A light cardigan. The weather was nice, she would wear her shades. She was nervous, but nowhere near as nervous as her foray into the surgery the other morning.

Lee had gone off to school with a smile on his face, he was being presented with yet another award in assembly for his England call-up, so he had been told by Mr Trustbrook. He really was 'cock of the north' at the moment.

She drove to Eaton Park, she knew it well, even though she hadn't lived in Norfolk that long. It had been one of the first places her and Lee had ventured after Lee heard about the park from his friends. It was a vast area and great for sports, football, cycling and tennis, or in Lee's case throwing a rugby ball about.

She parked the car in the adjacent car park and walked towards the cycle track which was in one of the corners of the park. The track was an oval and was used as a cycle-speedway racing circuit. She had seen the track before on her walks around the park with him.

It was just before 1pm when Karen arrived, she could feel her heart beating fast and her palms were sweating. She sat on a bench overlooking the track, wondering if he would come. She didn't have to wait long to find out.

'Afternoon.' She turned her head but had already recognised Tom's voice.

Tom stood there, short-sleeved shirt and tie. He looked relaxed, a bit tanned. He looked dishy, she thought as she looked up at him. 'Hi, thanks for coming.'

The pair looked at each other for a few seconds. It was Tom who got to the point.

'Look, I don't pretend to know what this is all about,' he said, hands in pockets. 'I don't make a habit of meeting up with women who call me to say they have something to tell me, I hope this is good news and won't take long, I have to get back to work.'

She looked at Tom, he was striking, those blue eyes. 'You really have no idea who I am, do you? Or do you? I reckon you do and you don't want to say.'

Karen detected a look on his face when she said about him having no idea who she was. She was starting to suspect he had an inkling.

'Okay, let me remind you, Tom. Crete, 2006. Remember it?'

The look on his face gave it away, he knew exactly who she was. He had half-guessed when going through his summer holiday 'conquests'. Karen had been one of several flings. Most he didn't, or couldn't, remember. And certainly he couldn't put names to faces now, but he looked at Karen. He remembered her, she had been different.

The pair had met on the first week of their two-week holiday. Karen was there for the same period of time as he was. They were both in their own groups of friends, but Karen and Tom had hooked up. Tom had already slept with one girl on the first night, but Karen came along and changed all that and he had spent almost every night with her after they had met. They had got on so well, he remembered her laugh, remembered how they would meet up in the afternoon by the pool. He remembered how his mates ribbed him that 'he'd pulled a cracker there'. He remembered her body. He even remembered the sex, which was something he rarely did with any of the other girls he met. She was very dominating, very passionate. He had loved it.

It had all come to nothing. They had exchanged numbers on their return to England but he wasn't keen on keeping the relationship going, it was just a holiday fling, that's how he saw it back then and, after not returning her calls, they became less frequent, until they stopped. They had gone their own ways.

She was pretty then and was pretty now, she had something about her that Tom still found attractive as she stood there in the sunshine, her low cut dress showing off her cleavage, her shades on her head, hair flowing, lovely legs. If his memory served him right, she came from London. He even remembered where, Woolwich.

'Well, yes, Karen... Karen Harding. Yep, I remember, it was fun. So how are you?' Tom tried to make light of the conversation. 'Oh, please don't tell me you have called me here to talk over our holiday? That's a bit random, isn't it?'

She eyed him up and continued her calm response. 'No, I'm not here to just talk about that, I've been wanting to speak to you for a long time, actually. Do you know it has taken me years to track you down?'

Tom looked concerned and surprised in equal measure. He felt his voice raise slightly.

'What? Track me down? It was a holiday romance, I'm married now, I'm sure you are. Please don't say this is about rekindling some sort of thing between us, because that isn't going to happen, it was fun. We've all moved on.'

'Don't flatter yourself.' Karen remained in control. 'I'm not interested in rekindling anything, Tom. Yes, I know you've moved on, we've both moved on.'

'So, what the hell is all this about?' Tom was getting slightly irritated.

Karen was quick to reply. 'Well, I've got some news for you. When I got home from that holiday in Crete, a couple of months later, I found out I was pregnant. Pregnant with *our* child.

'Your child, Tom. You have a son.....'

FORTY TWO

TOM stared at her.

He couldn't believe what he had just heard, he wouldn't believe it, this was a hoax, must be. In a minute she would laugh and say, *'only kidding'*, or something similar. All the time she had just wanted to say hello again, hook up and talk about old times.

'You're joking me, right?

'You're not seriously telling me you've called me up after what, 14 years, to tell me I have a son? Bullshit. I don't believe it, this is a wind-up, right?'

She shook her head and kept shaking her head. Karen looked deadly serious.

Tom was agitated. 'I remember. You said you were on the pill. I know you did and I used protection most of the time, I do remember that bit if nothing else. No, fuck off, stop shaking your head, I don't know what all this is about and I don't know what you want. But I'm happily married now, you can't just butt into my life and invent this shit up and hope to gain, I don't know what, gain something. Come on, what's this really about? You are winding me up?'

Karen wasn't surprised with his attitude, she knew it's what he'd say. How would she have felt if someone called up from the past and told her something like this? Oh yes, she knew about the life he led now. She knew all about his wife, their job, their wealth, their friends. She knew it all. *She had been told it all.*

'I knew you would act this way.' Karen continued to stay calm. 'I knew this is what you'd say. It was obvious.'

'What I would say!' Tom could feel the rage surging up inside him. A mixture of fury and confusion as he tried to grasp what the hell was happening.

'What, you mean expecting me to react a bit pissed because some woman comes out of the woodwork fuck knows how many years after we had sex together on a summer holiday when we were just kids and tells me I have a son. You mean something like that, do you? Are you mad? I don't know what your game is, but as I said, you can fuck right off, I don't believe you. I don't know what your motive is. This is just a joke, isn't it? It's a fucking joke. No, let me guess, it's not a joke and you want money. Please, don't let that be true. Please?' He raised his arms, his voice patronising.

She moved forward and slapped him hard around the face. It struck him to the core and even knocked him slightly off-balance. Karen was looking at him, her eyes wide. Raging.

'How dare you, how dare you,' she said as she moved closer.

'You arrogant bastard. You think I've called you up to meet me here to make up some cock and bull story about you having a son, our son, you think about that for a minute? Why don't you just fucking think about it? Why would I do it? What am I gaining? I don't want your money you precious bastard, I don't want your fucking flash house, I don't want anything off you. I certainly don't want you, but I do want you to know the truth. You are going to know the truth, whether you like it or not.' Karen wasn't holding back.

'I've lived with this secret for years. What have you been doing all that time while I've been bringing up your son? Where have you been? You have no idea what I've been through, no idea at all. Okay, so you didn't know, I get that. But you're a bastard for even thinking I'm here for money, you don't know me. I've spent all the time trying to forget all about you and yet I look at my son, our son, every day and can only see you in him.

'Do you think he's not now asking questions? He's been asking questions since he could start to understand why he had no proper dad. I've been beaten black and blue by other men, I've been cheated on, I've had to survive, we've had to survive. Just me and Lee. And now I've tracked you down to tell you. I knew you wouldn't believe me and I didn't expect you to. But you had better wake up and smell the coffee, Tom. Have a DNA test. The truth will then be out and you can then deal with it how you wish, I'm not here to tell you how it is going to be. That can be decided, but you had better believe it, you have a son.'

Tom was silent. He put his hands in his pockets and walked in small circles. The slap around the face had a sobering effect. He looked at her, she had tears in her eyes. They stood in silence for what seemed like five minutes, but was probably no more than 30 seconds.

'Lee, you say?' Tom said quietly, nodding his head. 'Lee Harding, the rugby player.'

She nodded. 'I know what you are going to say, yes, by some crazy coincidence you met him at the rugby on Saturday. I was there, I saw you present him with the award. I had no idea you would be there. I knew about him getting the award and while I was so proud, I knew he wouldn't want his mum there, not a teenage boy with mum in tow. So I tucked myself away.' Karen feigned a slight smile.

'And then I saw you, I couldn't believe it. Can you imagine how I felt seeing you with your arm around Lee? Can you imagine how I felt seeing you talk to him? All these years I've been trying to find you and only in the last few have I known where you were. That's why I came to the surgery in the first place, to see you, to know it was you. But I couldn't go through saying too much that day, so that's why I ran out, it was all too much.'

Tom looked at her. He was starting to believe her.

'Why are you so sure, he is my child? I will have a DNA test, I'm not going to take your word for it.'

She nodded. 'Look, I was no tart who slept round with lots of men. Yes, I had fun with my girlfriends, drinking and chatting to blokes but I had no boyfriend before I went to Crete and I had no boyfriends when I got home for months, I wasn't on the pill, I lied.'

Tom looked blankly into space. 'Fucking brilliant, thanks.'

He looked at the cycle track, the brown dirt scuffed up where the bikes had raced around. He looked across at the green hedge opposite. Part of him felt he would wake up from all this, it had to be a dream, a nightmare, it couldn't be true. He wanted the ground beneath him to swallow him up. If this were true, all he could think of was one person, Polly.

He regained his composure.

'I want a DNA test. For all I know you could be spinning me a load of shit.' Tom's aggressive tone returned.

'You just name the place, the day and the date and I'll be there, Tom, I promise you.'

He looked at her. 'Why are you doing this? 'Why now? I'm married, have you any idea what this will do to my wife? Have you any idea what this will do to my life?'

The conversation was edgy again, but she was ready. This was 14 pent-up years of hurt, she wasn't going to lose this opportunity.

'Listen to yourself?' Karen said. 'Listen to you. Me, me, me. What about Lee? I would say what about me? But I know you don't care a shit about me, I'll live with that. I can't expect you to want to have anything to do with me, I don't want anything to do with you. But when you get that bit of paper that says Lee is your son, I expect you to live up to being his father.

'Just like I've had to jump through hoops for the last shit knows how many years, so you will have to start doing the same. Are you going to man up to your responsibilities? I know you hope I'm making this up, but you couldn't be further from the truth, Tom. Let's get that DNA test done, then you can start thinking what you are going to do next. Because if you think you are just walking away, you can forget that. I'll make sure everyone knows about your love child. And Polly will find out in a way you couldn't even begin to dream of.'

'Oh, you know my wife's name then? Well, you leave her out of this.' Tom moved forward towards Karen. 'She'll be destroyed if this is the truth.'

'If? There's no if, you are the father, deal with it. Why should she be destroyed, anyhow? You knew me before you knew her, when you met her she had no idea about me. You haven't had a fling during your marriage, not with me, anyhow?' Karen smiled sarcastically.

'You bitch. That's enough.'

Tom stood up and started to walk away. 'This conversation is over.'

Karen followed him. 'Okay, this conversation might be over now, but the conversations we are going to have are only just beginning. If I don't hear from you in a week about a test, then I'll keep badgering you until you do take responsibility and I won't give a toss who I call, or bump into, or text, or meet at the gym, I'll tell them.'

Tom spun round. He was angry now.

'So, it's you who has been bombarding my wife with phone calls and texts, is it? You really are an evil slag, what has she done to you? Nothing. No more, no more calls, no more text messages. You leave Polly out of this.'

Karen looked surprised. 'What do you mean bombarding your wife with calls and texts? I haven't done that. I only know her name. I don't know what you are talking about.'

He looked closely at her. 'Have you been calling Polly, leaving shitty messages on her phone? I want the truth, you want me to deal with what might be the truth with Lee, then you tell me the truth about that.'

'I promise you, I don't know what you are talking about.'

As if he didn't have enough going through his head, her words confused him even more, Karen sounded genuine.

'Well, you just keep away from her. She's done nothing to offend you. I'll call you about the DNA test and we will get this sorted once and for all. And one thing. If the test proves I'm not the father, I don't want to hear anymore from you. Do you understand?'

She shook her head and, in a quiet voice, lent forward just a few feet from his face. 'You really don't want to believe it do you, Tom?

'You really don't want to believe it.'

FORTY THREE

'WHAT the hell is wrong with the pair of them? Getting on my bloody nerves, this. I will get it out of Tom if it continues.'

Polly was in the car driving home from the hairdressers. Josh had weaved his usual magic on her hair and she knew she it was looking a million dollars. It was a shame she wasn't feeling the same, a call to Jody meant she could vent her anger.

'But Tom isn't usually quiet about anything.' Jody sounded surprised. She was in the shop and had no customers. 'Neither is Craig. God, perhaps it's us imagining things. Are we paranoid? I mean, men are allowed to have mood swings.'

'Mood swings? I'll swing for Tom if he doesn't tell me what's his problem, he seems away with the fairies just lately. He says it's work, he's been getting up really early lately, says he's busy. But so what? He doesn't talk much about work at home, he likes to keep it to himself, but that doesn't make it right. He's the opposite of me. I'm always talking about work, I've got the footballers coming to the gym tomorrow. Had my hair done and everything.'

'Oh, that should be fun, Pol. Watch those footballers. They fancy themselves a bit. And remember, just because they are on zillions of pounds a week, your Tom is worth far more in love and understanding.' Jody laughed.

'Not at the bloody moment he isn't. If he doesn't cheer up a bit, I might look to swap him for a younger model with less money, but more go.'

'You don't mean that darling, you know how much you love him. Oh, and are we going to Vegas? Please tell me you at least managed to have that conversation with him.'

'Yes, we're in. I told Tom we're going, I didn't give him a choice to be honest. He can close the surgery down for a week, that won't hurt, I'll let you know some dates. We could do with a break, all four of us from the sound of things.'

'It will be fun. We can play on the slot machines and do some crazy stuff. You are right, I think we all need a break.' Jody looked up as a customer walked into the shop.

'Anyhow, look, I've just pulled into the drive and Tom's already home from the look of things. Perhaps he's feeling guilty and taking me out for dinner again. I'll go and see if I can beat anything out of him. Polly laughed. 'And if that doesn't work I can always resort to my speciality which he always gives into. Get him in the showers, never fails.'

'You are a naughty girl, Pol. Love you.'

'Love you too.'

Polly got out of the car and turned the key in the door. She walked in but there was no sign of Tom. It was 5pm, he must have left off early because he wasn't usually home by now. She walked into the kitchen and put down her phone and keys, Tom was sitting in the garden, with a glass of beer in his hand.

'Hello darling, had a good day.' Tom looked up.

'Hi. Yep, not bad. Bit busy and I think I'm still tired from not much sleep last night, how about you?'

She looked at him. He did look tired. 'Yeah, I'm okay. Things for the footballers' visit tomorrow are going well. James and Kevin had another set-to, James asked if he could borrow Kevin's fake tan as he was thinking of wearing a pair of football shorts when the players came, but his legs were too white. Kevin, as usual, fell for it, going on about he hasn't got a fake tan. James then asked to see his 'white bits', Andy had to step in. I honestly thought Kevin was going to deck him this time. It was funny, though.'

'Well, you have more fun than I do at work. If it wasn't for my staff doing crazy things nothing funny would happen in the surgery. Susan announced today that she was going vegetarian, but she was still going to eat fish. That set Emily off. She's a veggie and said real veggies don't eat fish. Susan told her real veggies didn't get pissed out on the town every Saturday night.'

He smiled and looked at his wife, she sat beside him on the bench and put her arm around him.

'Are you okay? It's just you've been a bit quiet lately and I don't like it, you do love me, don't you?' Polly kissed his ear.

He looked into her eyes and put his fingers through her hair. 'Now don't start all that. You know I do, I don't know why you ask. And your hair looks beautiful by the way, good old Josh to the rescue again?'

She nodded. 'But I love you so much and I don't like it when you are a bit quiet, which you have been lately, and don't deny it, or I'll pinch your thigh.'

'No, don't do that.' Tom covered his leg with his hand. 'No pinching. But please stop saying things like 'do I love you?' You know I do. Okay, so I'm not saying I agree to promise never to sleep with that bird I fancy on Corrie if the chance came up. But, that apart....' Tom didn't manage to get the rest of the sentence out. She pinched his thigh so hard, it made him yell out in pain. 'I'm only joking,' he screamed. 'I don't even watch Corrie anymore.'

'Button it Armstrong,' Polly smiled. 'You even think such thoughts and I've told you what I'll do.'

Tom laughed. 'You've got a thing about cutting it off at the moment, I'm getting worried.'

She got up and kissed him on the lips. 'You have no need to worry. What would I do without it!? I'll get the dinner on.'

He finished his beer and looked out into the garden, he put his head between his legs and breathed in. *What the hell was he going to do if Lee was his son? What the hell would Polly say?*

Tom was worried. He knew Karen wouldn't have tracked him down after all these years for no reason, he could see it in her eyes. She believed he was the father.

He would have the DNA test.

Jimmy Alban was 24 and one of Merseyside Police Force's 'up and comers'. He had been an outstanding cadet and, while full of himself, he had begun to control his cockiness and full-on attitude, Dan Swan had been a mentor in helping him.

The Police was everything to Jimmy, and his promotion into CID two years ago had been a dream come true for such a young lad. He had not spent nearly as much time as many of his fellow cops pounding the streets in uniform. Jimmy was now away from petty anti-social behaviour, domestic rows and pub fights. His world, the world of CID, was big-time crime, sexual assaults, murder, shootings and drugs. In a big city like Liverpool, he had a big job.

Jimmy had learned that looking after those who look after you was a basic life skill, and one that was useful in his line of work. Not just among fellow officers, but among other criminals. Already he was drawing up quite a list of 'good'un's and 'bad'uns', both active and former ex-cons, as well as current and ex-cops, who he could search out when looking for a bit of information.

So, when Dan Swan called into his office and asked to meet him for a drink in Liverpool city centre after work, he thought nothing of it. Dan had been a help to him, a father figure in many ways, a man who had knocked the stuffing out of him acting the 'big-time Charlie'. The man who had aided his career and shown him a good path.

'Hi, pal,' said Dan, as Alban approached. 'What do you want to drink?'

The pair were meeting in a pub in Liverpool and although it was 6.30pm in the evening, it was already busy.

'I'll have a pint of Fosters. Just the one, I've got the car.'

Dan went to the bar and returned with two pints, one for himself as well. He had found a corner of the pub that allowed them a bit of quiet.

'So, what's all this about?' Jimmy looked rather excited. 'Don't tell me, you're getting married and you want me to be the best man!' He laughed.

'You're joking aren't you? I'm not getting married any time soon, and even if I did I could hardly have you as a best man. You'd be too pissed before the speeches. And you'd tell the most outrageous secrets about me, my wife would likely walk out.'

Jimmy nodded in agreement, 'Fair point.'

'No, listen up, I want a favour Jim and it's a big one.' Jimmy looked suspicious. 'Oh yeah, what?'

'You know that Stuart Archer case? The drugs baron. You were on it, or on the edge of it, weren't you?' Jimmy gave nothing away, he just continued to stare at his pal. 'Well, I know the reason he was put down is because an insider in his gang stitched him up, that's hardly news. But what I want to know is, who was the guy who grassed up Archer? Who was the guy who got us in on Archer's gang?'

Jimmy looked at him, he didn't know what to say. Here was a mate, a good mate, asking for information that was so secret, very few coppers on the actual case had ever been told the bloke's name. There had even been talk of the guy getting a name change, such was the danger he had put himself in.

'Jesus, Dan, are you serious? What the fuck you getting involved in this for? This is top level secrecy man, the guy has just helped put down one of the city's biggest drug barons. He's got anonymity. I can't go giving his name out, even if I can find it, you know that.

'Look, I'm not going to beg, I'm not going to plead,' Dan stared at him. 'It's not life and death for me, but it is still quite a big deal. You know I wouldn't ask if it wasn't important to me, and others.'

'And others! Fuck me. You aren't in any hassle over this are you, Dan?'

'Look mate, calm down, no, I'm not in any bother and if you don't tell me, you don't tell me. No problem. But, you know me? You know what I've always taught you, life is built around loyal friendships and trust and I would like to know that name. You have to believe me. You don't have to know why and you don't have to be involved in any shape or form. The one thing you can guarantee is that if you tell me, I will tell no-one where I got it from.'

Jimmy knew he could trust Dan, but he still didn't know what to do. The Stuart Archer case had been one of the Force's biggest for years and, while Jimmy wasn't front and centre of it, he'd been on the periphery. He'd found out a lot during hours of typing in reports and dropping in on the odd meeting. It was a huge relief when Archer went down, the copper who had infiltrated the gang and been given a secret commendation, a new identity, a big pension and had moved abroad with his wife.

It had been huge stakes. If his memory served him right,

the guy who had tipped the cops off hadn't got the same deal, apparently they already had something on him and said they would drop it if he helped them.

But still, the informer expected anonymity.

He looked again at Dan, someone who had been good to him. A man he knew he could trust, but what he was asking was out of order.

Shit. What a dilemma.

FORTY FOUR

SHE had one call to make and one text to send. But it was getting late.

It had been a stressful day but one Karen felt had gone as good as it could. She looked at her watch, it was almost 11pm and she was enjoying her third glass of Merlot while watching an episode of 'A Place in the Sun'. Of all the dull shows that made up the ridiculous amount of TV these days, 'A Place in the Sun', did at least hold her attention. That and 'Judge Judy'! How she would like a place in the sun right now. Just her and Lee, a small apartment on the beach, lots of money in the bank, a car to potter about in, 300 days of sunshine. She could but dream.

Her conversation that afternoon with Tom had thrown her emotions into a frenzy. On the one hand she was glad she had confronted him, it had taken far too long to get to this point but that had been partly her own fault. It was a relief to get her biggest secret out in the open to the man who should have known years ago.

His pig-headed attitude about a DNA test and 'if he wasn't the father', had made her more determined. Then again, what did she expect?

It was 8am in Sydney, but she was sure Jane would be up. Her boys would be going to school she was sure of that, Karen had to tell her sister the news.

She decided Facetime would be the best option, she would be able to tell how busy her sister was because she would be able to see her. She rung the number. As the call was picked up, Jane's face came into view.

'Oooo! Look at you sis, calling me up first thing in the morning. How are you and what do you want my darling?' Karen smiled at the sight of Jane, her tanned face and the sound of her voice. They had been so close growing up. Karen had been pleased to see her sister happy with Peter, but inwardly upset when the pair emigrated Down Under. She had always supported her decision and at least they kept in touch regularly.

'Hi sis. Yep, I'm great thanks, how are you?' Karen turned the sound down on the television. 'Look, if you're busy getting everyone off to school and all that, just say so and I'll call a little later. But it's 11pm here, so I thought I would try before I fall asleep, I've had three glasses of wine.'

'No probs,' Jane said, forcing a piece of bread with peanut butter on, into her mouth, before adding, 'Peter has already taken the boys to school, they were having early rugby practice this morning, they have a game later today, so, they've gone. I'm home alone. I'm not at work till 10, so good timing.'

'So, how are you, sis? 'Everything okay?' Karen smiled into the phone.

'Yeah, all good Kaz. We're all working hard like you are I imagine. It's autumn here now so the weather isn't quite as warm as it was, but still good enough the odd 'barbie'. Anyhow, how are you and Lee? Or should I say Lee, 'the rugby champ'. Thanks for letting us know about his England call-up, Zac and Jake were most impressed about their cousin. They were asking if he was eligible to play for Australia.'

Karen laughed. 'No, I don't think we could stretch his allegiance to Oz just because his auntie Jane lives there, although Lee does like a good barbecue. He and his mates often go for one down by a lake near here, he'd suit life in Oz. Anyhow, I've got some news.'

'You haven't won the lottery, have you sis? If so, yes you can come and live with us.'

'No, I wish. It's not the lottery, I've got news about Lee's dad. I've got news about Tom.' Karen let the sentence settle.

'Tom. Lee's dad?' Jane pushed away her plate of food and got closer to the screen.

'What about him? Don't bloody well tell me you've tracked him down?' Karen sensed the excitement in her sister's voice. 'You bloody well have, haven't you?'

'I have, and I've spoken to him, and I've told him about Lee, and I've said I expect him to step up to the plate about being his dad.' Karen sounded excited and assured, in equal measure.

Jane put her hands on her head. 'My God. My God. How? Why? When did this happen? What did he say? Oh Kaz, how do you feel?'

Jane was happy, yet fearful for her younger sister as she fired questions at her. She knew the hurt and anguish she had gone through and she'd often felt guilty about moving to Australia after Lee was born. She had always felt maybe she should have stayed to be alongside her, but Peter's job couldn't wait. To have to choose between her sister's predicament and her family's new start, had been one of the toughest decisions of her life.

'Let me take it slowly.' Karen took a deep breath. 'I met him today at a park in Norwich and basically I told him everything, well, almost everything. He tried to make out at first he didn't know me, but I could tell he recognised me and not just from my visit to his surgery last week. Remember, I told you he was a dentist? Well, I made an appointment to see him, so I could be definitely sure it was him, but I didn't say much then. And if he did twig it was me, he didn't show it. So, I got his mobile and called him up to meet, and today we met. I told him about Lee.'

'Jesus, what the hell did he say?' Jane was wrapped up in her sister's news. 'How did he react? He must have wondered what the shit was going on, you certainly pooped on his day, or was he happy about it? Sorry for all the questions.'

'Oh, he wasn't happy. Oh no, certainly not to start with. He mellowed a bit for a while then got all bullshitty again about a DNA test and if Lee wasn't his, he never wanted to hear from me again, you know, that sort of thing. But I wasn't going to back down.'

'That must have been difficult to listen to, sis.'

'It was, but when he was in full bullshit mode, I gave him a slap around the face. A real one. Bloody hard as well. A bit of 'London chin music', I've never forgotten how to hit. Remember that girl, Amelia I slapped at that disco in Camden that time? Well, it was harder than that.'

Jane laughed, nodding her head, her sister was no shrinking violet.

'I bet that shut him up.' Jane laughed again.

'Well, I think it pressed a reset button.' Karen took a sip of her wine. 'He was starting to fly away with the idea I was some sort of money-grabbing woman trying to stitch him up and take all his belongings with some ridiculous story about a love child. I don't know why he should think that, I never mentioned anything about money. But listen to this, this will make you laugh. He only met Lee on Saturday, and he didn't even know it?'

'What? Are you kidding me? How did that happen? Are you making this up?'

Karen relayed the story of the afternoon at the rugby. How she had hidden in the corner of the hall to watch Lee get his presentation, then watched as Tom presented him with the certificate, oblivious to who he was presenting the certificate to. Jane was staggered.

'That's unbelievable.' Jane turned to put the kettle on. 'I mean, what a coincidence. What are the chances of that? So, what happens now?'

'Well, I'm going to text him tomorrow to arrange for a DNA test. I have already had Lee and mine done years ago, so I have all the documents from those tests here, I had it done when Lee was about six, I'll take them with us and have another test if he insists.'

'He's married isn't he?' Jane said. 'Does he have kids? Do you know his wife?'

'Yeah, he's married, but he has no kids with her. His wife's name is Polly. I saw her at the rugby on Saturday, she was there with him, very glamorous to say the least. This will make you laugh, you'll never guess what Lee said after he got his certificate from Tom? He only went and said that bloke's wife is a bit of alright, talking about Polly! Bloody hell. What could I say to that? I had to keep my mouth shut.'

'Jesus, talk about keeping it in the family.' Jane laughed. 'Sorry, I shouldn't say that.'

It was almost 11.15pm and Karen knew she had to be up early

the next morning, as Lee needed a lift into school.

'Look, I've got to go,' Karen stifled a small yawn. 'I need to be up early tomorrow, I'll keep you informed on what happens.'

'Well, look, please be careful,' said Jane. 'He's not going to take all this lying down, I imagine. Not until he's had the test will he believe anything. And even after that, the shit will likely hit the fan, so go careful. I know you have waited a long time for this, but if you need any help, you call me. Or, Tonya, or Tricia come to think of it. Is Tricia still about in Woolwich?'

Karen nodded. While she didn't speak to Tonya anymore, Karen had never even told anyone why, Tricia had also been one of their gang back in the day. They did keep in touch, but Tricia had been sent to Holloway Prison 14 years ago for a stabbing outside a disco, the two sisters were both there at the time. Tricia was their friend but had a very short fuse. The fight she had got involved in had started after Jane had been pushed by a girl who had accused her of staring at her boyfriend. Tricia had intervened, no-one knew Tricia had a knife. The girl was stabbed in the arm and Tricia had been put away for six years. She was out now.

'Yeah, I ought to speak to Tricia, anyhow,' Karen said. 'I'd like to catch up with her again. See ya Janie, got to go.'

'Bye sis. Love you,' Jane waved at the camera and blew kisses. 'You're a brave girl, you're nearly there.'

Karen smiled back and raised a glass of Merlot.

'Shame, it's a bit early in the morning for that over here. See ya darling. Keep in touch. Let me know what happens.' They pressed their off buttons.

Karen relaxed back in her chair and looked up as the couple in 'A Place in the Sun' were making an offer on a three-bedroom house in Valencia. The asking price was £200,000 and they were offering £165,000. She could never understand why people did that. Like a house but don't want to pay the price of it. Ah, good, the offer was refused. She picked up her phone again and finished her drink. She still had a text to send and although it was late, she knew the recipient would still be awake, although likely pissed.

'He knows. He knows. No hiding place for him now. Thanks for your help.....xxx'

She sent it and within 30 seconds a love heart emoji came

back with a kiss.

Karen, smiled and headed up the stairs.

FORTY FIVE

ANDY was sitting at the table in the boardroom with a big smile on his face with Polly, Tina and Valerie. The Norwich City team had come in early for photos and interviews. The press had been all over it, TV, radio, the newspapers.

It had helped that Norwich's new £33m star striker had been there. James had taken more than a passing interest in the man everyone seemed to want to have a few words with... *'He's got nice legs,'* he had whispered to Polly as he walked by, with cameras flashing, while a journalist from the local radio station held a microphone inches from the player's mouth.

'I don't think that could have gone much better,' said Andy.

'I have to congratulate you Pol, you're a star. That went smooth as clockwork. And how on earth did you get the BBC here? I mean I know Norwich City are important to the area, but it takes a lot to get the Beeb anywhere, I always thought.'

'It depends what you tell them.' Polly gave Andy a sly smile. 'If you tell them all the press are coming, including ITV and Sky, then you know the Beeb will come, they can't afford to miss out on a gig like that.'

'But Sky weren't coming I thought you said.' Andy frowned.

'Oh, yeah, so they weren't. Damn my little white lies.' Polly winked at Andy then nudged Tina.

'Anyhow, the guy from the Beeb was really nice, I think he was glad he came. And he stuffed about three croissants.'

'Well, thanks again Pol. Thank you everyone.' Andy looked so delighted that just for a second Polly thought he was going to lean across the table and give her a peck on the cheek.

'Who was the player with the dreadlocks? I've seen him before somewhere and I don't mean on the football pitch because I never go to football.' Tina's question received blank looks from both Polly and Andy. It was James who answered, having caught the end of the question as he entered the boardroom.

'He's in that pop group, BombBastic EIC. I've got all their records and now I've got his autograph because I asked for it in the car park. Did you see his thigh muscles? Like tree trunks. My David will never believe it when I show him the photos of him getting into his car.'

'What are you talking about?' Polly said. 'He's not in a pop band, he's a footballer. They were all footballers.'

James looked crestfallen. 'I only saw him in the car park when he left. Oh, how embarrassing, I asked him for an autograph and told him I had all his downloads. No wonder he gave me a funny look, I feel a plum.'

Andy shook his head. 'James, I despair.'

Kevin joined them in the boardroom. 'Have that wet set of lettuces gone, yet? Pity they didn't come into the gym, I had a couple of two pound dumb bells ready for them. Don't reckon they would have managed much more, most of them looked right twigs.'

Polly refused to take the bait, but instead stood up to go out of the room just as her phone went off. It was a text, from an unknown caller.

Oh shit.

'You must ask him now Polly sweet. Tom's a naughty boy not telling you. Secrets, dirty secrets.'

Her stomach knotted. Why the hell hadn't Tom got her number changed? How long did it take to change a bloody phone number? Then she remembered. Tom had told her to call Mike Gremshall that morning, she had been so busy she had forgotten.

She went out of the door and through reception, before sitting on a bench outside. She looked again at the text, what the hell did all this mean? *'Secrets, dirty secrets.'* If whoever was sending these texts was trying to live rent free in her head, they were succeeding.

She texted Tom. *'Call me ASAP.'*

She didn't bother with any kisses.

Tom wasn't especially talkative. Emily thought about asking why, but decided against it. She went upstairs and saw Jill making coffee in the staff room.

'Hi, Jill.' Emily had a smile on her face. For someone who often went to bed late, she was still an early riser and a good morning person.

'Come here,' Jill said, flicking her head towards her and looking over Emily's shoulder. 'Listen, I don't know what the matter is with Tom this morning, just to say he is not in a good mood.'

'Really. Why?'

'I don't know, but if I was you I'd play things a bit cool this morning. I'd keep the wisecracks down and don't go moaning about the music he puts on, if he puts on any at all. He's been over to see Mike at the phone tech shop twice already and he grunted something to me about why we only have four appointments this morning, as if that's my fault.' Jill handed her a coffee, just as Tom went past the door.

'Ah, Emily, you're in. Good, can you prep stuff for Mr Lightwater, he's having a filling and will be in at 9.15am, he's our first appointment for some reason. Has anyone cancelled, Jill or are we just starting later now on a Wednesday?'

Jill had to bite her tongue.

'I told you, no-one has cancelled, I can't force people to come to the surgery.'

'No, you can't force people to come, you're right, but filling up bookings is useful for revenue don't you think? It secures jobs.' And with that Tom strode back upstairs and into his surgery.

Jill looked at Emily, who shrugged her shoulders. They exchanged glances as much as to say, *'what was that all about?'* Jill went downstairs to reception, Emily followed Tom up the stairs and into the surgery.

You could cut the tension with a knife that morning. It was nothing Emily had experienced before in all the time she had been working with Tom. He didn't put any music on, he snapped her head off for not refilling one of the mouth washes, and when Mr Lightwater wanted to exchange pleasantries about how he thought

Arsenal would get on for the rest of the season. Tom batted him away with hardly a word.

It was just after 12.30pm when Sheila Gregg left the surgery after a brush and polish that set her back £60. Tom was washing his hands when his phone bleeped, he went over and read the text. *'Call me Tom… Karen'.* He also had a text from Polly. That would have to wait.

'I'm just popping out for a moment Emily, I won't be long. We haven't got anyone until 1.30pm, be back by then, won't you?'

She nodded as Tom left. He walked into the car park at the back of surgery, stood by his car and made the call.

'Don't push me, Karen.' Tom's voice was threatening.

'You're not just going to walk into my life and try and fuck me over just like this. If this is all true, have you any idea what this is going to do to my life? Any idea?'

'Don't give me that.' Karen wasn't going to be intimidated.

'I knew you'd wake up this morning and try to convince yourself it was all a horrible dream. Well, it's not, I'm still here and Lee is still here. And you and I are going to get those DNA tests done. Because if you don't. Well, if you don't, you'll wish you had. That's all I'll say.'

'Don't threaten me.' Tom was aware the car park wasn't the best place for a private conversation. Perhaps he should have chosen somewhere else to speak, too late now.

'I'll get the test done in my own good time, when I'm ready. Do you understand?'

'Oh, I understand. I understand just fine. You have a week to organise a trip with me to get it done. You see, I've already had mine and Lee's DNA recorded, we're just waiting for you now. One week Tom, one week.' The phone went dead.

He tried to redial Karen's number, but she had already turned her phone off.

'Fuck!' He banged the roof of his Audi.

He put his hands on his hips and took a deep breath. What the hell was he going to do if this nightmare proved to be true? The only way was a DNA test whether he liked it or not.

As he began heading back into the surgery his phone went

off again, this time it was Polly. Shit, he hadn't got back to her. Hopefully her morning had gone well. But when she began talking, his mood darkened even more.

Emily smiled to herself and closed the staff room window that overlooked the car park.

She'd heard more than enough.

FORTY SIX

JIMMY Alban was a smart cookie and he knew what he was doing was dumb.

You didn't get into CID by being a bit behind the times or slow on the uptake. And you certainly didn't get into CID by not knowing what protocol was. This was *not* protocol. *So why are you doing it Jimmy?* That thought whirled through his mind as he opened one of the large metal drawers containing the information on the Stuart Archer case.

Jimmy had blagged his way into the vaults on the ground floor of the Merseyside Force's HQ in Liverpool. It wasn't difficult to convince Sergeant McManus he was just looking for one of his previous cases. McManus was a kindly man, nearing retirement, he had a massive set of keys hanging from his waist and he valued his job, he was happy to let Jimmy in for a short while; 'no more than 30 minutes'. McManus left him to it.

Fifteen minutes in and Jimmy was starting to panic, even the plastic gloves he was wearing were starting to sweat on him. At least the CCTV wasn't working, or it wasn't last time he was down there.

He knew he only had one shot at finding the Archer file, there was no way he could blag his way in again without questions being asked. He was still only a kid in police terms, his presence in the vault wasn't viewed as suspicious by McManus. A second request however, would likely be.

Then he spotted it.

Archer, Stuart, November 2018. He had found it. But it was a thick file and Jimmy was running out of time, he flicked through the opening sheets of paper as quick as he could. Most of it was routine stuff, the real evidence and what he was looking for would be further back. He looked at his watch, he had 12 minutes.

As he flicked frantically through the masses of paper he was confident he knew the name he was looking for, yet he had to be sure. No guess work, this was all highly irregular, but it was too late now, he was in. Then he saw it... High Classified — CRAIG BALDINI.

He gobbled up as much information as he could where Baldini was mentioned, a total of about five pages. Someone had highlighted Baldini's name throughout, so it was easy to capture the snippets. Baldini was the name he had suspected and had heard mentioned in the few private briefings he had attended.

He read the name again and re-read some of the pages for a third time, it was all there. Baldini had been targeted by CID after footage of him emerged carrying drug packages from a van into a house in Birkenhead. He was arrested but never charged because he turned informant. *What a cad.*

He looked at his watch, McManus would be back in a couple of minutes. It would look better if Jimmy was outside the vault and waiting for him to return, he knew McManus would frisk him.

McManus came round the corner.

'You done then lad?' he said, swinging his huge set of keys from side to side.

'Yep, thanks Sarj.' Jimmy hoped he looked calm. 'I didn't find it, but no problem. It wasn't anything that important, it would have just been nice to check on something, thanks again.'

McManus patted Jimmy up and down just in case he had tried to sneak off with something. 'You know I have to do this,' he smiled.

As Jimmy walked off, McManus stuck his head in the vaults and went to turn the lights off but noticed one of the file drawers was still open a fraction. McManus was always meticulous in making sure every file was closed tight, he shook his head, walked in and went to close the file. He noticed it was the Archer case drawer that had been left slightly ajar, he closed it and locked up.

That lunchtime, Jimmy went into Liverpool and sat inside

Greggs he picked up his phone and made the call.

'It's Craig Baldini,' he said to Dan Swan. 'Okay, that's it Dan. No more on this, I'm shitting myself a bit to be honest. I didn't like doing that one little bit, just hope I've raised no suspicions, I'm fucked if I have.'

'You'll be fine pal, little bits of info like this are often exchanged, you're in CID now, remember?'

'Maybe. But this Baldini guy was a snitch on a very big case with very undesirable people. You know, and I know, some arsehole is going to get hold of his name and that puts Baldini in huge danger. What are we playing at here?'

'Jimmy, forget it, it's done. Go and get a thick shake from McDonalds, speak soon.' Dan ended the call.

It didn't take long for Billy Wade and then Tony Statton to find out who the snitch was. Swan called in immediately. All communication was done over the phone, it had been up to each man to remember the name and pass it on.

'Thanks Billy,' Statton said. 'I'll pop 5K in your account if you tell me your bank details, I've got a pen and paper here.'

'No thanks Tony.' Billy was sitting outside a petrol station in Peterborough when he had called Statton. 'I'm just passing you on the name from my man in Liverpool, I've decided I don't want anything for it and don't take this the wrong way but I don't want to hear from you again, ever. You understand, my friend?'

'I do mate.' What Statton had asked Billy to do had been bang out of order, especially as they hadn't spoken for so long, but Billy had come through. 'Look, enjoy life and thanks mate. You know I appreciate it,' Statton finished the call.

Billy sat in his car, turned his phone off and went to fill up with petrol. He would drive to a secluded spot he knew, smash his phone into pieces and throw them bit by bit into the large lake nearby.

He should have done it years ago.

FORTY SEVEN

'TOM'S a naughty boy not telling you'. What the hell does that mean?

Polly's words were ringing in Tom's ears as he drove home from the surgery. He had told her he couldn't talk when he had called her back in the car park, they would talk when he got home. Polly had told him about the text. At least putting their conversation off in the car park, had bought him some time.

The traffic was light as he drove home along the city ring road. He was feeling anxious as he walked into the house, it was no good hiding anything, not from Polly. The longer he hid it the worse it would get. Lies upon lies upon half-truths.

Tom put his briefcase down in the hall, Polly was sitting in the garden. He forced a smile as he went to greet her.

'Hi, love.'

She looked up saying nothing, he could tell she had been crying. There was a cup of tea on the floor, next to the hammock she was sitting in. Polly's tears had smudged mascara on her cheek and her hair was all over the place.

Tom sat down alongside her, he hated seeing her like this. She was usually so effervescent, so much fun and now he knew what he was going to tell her was going to cut deep.

'So, go on then, *'Tom's a naughty boy not telling you. Dirty secrets'*, the text said.' Polly turned to face him.

'You didn't want to discuss it earlier, well we are going to now because I'm getting really pissed off with all this, Tom. And don't keep telling me this is a crackpot who has my number, talk to me. What's going on?'

He looked at her and took her hands. He gazed into her eyes, his face sombre.

'I do have something to tell you.'

She pulled her hands away and stared at him. Her eyes were wide, she started to cry uncontrollably, holding her hands in her face.

'Oh no Tom, oh no,' she pleaded through the tears. 'Please, no.' The tears began to flow. 'Don't leave me, don't do this.'

'Listen, Pol. Listen.' He was trying desperately to calm her down and get a word in. 'It's not what you think, it's not about us as a couple. I love you, I love you desperately. Please just listen.'

His voice calmed her down long enough for him to begin to tell of Karen's appearance in the surgery. He told of their meeting in the park and of the accusation he was her son's dad. He admitted he knew Karen and yes she had been a holiday fling, he watched Polly's face, but it didn't change, although the tears had stopped.

He decided not to tell her about the pair of them having already met Lee at the rugby. She had more than enough to cope with.

'So, I'm going to have the DNA test to get this sorted once and for all. If the test proves negative, which I'm sure it will, she can get lost and we can get on with our lives. It's you I love.'

Polly had remained silent while Tom had been talking. He went to hold her hands again but she had shrugged them away. Her emotions were all over the place.

'So, you have a son? It's this Karen woman who has been sending me the texts, calling the home and hanging up. All along it has been some bird you shagged on holiday. Her *'dirty little secret'*. And now she wants you to know about her son, your son, after all these years, the fucking bitch.'

She shook her head and went to stand up. Tom went to say something, but Polly was having none of it.

'No, Tom. Shut up, I'm talking now. I've listened to you and your sordid little slag's secret. Now you listen to me because if you don't...'

'Oh, come on Pol, that's unfair,' Tom jumped in. 'I had no idea about this, it was before I met you. If I had an inkling, I would have done something, said something and got something sorted.

She's kept this secret for years, you can see that, and now she's popped up out of the woodwork and chucked it at me.'

He stretched out his hands to hold her, she pushed him away and then stood up, as the tears flowed again.

'Fuck you Tom. Who the hell are you to say to me, it's unfair. You have just walked into this house, sat down and told me, *'oh by the way I probably have a child with someone else'*. Think how that makes me feel after seven years of fucking marriage. Someone from the past who has suddenly 'popped out of the woodwork', according to you, and you expect me to understand because it was before I met you. You don't even know if this kid is yours and all the time this slag has been hassling me with texts and calls. I'll fucking kill her.

'You are clueless to my thoughts. You have no idea how much those texts and calls have been hurting me. Now I have to deal with the thought you may have a son you didn't even know about. We didn't know about, how am I, how are we, supposed to live with that, if it's true? What next? Is this woman who's been taunting me going to be dropping him off outside our house for you to go and play happy fathers? Because if you think that's going to happen, you are wrong, I'm not sure I will be able to handle it if you are the father. I don't know what I feel right now to be honest, I'm just numb.'

'No, come on, please,' Tom pleaded. 'I understand, I truly understand. This is killing me as well. I don't want to be this kid's dad, I love you. You are all I want. Please, you have to believe me. I'm as upset as you and I haven't known what to say, or when to say it.'

Polly wiped away her tears. She felt drained, mentally and physically. Tom again tried to hold her.

'Go away, I don't want you near me, just, go away.'

Polly brushed past him and went indoors. She went upstairs and sat on the bed, looked at herself in the mirror and went into the bathroom to wash her face. After coming out, she sat and thought, and then picked up her phone.

'Hi, my darling, how are you my little hun,' Jody was locking up at her shop when her phone had gone off.

'Hi Jode. You okay?'

'Yes Pol, I'm fine, what's wrong? You sound very quiet.'

'I'm not okay. Can I come up and stay with you for a couple of days, I'll call you on the way up in the car? I'm coming tonight.'

'Polly love, what on earth is wrong? Of course you can come up. Oh hell Pol, what has happened? Speak to me.'

'I'll tell you on the way up in the car. I'm going to pack a few things now and get going as soon as I can, I'll speak soon.' She finished the call.

Polly got out her small travelling case that she kept in her wardrobe and started to pack a couple of changes of clothes, as well as toiletries and a few other essentials. She hadn't noticed Tom come into the bedroom, he stood at the door.

'What are you doing?' He looked at the case on the bed. 'Where are you going?'

She continued to pack and talk at the same time. 'I'm going to Jody's for a few days and don't even think of trying to stop me.'

'No, don't, no please. Stay with me, I need you here with me. Please.'

She looked at him and stopped what she was doing. 'Don't worry, you call your little tart up for a chat. She has your future in her hands, talk to her, and tell her what you are going to do about all this. Tell her what you will do if that kid is yours, you don't need me around. And you can tell her that I now know it's her who is sending the texts, so she had better stop, her work is done, I'm going now and you're not going to stop me.'

She clicked the case shut and barged past him. He knew it was useless trying to stop her, once she had made up her mind she rarely went back on it. He felt utterly deflated, utterly sick. He followed her down the stairs and stopped her in the kitchen as she picked up her keys, he grabbed her arm as she went to walk past him once more.

'Please don't go, you're my life, I love you.' Tom felt the tears well up in his eyes.

Polly looked at him. Her eyes were harder now. She had gone past the hurt and upset stage and now she was angry. She was angry at the mug she felt she had been made to feel, angry her husband had brought this into their lives.

'Let me go.' Her voice was cold and calm. 'I'm going, don't try to call me.' And with that she walked out of the door and put her case in the boot of her car, started the car up and drove out of the driveway.

He watched her go as tears fell down his face.

Tom closed the front door and walked back into the house. He went to the fridge and opened a beer and sat in the garden, put his head in his hands and began to cry.

The house was already so empty without her.

FORTY EIGHT

IT was only 20 minutes into her journey when Polly called Jody. The phone only rang once.

'Hi,' Polly said in a quiet voice.

'Polly, love, what's happened?' Jody had been holding onto her phone waiting for the call.

'Are you okay? You're not are you?'

Polly re-laid the conversation she had with Tom. A couple of times she began to feel herself well up, especially when she told Jody about the texts and of course the damning news that Tom may have a son. Jody listened in silence.

'I told you something was wrong a couple of days ago, when he kept seeming distracted,' Polly said, her eyes concentrating on the road.

'If that child is his, what am I going to do, Jode? Because I don't know if I will be able to handle it. That's what's worrying me more than anything, and I can't stop thinking about that little bitch, her knowing all the time she was going to come and do this to us. I want to confront her, but I also want to be as far away from her as possible.

'Oh, Jode, this is so unlike me, I'm usually so in control, so happy with life. This is just a total bombshell and I'm not coping with it very well.' Polly's voice started to break.

The traffic was heavy as she left Norfolk and headed onto the A14. It was 6pm, commuters were leaving off for the day and heading home. It wasn't a great time to be on the road, but Polly knew traffic would get lighter the closer she got to Chester, which the sat nav said would be 10.44pm.

Jody's response caught Polly by surprise.

'Darling, listen to me. And please don't cry. I'll tell you what I think. You know I love you to bits so please listen to me.

'Why are you running away, darling? Why are you leaving the man in your life you truly love? Why are you letting this woman, who may not even be telling the truth, come between you and Tom?'

Polly began to say something, but Jody wouldn't let her. 'No, listen a minute, please.'

'You and I, and no doubt even Tom, don't know anything about this woman's motives and only he knows anything about her at all. So, he met her on holiday, a holiday fling, before you came along. How many holiday flings did you have? And think of the fun we had in Brighton with the parties, all before you met Tom and I met Craig. That was our life then. But it all changed when we met our men and now you're running away from yours. I know not forever and I know you're hurting. You're hurting so much because you think your wonderful life with Tom is about to change, but you don't know that.

'And what about Tom? Did he ask for this? Don't tell me he was waving you off as you drove away, I bet he is in a terrible state. Perhaps this isn't what you want to hear my darling, perhaps you want me to tell you what a bastard your husband is and he had this all planned, but he didn't. Sorry, if I've hurt you with what I'm saying, but I think more of you than anyone in the world, including Craig, and I love him. Well just!' Jody feigned a small laugh.

'Pol, don't come up here. Of course you can if you want, but turn around, go home and hug Tom. Or, if you want some space, pull into a hotel and have a few drinks, stay a couple of nights, collect your thoughts. Give Tom a ring when you are there, see how you feel in the morning. If you want to keep driving, you keep driving darling, there's always a welcome for you here.'

Polly hadn't expected that from Jody.

Instead of lambasting Tom and Karen, her friend was telling her to go home and hug her husband. Polly was silent for a while.

'Pol. You still there?'

'I'm here. I'm here.' Polly was taking in what Jody had said. 'You are right, Tom didn't ask for this. And you are right, he may not be the dad. I just feel so upset. Our relationship is so strong and this seems to have, I don't know, punched a hole right through it. If he does have a son, how will we cope with that? How will it affect us? Will we still be the same couple? Will I want to stay with him? I'm so scared, Jode.

'I don't know if I can go home right now to be honest, but I suppose I could pull over and stay at a Premier or something. I seriously need a bit of space. What would you do?'

'It's up to you darling.' Jody was relieved Pol was listening to her. 'Look, if there is somewhere you could stay tonight, then why not pull over and get a room. Find somewhere, have something to eat, a couple of drinks, relax. You don't want to keep driving all this way tonight.'

'No, you're right. I won't come to Chester tonight, but I do want some time on my own, I'm not just going back home, I need to clear my head. I know Tom didn't ask for this. It's not as if he's had an affair or anything. I suppose I just feel I've had the piss taken out of me and those texts were doing my head in.'

'I never knew about them, you should have told me,' Jody sounded surprised.

'I know, but I just thought they would go away. But they haven't and that's why I hate this woman so much, and I don't even know her. Not only is she trying to ruin me and Tom's relationship, she is trying to get at me. Perhaps she wants us to split, maybe she wants Tom. I never thought of that.'

'Don't even go there.' Jody was dismissive.

'What was it you said Tom said to you about loving you and this was nothing to do with you as a couple? He doesn't want her, he loves you. You can see it in his eyes all the time, don't doubt him. And call him up tonight, don't leave him in limbo. I know you are hurting, but you are a wonderful couple. You will get through this, unless of course you don't want to.'

'No, no, that's not what I want, I want to get through this. You know how much I love him, I'm just so unsure of so much. You understand that, don't you?'

'Yes, of course I do, I totally understand. So, there you go. You want Tom, that's all that counts.'

There was a short silence before Polly spoke. 'But I think you're right, I'll stay somewhere tonight. I might even stay for a couple of nights. I'm only 20 minutes from Cambridge, there are plenty of places to stay round there. I'll call you later.'

'And call Tom.'

'I will Jode. Thanks. Love you.'

'Love you as well darling. You'll get through this just fine, you are one mighty strong couple.'

'No, you're right. Speak soon.' Polly ended the call.

Polly had stayed in plenty of hotels, if not with Tom, often while away at conferences and training courses for the gym business. She knew of some of the best ones to stay, and one of them was just outside Peterborough. It was just 15 minutes away, she pulled into the car park and walked into reception, carrying her case.

It was 6.55pm and the girl behind the counter had a broad smile. Polly put her case down. 'I don't suppose you have a room available for a couple of nights?'

'Yes, madam, we have, a single is it?' the receptionist replied.

'Yes please. And can I book breakfasts as well? What time are you serving food until tonight?'

'We are serving until 9 and I'll book breakfast for two mornings. That's a total of £135, including the breakfasts.'

She paid on her debit card, thanked the girl and took her key to room 107. It was on the ground floor of the three-story building. She had stayed in enough rooms of this hotel chain to know what to expect when she walked in and, as per usual, it was clean and tidy, with a lovely big bed.

She put her case down and went into the bathroom, looked in the mirror and tried to force a smile. Her face was a bit of mess. What on earth had the girl on reception thought?

She went to lay on the bed, but decided against it, just in case she fell asleep and woke up after 9. That would mean no dinner and although she wasn't that hungry now, she knew she would be later on. Instead, she had a shower, freshened up and gathered up her latest *Sophie Kinsella* book — one of her favourite authors. She would eat dinner and read in the bar, for now she would leave her phone in the room.

The dining area was compact and Polly found herself a table in the corner that seated two. There were a few people eating, a couple of families, but mostly couples. There were three lads sitting at the bar enjoying a joke.

The menu was decent, not cheap, but not expensive. Polly went to the bar and ordered the Hunter's Chicken and got herself a large gin and tonic, then noticed the three lads look at her and smile. The one on the end gave her a wink. She smiled to herself.

Sitting back at her table she began reading her book, rather aptly named, *'My Not So Perfect Life'*, taking the odd sip of her drink. It wasn't long before her dinner arrived and she was surprised how hungry she was, the shower had released a bit of tension in her body.

Putting the book down to eat, she thought of what Tom had said. She knew it wasn't his fault this woman had appeared in his life, she knew he loved her. But what if the child was his?

She went back to the bar after finishing her meal and ordered another G&T. The lad who had winked at her smiled this time, Polly smiled back.

'I'll get that,' he said. 'I'll get that drink.'

He could have been no more than mid to late-20s but he had a handsome smile. He had fair hair with an Alice Band in it, he was tanned, really quite good-looking.

'Um, no, that's okay. I'm fine, thanks anyhow.' Polly smiled.

He shrugged his shoulders and smiled. 'Okay, no problem.'

She went and sat down, feeling slightly flattered by the offer. Not that it was a new experience for Polly. Men had always been falling over themselves to get to know her. What a wild and exciting single life she had led, there had been plenty of men but few steady dates. Not that she was a one-night stand girl, apart from the few on her summer holidays.

Yet, when it had come to serious relationships before Tom, Polly's longest ever had been just six months, with a guy named Brendan when she lived in Brighton. He was so cool, laid back, a bit of a drifter and that was his attraction. He had asked her to go travelling with him for a year, maybe two and it had been tempting, but in the end her work came first. She'd already done a bit of travelling after university and Brendan, for all his good points, didn't appear the most reliable.

She carried on reading before finishing her drink. Getting up to leave, Polly walked by the lads at the bar who were still drinking and making a bit more noise than they had been when she had first arrived. As she went past, the one who had offered to buy her a drink got off his bar stool and walked over.

'Hi again', he said. 'And held out his hand as if to shake hers. As Polly held out hers he wedged a piece of paper into her palm and closed it, he smiled, winked and went back to his mates. She turned and walked off, not looking at the piece of paper until she was out of view of them. She half-guessed what was written on it, she'd been here before. On unfolding the crumpled note, it read.

'No ties, room 232'.

She smiled to herself. As if she didn't know she still had it!

She kept smiling as she slipped in the key card and walked into her room, throwing the piece of paper in the bin. Sitting on the bed feeling relaxed she looked at her phone. Tom had called three times.

He picked her call up after one ring.

'Darling, where are you? I've called you loads of times, are you travelling still?'

'I'm not going to Jody's. I've called her and we've had a chat, I'm staying over in a Premier near Peterborough for a couple of nights, I need a little space, I'm fine. I've had a drink and something to eat and I'm going to bed.'

'Where are you babe? I will come and join you, please?'

'No. Please leave me. I want to be on my own. But I'll be back on Friday, okay? I'm going to do a bit of shopping in Cambridge.'

'I love you so much, I'm so sorry for all this.' Tom was standing in the kitchen with another beer in his hand. His idea to go and meet her would have been an expensive one, he would have had to get a taxi as he'd been drinking.

'I love you to, you're my world. I'm turning my phone off now.'

'Love you, so look forward to seeing you.' Polly didn't reply. She ended the call before texting Jody.

'I'm staying in Peterborough for a couple of nights. Thanks for the idea, it's a good one. I'm feeling a bit better tbh and I've just had a quick

chat with Tom. Speak soon. xxxxx'

Polly sent the text to her friend, before she went to turn her phone off and settle in for an early night. She sent one final text, this time to Tom.

'I just need space. But always yours..... xxxx'

FORTY NINE

TONY Statton read the name. He was pleased with his work.

Well, not so much his work, but those in the chain who had made it happen, Archer would be pleased as well. His pal in Strangeways had his suspicions about it being Baldini, but suspicions were all they were. Now he had confirmation.

But what to do next?

Statton had already been thinking about how to spend the 25K put into his bank account the day after he left Archer, his pal had a good 'financial' network outside prison. Another 25K was awaiting when he delivered Baldini's name. After that, he would make sure he was out of all this.

But he had a dilemma. Was it best to go up and see Archer again? He didn't want to send another cryptic letter, face to face was the best option once more. There was no way Archer needed Baldini's name written down on a piece of paper, he would never forget it. Anyhow, he quite enjoyed a couple of days in Manchester, the nightlife was always decent and there were plenty of good hotels and bars.

'Alice, I might have to go back up to Manchester again this weekend,' he shouted to his wife, who was outside hanging up the washing. 'I'll probably go up on Saturday, stay Saturday night, come home Sunday, if that's okay?

'Do we have anything on? If so, I can go another time, it's just that this guy is available for a chat this weekend. A bit of business and a bit short notice to be honest, so I can always fob him off.'

Statton was a superb liar, years of experience. The last thing he wanted was for his wife to start asking questions. He hoped his reverse psychology would work. Alice pinned the final piece of clothing on the line and walked in, this was the second time in two weeks her husband had to go to Manchester.

'Why do you need to go again? And at a weekend? What sort of business? I thought you just delivered things. I don't mind, we have nothing on, it just seems a bit unusual.'

Alice was a smart lass and while she trusted her husband, she could sniff something not quite as it should.

'Look it doesn't matter, I'll call the guy and let him know I'll come another time, I can rearrange.' His tone was convincing.

'No, it's alright, you go, I can do a bit of shopping with Jenny. I'll call her up.'

He smiled, walked over and gave her a kiss on the cheek. 'Are you sure?'

She smiled back. He felt a tad of guilt. His wife, who he loved dearly, had no idea what he was up to. But he had decided that when this was done, this was going to be it, and he would tell Archer just that.

So now he had the 'green light', he was soon on the phone. He made a call to book a prison visit and also book into that nice hotel he stayed in last time. Perhaps Baldini and his friends would be in the Maple Leaf on Saturday? Another chance to take a closer look at the man who set his pal up, and that good looking bird with the ferocious punch.

Statton looked in the mirror and combed his hair. He didn't know Baldini, but he hated snakes in the grass, sneaks, snitches were the lowest of the low in the criminal world.

He smiled to himself and called out to the kitchen... 'Come on Drake, let's go for a walk'.

A black and white border collie came into the living room with its lead already in its mouth. 'Good boy Drake.'

A bit of fresh air would do them both good.

FIFTY

POLLY lay in bed until 9am the next morning. She had enjoyed a great night's sleep.

She got up and took a shower before finding a change of clothes and heading out of her room. She turned on her phone, she had three texts. One from Tom wishing her good night, 11 hours ago, one from Andy telling him to give her a call. She had text Andy when she had arrived at the hotel last night to say she wasn't feeling great.

And she had a third text. She just looked at it, hardly daring to belief her eyes. *'So, now you know how it feels bitch'*. The number unknown, it had been sent this morning.

Polly deleted it, her mood had changed, no more tears. Yes, she was angry, but no way was this woman going to get the better of her. She knew where these texts were coming from now, there was nothing to fear. There was no psychopath out there stalking her, it was Karen who was getting at her and Karen was trying to wade into her and Tom's life and pull it apart, she wasn't going to let it happen. *'She won't beat me'*.

As she walked into the breakfast room, Polly almost felt a surge of strength. That text, that arrogant, ignorant text. Now she knew so much more, she knew what this was all about and she decided there and then, she was going to stand by her husband.

But first she was going to have a day or two in Cambridge and stay another night at the hotel, it would give her time to think things over.

As she entered the restaurant, the three lads from the night before who had been drinking at the bar were seated at one of the many tables, she decided to take a seat a good distance away. Getting up to get some orange juice, she felt someone saddle up alongside her. It was the lad who had given her his room number.

'You didn't take up my request,' he smiled. Oh yes, he was a looker, but at least he wasn't threatening, far from it. He was softly spoken and very tall, and very full of himself.

Polly turned to look at him, got close to his ear and whispered. 'I have a full glass of orange juice in my hand and I really couldn't give a toss to throw it in your face right now. You act cool and you seem a decent guy, but you would look a right dick standing here with orange juice all over your pretty face, because I would do it. Trust me, it wouldn't be the first time.'

Polly put a finger to her lips as he went to say something. 'Shhh! No, I didn't take up your offer because you would not have been able to handle the things I would have done to you last night in a bed.' She faked a smile. 'And before you splutter a word, I'm serious about this juice, so just go back to your little friends. You might also want to check something else out, your flies are undone dickhead. Nice speaking to you.'

The lad looked down at his trousers. Shit, she was right, he shook his head, smiled and went to say something, but Polly was halfway back to her table as a waitress came over to her to take her order. Polly went for the full English, minus hash browns.

The breakfast was decent and Polly ate it all, bar the hash browns, which had still appeared. She got up to get another juice and coffee and looked at her phone. Should she call Tom? No, she thought, she'd leave it today. She'd told him she would be home tomorrow, that's all he needed to know.

She sat back down with her drinks, her phone went off. It was Jody.

'Hello my little doll, how are you?' Jody's voice was low key and full of concern.

'Hi darling. I'm okay, thanks, just enjoying a good breakfast to be honest. Didn't get up until past 9, slept like a log, I think I needed it.'

Jody was buoyed by Polly's cheery voice. 'So, you're okay? You're not coming up here are you?'

'No, I'll go back home tomorrow, I've booked a couple of days stay here, do a bit of shopping in Cambridge, perhaps make that two days shopping, a bit of retail therapy.' Polly looked up at the three boys who were getting up from the table. The one who she had spoken to at the juice machine looked across, shook his head gently and gave her a wry smile and little wave, she smiled back and went back to her call.

'I've made a decision Jode, I've decided that whatever happens, I'm sticking by Tom. I'm going to be there for him, even if this child is his. I got another text from that cow this morning, calling me a bitch. My time will come.'

'You got a text saying what? She's got some nerve. Jesus, you're so strong, I really so admire you. Once you get it into your head what you are going to do, there's no going back. Well, apart from not coming up to see me last night. But I'll let you off for that, I had us some shopping lined up as well.'

'That would have been nice, Jode. Smash those credit cards again.' The girls laughed.

'So, I'm going back tomorrow and we'll chat over the weekend,' Polly said, as Jody listened, tidying up some stock in her shop, which was lying by the front of her desk. 'And we'll see what's next.'

'Okay, darling, I'm glad you are okay and sounding so much better. I've got to go, four customers have just walked in, I can't remember putting the word SALE up outside. I better go and check.'

'See ya.' Polly hung up, smiling.

She got up from the table and walked back to the room. She got her things together and went out past reception. It was a different lady who was behind the desk this morning, but she was as bright and polite as the one the night before.

In the car park, Polly got into her Mercedes, sat and thought. She thought she best call Andy just to let him know all was well and she would be back in on Monday. After that, a trip into Cambridge. There was a John Lewis last time she was there, she remembered it from a visit with Ann and Janie a couple of years back when the three had enjoyed a weekend away. What a weekend that had been. She had never seen Ann so drunk.

After her call to Andy who was concerned for her, as he had never known her to be ill, she started the car up and headed towards the city centre.

A night away had already cleared her head.

Karen Harding wasn't going to get the better of her. She was Tom's wife and she was proud to be so, they needed each other more now than ever.

'For better or for worse'....

Tom wasn't hungry, he hadn't slept well for a few nights now.

He had tried to call Polly all day Thursday but without luck. It had upset him and there had been more tears back on his own at home. He was a sensitive man and was never afraid to show his true feelings. Polly had always said that is what made him the man he was, the fact he could laugh and cry in equal measure.

At least she would be back today, they could talk more. It was the start of the Bank Holiday weekend, he had an extra day off, they would spend it together, take a drive to the countryside or the coast.

He hoped she'd had a good couple of days, they hadn't spoken since Wednesday night. He had thought hard about how this must be playing out in her mind. He had been selfish to only think of himself and how it was affecting him. *'Put the boot on the other foot, Tom'.*

Fortunately, the surgery would be finished by 4pm today, no-one had booked to want their teeth looked at late on Friday afternoon. It didn't bother him, not today. The quicker today went the better, as far as he was concerned, the sooner he could hug her again.

Tom left his house at 7.20am and hadn't been in the car more than 10 minutes when his phone went off. He looked eagerly to see who it was from, hoping it was Polly. It wasn't, it was Craig.

Did he want to talk to his pal right now? He knew Craig would know what was going on, Jody would have made sure of that. Polly and Jody had no doubt talked more. The four of them had few secrets at the best of times.

'Hi pal, how are you?' Tom tried to sound as bright as he could, even though he knew where the conversation would be heading the moment the small talk was out of the way.'

'I'm fine mate, more importantly, how are you?' Craig wasn't a gossip and Tom knew he would have been concerned for him.

'Well, pretty shit to be honest, mate, you no doubt know the story. It's come as a big, big shock, I can't even start to tell you how sick in the stomach I feel. And as for Pol, well can you imagine? She's distraught. She was coming up to see you, but she's coming home tonight now. She's stayed away a couple of nights at some Premier in Peterborough.'

'Look mate, I'm not here to pry. You know me, just to say, I'm here if you want a chat. I've needed you to chat to in recent times, so call if you want, you know where I am. I'm sure it will all work out. Jody did say it wasn't 100% defo about this woman and kid, anyhow.'

'No mate, it's not. Not definitely, but the lad is 14 apparently, or 15. I met this Karen 15 years ago on holiday, the dates stack up. She seems certain, I'll just have to deal with it when I know. I'm prepared that the boy could well be mine.'

'Okay, pal,' said Craig, looking to change the subject. 'I'm going to Man City tomorrow night. Going to give our boys a cheer. We doubled them last season and beat them at home in November, they are almost as rubbish as us at the moment!'

'You enjoy, should be a good game. I would come up but seeing as Pol is on her way home, I don't think it would be a good idea to tell her I'm off to see Arsenal at Man City, don't think she would laugh much.'

Craig laughed out loud. 'Ah yeah, our ninja chick! Good idea. Keep her sweet, unless you want your nose broken. Look mate, keep in touch and all the best. It will work out, I know it will, I'll let you go now, speak soon.'

'Cheers Craig. By the way, you working today?'

'Yep, same shit, different day!'

FIFTY ONE

JIMMY Alban wished he hadn't listened to Dan Swan.

His foray into the vaults to search for the Archer file was about to land him in the biggest heap of shit he had ever been dropped in. His job was on the line and he knew it.

Why had he done it? Fuck knows. He knew all along it was wrong. Now, here he was, sitting in front of Detective Inspectors Peter Harold and Steven Posselwhite, sweat already beginning to bead on his forehead. The question the two DIs wanted answering was simple: What was he doing looking through the Stuart Archer file? A fact they knew based on two things.

1. Jimmy had left the Archer file drawer slightly ajar after finishing. Sergeant McManus had spotted, and reported it.

2. The CCTV that Jimmy thought was not working was very much alive and kicking.

So, now he was going to have to wriggle his way out of a situation all of his own making. He was bang to rights about being there, he had no defence. It was now a case of could he bluff enough?

'Okay, sit down Detective Constable Alban and listen carefully.' DI Harold was going to be lead on this. Both he and DI Posselwhite were in their 50s, both had done 20 years plus in the Force, Jimmy knew them both, but not that well. Neither appeared aggressive in their general demeanour, but both hadn't got to the positions they had at Liverpool without being both talented, and ruthless. This wasn't going to be pleasant.

It was late afternoon and Jimmy had been made aware of the

meeting with the two DI's at lunchtime. He had been told he could have a 'Fed Rep' to listen in, but he just wanted it over. The meeting was being recorded, he felt asking for a rep may make him appear guilty before he even started.

'I'm sure you understand why you are here, DC Alban, but if you don't I'm going to tell you.' Harold took a sip of his coffee. Posselwhite also had a cup of coffee. Jimmy had requested water.

The room they were in was light and airy with a big window at the rear. The two DI's sat at a table alongside each other, while Jimmy sat opposite.

'CCTV picked you up searching in the vaults looking at files,' Harold continued. 'We are aware of this because Sgt McManus said he let you in on the pretence you were looking for something. He couldn't remember exactly what. Is he correct?' Alban nodded. 'Yes, something like that.'

'So, what were you looking for, Jimmy?'

'I was looking for a file on an old case I worked on, but I didn't find it.' He didn't sound convincing and he knew it.

Harold nodded. 'Really? Is that right? I don't think you should have been in there, should you? McManus was wrong to let you in on some flimsy excuse to wade through the files. But you cocked up pal, you left the Stuart Archer file ajar and McManus spotted it, we've checked the CCTV. That was the file you were rummaging through wasn't it? But that wasn't one of your cases. You said you were looking for one of your old cases. Yes, you may be part of CID, but the Archer case wasn't one of *your* cases. We've checked, you were not assigned to it. Correct?'

Jimmy nodded.

DI Posselwhite took up the interrogation. 'The CCTV footage, of which we are happy to show you by the way, shows you didn't take anything, or so it appears. Or look to photograph anything. But you were looking through the Archer case. Why?'

Jimmy wiped his forehead, he was feeling uncomfortable. He knew his police career was about to end right here, right now if he couldn't dig himself out of this.

He wasn't an arse, he was bang to rights and he would go down alone. Bringing Dan Swan into the equation was a 'no-no'. He had to take responsibility for his own actions, he could lie, but what was the point? He was a shit liar, it was over.

'I will be honest with you because, believe it or not, I'm an honest copper,' he began. 'But what I've done is wrong, I know that. I did it for all the right intentions I was trying to be loyal, I felt I owed people who had been good to me, but I've cocked up, big time and I'll take the wrap. I have no excuses, I went to the files to get a name, the name of the guy who was the insider who led us into Archer's gang. And before you ask, I'm not going to tell you who asked me to do it, if I get booted out of the Force, then it's my own fault. But I won't drop others in it, I knew what I was doing.'

Harold and Posselwhite looked at each other. It was a shocking confession, and with little effort from them. What a mess this boy had got himself in, an up-and-coming young copper on the verge of great things and what had he gone and done?

'So, DC Alban. You knew what you were doing you say, you wanted the name of the insider. Why?' Harold took up the conversation again.

'Because someone else wanted it. I didn't. They asked me as a favour to get the name, I got nothing out of it. Look, I've fucked myself over big time here, I can see that. I apologise and I regret ever agreeing to do what I've done, so that's it. You have me on tape, I have no intention of spinning you a web of lies, but neither will I tell you who wanted the name. Because actually, I don't know myself. I do know who asked me for it, but it wasn't them who wanted it in the first place.'

Posselwhite shuffled in his seat. Jimmy was spilling the beans at a rate of knots. Harold stood up and took his coffee with him, he was tall and had short cropped black hair. He, like Posselwhite, was dressed in a white shirt, Harold had his sleeves rolled up.

'You sure you don't want a Fed Rep, Jimmy?'

Jimmy shook his head.

'Okay, so what you are saying is that someone approached you and wanted this name? That's it. Nothing else, nothing at all, no money? Have you given him the name?'

'Yeah, that's it sir. I gave him the name. There was no money in it for me.'

The two DIs looked at each other, staggered. There was only one more question they had, but they already knew the answer, as

Posselwhite spoke.

'And the name in the file that you gave your man was....?'

Jimmy looked blankly ahead. 'Craig Baldini, sir. Craig Baldini.'

Posselwhite and Harold looked at each other and then back at him.

'You know what you've done, don't you?' Harold's arms were folded. 'You do know Baldini was an informer on one of the biggest drug cases this city has seen in decades? He was guaranteed anonymity because he helped us put Archer away, have you any idea what you've done, you idiot?'

The mood in the room changed as Harold raised his voice at the end of his sentence and banged the table with force, as he came up close to Jimmy's face. He continued to shout.

'You have likely put Craig Baldini in immediate and serious danger. A guy who was no more than a fucking drug runner for Archer, a foot soldier, but who was prepared to help us for whatever reason. And we've let him down. You think it's just your head that is going to roll for this do you? This will go to the top Alban, the bloody top, you hear me. You better hope nothing happens to Baldini because I don't know what your part in it might play in a court of law. You understand? You idiot.'

Jimmy sat there, motionless, he had nothing to say. His mouth was dry, he was sweating profusely. What could he say? He knew at this point his career was over.

'You're suspended on full pay for the time being until we know what to do next,' Posselwhite now standing up, picked up the files that were on the table.

'Don't come anywhere near HQ unless we say and certainly don't try to be some sort of hero and track down Baldini. And if you do ever fancy letting us know who got you into this fuck fest, feel free to call. Not that it will help your case much, go on and get out of here.'

He got up and walked out, he bumped into one of the canteen ladies as he walked down the corridor, his mind all over the place.

'Mind out Jimmy.'

'Sorry Martha, didn't see you there. Sorry.'

He walked to the car park and got in his car. As he drove out of the headquarters he felt sick. How would he explain all this to his mum and dad? They had been so proud of him, the day he joined the Police, that day he was promoted to CID.

And now look what he'd done, he'd let everyone down.

'Open wide. I'll have a quick shufty in the gods first.'

Jane Tungate was Tom's last patient of the afternoon and if the truth be told he hoped he would find nothing untoward with her teeth, he was keen to get home.

'Let's take a look downstairs.' A couple of minutes later he was satisfied all was well.

'Well, that all seems good, Jane.'

Jane was a similar age to Tom. Her and husband, Alex, were occasional visitors to the Queen's Head in Melsham. They lived about six miles outside in a village called Alton, but the Queen's Head was a pub they enjoyed eating at. Tom and Polly had seen them in there on the occasional Friday.

'How's Polly?' Jane got out of the chair. 'I went to the gym today where she works and was going to say hello, but someone told me she wasn't well, I hope she's okay.'

'Oh, no she's fine.' Tom was caught a little on the hop. 'Just a bit of a migraine that she couldn't shake off. She was feeling better at lunchtime, might even get her down the pub tonight.'

'What, the Queen's Head?' said Jane. 'We do like that pub, such good food, you are lucky to have such a pub in your village. The closest we have to any pub food in Alton is the fish and chip van that comes round on a Thursday. Chips are bloody awful though. Oh well, love to Polly and I'll catch up with her soon.'

And with that she was off, picking up her handbag on the way out.

It was 3.50pm and Tom followed her down the stairs. He waited for her to make another appointment with Jill and then asked Jill if that was it for the day, which it was.

'So, let's go, then,' said Tom, clapping his hands together. 'I could do with going home, sitting in the garden and having a drink to be honest, Jill, what about you?'

'I don't need a garden to sit in to have a drink,' she replied with a cheeky smile. 'Anywhere for a G&T is good enough for me, especially in bed.'

Tom frowned and then laughed. 'You are getting worse Mrs Jill Jacobs.'

'Um, that's Miss Jill Bramshaw if you don't mind please Mr Armstrong.' She raised her eyebrows. 'Since that pond life Robert has vacated my life, I've resorted to my maiden name, Bramshaw. But don't worry, I haven't changed my sort code or bank account number, so no excuse for my wages not being paid.' She winked at Tom, as she turned her computer off.

Emily had tidied up and came down to see what was going on.

'Are you done upstairs, Em?' Tom said. 'If so, you can go, see you Monday.'

Emily already had her coat in her hands, Jill had told her it could be an early finish after Mrs Tungate had been seen.

'Okay, thanks. Did I hear you say Polly wasn't well?'

He looked at her. 'Um, yes, she hasn't been feeling too good, why do you ask?'

Emily shrugged her shoulders. 'No reason.'

FIFTY TWO

CAMBRIDGE proved a nice release for Polly. She always enjoyed the city, her dad had always hoped she would go to university there.

It was just gone 5pm when she left for the journey home to Melsham. She'd bought a new dress and a hat, as well as a couple of small lamps for the bedroom. She had been looking for months for a classy pair of grey ones.

As she headed along the A14, she turned the music up and thought about Tom. She tried to imagine how he must be feeling. Up to now, perhaps she had only thought of herself, although with good reason. But a couple of nights away had made her think. She knew Tom was just as distraught about this situation as she was, he hadn't asked for Karen to come into his life, she knew he was hurting to.

That last text from '*that woman*' had been the final straw. When she got in tonight Polly would hug Tom so tight.

Her mobile rang as she drove along. It was Tom, should she let it ring off and surprise him when she got in? No, that would be unfair. They hadn't spoken for a couple of days and, anyhow, she wanted to talk to him.

'Hello, Polly Armstrong's secretary.' She grinned to herself as she imagined him looking at his phone smiling at her cheek.

'Polly. Is that you?'

'Of course it's me, who did you think it was?' She sounded great. Tom was so happy to hear her voice.

'Oh, honey, I was just checking to see when you would be back?'

'Why? Have you got the dinner on? If so, I'll be home in 35 minutes, if not, I'm staying another night.' Polly laughed.

It was Tom's turn to laugh, in relief at her mood. The way she had left the house on Wednesday had filled him with worry. Hopefully the break had done her good.

'No, no. You're not spending another night away. You get back here, I want you here with me. Dinner is on, salmon-en-croute, don't you know? And a bottle of Prosecco. And a big kiss.'

'That sounds so good.' She hadn't had much to eat in Cambridge that day, just a small takeaway salad and drink at lunchtime.

'See you soon, then darling, don't forget to warm the plates. Love you.'

'Oh is that it?' He wanted to talk longer, but she was driving, so he understood. Short and sweet. 'Okay, I love you to, don't be long.' He hung up.

Polly continued to stare at the road. She enjoyed driving and often had to take herself to far-flung parts of the country when she went on various marketing courses. She began to sing along to ABBA on the radio, 'Money, Money, Money'. It was a great karaoke song. She smiled to herself as she remembered the night Milky had tried to play this on his guitar during one Open Mic session in the Queen's Head, he was so pissed.

She was winding her way along the Norfolk country roads, looking at the sat nav, not that she needed to, she knew her way home from here. It showed she was 20 minutes from an embrace with hubbie.

It was a pleasant evening, they could have dinner and sit in the garden and talk. She needed to assure him she was with him all the way. They wouldn't go down the pub tonight.

There were plenty more Fridays for that.

Sammy Jenkins' mum was always telling him he drove too fast. At 18 years old he didn't listen. At 18 years old he was invincible, as were his two mates. They could look at their phones, sing music, drink energy drinks from a can and pat driver Sammy on the back as he sped them along roads he, and they, all knew well. Born and bred Norfolk boys. But he was going too fast again, he leant across to pick up a packet of gum that had fallen into the stairwell of the passenger seat. Why didn't he just ask Brad to pick it up? It was a fatal decision. Distracted, by the time he looked up, Sammy had missed the corner, clipped the kerb. His car flew across the opposite side of the road.

All Polly could do was react as quickly as possible. But she had no chance... She screamed.

But no-one heard.

FIFTY THREE

BLUE Watch were coming to the end of their shift.

One of two Norwich-based full-time fire departments, the day shift were just 15 minutes away from clocking off and handing over to their night colleagues. They had enjoyed a quiet day, there had been no 'shouts', so there had been plenty of practical work at the station, making sure the three engines were spick and span.

Station Officer Stuart Betts had been on the phone only ten minutes previous to Janie, discussing what was for tea and deciding what time they would head down the Queen's Head that night. They were still waiting to hear from the babysitter who had said she could 'definitely' come, but didn't know exactly when. Janie was desperate to know how Milky's wedding arrangements were coming along, if nothing else.

The call came through at 6.47pm, 13 minutes before the shifts were about to change. Stuart and his crew flew out of the canteen and straight towards the fire engine. There was no pole at Norwich West. The sirens went on, it was an emergency. James was driving, with Stu sitting alongside, getting more details over the phone about the incident. He listened intently.

'Okay, guys,' Stu shouted to the crew.

'It's an RTA on the B1122 towards Melsham. Police and ambulance are already on scene but people need cutting out, maybe one, maybe two. ETA nine minutes. Soon as we get there, get the cutting gear ready and let's move quickly.'

Stu and his crew travelled in silence towards the crash.

Road traffic accidents were considered by most firefighters to be the worse incidents to attend. You never knew what you were going to find, especially the thought of children involved. The fact they had been called to an RTA usually meant it was bad. They all had families. While no-one spoke, everyone in the engine was hoping it wasn't going to be one of those nights where they would deal with the crash, go home but be unable to sleep. The heart-breaking sights and terrible sounds replaying through their minds.

As they headed up the B1122, just three minutes away they hit traffic.

The country road was stacked up on one side with cars and there wasn't much room for the engine to pass. Cars were forcing themselves up the banks on the side of the road to let the fire engine through. Some people had already pulled over and were out of their vehicles. It was slow going but eventually Stuart and James could see flashing blue lights ahead. He could make out two ambulances and two police cars, they parked behind one of the ambulances. Stu jumped out.

'Afternoon officer, what we got?' Stuart got straight to the point as a constable came over to speak to him as he saw the engine arrive.

'It's a two-car crash,' the young constable said. He had taken a deep breath before speaking and was slightly ashen-faced. Stu guessed he wasn't going to hear good news.

'We have one fatality and three others injured. Looks like one car has come across the road and ploughed into another, it has flipped over the car it hit and rolled into a field. There were three lads in it, one is dead, one is walking wounded and the other is being attended. I think he's unconscious, but he's out of the car.

'Come with me.' Stuart began walking towards the scene with the policeman. 'It's the lady we need help with in the other car,' the constable continued. 'She's trapped, in a bad way. Car is wedged against the hedge. The paramedic won't move her until we can get the roof off. Air ambulance is on the way.'

Stuart continued to walk towards the car and glanced to his left to see the other car on its roof in the field. He looked back in front of him at what looked like a Mercedes. He looked again as he got closer. '*Shit, no*', for a second he had a horrible feeling he recognised the car, every firefighter's nightmare.

As he continued to walk he could see two paramedics working on the driver, he was now just 10 yards away. His chest tightened and his heart began racing. He did know the car, he'd seen it enough times in the village. He'd seen it enough times in Tom's and Polly's driveway. As he got close to the scene and looked between the two paramedics, he saw her, Polly, and she was in a terrible state.

'Oh, shit, no.' The paramedics looked up at him. 'You know this woman?' one of them said.

'Yeah, I know her,' Stuart tried to keep his composure, but it was very difficult for him to talk. He took some breaths. 'Oh, God. How bad is it and what do you want us to do?' Despite his shock, he knew he had to snap back into action.

The paramedic looked at him. 'She's in a very bad way, head injury, goodness knows how bad her right leg is. It's shattered, she's clinging on. So, let's get this roof off and steering wheel if we can. I'm not moving her until then. Let's get going and as soon as the air ambulance lands, I want her out of here and off.'

Stuart ran back to the engine and began organising his crew straightaway. He looked like he'd seen a ghost.

'You okay, mate,' James said. 'Is it a bad one?'

'Yep, and I know her. Now let's get the fuck moving. Please.'

James looked at him, they had worked together for 15 years but he hadn't seen his friend like this before. 'Come on guys, get the cutting equipment and let's get moving. NOW,' James shouted.

One of the paramedics moved aside as Stuart, James and the crew got to work. All the time Stuart tried hard not to look closely at Polly. She was covered in blood, had an oxygen mask on, such a beautiful girl, now look at her, battered and bloodied, her eyes closed, her head slightly tilted, her clothes shredded and damp in blood. Stuart's emotions were all over the place.

But he had to bat away all his thoughts and feelings. He had a job to do and the quicker he could do it, the more chance Polly stood, she was still alive. It took 15 minutes to get the roof off and another five to snap the steering wheel, the air ambulance had landed in the field opposite, dust flying all around. Not that Stuart and his team were distracted or stopped for one second.

'How is she holding up?' Stu looked at the paramedic as they twisted the steering wheel aside to free Polly's chest. Stu was right alongside Polly now. He could barely glance to look at her. *'Come on Pol, hang on in there.'*

'She's as stable as we could expect, you guys are doing a great job.'

A doctor had arrived and he and the paramedics slowly began to move her out of the car, she remained unconscious.

Stu helped move her onto a stretcher, her beautiful smooth legs covered in blood, one of her ankles at the most grotesque of angles, her gorgeous flowing hair matted and bloodied. And her terribly bloodied face. After they lay her down, he walked away and put his hands to his face, he could feel himself welling up.

As a firefighter Stuart had seen many terrible things, but in all his years in the service, he had never had to cut free a close friend from a car. As she was rushed away towards the air ambulance, he went over to the other car in the field to see if any help was required there. But all three occupants from that one were on their way in ambulances, two to hospital and one to the morgue.

Stuart gathered his team near the engine, they would all stay here and help tidy up if the police needed any help. James put his hand on his friend's shoulder.

'Are you alright mate?'

Stuart nodded his head. Firefighters knew not to ask questions at the wrong time, especially in situations like this. While their world back at the station could be banter and fun, on a job all that went out of the window. Stuart would talk in good time.

The young police constable came over to him.

'One of the paramedics said you knew the lady in the car. Have you a name or someone we can contact? We assume it's Polly Armstrong. She's the registered keeper of the car, we have an address. We can go knock on the door, but just in case no-one is in.'

'Yeah. It's Polly Armstrong,' he said, shaking his head with dismay. 'They live in Melsham, a couple of houses down from the chip shop, I think they have a blue garage door. Her husband is called Tom, I don't know the address, but I can get a mobile number for him.'

'That would be helpful thank you,' the policeman replied. He could see the upset in his eyes. 'We will be on the way to the house shortly. I'm sure we'll find it, Melsham isn't that big a place.'

Stuart went back to the engine as the rest of his crew were helping out with the cars. He noticed oil on the road as he walked past the Mercedes, they would be here a while to clean up. This road would be closed for hours. He called Janie.

'Hello darling, where are you? I thought you left off at 7.' Janie knew firefighters' jobs were never 9-5, but she was always concerned if Stu wasn't home when he said he would be.

'I've had a call out, love, a car crash and it's a bad one.'

'Oh, no.' Janie had got used to her husband having to deal with bad situations. But she still never got used to hearing him say so. She also knew when he said about it being a bad one, it was usually a fatal.

'It's fucking terrible,' Stu's voice was almost breaking as he walked away from the engine to talk on his own out of earshot of anyone. 'It's Polly and she's in a bad way, really bad.'

Janie breathed in and put her hand to her mouth. 'Jesus, no, Stu, not our Polly? Polly and Tom. No, please God.'

'Yep, our Polly. She's still alive, but it's not good. She's in an air ambulance on her way to Cambridge, I had to cut her out. I had to bloody cut her out Janie, it was horrendous.' Janie could hear his voice start to break. She was worried for him, this was so unlike him, but she could understand why. He thought the world of Polly, as they all did.

'Darling, are you alright? Where is this crash? Get some help if you need to.'

'I'll be fine, it's on the Melsham road and it's blocked and will be for hours. I won't be home until much later. Look, the police are going to Tom's house, so text me his mobile and address. Don't go over to see him at the moment, let the police deal with it. We can be there for him over the weekend. Keep quiet about all this for the moment love, I've got to go.'

Janie was in a state of shock. She found Tom's number and then the babysitter's, they wouldn't be going down the pub tonight.

He received his wife's text and took Tom's number over to the constable. 'Here you go. It's Tom Armstrong, her husband. That's his address, his mobile. Okay, I'll go and give my guys a hand cleaning up. Give me a shout if you want anything else.'

In the air ambulance Polly's heart-rate and blood pressure were both becoming erratic. She had taken a terrible bang to the head and that was the paramedics' main worry. Two were travelling with her. There was little doubt she had broken lots of bones, especially on the right-hand side of her body, but they would mend. On landing, she was rushed into intensive care where the nursing staff and doctors were waiting.

It was now a race against time.

Tom looked at his watch. It was 7pm, where was she?

She had said she would be home by now. Perhaps she had been held up in traffic, perhaps she had decided to turn round and stay another night in Cambridge. No, he knew that wasn't the case. He smiled to himself as he remembered hearing her cheery voice again.

By 7.15pm he was getting more concerned. The dinner was now getting to the stage where he was turning the oven down as the pastry on the salmon was staring to burn. He had fiddled with the candles and cutlery about ten times on the table he had laid for the pair of them and he'd checked the Prosecco was in the fridge three times now.

Should he call her? He didn't want to spoil some surprise she had in store. Typical Pol, she was no doubt going to make some grand entrance with a bunch of flowers, for herself! That would make them laugh, they needed to laugh.

By 7.30pm, he was now worried. He called her mobile. He couldn't worry now if she was cooking up a surprise. Polly was late, and Polly didn't do late.

The call went straight to voicemail. He shook his head, she always had the phone on in the car. Maybe there was no signal.

At last he heard a car pull into the driveway. He was in the kitchen, but the gravel drive gave it away. Tom smiled to himself, best not to mention she was late. Let's get the night off to a good start, a big hug would suffice. He checked on the salmon once more, it would be fine.

The doorbell rang.

'Why on earth is she ringing the doorbell? She's got a key.'

Tom waited a second expecting to hear the key in the lock, but nothing.... the doorbell rang again.

He went to open it expecting to see Polly standing there with half-a-dozen shopping bags in her arms, and the flowers of course.

'Mr Armstrong?' the first policeman said.

'Can we come in please?'

FIFTY FOUR

HAROLD and Posselwhite knew the crap was going to hit the fan.

No sooner had Jimmy Alban left the meeting room, the pair decided they had to go see the DCI. There was no choice, they couldn't sweep this under the carpet. This had no chance of ending up well. The quicker they passed the information onto DCI Graham Cook, their boss, the better and he could deal with it, or at least he could begin to take responsibility for it. He'd go mad at the news but their heads wouldn't roll. This wasn't CID's doing, lone wolf Alban had caused this.

'We need to tell the DCI and we need to tell him now,' Harold said. 'What that idiot has done has put Baldini in real danger. We will need to get to Baldini ASAP. What a nightmare, what was that dickhead thinking of?'

'I remember saying when he was promoted to CID he was too young,' Posselwhite said. 'I'm not trying to be a smartarse after the event, but you need some life experience in CID. Far too many young kids are getting pushed up the ladder just because they are good at social media, computers and shit. When it comes to common sense most of them have none.'

'We need to go and speak to the DCI, Steven,' Harold said. 'Come on.'

DCI Cook was in his late 30s and had been a copper since the age of 18, he was another who had done his time pounding the streets. But he was a high-flier and was always destined to go places in the Force, a likeable man the CID team gave him their backs, just as he gave them his. However, he was also a man not to piss off.

It was 4pm and Cook was hoping to leave off early.

'Can we come in sir,' Posselwhite said. 'We'd like a quick chat.'

Cook smiled at them. 'Of course you can, but make it quick gents, I'm taking Emma to the cinema tonight and then a meal afterwards. It's our 10th wedding anniversary and yet I don't appear to have had any congrats cards from you two.' He laughed. 'I'll let you off. We even have a babysitter, how good is that? So, what can I do for you two?'

Cook's good mood went rapidly downhill as Harold told his boss the story, leaving nothing out. When he had finished, Cook just stared at the pair of them.

'What a balls-up, what a total and utter balls-up.' He got up from behind his desk and began pacing around the room. 'Well that's pissed my weekend up, hasn't it? And yours.' He pointed at them.

The two DIs said nothing.

'Well, he will have to know. Baldini will have to know,' Cook was shaking his head furiously. 'We can't hold onto this information and pretend we never knew of it. If something happens to him we'll be hung out to dry.'

Still Posselwhite and Harold said nothing.

'What was the dick playing at?' Cook continued pacing about trying to work out a strategy in his head as he did so. 'Baldini's name will be heading straight back to Archer as we speak and then Baldini is in serious danger. It must be Archer, or one of his close mates, who wants to know. Jesus, that bloody stupid kid.'

Cook was in full flow: 'Well, do we know anything about Baldini? Is he still living around here? I don't suppose by any chance he has taken himself off to some far-flung island? We can only hope. At least tracking him down would be a good vacation.'

The DCI's quip broke the ice.

'To be perfectly honest sir, the last time any of the squad saw Baldini was before the trial,' Harold said. 'I remember going round to talk to him at his work, with Churchman, he never wanted us to go near his house. That must have been about 10 months ago. He was a little edgy about it all if I remember, more worried that if

Archer didn't go down, he might come calling. The fact Archer did go to jail should have made him feel safer.'

'Remind me again, what was Baldini's role in all this?' asked Cook.

'He was caught shifting drugs for Archer.' Posselwhite had his hands in his pockets. 'But he was just a foot solider, nothing more. He has a good job and settled life. Archer had something on him, something about a sex tape, so Baldini told us. Anyhow, long story short, we caught Baldini and were going to charge him, he was looking at three years, but he turned informant. Baldini had phone numbers and texts and we got one of our own men into Archer's inner circle. Boom! Job done.'

'So Archer knew a copper had infiltrated the gang but he never found out how that came about.' Cook had his back to the two men.

'Exactly,' said Posselwhite. 'But he will know someone snitched on him to get us in, he's no fool. It's got to be Archer who wants Baldini's name. Who else? We will have to get Alban in here again and extract as much information as possible out of him.'

'Who asked Alban to get Baldini's name? Cook turned back to face them.

'He won't say.' Harold shrugged his shoulders.

'Won't say? What to do you mean won't say? He will fucking say, make him say.' Cook started pacing around the room again. His mood getting darker. Even if he did get away to the cinema tonight, this was going to be whirling around his head all evening. Emma would notice. *'Bloody police force, you can never get away from it.'*

'Okay, so here's what we'll do.' Cook said. 'We'll contact Baldini and meet up, you two go and see him, where and when is up to him, but tell him it needs to be sooner rather than later. You are going to have to tell him what's happened and anything suspicious, he needs to tell us. Tell him we are available 24/7. Also, speak to the prison governor at Strangeways. That is where Archer was sent, wasn't it?' Harold nodded.

'Ask him to keep an eye on Archer's visitors, letters or phone calls he gets or makes and let us know straightaway. We'll get Alban back in here first thing Monday morning, I assume you have told him to stay away from HQ?'

'Yep, suspended on full,' Posselwhite said. 'But we can get him in here easy enough.'

Cook leant forward and got in the two faces of the DI's. 'Make Alban cough, he will tell us who he has passed Baldini's name onto, do you understand?'

The pair nodded.

Sitting his bedroom at the home he shared with his parents, Jimmy Alban was a broken man.

Suspended on full pay was going to very quickly turn into sacked and no pay — he knew that. But it wasn't about the money, he was going to be interrogated. They are going to want to know why he had done what he had, he knew the ropes as well as anyone. Already McManus was in trouble for just letting him into the vault, and if Jimmy's peers in CID got their way he knew he will be expected to spill the beans. If he didn't he could be facing criminal charges, and, if anything happened to Baldini, he certainly would.

He buried his head in his hands and began to sob.

He had brought shame on his family, friends, himself, the Force and anyone who knew him. Life was going to be very different for Jimmy Alban from this moment onwards.

As the tears flowed, he looked up from the bed at the shelves in his bedroom. There were scattered photos of him playing football as a kid, hugging his mum and dad, photos of his mates at university, one of him proudly posing in his police uniform. But that was worth nothing now.

And he was no longer thinking straight.

FIFTY FIVE

THE two police officers had convinced Tom to take 10 minutes to get a few bits and pieces together before driving off to the hospital in Cambridge.

Tom had wanted to shoot straight past them, get into his car, and head off as soon as he had heard the news. Fortunately the officers were experienced enough in these type of situations to know that calming someone down first was most important. People could do the most silly of things when told news they weren't expecting. The shock Tom was feeling was obvious, but he had to clear a little bit of space in his head to gather his thoughts and senses before driving, he knew that.

'So, you can't tell me any more than the fact she is seriously hurt.' Tom looked pleadingly at one of the officers as he hunted round for his wallet, keys and phone.

'No Mr Armstrong, we can't, I'm afraid.'

'But how seriously hurt?' Tom looked at the other officer.

'I don't know. We are just here to tell you what has happened and where your wife is and we want to help you get to Cambridge as smoothly and safely as possible. We are happy to drive you there ourselves if you want, is there anyone you want us to contact?'

'No, no, I'm fine. Okay, right I'm going to go now. So, just, okay, I'm off.'

And with that Tom led the officers out of the front door, closed it and jumped into his car. He knew the way to Cambridge from Norwich, he would put the sat nav on when he got closer to Addenbrooke's, the hospital Polly had been flown to.

The officers followed him out, closing the driveway gates behind them. They left him to drive to Cambridge alone.

He drove the 60 miles in silence, he neither put the radio on, nor did he speed. All he could think of was Polly and getting to see her. What would he do if she didn't pull through? The officers had been so vague, but he expected that, he knew they had to be. Polly was airlifted to the hospital still alive, which was the positive. It didn't mean to say she was still alive now, Tom couldn't bear the thought and he found himself wiping tears from his face as he drove along. The weather had deteriorated and it began to rain hard as he got closer to Cambridge. He had no idea where the hospital was, so he pulled over and set the sat nav up.

As he got closer, Addenbrooke's was well sign-posted. He pulled into one of the many car parks and decided to head towards Accident & Emergency, it seemed the best place to start. But he didn't know where it was, thankfully a car park attendant was nearby. He directed him.

Tom walked in. The department was big and full of blue leather chairs, there must have been 30 people sitting around, he headed straight to the reception, his heart racing.

'Hi,' Tom said to the lady behind the counter who looked up as though surprised to see someone. She smiled. 'Can I help you?'

'Yes, my wife was brought here by air ambulance only a little while ago. She had been in a car accident.' He was gabbling his words. 'I need to see her please or know how she is. Please help.'

The lady could see he was agitated. 'Of course. What's the name?'

'Her name is Polly Armstrong and it was a crash near Norwich, I'm her husband, Tom.'

The lady got up from her desk and walked across to another lady sitting behind a computer on the far side of the reception area. As the pair spoke, they turned round to look at him. It was only a couple of minutes, but felt like half-an-hour, as Tom awaited the lady's return. When she did her face gave away the seriousness of the situation.

'Mr Armstrong, your wife is currently being assessed by the doctors. My colleague who I was speaking to has gone to find out more. I don't want to speculate any further, I'm sure you understand. But please take a seat and I can promise you as soon as we are able to tell you anything. Anything at all, we will.'

It was what he had half expected to hear. He couldn't barge past staff and go find Polly, she was in the best hands, but that didn't' make him feel any better. He wanted to be with her, he wanted to be holding her hand, stroking her hair.

He went and got a drink of water. His chest was tight and his mind was spinning as he took a seat close to the reception area. For the first time since he had left the house, he looked at his phone. There was a message from Janie.... *'If you want to call me, please do so darling. Thinking of you xxxx'*

Tom looked at the text. Did he want to call Janie? How did she know? News spreads fast, he decided to leave it for now.

Polly had been rushed into intensive care as soon as the helicopter had landed, she was in a bad way and was still unconscious. The medical team had been awaiting her arrival, while Dr Surtees took control of the situation. She had lost a lot of blood from the awful leg injuries she had suffered. Her heart rate and blood pressure had stabilised although she was having help with her breathing. The next few hours would be crucial. Dr Surtees decided to take x-rays and do an MRI scan, that is all he could do for now. Keep the patient stable and let the healing begin, keeping an eye on her all the time.

Back in the A&E waiting room, two police officers arrived and headed to reception. They spoke to the same lady Tom had spoken to and turned around to look at him.

'Mr Armstrong,' the first officer said. 'I'm PC Little, this is PC Underwood. We are from Norfolk Police and were at the accident this afternoon which your wife was involved in, the lady behind reception tells us she is with the doctors now.'

'Yeah, that's all I know,' Tom remained seated.

'We just have a couple of questions if you don't mind. Nothing too detailed, we appreciate this is a very difficult time.' Tom nodded.

'Was your wife on her way back home from work?' PC Little was the smaller of the two men, but appeared to be the more senior as he led the questioning.

'Yes, I mean no,' said Tom, who was hardly thinking straight.

What did they want to know that for? 'She had been away for a couple of nights, to Cambridge but she was on her way home.'

'Okay, and the Mercedes is that her car, or yours?'

Tom looked up at the officer. 'It's our car, we both drive it. I'm sorry but you've lost me here, what is the relevance of whose car it is?'

'It's just routine, Mr Armstrong. Nothing more. Look, we'll head off now. We will likely need to speak to you again, but we'll leave you for now and hopefully good news on your wife is just around the corner.'

They both smiled apologetically as they walked off.

Tom's mind was still spinning, should he phone someone? Polly's parents need to know. But he would scare them witless if he told them the situation. They were both in their 70s and she was their only child and he needed facts not half-truths before calling them. He decided to keep quiet until he knew more. He didn't know what was going on himself as yet.

He had been sitting in the A&E department almost an hour when the lady behind reception came and sat down beside him.

'Mr Armstrong.' Tom looked at her, she smiled.

'I have just been to see how your wife is and I've spoken to the doctor and team who are working on her, I can't say too much but the doctor has told me to tell you that your wife is stable. She's still unconscious and is having x-rays. He will be out to speak to you very soon. Would you like a coffee or something? Or you can wait in another room, rather than in here.'

Tom shook his head. 'I'm fine here, thank you, but he was feeling sick. He hadn't eaten, it was nearly 10pm. The not knowing was becoming too much. He had a headache as another text on his phone arrived... *'Hi Tom. You lot all in the pub? Piss heads! Is Pol about? Can't seem to contact her. Love u.... Jody x'*

He was going to have to contact someone soon.

Janie knew what had happened. How? He thought hard. Oh, of course, Stuart was a fireman. Maybe he had been called out to the accident, it was a long shot. Tom decided to call her, maybe Stuart would know something. He wasn't being told much here in the hospital. She picked it up on the second ring. 'Tom, Tom, oh my love, how is she?' Janie's voice was desperate.

'I don't know fully as yet, she's still in with the doctor. The receptionist has told me she is stable and the doctor will speak to me as soon as. You knew quickly, how did you know? Was Stu there?'

'He was darling, he's been in about 30 minutes now, and he's upstairs having a shower. Do you want to talk to him?'

'Please. He won't mind, will he?'

'Of course he won't mind.' Janie headed up the stairs with the phone in her hand.

Stuart was in the bedroom with a towel wrapped around him. He was sitting on the bed staring blankly, Tom wasn't the only one who hadn't eaten, or felt like eating. And like Tom, Stuart's head was spinning. Janie came in with the phone and mouthed *'it's Tom'*, to him. Stu looked up and nodded his head.

'Hi Tom.'

'Stu, were you there?'

'Yes mate, I was. I'm so sorry, how is she?'

'I don't know yet.' Tom was walking around the reception area. 'She's still being seen to. She's stable, alive at least, I can't believe I'm saying that. Oh, Christ Stu, this is just so bad.'

'Mate, do you want me or Janie to come over to the hospital, it's only Cambridge. We will come if you want someone there.'

'No, I'm fine, what happened? Please tell me.'

Stuart didn't tell Tom everything he had seen, but he knew his friend would want some sort of picture.

'It looks like the other car clipped the kerb on the other side of the road and flew across into Polly's path. It hit her car and then flipped over into the field opposite, we got there about 20 minutes later. Polly needed cutting out of the car mate... Look Tom, do you really want to know all this? Are you sure you don't want us to come over?'

'No, I'll be okay. I do want to know, but I better go just in case I get a call to go and see her. I'll let you know more when I know more. In many ways it's reassuring for me to know you were there. Polly thinks the world of you Stu, thanks mate.' He hung up.

Stuart put his hands to his face as Janie sat alongside him with her arms around him. There were tears.

Tom put his phone down and got a coffee, he looked at the

television set that was blaring out the latest news, but he wasn't taking it in. It was 10.45pm and he was about to go over to the receptionist he had spoken to earlier, she was still on duty, to ask if there was any more news. He had been there more than two hours, there were now less than 20 people waiting for treatment. The pubs hadn't shut yet though, it was a Friday night and he guessed it would likely get busy.

'Mr Armstrong.' A doctor in a white coat appeared from around the corner, Tom had seen him just a couple of minutes ago talking to the receptionist.

'I'm Dr Surtees.' The doctor held out his hand. 'Please come with me a second.'

Tom's heart was racing as he followed the doctor down a corridor for about 50 yards. They turned into a room. It wasn't an office, or certainly didn't look like one. It had a bland four walls, with a table and four chairs, they both sat down.

'Mr Armstrong, I have been treating your wife and she has suffered some serious injuries,' Dr Surtees began. 'And when she arrived she was in a critical condition, but she has come round now, is breathing unaided and is stable, which is good. She has opened her eyes, but only briefly.' He smiled at Tom, as he watched the relief drain from his face. Tom went to speak, but decided against it.

'She has been unconscious for a few hours which is just about okay, but we would not have wanted it to go on much longer, so we are glad she is back with us again. She's had an MRI scan which shows no head injury, but she was knocked out by the force of her head being whip-lashed in the crash.

'However, she has a broken ankle, kneecap, shoulder and severe bruising and likely a few other bangs and smaller broken bones we are not as yet aware of. Your wife is a strong woman. We will be keeping her in intensive care for 24 hours at least just to be sure all is well, I'm confident and hopeful she will go on to make a full recovery, although it won't be a quick recovery.

'You are welcome to pop round the corner and see her, I will take you, but please no more than five minutes, she needs to rest. That is her best medicine right now, let her body heal itself.'

Tom went to stand up and went to shake the doctor's hand

again. The relief that she had come round, even for a few minutes, was overwhelming. He was feeling shattered, now, he just wanted to see her.

'Thank you doctor.'

Dr Surtees smiled.

'Before you go and see your wife, Mr Armstrong, I do have other news I am sure you will be pleased about.'

Tom looked at him. 'Sorry, doctor, pleased about? What news?'

Dr Surtees looked surprised. 'Well, thankfully, your baby is safe and well.'

Tom looked stunned. 'Baby, what baby?'

'Oh, Mr Armstrong, I'm sorry. Did you not know? Your wife is pregnant, almost three months I would say.'

FIFTY SIX

PREGNANT!

Tom's head was all over the place as he walked with Dr Surtees towards intensive care.

Polly was in a large room on her own and the door was closed as the doctor and Tom got close to where she was being treated. A nurse was in the room taking notes with a clipboard and standing over her.

'Please, have just five minutes, Mr Armstrong, I'm sure you understand.' Dr Surtees smiled before walking off.

Tom nodded and opened the door, the nurse acknowledged him and also smiled. She had seen Dr Surtees point him in, so knew he must be a close relative. Buried among machines and with wires attached to her at all different angles, he could just make out Polly. He felt sick. She looked terrible.

He went alongside the bed and sat in a chair.

'She opened her eyes about 20 minutes ago,' the nurse said. 'But not for long. It was a very good sign though, I'm sure the doctor has told you.'

Tom nodded and held Polly's hand. He looked at her closely but kept his emotions intact. She looked so peaceful, although she had a bandage around her head, much of her hair was exposed and he lightly touched it, putting his fingers through it. It felt soft, although matted, the first thing she would want to do when she fully came round was sort her hair out. Her face was full of cuts.

It was nearing 11.30pm and Tom was shattered. He kissed Polly gently and held her hand. He wanted to spend the night alongside her, but that wasn't going to happen. Quite where he was going to spend the night, he had no idea. He hadn't even thought about it, there was no way he was going to drive back to Norwich. He wanted to just lay his head on the bed alongside her and go to sleep with her, wake up tomorrow, be with her when she woke.

But he knew he couldn't.

'I don't suppose there is a room I can spend the night here, is there?' Tom looked at the nurse. 'I hadn't even thought about it until now, I live in Norwich and I don't want to go home at this time of night.'

'I'll make a call, we do have rooms, but they often get full. I'll see what I can do.' The nurse smiled and walked out of the room.

He was left on his own with Polly, he leant over and kissed her on the cheek again. As he kissed her, he thought he saw her eyes flicker. But no, he was just hoping.

He whispered in her ear. 'Love you darling, with all my heart. And our little baby inside you, keep safe, keep fighting, both of you. Love you both, see you tomorrow.' He felt himself begin to well up again. He wiped his eyes.

The nurse came back into the room and smiled at him to leave. She had managed to book him a room within the hospital, she gave him directions.

'Thank you, thank you,' Tom said, before looking back at Polly as he left.

He checked his phone as his walked down the corridor. He had received a host of messages, although none were from Polly's parents, the people he knew he must contact first.

But it was far too late to disturb them now. And the rest of his friends will just have to wait until tomorrow, he was too tired to go through it all with so many people right now. Polly was in good hands. He just had to pray all would be well.

The room he had been booked into was basic, but cosy. He hadn't eaten all night, so was grateful for the complimentary tea and biscuits. He set his alarm for 7am and he would get up and go over to see Polly as soon as he was allowed the next morning and then make a round of phone calls to family and friends.

He didn't bother getting changed, he just crashed out on the bed. He was soon asleep.

FIFTY SEVEN

TOM slept well considering how his mind had been racing.

In the end it had all been too much and his body had said enough is enough. But he was still awake early. It was 6.30am and his alarm hadn't gone off, not that it mattered. As soon as he awoke he jumped out of bed and headed for the shower. His first thought was to go over to the ward and see how Polly was.

He turned his phone on and the texts and messages started to come through. There were missed calls and WhatsApp messages, texts and voicemails. He knew he had to begin to answer them soon but now it was too early and most importantly, Polly's parents Jonathan and Margaret needed be the first people he would phone.

Tom stripped off and headed for the shower. But just as he went to get in, his phone rang, it was Jody. He'd already missed four calls from her and had three texts he hadn't as yet read.

'Hi Jody.'

'Tom, Tom, what the hell has happened? We've been worried sick. Polly. What's happened? We called Janie in the end late last night because we couldn't get hold of either of you. And she told us about Polly, in a car accident. Oh, my God, how is she?'

'I'm sorry I didn't get back to you last night, but I was with Polly till late. She's in a bad way, it was a horrible accident, but she's come round, although I only saw her for five minutes and she was back asleep then. She was critical, but is now stable and has lots of broken bones. I'm going over to see her shortly'

Before he could continue his update, Jody was off. 'I'm coming down. Coming down today to stay with you. I will come to Cambridge first, that's where you are Janie said. You'll be there all day, won't you? Then I'll go back to your house and get things for you if you need.'

'No, you don't have to do that.' Tom was putting on his shirt. 'I'm fine here and I can come and go back to Norwich, I'll manage.'

'Sorry, Tom I don't give a shit. Polly is my best friend and I want to be with her. God, I haven't slept a wink and I want to be there for you as well, I love you both so much. I told Craig about me going down to be with you.'

'And what did he say?'

'No, I *told* Craig. I didn't ask him. He said he'll open the shop and I've got a friend who can run it. Anyhow, how are you coping? I'm so sorry to be so abrupt, but I'm so upset, I can't believe it. She is going to be okay, isn't she?' And with that Jody began to cry.

'Jode, darling, listen. Yes, she's in a bad way, but the doctor was very positive about the fact she has already come round and is breathing unaided. She has broken bones, but they will mend. She's had an MRI scan and her head is okay, I'm going to get some breakfast and will call you as soon as. If you want to come down, of course I'd love to have you around. But please drive carefully, don't rush, I'll text you the postcode of the hospital.'

'You sure you don't mind me coming?'

'What have I just said?'

'Okay, I'll be leaving about 9. Call me when you see her again, I'll be hands-free. Give her all my love.'

'I will, see you later.' He hung up.

Tom made his way out of his room and handed his key into reception. It was almost 7.30am and he decided to make his way to the intensive care ward. If he wasn't allowed to see Polly, then so be it.

He felt odd walking around a hospital at such an early hour of the day. The only people he passed were either nurses, doctors or cleaners, no members of the general public. He entered the IC ward and went straight to reception where a nurse sat filling out forms. She looked surprised to see him.

'Hello, can I help you?' She smiled.

Tom explained who he was and that his wife had been rushed in last night. He had no idea if he could see her or not but the nurse was most helpful.

'Polly is awake and talking to my colleague, I believe. Would you like to see her?'

He couldn't hide his joy. 'Yes please. I would love to.'

Tom followed the nurse, even though he knew where he was going. Sure enough, as he looked through the windows in her room, he saw Polly talking to another nurse. The nurse from reception opened the door. 'Polly, you have a visitor.'

She turned to Tom, 'just 10 minutes Mr Armstrong.'

Tom couldn't hide his emotions as he walked over. The young nurse who had been speaking to Polly got up and left, he just sat on the bed and put his arms gently around her. For a few seconds neither said anything, he shed a tear but wiped it clear so Polly didn't see him upset.

'Oh, darling, I love you. How are you feeling?' Tom looked closely into his wife's eyes. She still looked tired and she had a bruise coming up under her right eye that was going to be a right shiner.

'I'm a bit tired, but I don't feel too bad.' Polly spoke quietly, but smiled. 'I reckon it's all these drugs I'm on, I'm floating a bit here. Are you okay?'

'Don't worry about me, I'm just so glad you are, well you're here. I can't believe it. Do you remember what happened? Don't worry yourself to think about it, though.'

'I don't remember anything, which is what the nurse was talking to me about. She has been with me for about 10 minutes, telling me what happened, a crash apparently, asking me if I knew my name and such stuff. But that's all fine, I know who I am. But I don't remember much about the accident.'

'Good, well don't think about it.' Tom could only stare at his wife, broken and shattered. 'Just rest and we'll get you home when the time is right.'

There was a few moments of silence as the pair looked at each other. Polly was exhausted and as much as Tom wanted to stay longer, he knew it best to leave her to rest for now. The nurse who had been sitting with Polly came in and looked at Tom, suggesting he leave.

He kissed Polly very gently on the lips, then the head and

finally her hand, he kept looking at her. He loved her so much, his life was nothing without her. As he went to leave it dawned on him what the doctor had said about the baby. But no, now wasn't the time to be talking about that, did Polly even know?

'I love you Pol. Have a sleep, I'll be back soon.'

'Love you,' Polly whispered back.

Outside the room the nurse spoke to Tom.

'Your wife had a good night but she is going to be in here a few days at least, maybe more. The doctor will be coming round to see her soon. Can you call the ward before coming to see her, just in case she is resting? She is going to need plenty of rest, you can come any time of course. Hopefully she'll move onto another ward and out of IC soon.

'I'm nurse Beazeley by the way, so ask for me, if not any of the other nurses will help, here's the direct line number.' She scribbled it down on a piece of paper.

Tom nodded and walked out, looking for the signs for the canteen. He was hungry, he couldn't remember the last time he had eaten. Fortunately it wasn't that far away and he was surprised to see so many people already sitting at tables, the smell of eggs and bacon, sausages and toast was a treat and Tom sat down enjoying a couple of cups of coffee after ordering the full English. He picked up a paper, the local one, flicking through it as he ate his breakfast.

He noticed a headline on page five, down the right-hand side. *'One dead in two-car crash'*. It was the crash Polly was involved in. He was surprised to see it in a Cambridge paper, seeing as the crash had taken place in Norfolk. Then again it was only an hour away and Ben had told him how newspaper's liked to editionise pages to make them more local.

'One man was killed and three others were injured in a horror crash just outside Melsham, in west Norfolk, yesterday afternoon,' the story read.

'The crash involved two cars on the A1120. An 18-year-old male was declared dead at the scene, while a woman was rushed to Addenbrooke's Hospital, in Cambridge, with severe injuries. Police are appealing for witnesses. Two ambulances and a fire crew from Norwich attended the scene.'

Tom read the story again. The severity of the crash hit home, one poor lad was dead. Tom hadn't even thought about the people in the other car.

By the time he had finished his breakfast, he knew a round of phone calls needed to be made. He bought a copy of the newspaper, before phoning Polly's parents first. At least he could reassure them and then the rest of the people he was about to call, that Polly was awake and talking.

He didn't worry about Jody for the time being, it was family first. Jody would be halfway down the M6 anyhow. She had said she was leaving at 9, but as soon as Tom had said he was happy for her to come, she had likely jumped in the car. He smiled to himself, poor Craig having to look after the shop, hardly his cup of tea!

Tom got to work. Janie had left a couple of texts, as had Alison and Ann who had no doubt been in the pub last night when they heard the news. Gosh, the news had no doubt ruined their evenings. He had missed a call from Jill.

They must all be worried sick and he could understand.

Tom began making calls.

Tony Statton was up early on Saturday morning for his trip north to visit Archer.

He travelled first class with no stops, it wasn't cheap, but with another 25K on its way after the information was delivered, he could afford it. He would treat himself to a new car when he got home, nothing too flash, perhaps upgrade the Merc.

He arrived at Manchester's Piccadilly just before noon. His visit was already booked and he wouldn't be long with his old friend, there would likely be plenty of time for an afternoon in the pub watching a bit of footie, before a pleasant evening meal and more drinks at the Holiday Inn.

The visit was arranged for 1.10pm. Archer didn't have many visitors, only his son Liam, who would come to see his father once a week, every Friday evening. Liam was Stuart and Marie Archer's only child. It hadn't been a great upbringing for the young boy and he had left the family home as soon as he could at 18, attending Edinburgh University, where he graduated with a first in chemistry. He was now a teacher in north Wales. He kept his father's life history secret from pals, and girlfriends. Probably why, at 27, he was still single. Who could he trust?

Statton knew the drill as he arrived at Strangeways but he was pondering how he was going to get Baldini's name over to Archer. *'Just tell him I suppose,'* he thought to himself. It was what Archer had planned next for Baldini that most worried him, although Statton was sure he would be well out of this mess by then.

'Afternoon mate, how are you?' Archer looked better than he had the last time he saw him, Statton thought as the pair greeted.

'I'm fine, how are you getting on Stu?'

'I'm okay pal. Why we sitting at this table in the corner? You got something to hide?' Archer winked and smiled as he spoke.

'Well, they showed me here to be honest,' Statton mumbled back. 'Do you want to sit somewhere else?'

'No, I'm okay mate, only joshing with ya. So, how's tricks? How's Alice? Did you get the money?'

'Yes pal, thanks, I did get the money.' The look on Statton's face said it all. Like all those who had been in Archer's gang, money was the key driver. They all loved it, couldn't get enough of it. 'And Alice is well, we're both good. Looking forward to going to Switzerland for a couple of weeks next month.'

Archer smiled. He was pleased for his friend.

'So,' said Archer. 'You got me a name? Is it who I thought?'

Statton stared at his friend. 'Yep, it is exactly who you thought, Craig Baldini. I won't repeat it, he was the snitch who let the cops in. Got the name from the cops themselves. They can be so helpful!'

Archer smiled. 'That's great work, thanks pal, the rest of the money will be with you by Monday. I hoped you had that name, now I just need you to do me one last favour.'

Statton's face dropped. He didn't want to get involved in this any further. As far as he was concerned, it was all over as soon as he delivered Baldini's name. Friend or not, Archer wasn't going to keep toying him around like this.

'Hang on, no way. You wanted a name, you got a name Stu, I could easily have batted you away but I didn't. You said that is all you wanted, now play the game, my friend, my job is done.'

Archer put his hands up. 'Okay, okay, I hear you Andy.

'But what I want you to do is a piece of piss. When you leave here in a moment, I want you to go out of the main entrance and turn left. About 500 yards down the road is a red telephone box, you can't miss it. Charlie Cantwell will be waiting nearby. You remember Charlie? Big bastard, he'll be wearing a black hat and carrying a briefcase. Don't look at him, just give him the name as you walk past. He's expecting you, the rest is his baby. The 25K will be with you on Monday, oh, I've mentioned that, haven't I?' And with that Archer got up, held out his hand to Statton, who took it. They shook and went their own ways.

The pair were never to meet again.

Outside Strangeways, Statton did as requested. He turned left and continued walking. He couldn't see a telephone box ahead and he wasn't a good judge of how far 500 yards was. But then a box came into view and sure enough, standing alongside it, looking like a spare dick at a wedding, was Charlie Cantwell.

'Bloody hell. Could he look any more out of place?'

Not that it was his problem. And as he walked past the big man he whispered 'Craig Baldini' loud enough for Charlie to hear. 'Got ya', was Cantwell's response.

For Statton it was like the old days, going back in time, to his gang roots. Surreal. Delivering the name to Archer had been easy, but he hadn't expected to deliver it again to Cantwell, one of Liverpool's serious hard men. Well into his 50s now, Cantwell had already been in and out of prison, his longest stretch was nine years for GBH after he took a knuckle duster to a man's jaw in a pub in Stockport. He'd 'done him' for 'gawping' at his wife's legs as she walked by him, then nudging the mates he was sitting with to have a look, Cantwell took exception to the whole episode.

As Statton walked away, he carried on and headed towards the city centre. Relieved he had done his bit, he was now looking forward to a pint in a pub. He might also have a flick through the best Mercs to buy. How about one of those G-Wagons? Now that would get heads turning in Southampton.

He carried on walking for 10 minutes, checking his phone, oblivious to the car that had been shadowing him for the past minute or so. Eventually it pulled up alongside him and two men jumped out, grabbing his arm before he had a second to move.

'Mr Statton, Merseyside Police. We'd like a word, please.'

Posselwhite and Harold bundled him into the back of the BMW.

FIFTY EIGHT

THE two DSI's got either side of Statton in the back of the unmarked police car. Neither said a word.

The driver sped away with Statton's mind awhirl. *Fuck, he hadn't bargained for this, how did they know?*

'What's going on? What's happening?' Statton spoke, looking at one of the coppers, then the other, but neither batted an eyelid. They had their poker faces on and were looking ahead, the driver also said nothing.

'Come on. You can't just grab me off the bloody street without a word, this is not bloody North Korea. What the hell do you think you're doing?'

But his pleas fell on deaf ears, he knew he would get nothing out of either cop until they decided they wanted to talk. The car drove for about 20 minutes before coming to a halt at an industrial estate on the east of the city. It had started to rain and the mood outside reflected the dark mood in the car. The driver turned the engine off and, despite the rain, got out and stood outside lighting up a fag.

It left the three men in the back.

It was Posselwhite who spoke. 'Okay, Statton. We'll make this as easy and hopefully as quick as we can. We know you are a busy man and a long way from home, no doubt your wife will want you back in Southampton as soon as possible.'

Statton looked at Posselwhite. He was going to say something but decided to keep his mouth shut.

Posselwhite continued. 'So, we'll make it simple, you make it simple. And we can both go our own ways. I'm just going to say two words, one name, and I want your undivided attention please.

'Craig Baldini. Ring any bells that name?' The DSI's both looked at Statton. He stared back, but said nothing.

'Craig Baldini. I said, ring any bells Mr Statton. Don't piss us about.'

'Pizza restaurant?' Statton smiled.

'What?' It was Harold's turn to speak.

'Does he own a pizza restaurant? Sounds Italian to me.' Statton grinned. He had played the cops many times over the years, back in the day with Archer's gang, but not once had he been arrested. They didn't intimidate him then. He wasn't going to be intimidated by them now.

'Don't be funny, Statton,' Posselwhite said. 'We know you have been to see Archer and we know you know who Craig Baldini is. So, let's make this easy and you tell us what you know about him.'

'Good try,' Statton smirked. 'You two got nothing better to do? Don't try to make out you know Jack Shit. I haven't got a fucking scooby doo who Craig Baldini is and even if I did have, I wouldn't be telling you. You are barking so far up the wrong tree you are not even in the right wood.

'I know Archer because one of my pals used to be his gardener and we got friendly because my pal bought a car off him and asked me to check it over before he bought it off him. That was about five years ago. Archer called me up and wanted to catch up and I thought, 'why not?' Nice weather in Manchester. Go make a weekend of it.'

'Bullshit.' Harold got in Statton's face.

'Look pal, we'll make this as easy or as hard as you want. Craig Baldini, that's the name we want you to tell us about, we're not interested in you, although we could take interest. We're interested in what you know about Baldini.'

Statton remained dead pan. He knew they were only fishing.

'I don't know who this Baldini is and even if I did, I wouldn't tell you.' Statton flicked his eyes from one to the other. 'You are bang out of order dragging me off the street for this and you know you are, I can't imagine your superiors know what you're doing, you gone rogue you two? And for what? I have no idea and I don't give a shit. So, just take me back to where you picked me up and I'll say nothing more to anyone about this unfortunate episode.'

'You'll regret this,' Posselwhite said. Statton smiled.

The two cops knew it had been a long shot dragging him off the street. Even if he had known Baldini, he was never likely to say, but the fact Archer got so few visitors and Statton had come all the way up from Southampton, for the second time in two weeks to see him, meant they smelt a rat. Jimmy Alban's confession had helped in that.

The driver got back into the car and they drove Statton back to Strangeways. He clearly wasn't going to talk.

'Don't leave the country.' Harold smirked at him as he got out of the car.

'I may do, I may not.' Statton got out but then stuck his head back into it. 'Oh, and don't ever lift me off the street like that again for no reason, I know the rules.' He headed off.

Harold and Posselwhite looked at each other. Statton was right. Grabbing him off the street was bang out of order. All they could do now was speak to Alban again to try and get more information, get him to crack. That, and keep surveillance on Baldini. He was in the biggest danger.

They would have to speak to Cook again. Shit, he was not going to be happy one little bit about all this.

All this had shafted his weekend good and proper.

FIFTY NINE

JODY gave Tom a huge, tight hug.

'Can I go and see her?' Jody had driven straight from Chester to the hospital — no stopping.

'You can say hello to me first,' Tom said. He was pleased to see her, but knew he had to dampen down her desperation to see Polly, it was going to be a shock when she saw the injuries she had suffered.

Tom had been back to the ICU ward later that morning, but Polly was asleep. Apparently she had been awake for a short while, but he had been busy making calls and trying to organise his life, which right now was very much on hold. Polly's parents had been deeply upset when he phoned, but Tom put them off the idea of coming to Cambridge immediately, he would keep them informed with at least two calls a day. Jill was going to head into the dentist surgery tomorrow and cancel all appointments for Monday and Tuesday, a thankless task as she would likely not be able to get hold of everyone, especially if they didn't check their e-mails.

'Come and get a coffee and I'll let you know what's happening.' Tom gave Jody another hug. 'It's not as easy as just going to see her because she drifts in and out at the moment. I went to see her about two hours ago and she was asleep. Without actually sitting beside her all the time, there is not much we can do apart from wait, I've had to make lots of calls this morning, but I am going back to see her soon. We are only allowed a certain amount of time with her. Come with me then, let's get a coffee first.'

Tom filled her in on everything that had happened. He would

need to go home to Melsham today because he needed a change of clothes and he was booked in a room at the hospital for another night, but he couldn't get Jody a room there.

'I'm staying here, in Cambridge,' Jody said firmly. 'I'll find a hotel, I don't care. You go home and get a change of clothes or whatever you need, I've got everything in the car. I'll just book somewhere nearby, I don't want to get in the way, but I do want to be here as much as possible. I still can't believe what has happened.'

As they sat in the corner of the canteen what had actually happened hit Jody. For the first time since she'd left Chester for the journey to Cambridge, she began again to cry, and the tears flowed.

'I'm sorry.' Tom held her tight. 'Bloody use I'm proving. I've tried to keep it all in since I got in the car, you don't need me in a stupid wreck like this. I'm just glad she's, you know, you know, with us. She could have died, couldn't she?'

Tom nodded.

'But she didn't, Jody.' Tom held her hands across the table. 'Come on, let's finish this coffee and see if she's awake, you can hopefully be with her for a while this afternoon while I go home.'

Jody smiled. 'I will do. Is that okay? Are her parents coming up?'

'Not sure, they have told me to keep them informed. I don't think they are great at driving long distances these days, so I'll make sure they are kept in the know.'

As the pair sat, Tom's phone continued to bleep as messages came in from friends. He would reply to them all today.

The two of them went back to ICU and headed towards the reception area. They were told they could sit with Polly, but the doctor was arriving in 'about 45 minutes', so they would have to leave then. As Jody walked in, she held her hands to her face, there was Polly, gorgeous Polly, looking battered and bruised, her swollen face almost unrecognisable. Tom held Jody's hand, he could see she was shocked, Polly was asleep.

She went and sat next to her and took her hand. She kissed it, the tears welling up in her face. 'Oh, Polly, my darling. I love you.'

She looked up at Tom, who was standing on the opposite side of the bed. He smiled at her and nodded and then looked back at

Polly, just as Polly's eyes opened.

The pair of them perked up and Tom went and sat opposite Jody, who let him speak as Polly turned her head to him.

'I'm here.' Tom smiled at his wife and Polly's lips moved to smile back. 'And so is someone else.'

Polly didn't answer, Jody still had her hand. Polly turned to look at her. 'Jody, Jody.'

Jody put her hands to her face, but kept the tears in and kissed Polly on the hand.

'I'm here, Tom's here. We're all here. You are going to be fine. You know I wouldn't miss a party, Pol!' She smiled and Polly smiled back, 'You never have done,' Polly whispered.

Jody was struggling seeing her friend like this. Her badly bruised eye and cuts to her hands and chin may have been superficial compared to the broken bones, but for Jody it masked her friend's beauty. A nurse entered the room and marched across to look at Polly. 'Hello my dear, how are you?' She said it in an abrupt manner that made Jody recoil from holding Polly's hand. 'Would you like a drink?'

Polly looked up at the nurse and nodded. 'Yes, please, a drink.' Tom smiled. Polly looked round at him and then turned to Jody. 'Have you been here long?'

As she spoke her face contorted in pain.

'Shhhhh,' Jody said, putting her finger to her mouth. 'Don't try to talk too much, I came down from Chester today and I'm staying for as long as it takes.' She held her hand again.

The nurse came back into the room with some water.

'The doctor is on his way to do his rounds sooner than we thought, so do you both mind if you wait outside for a while, or perhaps go and grab something to eat?' The nurse continued to be her efficient self, something Tom found slightly irritating.

'The doctor will be with her a little while I suspect, so don't hurry back, you are allowed to pop in and out all day if you wish, as you know. Just please don't stay too long at a time.'

As the nurse went to walk out, she turned to Tom and smiled. 'It's good to see her talking.' Tom smiled back and felt a tad of guilt about his previous thoughts of her over-efficient demeanour.

Jody and Tom kissed Polly before leaving to get something to eat.

'You said you would call when you got there.'

Craig was on the phone to Jody. It was the middle of the afternoon and he knew if all had gone well she would have been in Cambridge well before then, but he'd given her the chance to call him first. She hadn't.

'Oh, darling, I'm sorry. I've been talking to Tom and getting all the lowdown on what's happened. I've seen Polly, she's a terrible mess. It's horrible. But the good thing is she's talking now. She spoke to us when we were in there, I've just come out of her room. Tom are I are going for a bite to eat.'

Craig wasn't cross with Jody for not giving him a call, despite her saying she would text him as soon as she got there. 'You could have dropped me a quick text to say you had arrived, Jode, that's all. Anyhow, how bad is our Pol?'

'Very bad. She's black and blue, she's broken her ankle and other places, her shoulder, I think. It's going to be a long while. She's still in Intensive Care, but Tom reckons she will be moved soon. At least she recognised me, she woke up about 30 minutes ago. She's been awake a few times, it could have been worse.'

'Well, I checked the website of the Norwich *Eastern Daily Press* and they had the crash down as one of their main stories. One poor lad died.' Craig was drinking a cup of coffee in the kitchen looking at his tablet at the story.

'I know,' Jody said, looking around for Tom, who had said he was popping to the loo, but seemed to have been gone a while. 'We haven't really spoken too much about the crash and I won't unless Tom wants to talk about it. All he told me is that their friend Stuart, do you remember him? The firefighter, well he's Janie's husband. We have met them. Anyhow, he attended the scene and helped cut Pol out of the car, gosh, that must have been horrible for him.'

'Weren't Stuart and Janie at Polly and Tom's for New Year a couple of years ago?' Craig thought he could picture who Jody was talking about.

'Yes, Stu was the one who brought the fireworks.' Jody smiled as she remembered Stu, Tom and Craig getting in a right panic as they set off a rocket that only went about six foot off the ground, but straight at Tom's garden fence. It hit it with such force it left huge burn marks, luckily no-one was in its line of sight as it took off.

'Oh yeah, Stu sent that rocket into the fence.' Craig said. 'Oh, wow, yes, that must have been terrible for him to have to be there, how horrible.'

Tom returned from the loo and Jody handed him the phone. 'Do you want to chat with your friend?'

'Hello mate, how are you?' Tom sounded more upbeat than Craig had expected.

'Alright pal, thinking of you to be honest. Hope Polly is on the mend. All very nasty, I hear.'

'Yep, very bad, could also have been worse to be honest. But it's nice of Jody to come down, hope you will cope without her. Pub tonight, I imagine, and tomorrow night and the next night.'

The pair laughed, it was a light moment for Tom. After the previous 24 hours or so he'd been through, he needed it.

'Yeah, not wrong, pub here I come. But look, take care and if you want anything, just ask Jody. She'll have an answer. Oh, by the way, as I said, I'm off to the Arsenal game tonight. My mate Terry has a couple of tickets, I'll give the boys a cheer for you.' Craig went to finish the call. 'Pass me back to the trouble and strife. Love to Pol.'

'Yeah, give them a cheer mate. See ya.' Tom passed the phone to Jody. She and Craig said their goodbyes.

'Well, where do you want to eat?' Tom said. 'Are we going for a cheap and cheerful McDonalds or a bit of pub grub?'

'Oh, a bit of pub grub please, I'll pay. Not McDonalds,' Jody pulled a face at the mere thought of the idea.

He smiled to himself, he knew that's what Jody would say. She hated junk food. She was a lot of wonderful things was Jody, but she wasn't Polly, who would always get down and dirty in the food stakes.

Charlie Cantwell and Stuart Archer were High School pals.

Having gone their own ways for a few years after they left

school, the pair met up in a Liverpool nightclub, almost coming to blows over a girl. The bizarre thing was that confrontation, which came to nothing in the end that evening, saw the beginning of a friendship that lasted from that day onwards, and now almost 30 years.

Both men were crooks, both got deeper and deeper into it, Archer was a planner, Cantwell an enforcer. They bonded, and although the pair's paths rarely crossed in criminal terms, they always knew where they could find each other if needed.

When Cantwell had been banged up for destroying the guy's jaw, 15 years ago, Archer had helped keep protection on Cantwell's wife and kids, even though it wasn't really any of his concern. He also saw that they stayed financially stable. Cantwell had never forgotten what Archer had done for him and his family during those difficult years.

So, he had needed no second invitation when Liam had passed on the information about Craig Baldini, *'which would be confirmed'* by Statton's message at the phone box. Cantwell was mad, very mad, that someone could snitch his pal up, a pal who had done so much for his family during his hour of need.

Cantwell was determined to make sure the bastard paid for what he'd done.

After Statton had passed on the name outside Strangeways, Cantwell had headed into Manchester to his favourite pub and ordered his favourite lunch, lamb shank, potatoes and veg. He liked his food, but he liked a drink more. As he sat down to enjoy his second lager of the afternoon, an afternoon of drinking that would extend well into the evening, he spent the next hour hatching a plan. Archer had given him a blank canvas.

'Alright Charlie,' said the female voice, as she draped her hand around Charlie's shoulders and neck, fiddling with his ear as she did so. You up to no good? You must be.'

Charlie smiled. 'Bloody hell, Marie Archer, looking gorgeous. How are you love? I thought you were on a different continent, far, far away, I think Stuart thinks you are as well. Glad you came though. You got the message, then?'

'I've been back two months, Charlie. I've thought about going to see Stu, but we've been doing our own thing for years now.

Let sleeping dogs lie, I say, I don't need to see him. He won't be bothered about seeing me, so long as I'm not haggling him for money, he's happy. And right now, I've plenty. Anyway, I got your message from Liam, bet you thought that was a long shot asking him.'

'Too right I did. You want a drink?' Charlie got up to go to the bar. 'Vodka and lime, Charlie. Make it a double, for old time's sake.' She winked.

Charlie came back and sat down, they looked at each other. She was still an attractive-looking woman, even now into her early 50s. Cantwell had known Marie through Archer, but only as acquaintances. A few hellos here, a few goodbyes there, Marie had been a schemer, wife of a drugs baron, she knew the ropes, she knew how to play men, how to keep her man happy, what to say and how to say it. A proud scouser, Marie was more street-wise today than most of the current criminal fraternity in Liverpool.

Archer had been on the phone to his son within hours of Statton giving him Baldini's name. He wanted to move fast, Liam had passed on to his mum the news that she could help. She didn't have to, but Marie said she would, although it would cost her husband 300K, he had the money. Liam returned the message to his dad and the cash arrived in Marie's offshore account within hours, it never ceased to amaze her how many people her husband knew.

'So, you know what this is all about, don't you?' Charlie looked closely at her.

'You bet I do,' Marie's smile had a vengeful look to it, Charlie liked her manner. 'Stu has already put the money in my account, bloody hell, it must be serious.'

Charlie returned the smile; 'It is. So, have you got it then?'

Marie opened her handbag and pulled out a DVD, she flicked it in his face. 'It's all here. Me and Mr Baldini making very big drunken love. Great sex tape, I'll let you watch it one day if you're good.'

'You behave Mrs Archer.' Charlie supped his pint and pointed his finger in fun. 'I just want you to get Baldini for me. You have the DVD, he'll come, and then when you got him there, you can fuck off and go get you nails done.

She smiled. 'Cheers'. The pair clinked glasses.

An hour later, Marie left the pub and grinned to herself. *'Charlie Cantwell, you old dinosaur. Taking candy off a baby.'*

Her phone rang, Marie looked at the number and smiled, she loved hearing his voice. 'Are we all set then, love? Oh, and by the way, you are not going to believe what's fucking gone and happened, babe?'

SIXTY

EMILY'S head was aching on Sunday morning.

It had been a raucous night out with her friends that had ended with them all at Baristas nightclub until 4am.

She looked at her phone, it was 10.30am. She had to be at the rugby club at noon but at least she could have another 20 minutes in bed.

Emily lived in a flat in the town centre. With her latest boyfriend now *persona none gratis*, she was enjoying her freedom once more. Her memory of last night was sketchy, had she met any new blokes? Maybe one or two she had danced with at Baristas. But, overall it had been a girl's night out, Gwen had been there.

As Emily pulled the covers over her head looking to enjoy a final few moments in bed, her phone rang. It was Jill.

'Shit, Jill, please don't tell me it's 10.30 on Monday morning and I've slept all day Sunday and now I'm late for work, please tell me it's still Sunday.'

'Yes, it's Sunday, let me guess, you're in bed after a late night.'

'Yeah, it was a late one, but a fun one. I'm working at the rugby club later, seeing as it is Sunday. Why are you calling?'

'There's been an accident, a bad accident.' said Jill, Emily sat up in bed.

'Oh, no. Who? What?' She flicked her legs off the bed.

'It's Polly, Tom's Polly. She was involved in a car crash on Friday night and is serious in hospital. Tom's with her but he is closing the surgery down tomorrow and on Tuesday, so we need to contact all our patients who are booked in for those two days to tell them their appointments are cancelled. Do you think you can give me a hand with Tuesday's patients some time later today? I know you're going to the rugby club, but if I get tomorrow's appointments cancelled, can you help me with Tuesdays when you come home?'

'Of course, of course I will. How bad is Polly?'

'Well, she's bad, I had a quick chat with Tom yesterday. She's broken several bones from what I could gather, hopefully I'll speak to him tonight to find out more.'

Emily was wide awake now, taking in the news.

'Okay, that's fine. I'll call you tonight and you can let me know what you've done and then I can help you with the rest. That's awful about Polly, I can't believe it. Tom must be devastated. Where did it happen?'

'Near their home apparently, and he sounded upset.' Jill was turning her computer on. She could access the surgery rota remotely, so she would work from home.

'Hopefully she will be okay but be prepared for Tom to be off more than just tomorrow and Tuesday, it could be all week, maybe longer. He will be with her for as long as it takes, I'm sure of that. Look, it's important we both help him through this, I'll give Susan a call about Tuesday and not to come in. I'm going to go in tomorrow because some patients will turn up, you can come in as well if you like.'

'Of course,' Emily replied. 'Anything to help Tom, I'll call you tonight, bye.'

Emily hung up and put down her phone. Poor Polly, poor Tom. She looked at the wall in front of her and went over to a photograph on a shelf one of her former boyfriends had put up. A photo she cherished more than any she had in her flat.

The picture of her and Tom in the surgery, smiling. The one Jill took on Emily's birthday back in November. He had his arms around her. She picked it up.

'*I'm here, don't worry,*' she said to herself before kissing her finger and placing it on Tom's photo.

Showered and changed, Emily arrived at the rugby club at 11.45am.

It was mostly junior rugby on a Sunday morning but the clubhouse was always heaving. There were loads of youngsters enjoying the game, almost all with their parents, although the clubhouse was quiet when she arrived, but as soon as the games and the training finished, the place would become an amphitheatre of noise.

She enjoyed her work and got to meet lots of people.

'Morning, or is it afternoon?' Karen walked up to the bar, smiling and looking very glamorous, so Emily thought.

'I think it's still morning Kaz. You alright?' Emily bent down to put a glass away she had been cleaning. 'Lee up here today?'

'Yes, he's got a game, starts at 12.15. Saw you over here, so thought I would come and say hello, how is everything at the surgery?

Emily looked at Karen. 'Everything's fine. But you obviously haven't heard about Polly, have you?'

'Polly, Polly who?' Karen looked bemused.

'Polly Armstrong, Tom's wife, she's been seriously hurt in a car crash.'

Karen didn't say anything, she looked away and then back at Emily. 'Oh, that Polly, how awful, when did it happen?'

'Friday night apparently,' said Emily, who had turned to serve a customer who had asked for a large coke. 'I'll tell you more in a minute but, as you can see, I'm going to be busy for a while. Just thought you might like to know.' She raised her eyebrows. 'Hope the news hasn't upset you.'

Karen walked away from the bar and out of the clubhouse towards the pitches where Lee would be playing. As she did so, she made the call, this was her time and nothing was going to stop her and certainly not Polly Armstrong. The call went to voicemail.

'Hi Tom, its Karen. I've booked us in on Wednesday at a clinic in London, 10am. They can hopefully get us the results that day. I'll text you the details. Oh, and sorry to hear about Pol. Hope all well.'

SIXTY ONE

TOM and Jody were seated on opposite sides of Polly's bed.

When he had walked into Polly's room that morning, the sight of her awake and smiling had welled him up again, but this time with joy.

'Your wife woke up at about 6am and has been awake ever since. As we often say, all her lights really came on,' nurse Beazley had told him as he arrived at the ward. 'This does often happen, things can change quickly, although it's only strong painkillers that are keeping her from feeling too much pain. She still has a long way to go, but she's far more with it now and you can spend a bit more time with her.' She smiled at him.

Tom had been thrilled to see Polly and had called up Jody to come over to the hospital. She had been staying in a hotel in Cambridge, but was eating breakfast herself. She finished that up and headed over.

So, now the pair of them sat looking and chatting with Polly, who still looked a mess. She would be horrified if she could see herself. But her eyes were more sparkling and she was talking coherently, Tom could not believe the overnight improvement.

'You didn't have to come to be with me.' Polly was holding her friend's hand. She was trying to smile, but it wasn't easy with all the cuts and bruises. 'Tom could have coped on his own, pretty badly. But he'd have coped.'

'If you think I'm sitting up in Chester waiting for up-to-dates from *him*, which would likely be every 10 hours', Jody smiled at Tom, 'you must be joking.'

'She's been a real trooper,' Tom smiled. 'Hasn't got in the way at all.'

'So far, she has sworn at me when I said she didn't have to come down straight away, then when she did turn up, she demanded a room in the hospital to stay overnight. When she was told there weren't any, she threatened to report the staff.' Jody looked at Polly, shaking her head and smiling.

'Then, to make matters worse, she sends me home to get my clothes and last night when I returned, she asked me over to her hotel room for a late nightcap. I said no.'

'You wish,' Jody laughed, puffing out her cheeks. 'He tried to take me for a McDonalds, yesterday lunchtime, can you imagine that? Me sat in a drive-through at McDonalds? Whatever next?'

It was Polly's turn to force a smile and the three chatted away for almost an hour before it was clear Polly was tired, as the conversation waned.

'Have a sleep, love?' Tom looked into her eyes, she nodded. 'I think I will to be honest.'

'Look, we'll leave you now and come back this afternoon, have a sleep, so proud of you darling.' He kissed Polly on the cheek as she raised her hand to touch him.

Jody hugged her and then smiled at Polly, flicking her head towards Tom. 'Don't worry babe, I'll look after him for a while. I'll take him back to yours tomorrow and get him to do a bit of housework, I bet you look good in a piny and no pants, doing the hoovering, I'll send you the photos, Pol.'

She held out her hand again to Jody, who leaned forward and kissed her. 'We were so worried about you, my darling, but I knew you would pull through, tough little cookie, you.'

Tom and Jody walked out, turning at the door and waving back. It was good timing, the doctor was doing his rounds. It was Doctor Surtees, who smiled at Tom as he came towards the pair of them.

'Well, that's a big improvement,' Dr Surtees said to Tom. He was happy with Polly's progress. 'I called in to see her this morning after one of the nurses bleeped me to say she was awake. There is a long way to go as I know you know but this is a very good sign.'

'Thanks doctor, it's such a relief. Oh, by the way, this is Jody,

Polly's friend,' Tom put his hand out in Jody's direction. She smiled.

'Oh, one more thing Tom, have you got a minute, over here.' The doctor beckoned him away from Jody and nurse Beazley who had been standing with them. He looked at them. 'Nothing to worry about ladies, just need a chat.'

The two walked over to the water dispenser.

'You sounded surprised on Friday when I mentioned about the baby, Mr Armstrong, are you telling me you didn't know?'

'I had no idea. And I have no idea if Polly knows, she hasn't mentioned it to me, obviously.'

The doctor looked concerned. 'The reason I ask is because I checked again last night from her bloods and all is well, but I didn't know if she knows, so I haven't said anything. Obviously the nurses will find out, but if your wife doesn't know, it would be best coming from you, however that's up to you. I just didn't know how you wanted to approach it. The chances of keeping it quiet in here are going to be tricky as she is going to get regular tests. I will tell the nurses the situation, hopefully no-one will say anything and I'll leave it up to you, but don't leave it too long. Oh, I assume congrats are in order.'

'They are, doctor, leave it with me, I'll tell her.'

Tom returned to Jody who was standing on her own looking through the glass at her friend, Polly had dropped off to sleep.

'What was that all about,' she said, as Tom joined her by the window. 'Nothing serious, I hope.'

'Oh, no, nothing serious. I promise you,' Tom began to walk off. 'Come on, I'll get you a coffee.'

'Everything is okay isn't it? You better not be hiding any secrets from me, Tom Armstrong because if you do, I'll get them out of you, you do know that?' She nudged him as the pair walked down the hospital corridor, arms linked.

'Everything's fine, Jode, how could I possibly keep a secret from you anyway? You and Polly know everything there is to know about each other, you probably know more about me than I know.'

'Including your favourite sex position.' Jody winked. 'I would never have thought it, either. Even Craig wouldn't try that.'

He nudged her back as they smiled at each other. Polly's

improvement had given them both a big boost after all the worry of recent days.

'Do you two really tell each other everything?' They headed towards the car park.

'Oh yes, everything,' Jody had a beam on her face.

The pair got into Jody's car and went for lunch.

'She was looking a bit more like her old self?' Jody was talking as she drove. They were heading into the Cambridgeshire countryside and had agreed to find a quiet pub where they could talk, while Tom could also make more phone calls. He needed to call Polly's parents again.

'I must admit, I feared the worse when I first got there on Friday night.' Tom said as he fiddled with his phone and read texts. 'It was hours before they would let me see her.'

It was nice for Tom not to have to drive. He looked at his phone. He had four missed calls and five texts. As he flicked at the screen, he pressed 121 for messages. He had two, the first one from Polly's parents asking him to give them a call ASAP, then came the second one, from Karen. He listened to it once, then again.

He couldn't believe it, she'd even had the gall to mention Polly's accident — *how the fuck did she know?* And Wednesday? He couldn't make Wednesday, he would still be here with Polly.

'So, what do you think?' Jody looked at him. 'Tom?'

He was miles away. Think? The only thing he was thinking about was Karen's message.

'Sorry, Jody, what do I think about what?'

'Dogs?'

'Dogs?' Tom looked confused. 'What about them?'

'What I just said about Craig saying I should think about getting one, I'm not sure though. Don't know why he thinks I need a dog.'

Tom didn't know what to say. He hadn't taken in Jody's talk about dogs but he soon managed to work out what she was talking about.

'Well, if you want to know, personally I love dogs, but only other people's. I wouldn't have one, Polly would, which I know doesn't surprise you. But not me, too much of a tie. Why would you and Craig want one, anyhow?'

'Well, we chatted the other night and he mentioned having a dog, security and all that. He went to the Arsenal game with a mate of his who is a breeder of Alsatians. He said we could have one for a small price.'

'Oh, shit, the Arsenal game. Well done Jode, how did they get on?' He looked at her. She shrugged her shoulders. 'I don't know.'

Tom got frantically back on his phone to check. Manchester City 3 Arsenal 3. Sounded a bit of game. Craig had watched a good one, even more so when Tom noticed that Arsenal had been 1-3 down with 10 minutes left.

'Wow. It finished 3-3.' He sounded excited. 'I bet Craig enjoyed that.'

Jody looked disinterested. 'Whoopee do, who cares? Wouldn't it be better if you made a few phone calls, rather than worrying about football?'

He smiled. She was right. He would talk to Polly's parents and he would text back Stu, Ben, and Polly's boss Andy, he must remember to call Jill sometime tonight as well.

That just left Karen. She could wait.

PCs Kevin Rigby and David Shoreditch didn't think much would come of a call to go and investigate a suspicious car that had been left in woods near a country park, not far from Bootle Golf Club. It was early Sunday morning.

The car was likely a stolen one, left by kids who had been joy-riding around Merseyside on Saturday night before dumping it, although why they would abandon it where they had was not immediately obvious.

The car was well hidden and the pair of them drove past it to begin with, although Rigby thought he'd spotted the glint of silver of a wing mirror.

'Hang on, there was something back there,' said Rigby. 'Turn around.'

The pair pulled up near to the spot where the car had been reported tucked into trees. It must have been reversed in because the car's front was slightly sticking out, someone had certainly tried to get it out of sight. It looked like a VW Golf.

The two officers approached the car in a casual manner,

expecting to see it damaged, windows broken, the usual unnecessary hooliganism that followed joy riding. But it didn't look that bad from the front. Shoreditch took the registration number and went back to his car to call it in, they would soon know who the abandoned vehicle was registered to.

Suddenly there was a shout from Rigby

'Dave, get over here, quick. There's a bloody body in here.'

Sure enough, slouched on the back seat was the body of a man. Rigby had opened one of the back doors, they didn't need to look any further. He was a mess.

'Shit,' said Shoreditch, as he joined his partner. 'Don't touch anything else Kev.

Shoreditch got away from the car and got onto his phone again, calling for more officers and an ambulance. He couldn't be sure what had happened here, but one look at the gun alongside the body suggested the guy had taken his life, or it was a gangland killing.

The two officers knew they had to make sure no-one got close to the car, not until help arrived. They would have to block the road off.

Shoreditch's phone crackled into action again, it was HQ.

'Dave,' the policeman on the other end said. 'The reg number of that car you wanted.

'It belongs to a Mr Alban... a Mr Jimmy Alban.'

SIXTY TWO

HAROLD and Posselwhite were always on duty, even when they were not.

The life of a copper in CID was anything but 9-5. Harold and Posselwhite knew it, their families knew it. So a call at any time of the night or day was never a surprise, 9am on a Sunday morning for instance.

'Pete, it's Graham Cook, I need you and Steven out to an incident at a country park near Bootle. I'll text you the post code and the road name, give Steve a call and be there ASAP, bad news Pete.'

'Bad news?' Harold looked surprised. 'What bad news?'

'We'll speak when we get there.' Cook was in a hurry. 'I'm on my way now.'

Harold got hold of Posselwhite and the pair met up at a garage on the way to Bootle. Harold had the directions, while Posselwhite drove. Both were intrigued. Cook's involvement was significant, so this must be important. The big cheese didn't come out on a Sunday morning for a garden ornament being stolen from someone's front garden.

The two DIs drove through the cordoned off road, flashing their badges as they did so. The incident was about half-a-mile further on, they pulled up and they could already see Cook standing talking to a couple of uniforms.

'Morning guv.' Harold clapped his hands together. There was a nip in the air. 'So, what's this all about on a Sunday morning? Thought you played golf Sundays?'

Cook's face never cracked. 'Take a look at this boys.'

The pair followed him towards a car they could see was buried in woods off the road, there was tape around it and a couple of SOCOs were beginning to put white coats on. As all three got closer to the car, Cook stood back.

'Take a look, in the back.'

Posselwhite went one side of the car and Harold the other. The door on the side Harold went round was still closed, but Posselwhite's was open.

'Fuck, shit,' Posselwhite exclaimed. 'Shit, its Jimmy Alban, isn't it?' He turned round to look at his boss who was standing behind him.

Cook nodded. Harold put his hand to the window to peer in, he didn't have as good a sight of Alban as Posselwhite, but he could see enough. He came round to Posselwhite's side for a better view. Alban's face was a mess, but you could tell it was him. Harold looked round the car just to make sure, but it was Alban's alright, Harold had seen him pull up in it at work on occasions. Anyhow, that had been confirmed.

'What a right balls-up this is turning into.' Cook looked at them both. We've got a young cop taking his own life, well it looks that way, just a few days after telling us he's infiltrated police records on one of the biggest investigations we've had in a decade and gone and told someone who the informant was. And if that's not bad enough, you two guys had him in your office interrogating him. Was it all on the record? Was it recorded? Or did you just sweep him up and 'have a chat?' Because if you did, you'd better keep that to yourself, there will be an investigation into what led to this, you do know that? Maybe Alban left a note somewhere, then again, I'm not sure if that would be good or a bad thing.'

'We taped the meeting.' Harold said. 'We asked him if he wanted a Fed Rep and he said no. He was fucked sir. As we told you, he coughed up all what he'd done about going to the vaults and finding Baldini's name, the only thing he didn't, or wouldn't, tell us is who he told Baldini's name to.'

'Okay', said Cook, relieved that his two officers had at least had the common sense to do things by the book. He walked away from the car, beckoning the two to walk with him. 'Well, I'm glad you did things the right way. But now we have to sort this poor kid's family out. If it is suicide, which we are assuming at the moment, then it could be about Baldini and what Alban has done, then again, it might be his girlfriend packed him up last night and he couldn't handle it. It could be one of Archer's mob that think he's grassed them up. I really don't know. But if he's been shot, then we have a murder on our hands, either way, this isn't nice.'

Harold went back to the car to take one last look at Alban. He was pretty sure the young lad had taken his own life, there was a gun lying on the floor and Alban was sprawled back in the seat. Either he, or someone, had put the gun under his throat, there was a bullet hole coming out of the roof of the car.

'It might not be suicide, boss?' Posselwhite had taken another look inside the back seat. 'I mean Alban was messing around with a big case here, looking for names. Someone has put him up to finding Baldini's name, what if that someone got the name and then wanted Alban out of it?'

'There are lots of possibilities.' Cook nodded his head. 'Perhaps all is not as obvious as it seems. Then again, as I said, maybe he has left a note, let's hope so, because if not, we may have a bigger case on our hands than we are aware of, and it could involve Archer again.'

At the sound of Archer's name, Posselwhite and Harold looked at each other. Harold nodded at Posselwhite, who nodded back.

'Sir,' Harold called out to Cook who was starting to walk away. 'There is one thing you need to know.'

Cook showed no emotion as he walked back towards them. 'And what is that?'

'Yesterday, we picked up a bloke called Tony Statton, lifted him near Strangeways prison and said we wanted a word.

'Oh, did you?' Cook looked unimpressed. 'And why did you do that?'

'Well, Statton had been to see Archer in prison, the governor called us yesterday to say Archer had a visitor. Remember, we'd told him to look out for visitors. Apparently it's unusual for Archer to have any, only his son Liam visits regularly. This was the second time in a week or so this bloke Statton had been.

'So, we looked into him. He used to live around here, in

Liverpool, during Archer's 'reign'. Not that Statton has a record, not even a speeding ticket, he now lives in Southampton, left to go there about 10 years or so ago. So, what is he doing travelling from Southampton to Manchester to visit Archer? Twice.

'We kept an eye on him as he left the prison then we picked him up. Drove him to Jenkin Bush Industrial Estate and asked him if he knew Baldini, or has heard of him. It was a long shot but he wouldn't give us anything, so he gets arsey. But I smell a rat with him. You don't come all that way to visit someone without it meaning something, he could just have phoned.'

Cook looked at the pair of them. 'Okay, well you were right to speak to him, I had hoped this Archer case was closed. At least Alban gave us something, the news that someone or some people are after Baldini's name, we need to keep an eye on Baldini.

'He's in real danger.'

SIXTY THREE

THE improvement in Polly continued apace.

Monday lunchtime, Jody and Tom were at her bedside chatting and smiling, both holding Polly's hands, not that the poor girl wasn't still in a lot of pain. The right-hand side of her body had taken the full impact of the crash, her ankle, kneecap and shoulder that were all broken and, despite numerous pain-killers, she could feel the hurt. At least she was no longer wired up to any machines and the doctor said she would be moving onto a general ward later that day.

'What happened to the other car in the crash?' Polly looked at Tom.

Tom looked at Jody who raised her eyebrows. 'Come on, I know what happened, well sort of what happened. So?'

Tom took her hand. 'Well, there were three young lads in it and one died, the other two were walking wounded and I don't know anything about the boy who was killed.'

Polly looked into space and away from both of them. 'That's so awful, I was lucky then. Very lucky.'

'You were. But the crash wasn't your fault.' Jody said. 'They were on the wrong side of the road, you were the innocent victim. So, by all means think about it for a little while, but not too long, you need to get yourself better and back to work and back to that pub in your village. Oh, and Las Vegas.'

'Ah, yeah, Vegas,' Polly's face lit up. 'Are we still going? What's happened with it all? Don't stop looking at brochures because of me, I'll be there.'

Tom looked at Jody who knew more what was going on with the trip than he did. 'Well, Craig and I were about to book this weekend, but then for some reason we just haven't, something else has come up.' She raised her eyebrows at her friend. 'No, only joking darling, we will look to book when you are able to fly, which won't be just yet I don't reckon. Although I've been on planes with people who have come hobbling on them with crutches.'

'Oh no, I can't be doing that, Jode, I'd rather wait and be able to walk myself than have everyone getting out of my way, or being pushed around the airport on one of those little carts that bleep.'

'But think of all the attention you will get?' Tom said. 'All those pilots and cabin crew making sure you are safe and well when you arrive on the plane and you get to go on first.'

'Yeah, but you have to go off last, don't you?' Jody said. 'Although do you get pushed to the front of passport control? In fact, I hadn't thought of that, it could be useful. We could all say we're with you and get to the front of the queue.'

The girls grinned and Tom was pleased to see his wife back in good spirits. He knew there was a long way to go, but he felt more comfortable. Anyhow, he had to get back to work. Perhaps he would have tomorrow off and go back Wednesday, then he remembered Karen's message.

'Have you spoken to Andy?' Polly wanted to make sure her boss knew her situation. 'He knows I'm in here I assume? ....Tom?'

He had been thinking of Karen, but snapped out of it. 'Yes, I spoke to him yesterday and he was most worried and concerned. He sends all his love and Kevin does too apparently, but misses your sparring in team meetings.'

'I bet he does. Do you know what? I reckon me and Kev could be on a desert island together, just the two of us, and we wouldn't get on. We are chalk and cheese.'

'Is he really that bad?' Jody looked surprised.

'Is he? You bet. It doesn't matter what I say or do, he picks faults in it and he's always trying to score points with Andy. He's a hairy gorilla creep-arse.'

'Pol.' Tom shook his head. 'That's no way to talk about someone who has sent his best wishes.'

'You don't know him like I do. Kevin wouldn't like you

anyhow, you're too posh.'

'As if I am. Crikey, I can see you're better... *too posh*. Who you kidding?'

All three smiled. Life was on the mend.

'Have you spoken to Craig?' Tom and Jody had left Polly having lunch. She was starting to feel tired after a morning of chatting to the pair of them and although she wanted them to stay, they had decided to go and find something to eat and leave her to rest.

'Yeah, I spoke to him last night.' Jody was marching alongside Tom, trying to keep up with the pace of his walk. 'He was fine, just nipping across to the pub for a quick couple of pints, so he said. I think he quite likes it when I'm not there, he was happy to hear Polly is on the mend.'

'So, you two getting on just fine?' Jody spun her head towards him.

'Ah, yes, we're fine. Why do you ask?'

'No reason. It was just a question, nothing more, really. I don't know why I said it like that to be honest.'

She linked her arm in his as they continued to walk. 'We're fine my darling, don't you worry about us, you just look after our Pol.'

They smiled at each other and carried on walking. But Tom felt awkward. Why did he say that?

Marie put her phone down. It had rung six times and he hadn't answered. She would wait until the evening to call him again.

But first she had to catch up with Charlie as she headed into Liverpool city centre.

'Charlie, you in the pub again?'

'My darling Marie, twice in three days, I love listening to your voice. No, I'm not in the pub, I'm in the bookies and I've just had a nice little win on the 12.25 at Newcastle, so I'm in a good mood.'

'Oh, glad to hear that,' although she hated betting. Stuart had gambled thousands over the years. When he won, he was all sweetness and light, champagne, flowers, he even bought her a new Mazda sports car when he won big on the horses one time.

But when he lost it was a different story. He would sit around the house drinking, saying little. Stuart only ever hit her once, and that was after returning home from the bookies one Saturday afternoon. He hadn't even been drinking but he'd lost about 50K. Marie's comment about gambling being for jokers, saw him fly into a rage. He apologised and never hit her again, however that was the beginning of the end for them as a couple as far as Marie was concerned. She stayed for a few more years, she liked the lifestyle. But her heart had long gone.

'Mug's game, you know that,' Marie waited for his response, Charlie didn't let her down.

'Not always my love, not always, I've had plenty of big wins.' *'And plenty of big losses'*, she thought to herself.

'Anyhow, when you getting this arsehole to me. Baldini isn't it? You sure you can do it okay?'

'Of course I can. Anyhow, why are you doing this? I'm doing it for the money, what's your motive, Charlie?'

'I'm doing it for my friend. You know me and Stuart go back a long way. He's like a brother to me, so, don't you worry love about what I'm thinking or doing, you just get that bloke to me.'

'I'll text you the details. It will be in the next couple of days.'

She hung up and looked about. The city was busy with people running this way and that. It had started to rain as well. Charlie hadn't answered her question about what would happen to Craig if she delivered him to him…. *If she did!*

At least Stuart wouldn't be about for the next 15 years. It gave her a chance for a fresh start. She was playing with fire and she knew it.

But she was a big girl now.

SIXTY FOUR

JILL and Emily had managed to contact most patients in an effort to stop those making unnecessary journeys to the surgery, but not everyone. Although a Bank Holiday Monday, they had always opened in the morning for a few hours.

Both Mr Tuttle and Mrs Braithwaite had arrived, only to be told the news their appointments were cancelled. They demanded to know why. Jill had already spoken to Tom and he had told her to say on the email it was due to 'unforeseen circumstances'. But if people came to the surgery, Jill had been told to say, 'family illness'.

'When do you think he will be back?,' Emily said as she and Jill used their time in the surgery to tidy up a few bits and pieces they hadn't been able to get around to doing in recent months. 'Have you spoken to him?'

'I spoke to him last night. Just for a couple of minutes. He said he wouldn't be in until Wednesday at the earliest, but likely Thursday.'

'Can I call him, do you think?' Emily looked at Jill, who looked surprised. 'You call him? Why would you want to do that?'

'I'm just concerned, he is my boss as well, you know.'

'Well, it's up to you, I can't tell you not to. But don't be surprised if you can't get hold of him. He's spending hours at Polly's bedside.'

Emily began tidying up some books on the table in reception.

Craig knew there were still a few loose ends to tie up. But he'd be fine, he was a good organiser. Not everyone was in the office this

Monday morning and being a Bank Holiday, dress was casual.

'So, when's Jody coming back?' Lisa had put a cup of coffee for him on his desk. He had told her the news about his wife having to head to Cambridge to be with a friend who had been involved in a car crash.

'Oh, I don't know. I imagine she will lap it up down there, her friend is on the mend. It was a worry for a while. But now she will want to enjoy chatting to her endlessly, no doubt.'

'Well, I hope you are cleaning up at home. Making sure the house is spotless when that lovely wife of yours returns. She won't want to come home to your pants and socks scattered everywhere and don't say that won't happen because I know how it works when you men are left to your own devices. You make a right mess, I bet you haven't done any washing up either.'

'You can read me like a book. That's why I value you so much,' Craig winked at her. 'I don't suppose you are offering?'

'Offering what? Offering to tidy up your house? Are you kidding me? I'll tell you what, if you are serious, I'll do it, only to help Jody, she's such a good kid.'

'I'm only joking.' He laughed. 'My house is spotless. Even my shoes sparkle.'

She gave him a knowing look. 'Well, you had better done, okay, I'm going for lunch now, and then leaving off early if that's alright?'

'You know it is my little cherry.'

'Shut up Craig. I'll see you tomorrow.'

'See ya.'

Craig sat back in his chair and flicked the television on. All the directors had televisions in their offices and it was mainly the news channels he watched, although he was getting bored of all the negative stories that seemed to feature on mainstream media these days.

His mobile rang. He looked at the number, smiled to himself and took the call.

'Mr Craig Baldini,' he said.

'Hi Craig. I don't know if you remember me? But I'm guessing you will. It's Marie. Marie Archer. We got to know each other quite well at a weekend conference last year. Or was it the year before that? Do you remember?'

Craig looked up at the ceiling shaking his head.

'Marie Archer. Yeah, I remember you, now what the hell is all this all about?'

'Now, now. I just want to meet, that's all.'

'Are you kidding me? Why the fuck would I want to meet you? I tried to call you after that night but you never answered, a right little bitch you turned out to be.'

'You sound like a child, Craig. I thought you had more about you than that. Anyhow, I have something you will be very interested in. Now, listen up and listen good will you? Because if you don't.....'

Ten minutes later Craig put the phone down. His face was like thunder. A sex tape. Shit. He saw Jason's reflection in the window and banged the table, he knew Jason saw it, Craig waved him in.

'Hello mate, you okay? You haven't forgotten our meeting, have you?' Jason looked concerned.

'Um, yeah, I'm fine, I'll be there. Look, do you mind if we postpone the meeting till later this afternoon, I've got to go out, need a bit of fresh air to be honest. Can we say 4ish?'

'Of course. We were hoping to get away early today, but no probs. You okay? You look like you've seen a ghost. Come on man, if something is up, Pete and I are here, you know, one for all and all that.' Jason smiled at his Musketeer's reference.

'I'm fine. See you at 4.' Craig took his coat and walked out of the office.

As he strolled past the many offices and firms PJC Shipping shared that area of Liverpool with, he picked up the pace. He had things to do and he needed to crack on.

Marie called Charlie.

'Wednesday night, 7pm. But you know that don't you? Let me meet him first. I'll bring him to you, then I'm out of all this shit, Charlie, do you understand?'

'My beauty,' Charlie was smiling to himself. 'Stuart must be so proud of you. Yes, I heard the conversation. Very convincing. Bugging his phone like that. You are so naughty, that poor chap. Glad I haven't got a secret sex tape.'

She rolled her eyes. 'See ya Wednesday, Charlie.'

SIXTY FIVE

HE flicked through Karen's text.

'Klan's Clinic, 53 Upper Minster Avenue, The Thoroughfare, Wimbledon, SW1. 10am, Wednesday. It's £300. Bring ID. I'll bring mine and Lee's DNA results. See you there.'

He read the text again. He was happy Polly was on the mend but their lives was still on hold. He had hoped Karen would contact him and say she'd had a change of heart. That she had been wrong all along and she didn't for one minute think he was Lee's father. Clearly some hope. She was going ahead with this, and he had little choice. If he failed to turn up, Karen wouldn't let it go and he didn't want that, this would have to be dealt with.

Polly had been moved to a general ward and although she was set to be in hospital for another week, Tom was considering opening up his dental surgery again, possibly Thursday. What he had to work out was how he was going to get out of seeing Polly on Wednesday.

Jody was in with Polly on a general ward. Visiting hours were a bit less restricted, it was almost midday and she was chatting to her friend. A couple of policemen had been earlier to take a statement from Polly about the accident, now she was in a better way. They had as good as told her car's tyre marks on the road had suggested she was not to blame for the accident, they hadn't stayed long.

'So, what are you looking forward to doing most when you get home?' Jody was leaning excitedly into Polly's face. 'Let me guess, going to the pub?'

'Are you kidding? No, I'm looking forward to Tom having to

undress me very slowly. Very, very slowly and then giving me a good rub down on the bed. With those lovely oils you bought me for Christmas, remember the ones? We've only used the strawberry flavour.'

'You naughty cow. Is that all you can think of? What about a nice warm bath? That's what I'd go for.'

'Well, could do I suppose but I've already had two here. I'll still have my ankle in some sort of bandage, I reckon, which will make it difficult. Although they do put ankles in those plastic things these days, don't they? We'll have to see, so long as Tom has to undress me, I'll be happy.' The pair giggled.

'You sound happy,' said Tom as he saddled up to Polly's bed. 'What are we all laughing about?'

'Don't tell him Jode. You'll give him ideas.'

'What ideas,' Tom looked surprised.

'Naughty ones,' Polly replied. 'Very naughty ones.'

Tom gave her a kiss on the cheek and then smiled at Jody. 'Well, it's nice to see some things never change. Here you are, bought some flowers.'

'Ooh, lovely, have we got a vase, Jode?'

Jody got up and went to the side table next to Polly's bed. There was no vase inside, she got up to go and find one.

'How are you then, tiger?' He went to hold Polly's hand. 'You feeling good, those bruises on your face are going down.'

'I'm okay, looking forward to going home. Don't know when that will be though, hopefully soon.'

He leant over and kissed her. 'Oh, by the way, I've got to go to London on Wednesday. It's a dentist conference, I don't have to go, but seeing as you are on the mend, do you mind? I just need to find out if Jody is still going to be here.'

'A conference? Is it all day, or more than a day? Sounds dull!'

'It's just a day.' Tom was trying hard to keep the subject conversation to a minimum.

Jody came back with a vase.

'God, look at this,' she said. 'It looks like something from the Victorian ages, it's the best I could find though, but it will do a job.'

Jody arranged the flowers and put them on the side table.

'Actually, they're really nice,' Jody said. 'Where did you get them, a garage?'

The girls both laughed. Tom looked indignant. 'No, I bloody didn't. M&S if you must know and they weren't reduced before you ask.'

'The only time Craig buys me flowers is when he wants an early night,' Jody said, flicking her eyebrows up at Polly, who winked in return.

'Oh hell, not back on this subject again, are we for goodness sake?' Tom started to get up. 'I need a wee.'

As he headed off to the toilet, he turned round. 'Oh, by the way Jody, when are you thinking of going back to Chester? It's just that I'm in London at a conference on Wednesday, I'll be back later, but, you know, whatever you're doing.'

Polly looked at Jody, who looked at Tom. 'I was going to go home Thursday, probably just after lunch if that's okay with you guys? We still have a bit to catch up on, don't we Pol?'

Polly nodded her head. 'Lots.'

'Okay, well that will be great. I was only wondering.'

'Well, stop wondering and go for a pee,' Polly joked. 'At least I have one person I can rely on to be with me through all this.

'You go and play dentists with your friends.'

SIXTY SIX

After the meeting with his fellow directors on Monday afternoon, Craig went back into his own office.

The meeting had been one long blur, the sort of meeting he was now bored of. Talk of budgets, targets, new contracts, bonuses. Money, money, money, grind and grind again, he looked around the office. It had been his home for more than six years. He was sick of it.

It was 4.45pm. He looked out across the floor and saw Lisa laughing, good old Lisa. What was she still doing here? Thought she was going home early? Oh well, she's probably the only person in the office he genuinely liked. She'll be furious, not upset, but bloody furious.

Craig knew this was it. He'd danced with the devil and still was, but he had to do this. He wanted to do this, they both did. Craig knew whichever way the coin landed, he was going to hurt people. But this was about him, this was about them.

No-one knew Craig Baldini, like Craig Baldini.

His life had degenerated into one huge web of deceit and lies and now the final act was going to pass. He looked out at the office again and saw Jason chatting on the phone. No-one had a clue. He wasn't proud of himself, it had been in the planning for almost a year. Thank goodness Jody's IVF had failed. The thought of her having his children. He'd dodged a bullet there, not that it would have changed anything.

Tom would be his spokesperson if he so chose. He didn't know the whole story but he knew enough. Oh, yes, he knew he would be viewed as a coward, as a total arsehole. His name would be mud and the collateral damage would be catastrophic. But it would be too late then, it was too late now.

It was just after 5pm and it was time to leave, he had to be there by 7.30, he had time.

Lisa knocked on the door and waved goodbye. 'See you tomorrow'. He lip read her through the glass. He put up his hand. He thought about blowing her a kiss but no, he must keep everything together. Now was not the time to buckle. He would nip home, the few things he needed were already in the case in the back of his car. All his worldly goods.

He left the office not even bothering to say goodbye to Jason and Pete. What a fuck fest he was leaving behind. By the time they noticed the money, he'd be gone.

Craig looked at his phone before he started the car up and drove home, Jody had called and left a text, *'hey, give me a call lover boy!'*, it had said, along with a couple of bright red lip emojis. How he hated those emojis. He pulled in the drive and went in through the front door, looked around his house, he remembered all the times he had shared with Jody... Lovely dear Jody. The parties with friends, the laughter, the tears, the fun and the games.

But this was no time for sentiment. That had gone out of the window back in that hotel room *that* night during *that* conference 18 months ago. This was for the best, even the timing of Polly's crash and Jody's trip to visit her had worked out perfectly. He couldn't have planned it better himself.

Oh, and Polly. What would she say? Best not to think. He looked at a photo of the four of them on the sideboard in the dining room, it was from New Year's Eve three years ago. In fairness it was one of his favourite photos, the four of them laughing, glasses in hand, clearly drunk. He would miss them, especially Polly. If there was one woman on the planet he would have loved to have shagged, it would have been her. Lucky Tom, *the bastard.*

He positioned the note in the middle of the table, looked round one more time and walked out. He was taking nothing, Jody at least deserved a house in one piece, the way she had always known it. It just wouldn't contain him anymore. His final act was to position the letter in the middle of the kitchen table... *'To Jody'.*

He drove the 10 miles to the scrapyard and met up with the owner, the booking had been made. Craig was 10 minutes early, he got his case out of the car.

Craig handed over the money. It was not often cars were crushed at this yard for a £4,000 fee. But the owner wasn't asking questions, if he'd wanted to be a journalist he would have studied harder at school!

Craig looked on as his precious Z4 was turned into a small metal piece of mush. His phone was in the glove compartment, what was left of it. He loved that car as well. He left the yard and wandered onto the street alongside where the taxi was waiting. It would take only 45 minutes to the airport.

As he got out of the taxi and walked into the airport, he joined the queue for the flight to New York. He hadn't flown American Airlines before, but he'd heard good things about them. He was soon through customs and passports and after grabbing a sandwich and a cup of coffee, made his way to the gate.

This was it then.

Craig was glad to see the plane was on time and he boarded with 45 minutes to go. His ticket was 10A and was pretty close to the front. For someone who had spent far too much time flying on smaller budget airlines, he appreciated the extra leg room, and the TV.

He looked around and put his case in the overhead locker, then looked at his watch. It was 9pm.

As he sat back down and looked out of the window at the damp greyness of a typical Manchester evening, he didn't notice the case being put in the locker alongside his. Then, as he turned away from the window and looked up, his eyes met hers and they both smiled. She sat in the seat next to him, leant over and kissed him on the cheek.

'So, this is it then, Craig Baldini. You've done it, we've done it. No turning back now you know.'

He smiled and put his hand on Marie's cheek, pulling her close to him.

'Who wants to turn back?'

SIXTY SEVEN

THE flight to New York was just under eight hours. They would arrive early morning, which although wasn't great, neither were fussed. They had half a day to spend before the connecting flight.

'So, here we are then,' Craig smiled at Marie, holding her hand.

She may have been older than him, but Marie had charmed him the moment he saw her at the business meeting in Liverpool. 'Drunken sex', he had told Tom. Well, it may have been that first night, but after that it had been anything but.

'You called me a bitch,' She pinched him on the leg. 'On the phone, you called me a bitch.'

He laughed and put his head back. 'You told me Charlie would be listening, I had to act the part. I was going to start saying how the only good thing about you was the size of your tits. But I didn't want to get the poor old boy aroused!'

They laughed and she took a sip of her coffee. 'No, dear, you did the right thing.

'I'm just glad you trusted me about bugging your phone. Makes the story seem truthful. Charlie will have swallowed it. It comes with years of experience of being married to a man like Stuart. I know all his tricks. As I told you, even after your final run, you were still in his pocket, and you never even knew. You're just lucky he didn't know find out about us. Still don't know how he didn't.'

Craig smiled. 'You do know I ended up with three bloody phones in the end. I was mixing and matching them all over the place. How Jody didn't find the others I still don't know, but I'm glad that's all over with, I haven't got any phones now. I crushed the last one with my BMW. Just hope Stuart knows nothing about us.'

'He doesn't, so don't get wet on me, Craig. We've been through all this. You know the risks, I know the risks. All we can do is minimise the risk, I've booked six different flights out of the UK, with six connecting flights and six more flights after that. We could be anywhere in the world from Canada to New Zealand and we have a private plane waiting at JFK. Okay, it's not fool-proof, but it's a pretty good start. I can't imagine Stuart, or Charlie for that matter wanting to travel the globe looking for us. Not that Stuart can.

'Was Charlie really going to smash up my knee-caps?'

'Yeah, and the rest,' Marie took another sip of her drink. 'Knee caps, broken legs, even cutting off one of your ears. I know of at least three people Stuart 'got rid of' permanently. How he's only in prison for 25 years when it should be 125, I don't know. Still, that's another little string to my bow. I could put him away for life if I wanted to, the information I hold on him. That's one good reason he is likely to leave us alone, if he ever does find out I'm with you.

'He'll jump up and down for a while about you vanishing but he won't think you've run off with me. You've just gone. When he finds out, which he is bound to, will he be bothered? Maybe, maybe not, that's Stuart all over, he moves on, he'll have to move on. But he will be pissed about you stitching him up and me not showing up with you. Then again, that's the world he has always lived in, deceit, lies and taking chances.'

'And you've spoken to Liam?'

'Yes. He's fine. I didn't tell him where I was going and I never mentioned you. He wished me all the best. He did as his dad asked, getting me to set you up. Stuart loves Liam and he would rather he had nothing to do with any of this. So long as he says he knew nothing about us leaving, his dad will stick by him.'

'Which just leaves that bloody sex tape?' Craig looked at Marie with a wry smile, as a hostess came past asking if anyone wanted more drinks. The pair said no.

'Well, you should have sorted that. You got the car crushed.'

'Into a pulp, my darling,' Craig laughed. 'Perhaps we should have kept the DVD, reminded us of our great first night.'

Marie almost spat out her coffee. 'Great night? Are you kidding me? You were almost asleep trying to do it the first time and in the morning, you felt so guilty you were gone by 7.'

Craig sat back and smiled. Never in a million years did he think 18 months on it would have led to this.

After his first encounter with Marie, Stuart had contacted him to do the runs. Marie had also contacted wanting to meet him. He had refused, but she was persistent, it started off with her saying she would speak to her husband about letting him off from the drugs runs. Then it developed into a meeting for a drink and a chat, the chemistry was unstoppable, the affair began. The planning for all this had been a year in the making.

'Did you leave a note for your wife?' Marie looked at Craig, who was looking out of the aircraft window.

'I'd rather not think about it.' He returned the look. 'It's about us now.'

Craig kissed her on the cheek and sat back in his seat. He turned his television on to watch a film there were plenty of choices, but one caught his eye, *'Indecent Proposal'*. He hadn't seen it for years.

'This is an appropriate film to watch.' He nudged Marie who was still trying to work out how to get her TV to work.

'What is?'

''Indecent Proposal'. I think it stars Demi Moore.'

'Why is that appropriate?' Marie looked at him. 'What is it about?'

'Haven't you seen it? It's great. It's about this guy who offers a husband a million dollars to spend the night with his wife, they agree, but it causes all sorts of issues, great finale though.'

'Seems you know the film inside out, so why watch it? What it's got to do with us.'

'Nothing really but what a dilemma, don't you think? I mean what would you do if you were offered a million bucks to sleep with someone?'

Marie looked at him and grinned. 'Who says, I haven't? Well, not a million, but Stuart knew how to make money, for him and me. I was one of his biggest cash cows.'

'Are you serious? You haven't done that, have you?'

Marie took hold of his face and turned it to his. Her tone changed. 'Look, lover boy, you know my history, you know my story. I have done things with men most women wouldn't dream of watching on TV, let alone doing in their own bedrooms, I've told you all this. You've known the deal since we began planning for our lives together. I've told you I'll always tell you the truth, no questions, no ifs, no buts. It's you I love. No, it wasn't for a million, it was for £10,000, if you want to know, many, many years ago. And Stuart made sure I got a large percentage of it. Did I regret it? Maybe. But remember where I came from? Think of the wealth, the glamour and money I was, and still am, afforded, I'm the wife of a drugs baron, gangster, call him what you want, and it's a dangerous life. But with big rewards. Look what we are doing now. So, you sit and watch that film and think what you wish, I'll never duck any of your questions. But if we are to have a great life ahead, the past must be exactly that, the past.'

He kissed her hand. 'I know, it's all about the future, don't worry. I'm not a silly green-eyed kid. £10K? Blimey, I was desperate to sleep with my mate's wife and I'd have done it for nothing.'

'Well there you are then,' Marie smiled. And did you?'

He shook his head. 'Sadly... no!'

She smiled. 'And that's the difference.'

'Does Craig mind you staying here with me all this time.' Polly looked at Jody and leant over to get some grapes from the fruit bowl next to her bed. The ward she was on had 10 people in it, mostly with broken and fractured bones. It had plenty of windows in it though, was very airy and most of the patients were young or a bit older than Polly.

'Can't get hold of him. He told me he had meetings at work yesterday and today he was apparently travelling to Blackpool on business, so his work said, I'll just wait to hear from him.'

'Have you talked any more about surrogacy?' said Polly, taking the opportunity to mention it while Tom had gone off to make a call to Jill in the surgery.

'Not really. In fact we haven't talked about much in the last couple of weeks. I told you he'd been a bit quiet. I know him too well, something is bothering him and I reckon it could be to do with the IVF. You know what men are like? They are like swans. On the surface everything looks fine, but underneath they're flapping away.'

'At least Tom appears more relaxed. You should have seen him on Saturday when you were still out of it, he was a wreck. I honestly think he thought he'd lost you, he thinks so much of you, Pol.'

'I know.'

The two sipped the cups of tea the nurse had brought them.

'So, are you still feeling okay about Tom and this other woman? You don't mind me asking. It's just that you said you were going to see it through, you still feel the same? Especially after all this....'

'I know I did.' Polly took another sip of her tea. 'Easier said than done. We'll work it out, I'm sure. It won't be easy, but I don't want to walk away from our marriage. And I know Tom doesn't. The only good thing, if there is any, is that at least he hasn't had an affair, which I would not put up with. He could go fuck himself, if he thinks I'd stick by him doing something like that. That slag has been hiding this secret for years, I bet she knew Tom was the father all along. I don't know why she has waited, probably to see if he had any money.'

'You think she knows definitely he is the father?'

'Well, she seems pretty sure and he isn't denying it.'

Jody put her hand on Polly's arm. 'Don't be so sure. It was a holiday fling, you had plenty. How many flings did this woman have during that holiday? Just the one, just with Tom? Doubt that, she's probably been hunting down for years all the men she slept with that holiday and there's still probably 20 to go.'

Polly smiled at her friend. 'I love you Jody, you are my forever Miss Positive. I love your loyalty. And what's all this about my holiday flings? I bet you didn't do too badly, you little hussy you.' The pair both laughed as Tom walked in.

'Oh no, what are you two plotting now? I recognise the tones of those laughs anywhere.'

'Oh, nothing,' Polly said.

'That's good,' said Tom, sitting down opposite Jody. 'Well, the surgery is in good hands, I spoke to Jill and said I'd probably go back Thursday. Hopefully, they might move you nearer home as well, which would be nice.' He turned to Jody.

'Thanks for staying another couple of days. I sent your hubby a crate of beer from me to tie him over while his wife is away as a little thank you.'

'Ah, that's nice, thanks. He'll like that, he can drink himself stupid and think of me. I don't suppose you have spoken to him, have you?'

Tom shook his head and smiled. 'No, I just sent the beer.'

SIXTY EIGHT

KAREN had a lot to do to get ready for the trip to London.

For a start she had to arrange train tickets and organise Lee. She would be catching the 7.30am to Liverpool Street and Lee would need to be up and about early tomorrow morning.

Then there were the DNA tests, she mustn't forget them. They had the tests done almost two years ago, she had the print-outs and where the information was stored. It was getting late this Tuesday night and she was desperate to get Lee to bed by 9.

'Remember what I've said about getting up early tomorrow. I've got to be out of the house by 6.45, so I need to wake you at 6.30. Please make sure you get up for me darling, what do you need tomorrow for school? Anything?'

He came down the stairs, he had been playing on his computer for an hour.

'I need my rugby kit, we have a game tomorrow night after school.'

'Now you tell me. I thought it was just practice. I will have to iron your tracksuit stuff, thanks for giving me such good notice.'

He shrugged his shoulders and went into the kitchen, diving into the fridge. 'Have we got any more orange juice? Is this the last bit, because if it is I'm having it.' Before she had a chance to answer, Lee had filled a cup and was drinking it.

'Why are you going out so early tomorrow? Will you be back in the evening?'

She put the ironing board up. 'I'm going about a job, which is around here, but they want to see me in London. And yes, I'll be back, hopefully by 6ish, can you get home from rugby okay?'

'Yeah, should be able to, I think Jack Davis said his dad was coming to watch, he'll give me a lift home.'

'Are you sure? Don't get yourself in a pickle and can't get home.'

He ignored his mum's worries and headed up the stairs to bed. Karen finished ironing his tracksuit and put it on top of his rugby bag which he had put by the front door.

She made herself a cup of tea and sat in front of the TV. There was nothing that appealed to her, so her mind drifted. Tomorrow could turn out to be one of the biggest days of her life, it would certainly be the biggest day of Lee's life and he didn't have a clue it was happening. She started to wonder how she was going to tell him the news that she had found his dad. Should she make a big thing of it, or just sit down with him and talk him through it quietly? That could all wait.

First, she would have to gauge Tom's reaction. Goodness know what he'll say! *'Poor old Tom'*. Those nights of fun all those years ago and now it has come to this, all these years she was sure it was him and now she was just a few days away from confirming it.

Then again, what if he wasn't the father? Shit, she couldn't think about that.

He could maybe owe her thousands. He looked like a guy who could afford to give her child support. Hey, child support. That's a laugh. Lee is 14, no-one has been supporting him for all these years, apart from her two hapless husbands, and most of the time she was supporting them.

Karen looked at her watch. It was 9.30pm. She would have an early night. She put down the ironing board and put the iron on the kitchen table, went across to the photos on her window sill and picked her favourite one up of her and Lee. There he was smiling, he must have been about 10-years-old then. A day out at Southend, on the pier, both of them were eating ice-creams. She remembered now, Mark had taken it. Such a happy day.

Karen hoped it would all work out. She mustn't get ahead of herself, just in case. As she went up the stairs to bed, she looked in Lee's room, he had zonked out pretty quick. She smiled at him lying there.... *'So close now darling, so close.'*

Tom had left Polly and Jody playing 'hot or not' with some of the celebrity magazines Jody had bought for Polly to read.

If he needed any indication his wife was on the mend, the playing of a game where the pair whispered to each other 'hot or not' at each bloke who appeared in the mags, then this was it. So childish!

Tom had left at 6 and as he had kissed Polly goodbye, Jody had leaned across after he had finished... 'Hot or not, Pol', she said. Polly had rung her tongue around her lips... 'Hot'. Tom had got up shaking his head and walked out, he heard them laughing behind him as he went out of the ward.

'He is funny, your Tom. Is he as sexy in bed as he is in his shorts? Because I always think he's got a great set of legs.'

'Oh, yeah, he's great. Although I don't know what shape I'm going to be in when I get home, he's going to have to do most of the work from the look of things, which won't do him any harm. Talking of sexy men, you got hold of Craig yet?'

'Nope.' Not a word.' Jody raised her eyes. 'Which I must admit is starting to worry me. I hadn't expected him to call if he's on business all day, but a quick text wouldn't have hurt.'

'He'll be fine. I imagine he's enjoying a break, what do you reckon he's up to now?'

'Goodness knows Probably sitting in a bar boring the pants off some poor shipping container CEO, telling them that Liverpool Docks is the greatest port in the history of the universe.'

The pair laughed.

American Airlines flight AA4569 landed at JFK airport at 1.55am. Craig and Marie had slept for the last two hours, they had both been a bit dozy when the announcement came on to prepare for landing.

They looked at each other and smiled as Craig checked his watch.

After heading through customs and passport control, they walked out into the New York open air. It was a cool morning and damp, it wasn't raining, but it was threatening. Early morning it may have been, but JFK airport was still as busy as a mini city with bars and restaurants open and there were lots of people milling about.

Marie hailed a taxi.

"'The William', please,' she said, as the driver put the couple's two cases in the back of the yellow cab.

It wasn't a long trip to the hotel and, after booking in, they were settled in their room, both now wide awake. Craig went over to the mini bar. 'Shall I open it?' Marie nodded her approval. 'I'm just going to slip a nightdress on.'

As he was getting the drinks, he heard Marie's phone bleep, he knew she was still keeping hers for a day or so until they reached their destination. Then, like his phone, it would become history. Curiosity got the better of him, he leant over and read it... *'All set for tomorrow?'* It was from Charlie Cantwell.

Marie came out of the bathroom.

'You've had a text from Charlie.' Craig handed her a drink and the phone. Marie looked. She wouldn't reply.

'I'll leave it, I don't want him knowing where we are and if I return the text he could find out if he was clever enough, which he isn't. He'll just have to hope I haven't duped him. As if I would!' She pulled a smile and shrugged her shoulders. 'This phone will have to go.'

They were stood next to the bathroom door, as Marie stretched across to put her phone back down on the table, he took her arms, stood back from her, looking her up and down in her low cut, light blue nightdress.

'You have such a figure,' he smiled and leant forward. 'And I don't know about you but I'm still wide awake, what time are we being picked up?'

'10am.' Marie winked. 'We've got plenty of time. I must admit even with your clothes on and after an eight-hour flight, you still look good, my toy boy stud.' He laughed, *'toy boy stud!'*

Marie stood back further. 'So, lover boy, you like what you see?' She winked again. 'Over to you...'

With that, she slipped off her nightdress and let it fall to the floor.

Tom arrived home just after 7.30 and began packing a few things for the trip to London. He was going to drive and catch the tube in.

He didn't need much, but knew he had to take some forms of ID. He went mob-handed, bank statements, water bill, driving licence and passport, which should be enough. A small part of him was thinking it would be good to get all this over with, while a bigger part was telling him this could just be the beginning, of what, he had no idea. At least Polly now knew. And he'd left her in such a good mood.

Shit!

If he was the father, his and Polly's life was about to change forever. Yes, she said she will stick by him, but that's easier said than done. What if Lee wanted to see him each weekend? How would that work? What about money? Karen is bound to want money.

He poured himself a whisky and stood in the kitchen contemplating. The radio was playing and the washing up he had left a few days ago was still waiting to be done, he wondered if Craig had got the beer? He'd call him.

Tom pressed Craig's name on his phone and waited for the ringtone. There was none, it just went dead. Odd, perhaps he had no signal. No, he checked, he had a signal. He tried again, still nothing.

He shrugged his shoulders and put his phone down.

What a pair they both were. Craig with all his worries, Tom with his. He finished his whisky and headed upstairs. It was early for him, but there was a football game on the TV he could watch in bed. He went into the bathroom and washed his face, as he felt the water pouring down he looked into the mirror.

What would tomorrow bring?

SIXTY NINE

KAREN was up early and had managed to get Lee to stir. She left him awake with a cup of tea, he could sort himself out.

She had showered, made sure she had all her documents and was enjoying the ride on the 7.30am from Norwich to Liverpool Street. Trains were a good way to travel when they weren't overcrowded or late, thankfully this was neither.

She'd even found time to pick up a copy of Vogue from a news-stand at Norwich station. It wasn't usually her cup of tea, but an intriguing photograph of Billie Eilish on the front cover made her pick the magazine up, she loved Billie's music and was keen to read anything about the singer.

It wasn't long before the train pulled into Liverpool Street and as she got out there were plenty of people buzzing around. *'Welcome to rush hour in London'.*

She had more than an hour to get to the clinic, so she texted Lee to make sure he had got into school alright. An emoji 'thumbs up' showed he had. With time on her hands and a taxi trip to the clinic likely to take no more than 15 minutes, she left the station and took a stroll down Eldon Street. There were shops to browse and she did think about heading towards Finsbury Circus Gardens, but time would run out. Instead she picked up a coffee to go and jumped in a taxi, arriving at the clinic at ten minutes to ten.

He was waiting outside, she spotted him immediately.

Tom had driven down the M11 and parked his car at Mile End, before catching the tube in. It had only been a five-minute walk and he had arrived at the clinic at 9.40. He hadn't slept well and hadn't bothered to shave, which was unlike him. He was even dressed in scruffy jeans and a white casual shirt with a thin blue jacket while carrying his small briefcase. The forecast was for a sunny day, not that Tom was worried about the weather.

Karen half smiled as she walked towards him. It was an awkward greeting as they stood face to face on the pavement.

'Did you have a good journey down?' Karen looked to break the ice.

She had made an effort to look nice. A short pretty white skirt showed off her shapely legs and a white blouse and dark green jacket. She had her handbag slung over her shoulder, while her make-up was simple.

'Not bad, yourself?' Tom had already glanced her up and down as she had walked towards him. He spotted her a mile off. As much as he hated himself for thinking it, he could see why he had been attracted to her all those years ago, she looked good, and far better than when he had seen her in the surgery or at the park. Life had not been unkind to her body. Her flowing hair was tied back in a ponytail, it was a nice smile. Tom tried to dismiss such thoughts.

'Yeah, not bad, thanks. I managed to get Lee up, which is quite something at 6 in the morning.' She put out a nervous laugh. 'The train journey was good as well, I've been used to the underground for years, so to have a peaceful train with not that many people on is a bit of a novelty.'

There was an awkward silence before Tom looked at his watch. It was 9.55. 'Shall we go in?'

He put out his arm and gestured for her to walk in ahead of him. Once inside, they were met by a woman sitting behind a desk who must have been in her early 20s, she spoke with a slight Canadian or American accent.

'Good morning, can I help you?'

'Yes, it's Karen Harding and Tom Armstrong, we have an appointment with Dr Garden at 10.' Karen spoke for them.

The receptionist looked at her computer and tapped a few keys. Tom looked around the clinic reception area. It was quite big and looked old, a grand building. It certainly wasn't a clinical, drab, pristine white surgery, with boring pictures on the walls, this had far more character.

'Dr Garden will call you, please wait over there.' The receptionist smiled, while pointing to some sofa chairs surrounding a table with magazines to read. They walked over and sat down, neither of them saying anything. Tom picked up a copy of Autocar. Not that he intended to read any of the features inside, his mind was spinning.

'Mrs Harding, Mr Armstrong.' Dr Garden walked out of a door to left of both Karen and Tom. He was a short man of Asian appearance, with a broad smile, he was wearing a white coat and shook both their hands as the pair stood up and then headed into his office. Tom felt his hands begin to sweat and his heart began to pound as he sat down. He was getting anxious, Karen looked as cool as a cucumber.

'Morning, I believe you are here to have a DNA Paternity test?' began Dr Garden. They both nodded.

'Well, the test won't take long and the results will be with you in three to five working days. Seeing as it is a Wednesday today, they could be with you by Saturday. We e-mail them, and we assume you will both want to receive the e-mail, so we will send them to both of you. Is that satisfactory?'

'Can't we get the results any earlier?' Tom asked. 'Is there some sort of fast-track service?'

'We don't offer a fast-track service on legal paternity tests, which is what you have requested,' Dr Garden replied. Tom had hoped he might get the results that day.

'And is that okay with you, Mrs Harding?' Karen nodded. She, like Tom, had hoped it would be sooner.

'So, I believe Mrs Harding you have already had your DNA test done and your son, is it Lee? He has had a DNA test as well.' Dr Garden looked at his notes. 'It's Mr Armstrong who needs his DNA taken, is that correct?'

Karen nodded her head again. 'I've bought my results with me.' She handed over a file with the documents in. 'I had them done a couple of years ago.'

'Okay,' said Dr Garden. 'So, I need to obviously ask this, the test is about Tom possibly being Lee's father, is that correct?'

'He is his father,' Karen jumped in.

Tom glared at her. 'We don't know that, why do you think we're here?' He shook his head, Karen looked away. Dr Garden could sense the tension.

'Right, okay, I see feelings are running a little high. I understand,' he said.

'Let me just go through a few of the basics.' Dr Garden took off his glasses. 'The test will have to be 99.9% accurate to be fully sure Mr Armstrong is the father. If it isn't that high, we cannot be completely sure, but it is rare for it either not to be 99.9% or 0%. Basically in almost all cases you either are, or you are not, the father. Are you both clear with that? Because that is important. It's no good going through this and then not liking the result you get, or not believing the result you get. It does happen. People occasionally still won't believe the test result, all I can say is that in my 26 years of practice, the result *is* the result. Any questions?'

They both shook their heads.

'So, it won't take long,' Dr Garden added. 'We'll take a swab from Mr Armstrong and that is just about it. I assume you have passport-type photos and all the usual ID we asked for, Mr Armstrong? And we will invoice you in the next week or so.'

Tom nodded. He had tried not to look across at Karen, who he noticed had begun to glance at him as the doctor was talking....

.... Twenty minutes later the pair were standing outside the clinic.

'Do you want to go for a coffee?' Karen looked at Tom, forcing a smile.

'Are you serious? We're not on a date here you know, I need to get back to my surgery.' He went to walk off, but Karen pulled his arm. It caught him by surprise.

'Look, I know you hate me, I know you hate everything I've brought into your life, I understand, don't worry, I've been used to people coming into my life and hurting me, so I know exactly how you feel. But can't we talk? Just like a couple of adults, for a few moments. What harm is it going to do? Please?'

He looked at her, she had soft eyes. When they had met at the park the conversation had degenerated into a shouting match and she had held her own easily. Tom had despised the way she had flew at him that day but now she looked defenceless. He almost felt sorry for her. Maybe if he'd walked in her shoes for the past 14 years, he'd think different towards her, a coffee wouldn't hurt.

'Okay. But not for too long, I do need to get back home.'

Karen smiled and pointed to a coffee shop across the road. She placed her hand on his arm. 'Thanks.'

The coffee shop was not very big, but quaint with pictures of old London mixed in with photographs and pictures of London today. The young waiter bought their drinks over, Tom had Americano, Karen a latte. They both took a sip before Tom took up the conversation.

'So, how's Lee's rugby going? 'He's obviously a bit of a player if he's been picked to play for England.'

Karen beamed across the table. *'God, she had such a lovely smile'*. 'Oh, it's going so well, you'd be so proud of him....' As soon as she said it, she regretted her comment. Tom stopped drinking his coffee and stared at her. 'I mean, you know what I mean? You'd think he was a good player, if you saw him.'

'I think I should leave,' he began to stand up.

Karen put her hand on his arm again. 'I'm sorry, for goodness sake, I didn't mean to say it that way. It just came out, please, sit down, I'm sorry.'

Tom sat back down. But her comment, intended or not, had put him on the back foot, his defences were back up.

'Well, I'm pleased for him,' Tom said, as he took another sip of his coffee, before changing the subject. 'But, whether you like it or not, there is still a chance I'm not his father, you do know that? And I want you to think of that. Because that could well be the situation we end up with here.'

'I know that.' She wasn't going to go down the *'but I'm convinced he's yours'* route. She knew he would definitely get up and walk out this time.

Another silence followed, but this time not as awkward as the previous ones. Karen decided to change the subject. 'I'm sorry to hear about your wife, is she okay?'

'She's on the mend, it was a bad car crash, one lad died in it. In the car that hit her.'

She held her hand to her mouth. 'I didn't realise it was as bad as that. Gosh, that must have been awful, and there I was demanding you come to London for the test. Shit, no wonder you hate me, I'm sorry, I hope she makes a full recovery.'

'Can we stop saying how much I hate you?' He looked over her shoulder, just as three more people sat down at a table behind them. 'I don't hate you, what I hate is the uncertainty and heartache all this has the capability of bringing into my life, your life, Polly's life and Lee's life. Because trust me, this test is just the start of things, if it proves I'm Lee's dad. Nothing will be the same again, especially for Lee, you do know that? I have this feeling you think we are all going to be playing happy families if I am his dad. And while I don't know how I will react if I am, it isn't all going to be sweetness and light, which I think, you think, it will be.'

'I know,' she said. 'Maybe I do think it is all going to turn out for the best, maybe I don't. Quite honestly, I'm not sure what I think Tom, my life has been one mucked up story from the day Lee was born. I don't expect you to understand. It's not fair for me to expect you to understand, but for 14 years I've been wondering about his father, I've tried to put it out of my head. As I told you, two failed marriages. One bloke who beat the shit out of me in front of Lee when he was just a toddler.' Her eyes began to fill.

'I just seem to have been in the wrong place at the wrong time on so many occasions. And all the time, in the back of my mind I kept thinking of that holiday in Crete, and you and the possibility, the real possibility, you are his dad. So, while I was getting beaten up and getting married, and shit on by partners, I tried to forget about you, I tried to get on with my life. I wanted to hope I married a man who took Lee on as his own, but it never happened. So, he's never had a proper father, he hasn't had a father of any description. And the guilt, can you imagine the guilt I feel and have felt, every day of my life? Looking at Lee, knowing he ought to have so much more. Why didn't I chase you down after I came home from Crete? Why didn't I try and find you? I should have done. When I knew I was pregnant, all the dates stacked up to the holiday, I was sure in my mind that was when I fell pregnant. But no, I just carried on, had the baby.'

He looked at her. As much as he didn't want to, part of him felt so sorry for her.

'Hey, come on.' He put his hand on hers. 'You should have

tried to find me, I had no ties back then. Trouble is, now everything is more complicated.'

She half-smiled. 'I did try and find you,' she said, wiping her eyes. 'And I did find you.'

'What? When? You don't mean recently?'

'No, not recently. I found you when you lived in London, you did live in London didn't you? About 12 years ago. Lee was about two years old, I hope it was you because I followed you about. If it wasn't you, some bloke must have wondered if they had a stalker!'

They both smiled, it relieved the tension.

'About 12 years ago?' He was thinking aloud. 'Probably was me, I was studying dentistry in London at that time, I moved to Norwich 10 years ago. And you found me, you followed me? How did you do that?'

Karen laughed nervously. 'I found a photo of us on a beach in Crete. There were a group of us, some of your mates and a few of the girls I was on holiday with, you and I were on the end and you were hugging me.

'So, I looked on Facebook, to see if I could find a photo of you. And I did. I could tell it was you. Anyhow you also had a business address, which I clicked into and it said you were working in London at some dentist, I can't remember the name. Because I lived in Woolwich, I went and found the surgery, made an appointment with another dentist and, bingo, there you were. I saw you. I was going to say hello, but didn't have the nerve.' Tom admired her tenacity.

'I seem to make a habit of coming into dentist surgeries to see you. Like I did in Norwich, I do genuinely feel like a bit of a stalker!' She nervously laughed.

'Anyway, I went back to the surgery a few times to see if I could see when you left off. I didn't get lucky, so one day I went up to reception and asked the lady when surgery closed. She told me 6, I think. So, one night, I waited and I got lucky. I saw you leave and you walked back to your flat. I knew then where you lived and kept tabs on you, I used to get the tube from Woolwich, not every day, but about three times a week, you were in Chelsea, so it was a bit of a trip. But I didn't mind. It went on for about a week or two and I was plucking up the courage to talk to you.

'I was on the verge of doing it. Then one day you didn't come out of your flat and I never saw you again. I called the surgery to make an appointment asking for Mr Armstrong and they said you no longer worked there and for some reason I never asked where you had gone. Years later, I looked you up again, it was easier this time, I just put in Tom Armstrong, dentist into Google and up you popped, and with a photo.'

Tom was amazed. 'Well, I never knew we were that close all those years ago. That's mad, just think how close we were to things being very different? If you had spoken to me then and we'd gone for a test then, life could have been very different.'

He smiled at her. 'I'm starving. I'm getting one of those large cookies. Want one?'

She smiled back and nodded. 'Yes please.'

The chat turned to Tom's work and how he had become a dentist, while Karen told him about all the jobs she had held down in London, before telling him about her job at the pet shop. About Roger Tomkins, the owner and how the girls in the shop call all the rabbits 'Roger', after him!

'Did you enjoy the holiday in Crete, then?' She forced a cheeky smile.

'That's a bit of a naughty question, but okay, yeah what I remember of it, I think it was good. We had some fun didn't we?'

Karen laughed. 'We certainly did, I really enjoyed it. One of the best I ever had to be honest. It was my first holiday away without my sister, Jane. She lives in Australia now.'

Karen told him what life was like Down Under for her sister. How she had almost taken Lee with her to join them. Karen was fascinated about Tom's work, seeing as she was someone who hated going to the dentist and they discussed why she had run out of the surgery that time just a few weeks ago. They had been talking about families and jobs for 20 minutes, before the conversation changed.

'You do know if I'm not the father, I don't expect you to contact me ever again, don't you?' Tom sat back in his chair.

'And I certainly don't expect any more unpleasant texts to Polly. Having spoken like we have today, I'm surprised to be honest, I didn't realise you lacked such class because she's done nothing wrong to you and you shouldn't be trying to get at her.'

Karen screwed up her face.

'Why are you suddenly talking like this? We've been having a nice chat and now we are having this conversation. We had this conversation the last time we met and I told you, I haven't sent your wife any texts, I have never spoken to Polly and I don't care about her. This is about Lee, and you and me. Not Polly. I don't know what has been happening to her with these texts you are talking about but they are nothing to do with me.'

'Come on, I'm not stupid. The stuff Polly has been getting is only stuff you know about unless you'd been talking to other people. But they wouldn't have Polly's number unless someone had given it to them, I'm sorry, but I don't believe you, Karen.'

She shook her head. 'I can promise you, on Lee's life, I haven't been sending your wife any messages, texts, phone calls, emails, letters in the post, whatever else you want me to say. I don't care about your wife.'

He looked at her, maybe she was telling the truth.

'Okay, so say I believe you. Then who is it? Have you told anyone about us? Has anyone spoken to you about Polly? Help me out here, I'm trying to see your side of the argument, but you aren't helping just by swearing on your son's life.'

She thought for a moment, who had she spoken to about Tom? About Polly? About Lee?

Then it clicked.

SEVENTY

'ARE you alright, Jode? You spoke to him?'

Polly was sat up in bed. Her move to the Norwich & Norfolk hospital was taking place tomorrow and Jody was sitting alongside her. It was Wednesday lunchtime and Jody had only been in with Polly for 30 minutes as she had been trying to get hold of Craig for much of the morning.

'No, I haven't.' Jody looked concerned. She didn't want to worry her friend, but she was now getting worried herself.

'I can't get hold of him and no-one at his work has seen him this morning. I asked them about his business meeting in Blackpool and no-one seemed to know about it, I'm confused and worried something has happened. I know this sounds a bit dramatic, but I think I want to go home, this is all very unlike Craig. Would you mind if I went home, Pol? I know Tom won't be too long, he said he'd be back by tonight.'

'Of course I don't mind.' Polly reached across and held Jody's hand. 'I'm sure it's all fine. He's probably lost his phone, or overslept, or something daft, you know what men are like.'

'This is not him though, Pol. He's not the sort of bloke to lose his phone, and no-one seems to know about his Blackpool trip. If I could get hold of his PA, Lisa, she would know if he went to Blackpool, but she's off for a few days apparently.'

Jody cut a worried figure and Polly was not going to have her hanging around.

'Jody. Get going, what's the time? 1'ish, you'll be home this evening and you and Craig can have a good chat. There will be a perfectly good explanation. You're not staying here any longer, go on, and go, I'm fine. You've been a rock the last few days, but I'm not going to have you sit here worrying.'

She looked at Pol with desperate eyes. 'Are you sure? I feel terrible leaving you with no-one.'

'But you're not leaving me with no-one, Tom won't be long, I'll happily have a sleep this afternoon. Go on, get going my darling, and drive carefully.'

She got up and leant over her friend, they hugged. Jody stared into her eyes.

'I'm so glad you're looking and feeling better, I can't believe how much you have improved in the last few days.'

Polly smiled and gestured for her to go. 'Give me a ring when you get home, and let me know what that bloody husband has been up to. Tell him from me he's a plonker not calling you. He'll have me to deal with when I next see him.'

Jody stood at the door of the ward and looked back at her friend. She blew her a kiss and headed towards the car park, checking her phone once more.

She'd left him about six messages in the last 24 hours — *'where the hell was he?'*

Tom and Karen went their own ways.

There was little emotion between the pair of them as they said their goodbyes outside the coffee shop. He had told her if he saw the e-mail first, he would text her, and vice versa.

As Tom walked back to his car after his tube ride back to Mile End, he reflected on the morning. He had been surprised how they had chatted away over coffee after the initial coldness of their meeting outside the clinic, he was surprised how much they had got on. He was even more surprised how attractive he still found her.

Again he felt a pang of guilt about Karen, a woman who had clearly worked so hard to bring up her son... possibly his son. Then again, he couldn't stop thinking what Polly would have thought, seeing the pair of them chatting, even laughing, in the coffee shop, Karen was going to come right in-between him and his wife. And Polly wouldn't be okay about it, whatever she may say now. He unlocked his car and got in, there was a text message from Polly, hoping the conference all went well.

He hated lying to her like this.

'*On my way home*', he texted back.

Karen found herself day-dreaming on her way back on the train.

Her meeting with Tom had gone better than she could have hoped. She had been dreading it in many ways. While she had nothing to lose, it was a different situation for him, but it had gone well after the initial frostiness. She had thought he would be in and out of the clinic without even a 'beg pardon', and off back home. So the coffee, cookies and chat had come out of the blue. The conversation had flowed and she could see why she was attracted to him all those years ago in Crete, even his day-old stubble made him look sexy. She could see why they had got on. Much had changed in both their lives, but, as far as she was concerned, the chemistry hadn't.

But he was married, had a good job, no doubt a nice car and house and here she was about to throw a hand grenade right into the middle of his world. She could not feel guilty about that though, she had to be strong.

She began to daydream, slowly falling asleep as the train purred over the tracks. She pictured them all on a beach, Tom and Lee fooling around out in the sea. They were playing around in the water, the pair coming out of the surf and walking towards her, both pushing each other and laughing, Lee sitting down next to her... '*Dad's not a bad swimmer, mum, not as good as me, but pretty good*'... Tom patting his son on the head, telling him not to be so cheeky. She was opening up a picnic as all three tucked into the food and drink she'd prepared.

She awoke suddenly as she heard the announcement on the train that they were now coming into Ipswich station, it meant there was only 40 minutes to go. On looking at her watch, she realised she would be home by 3. She opened her handbag and had a quick shuffle, pulling out an old photo, the one she had looked at on so many occasions over the years, the one of her and Tom and friends on that beach in Crete.

The e-mail from the clinic couldn't come soon enough.

Tom arrived back at the hospital at 4.30pm and went straight in to see her. He found Polly asleep.

He went over to the nurse's station and asked how long she had been like it. They said she had been that way that since her friend left, just after lunch.

Tom assumed they meant Jody, but why would she leave? She had said she would stay with Polly until tomorrow. He'll worry about that later. He had to tell Polly about the baby, he had waited far too long. Maybe she already knew and was going to surprise him? It couldn't wait any longer.

He looked at her, still asleep. She looked so peaceful after all she had been through. He felt a surge of joy in the pit of his stomach about the baby and he remembered how she had only told him a couple of weeks ago she was coming off the pill, *'bloody hell that was quick work!'*

He pulled up a chair and sat next to her, Polly was his world, his future and now with a baby on the way to cement it all. He looked at her and moved closer, kissing her on the forehead as she began to stir.

'Hi, sleepy head. How are you doing?'

She came round and it took her a couple of seconds to work out who it was.

'You're back, what's the time? How long have I been asleep?' Polly pulled herself up slowly, grimacing with the pain in her shoulder.

'It's nearly 5, I've just got back. The nurse said you went to sleep after your friend left. I assume she meant Jody? But that's not right, is it? I thought she was staying until tomorrow.'

'Oh, she was, but she still can't get hold of Craig, she's getting a bit frantic, which I think I would if I couldn't get hold of you for that long, she's going to call us when she gets home, everything will be fine, I'm sure.'

'It will be. Knowing Craig, he's probably been on a four-day bender since she left. He better watch out when she gets home. If her temperature is right, it could be 'try for baby' time as soon as she walks in as punishment for not contacting her!'

'Don't say that, you are cruel sometimes,' Polly tried to look offended, but couldn't also help but smile. 'Lucky we don't have to worry about that, I'm not that desperate for kids, yet. We can wait a while longer. Well, we will have to while I'm stuck in here. Be rude to do it in hospital. We'll get caught.'

Tom smiled at the irony of the conversation, he couldn't have scripted it better. She either didn't know, or was a good liar... It was time.

'What are you grinning at?'

He leant in close to her. 'I want to ask you a question. Something very important, not just a bit important, but very, very important and I want an honest answer.'

Polly looked at him, not knowing what was coming next.

'What is it? What are you on about? What important question? Don't do this again, Tom.'

Tom took hold of both her hands and smiled broadly. 'What if I said to you, Polly Armstrong, you're going to be a mummy.'

She didn't say anything. She just looked at him and her eyes began to well up. He didn't need to say anything else, their telepathy was saying it all and even Tom's eyes began to water.

She nodded her head. 'I am aren't I? Oh, wow, I thought I might be, but I wasn't sure. And there was me saying we can wait a bit longer, I really didn't know. Are you serious?'

Tom's eyes gave away an enormous smile, he put his arms around her and hugged her tight. 'Oh, I'm serious, you're pregnant, you're going to be a mum and I'm going to be a dad.' Their embrace went on for minutes, he sat back and looked at her as she tried to hold back the tears.

'How do you know? You must know otherwise you wouldn't be telling me. I thought it was the woman who was supposed to tell the man she's pregnant not the other way round.' She was laughing and crying at the same time.

'Doctor Surtees told me on Friday when you came in.' Tom was holding both Polly's hands tight. 'He told me the baby had survived the crash, he thought I knew you were pregnant, but obviously I didn't, I think it rather shocked him. He wanted me to tell you as soon as, because some of the nurses knew. I'm sorry I've waited until today, but I just wanted you to get better before telling you, I know that seems stupid. Just a pity Jode isn't here, then again, she would have screamed the place down. Did you not know yourself?

'Come on, what's been going on Polly Armstrong? I thought you came off the pill only a few weeks ago? The doctor said you are about three months gone, there are a lot of unanswered questions here, my young lady and I want answers!' Tom pulled a stern face, then hugged her again.

Polly's eyes were still watery.

'I did wonder if I was pregnant, but I wasn't sure, I was going to take a test this week, or next, because I have missed two periods which is unusual for me. Then we had all the upset of last week, me walking out and obviously now I'm here, oh, my God, how close have I come to losing the baby in that crash?'

'Don't think about it. You're safe and baby is safe and although I don't remember us talking about starting a family.' Tom raised his eyebrows. 'I'm so, so happy.'

'I know, I'm sorry but I didn't think I'd get pregnant straightaway, I only came off the pill recently, well, about four months ago!' Polly bit her lip and smiled.

'Four months ago. That's hardly recently. You are one cheeky madam. Just as well I love you so much.'

Craig and Marie enjoyed a hearty breakfast.

Bacon, eggs, sausages, grit, toast, beans, lashings of coffee. The pair were both full and comfortable as they made their way down to reception to square up the bill. Outside, the taxi was waiting, to take them to a small airfield 40 miles south of Brooklyn.

'If this is the way it's going to be for the next 30 years, I'm happy,' Craig looked at her and kissed Marie as the pair sat in the back of the car.

'Well, my darling, we have enough money to last us that and another 20, how you want to spend it is up to you. If you like snorkelling and deep sea diving you'll be in your element. And golden beaches aplenty, I've showed you where we're staying.'

'And Cuba? You say it is all set up?'

"Everything is set up my darling. You know it is. Six months in Cayman, six months in Cuba. Or four in Cuba and two in Jamaica, it's all there my sweetie, the houses, cars and cash, happy days.'

The two kissed once more as the taxi pulled into the small

municipal airport. The Cessna aircraft was waiting, as was the pilot, who took their cases.

'Good to see you Madam Marie,' the pilot said. 'We will have you on the Caymans in time for evening lunch.'

'Thank you Armando.' Marie said. 'By the way, this is Craig.' She turned to him. 'You'll be seeing plenty of Armando in the years ahead, assuming of course Armando still wants to be my pilot.' Marie put her hand on Armando's face.

'Oh, yes Mrs Archer, I do, most definitely, oh, and find your favourite champagne aboard, I thought you might like an early toast.'

The plane took off and rose high above the New York skyline. Craig opened the champagne, the pair clinked glasses, kissed.... 'Here's to our future.'

Charlie Cantwell was pissed, very pissed.

He didn't like hanging around and it was gone 7pm and there had been no sign of Marie and no sign of Baldini.

He had called Marie five times, his watch said 7.33pm and he was starting to get a sinking feeling that he had been stitched up. And you didn't stitch up Charlie Cantwell. The two men he had bought along with him would get paid regardless of tonight's outcome but Charlie wasn't in it for the money.

By 8pm, he decided enough was enough. The light was fading and Marie hadn't returned any of his calls. He'd called Liam but all he had told him was he hadn't seen his mum for a couple of days.

He got back in the car and sat in the passenger seat.

'Fucking drive off, let's get out of here.'

SEVENTY ONE

DEAR Jody,

If you are reading this then you have picked up the letter on the kitchen table.

I not going to pretend to know where to begin, so I must get straight to the point, I've gone. I've left and I won't be coming back, our life together is over.

I've left not just you, but our house, my job, the life I have been leading. Parts of that life you are not remotely aware of, parts of it that are not good.

I know I am hurting you by doing this baby. I know you won't believe it, but it's true.

I'm so sorry for doing this to you, but things have changed in my life over the past 18 months. You may have noticed, you may have not. I'm a coward by doing this, I know that and I genuinely still love you with all my heart, but I've got to go. I couldn't face talking to you because you would have made me want to stay and that would have been the wrong decision, for both of us. I've lied to you so much.

I've taken nothing, apart from a few personal things. All our money and savings in the bank are yours. I've written out below all the bills I pay, so you can take them over. I've paid off our mortgage.

Our years together have been such fun, but you deserve someone better than me. You deserve someone much better.

Please don't try to hunt me down or find me. Don't waste your life worrying about me, I don't deserve it and you deserve so much more.

After the shock of this, I hope you find happiness again.

I love you Jody.

I know that seems the most arrogant thing to say. And again, I'm so sorry.

Please find it in your heart to one day forgive me.

Craig x

She stared at the letter.

Jody had sat down as soon as she began reading it, she'd only been home five minutes and it was one of the first things she noticed when she walked into the kitchen.

She put her hands to her face and sobbed and sobbed.

She read it again and screamed out loud.

'No, no, no, nooooooooo'

SEVENTY TWO

TOM and Polly were talking excitedly about their future together with a new addition to the family on the way.

'Crikey, you're hungry Mrs 'mum to be', do you want any more? I can go ask.'

'No, I'm fine. I've had enough, thanks.' She smiled at him. 'So, my hunky man, what would you prefer, a boy or a girl?' Polly took a sip of water.

'I'm not really bothered, so long as he or she is fit and healthy. I know that's what everyone says, but that's the truth. Only thing with a girl is, I hope she doesn't have your feisty personality because there is no way I could cope with two of you in the house.'

She pulled a face. 'I only get cross when I'm angry.'

'Oh, yeah? You mean or when you are tired, or hungry, or during your time of the month. Or when you have a hangover!'

She slapped his arm, before looking him in the face.

'I do have one question, though.' Polly had a serious look on her face.

'Don't worry. I know the answer before you ask. Yes, we can still have sex during pregnancy.' He smiled but her face didn't crack, as she shook her head.

'Not that. I want to know. Oh, shit, sorry to bring this up now but I want to know, what is the situation with Karen?'

Tom sat back in his chair, he knew this was coming.

'I was going to tell you tonight, you've just beaten me to it.'

Polly looked at him, her lips tight. She hoped what Tom was about to say wasn't going to spoil the moment.

'I met Karen today.' Tom watched the reaction on her face. 'Today, in London.'

'Today in London? You said you were at a conference.' Polly sat up.

'Please, hear me out, I wasn't trying to lie to you, but I didn't want to worry you, I just want to get this stuff with me and Karen sorted. I knew you were pregnant and I didn't want you worrying all day about me meeting her. And Jody was here, so I didn't want to mention it in front of her either, but I was always going to tell you today.'

Polly continued to stare at him.

'So, I've been to London for a DNA test, to see if I'm the dad or not.'

Polly shook her head. She knew this conversation had to happen. But the timing was painful.

'Fucking hell, the irony.' She was trying to laugh sarcastically. 'What? Trying to see if you are a dad to two different kids in one day, what a feat that would be, hey? What a man you are, Tom. I love you for that.'

He had dreaded this happening. He wanted to tell her when he felt the time was right. This was all going wrong.

'Look, Pol. Please, listen, we've been through this. You know how I feel about it, I don't want to be that boy's dad, but I can't do anything until I know for sure.'

'But you are the dad, aren't' you?' She shook her head. 'You bloody are, and you know it and she knows it. Our baby is going to seem no-where near as important for you, not with her precious little son around. Fuck, I knew being pregnant with our child was too good to be true.'

'That's enough.' Tom was angry. Polly could be such a strong and at times difficult person to deal with. He'd been here before on many occasions and it was times like this he had to be strong.

'I've been for the test because the test will tell us everything, yes there is a chance I'm the dad, there is a chance I'm not. Now, what did you want me to do? Sit on my arse and allow her to annoy and hassle us for years with little innuendoes about me perhaps being the dad. It needs to get sorted. When I found out about our baby it filled me with joy, you are my world, not her. You are my future, our baby is our future. Whatever happens between me and Karen, nothing is more important than our baby because we want this. I didn't want Lee.

'Okay, so we may have to deal with it if Lee proves to be mine, but we will. And we will in a way that won't impact on our family, I mean it. Come on, you said you would deal with this with me. We're a team, a strong team, and you're pregnant with our newest little recruit. And who knows? Maybe we will have another and another and another.' Tom was holding Polly's hand again breaking into a half-smile hoping he'd said enough to bring her round.

She leant back on her pillow and looked at him.

'I know, you're right, I'm just worried that if he is your child, he will come between us, that's all. I've tried so hard not to think about it, but how can I not?'

'*If* Lee is my son. *If*. There is no guarantee, Pol. Anyhow, we'll find out and then we'll deal with it.'

'How soon?'

'In a few days. So, for now, let's look forward to our new family and let me put my hand on your little tummy, which is going to get a whole lot bigger over the next six months.'

She had calmed down as she half-smiled and put out her arms. 'I'm sorry to fly at you like that. I know you understand. I can only hope he's not yours. And if he is... well, as you say, we'll deal with it. You are a good husband and you'll make such a good dad. And if it's a girl, I'll let you come shopping for clothes with us both when she is a teenager!'

'Bloody hell. You're living our child's life away aren't you? She's already a teenager. Assuming it's a girl, you two can go shopping and I'll take the three boys to football.'

'Three boys! Trying to start up a football team, are we?' Polly gasped, then laughed, smiling at him. 'I'll try and be positive.'

He smiled back, but inside he hoped desperately that Polly would deal well with the news that he feared was heading their way.

Tom stood up. 'Right, who wants a coffee or tea?' I'll go and ask the nurses if we can have one. Or I'll get one myself, in fact, I'll do that and go to the little shop downstairs. I'll pick up a paper as well. You okay for 10 minutes?'

'Of course I am,' she smiled.

'Look at the time, it's nearly 7. Jody will be home by now, I told her to text me, but she hasn't.

'I'll give her a call.'

SEVENTY THREE

TOM spent 20 minutes in the hospital shop.

He liked to browse at the books and newspapers and he treated himself and Polly to a couple of packets of their favourite chocolates.

On his return, his cheery smile was quickly wiped off by the sight of Polly, sitting upright in her bed on the phone, looking concerned. She mouthed to Tom, *'it's Jody, problem'*. Polly put her finger to her mouth to suggest him to say nothing.

He shrugged his shoulders and sat down next to her. *'Problem?'* Don't say Craig has decorated one of their ten bathrooms the wrong colour while she was away. He smiled at the thought.

'So have you any idea where he might have gone?' Polly was staring ahead, not looking at Tom.

'Do you believe the letter? Can you think of anything? Oh, darling, please don't cry, you're making me cry, I just don't know what to say. Oh, please, is there someone near you can go and see, any neighbours?'

Tom was looking at his wife now, but she was giving him no eye contact.

'Well, look, give me a call later on, don't worry about the time. I'll keep my phone on until 10, then I have to turn it off. Try some of his friends, try those guys he works with, his other directors. This can't be right, there will be some explanation. It's not just a sick joke is it?'

Polly was silent once more as she listened. Tom sat motionless. This sounded very strange. He was anxious for Polly to end the call so he could find out what the hell was going on.

'Alright Jode, love you, call me and keep in touch. Speak to your parents. Love you, speak soon. Bye.... bye.'

Polly put the phone on her sideboard and turned to Tom.

'That didn't sound great,' he said as he put down the paper he was pretending to read. Polly looked shocked.

'Craig's left her, he's bloody left her.'

'Left her? Left her where?'

'Left her Tom. For fucks sake, he's gone. He left a note saying he'd gone, left the house and it was no use trying to look for him. Something about parts of his life are not so good. What the shit is that all about? Jody's in hell of a state, I'm so desperate for her, but I can't do anything stuck here. What the hell is he thinking of? It must be a mistake. They hadn't had a row. When she came down here everything was fine. She's devastated. The letter says don't bother trying to find him, Tom, it's awful.'

Tom was shocked. He didn't know what to say, he knew Craig had a secret past, but he could hardly announce that now. Polly would kill him if he suddenly piped up that he knew Craig had an affair, or that he'd run drugs. *Bloody hell Craig, what have you done?*

'I can't believe it,' was all Tom could think of to say. 'It's unbelievable, poor Jody. So, Craig just wrote a letter? Has his car gone? I suppose it has.'

'Yes, he just wrote a pissing letter, the bastard,' Polly said, half filled with upset, half filled with anger. 'This better be some sort of joke. Because if it isn't....'

'Hey, calm, down'. Tom didn't want his wife getting angry, especially in her condition.

'So, I suppose you didn't tell Jody you were pregnant?' Polly glared at him.

'What do you reckon? Jesus, sometimes I despair with you, of course I didn't tell her I'm fucking pregnant, that's hardly the news she wants right now, is it?'

Polly's phone went off, it was Jody again.

'Hi, darling. Oh, okay, okay, you do that, I think that is for the best. You don't want to be on your own. Darling you know you can come and stay with us whenever you want. I know, I know. Just close the shop for a while, okay, well, if there's someone at the door, you go and we'll speak soon.'

Polly hung up.

'Her parents are on their way. I think they live in Chesterfield. She said they will be there in a couple of hours.' Polly shook her head. 'She's so upset, she thinks the world of him. All she has been through with IVF and stuff and he goes and does this, I still can't believe it, something's not right about this. Had he said anything to you?'

Tom tried not to look sheepish.

'Ah, no, no, he hasn't. Why should he?'

Despite all the things Craig had told him, never did Tom get the impression he was on the verge of doing this, the little shit must have been planning it. Maybe that is why he had told Tom, so, when it happened, someone knew.

'Probably best her parents come over,' Tom said in a matter-of-fact manner, his voice sounding cold. Something Polly clocked.

'Don't get me wrong Tom, I don't expect you to be sobbing your eyes out here, but you don't seem that bothered, she is my best friend and she's always been here for me. It's terrible news, you don't seem bothered.'

'No, that's not the case, not at all. I'm more shocked than anything else to be honest, I don't know what to say. I suppose just knowing Jody all these years she's had the odd drama in her life. Hopefully this will end up like the rest and all turn out okay, hopefully.'

Polly picked up a paper and went to read it.

'You can be quite cold sometimes, can't you?' she said as she began to scan the front page. 'Sometimes I think I don't quite know all of you.'

'What do you mean by that?' He looked aghast.

'I don't know,' Polly put the paper down and looked at him. 'Sometimes, it's just stuff. Oh, ignore me, it will be my hormones.'

Tom looked at her and held her hand.

'Look, I'm sad for Jody, and you know me, if I can help I will, but if I can't, well I can't. Which right now, I don't feel I can. But we are here for her, always.'

'I know we are and I know you are a good man, Jody deserves someone like you in her life. I can't believe Craig has done this, whatever is he thinking?'

'Don't know. What with you pregnant and Craig having vanished off the face of the earth, looks like Vegas is off, I suppose. Didn't want to go anyhow. If we were going next month, it clashes with the start of the World Cup.' Tom flicked his eyebrows.

'That's not funny, Tom.'

SEVENTY FOUR

THE post-mortem showed Jimmy Alban had taken his own life.

He'd left a note in his bedroom. In it, he'd poured his heart out over what he'd done, but he shopped no-one else. According to the note, it was all his own doing.

For the Merseyside Force, especially Harold and Posselwhite it was an uncomfortable and sad time. They had been the last coppers to speak to Alban. Yes, they'd given him a talking to about what he had done, yes, he had been suspended, but it was all done above-board. The played-back recording of the interview, showed they had done and said nothing out of turn.

For Cook it was a mess, however at least a mess he felt he could control. The full inquest into Alban's death wouldn't be for a while, but he was confident his officers had taken the right procedures, it was just a personal tragedy. A young copper doing wrong and not being able to cope with the consequences of his actions. What Cook needed to do now more than anything was find Craig Baldini, and that was proving difficult.

Posselwhite and Harold had tried to catch Baldini after work on Tuesday and on Wednesday. Waiting in their car near the work's car park, he hadn't been there, or if he had, they had missed him. Things had taken an ever more curious turn after Posselwhite called the Shipping company and asked to speak to him, only to be told he 'wasn't in today' and no-one could say when he would be back.

Baldini had to be told that his name had been leaked. If something happened to him and no-one had contacted him from the Force, then the shit really would hit the fan. So many questions would be asked, in the end they had no choice, and they had to go to his house. But seeing as he had told them his family didn't know about his involvement in the drug runs, they had to make up a story.

Posselwhite had decided he would go alone and say he was calling about life insurance. *'Is that the best you can think of?'* Harold had said. Not that he could think of anything better.

Jody had answered the door to find Posselwhite standing there smiling.

'Evening. Could I speak to Mr Baldini please?'

She'd looked at him, her eyes appeared red and Posselwhite thought she had been crying.

'He's not here. Who are you?'

'I'm Mark Williams from SNPP Insurance and your husband contacted us and made an appointment for tonight, but you say he's not here.'

'No, he's not here, I think I said that.' Her tone was ice cold.

'Do you know when he will be back, or can you get him to call me?'

'I don't know when he will be back, sorry, I can't help you.' And with that she closed the door.

Posselwhite stood on the doorstep. While he hadn't expected Baldini to be there, he had expected to find someone, and he assumed the lady he spoke to was his wife, although he had forgotten to ask. And not a grain of information.

Getting back in the car he looked at the house again, there had been lights on everywhere. The fact the lady had said she didn't know when he would be back was odd. Her words were almost exactly what had been said to him and Harold by the Shipping company, Baldini's car wasn't there either.

He can't have just vanished.

Tom said his goodbyes, kissing Polly on the head.

He was going home, Polly was being moved to the Norwich & Norfolk tomorrow. He said he wanted to be back in his surgery on Thursday and he'd told Jill not to cancel any more appointments, they already had a lot of catching up to do.

'Drive carefully and come and see me tomorrow night.' Polly had her pleading eyes all over him. 'Don't leave me and little baby alone for too long.'

'I won't, I'll have to catch up on a few things tomorrow though, and I've cancelled about 35 appointments. But we'll get there, Jill and Susan are troopers.'

'And Emily,' said Polly. 'Don't forget little Emily.'

He didn't say anything. He just looked at Polly and raised his eyebrows.

'Oh yes, little Emily.

'I haven't forgotten her, don't you worry.'

SEVENTY FIVE

'OPEN wide.'

Mark Wraggens was a keen golfer and Tom had known him well since he signed up to his surgery a few years ago, he was always trying to get Tom to have a round with him.

It was Friday morning and Thursday had gone by in a blur, not helped for Tom by Emily calling in sick and Jill being in an especially grumpy mood... *'Sorry, Tom, I'm menopausal again today, you'll just have to deal with it.'*

With Polly being moved to the Norwich & Norfolk, Tom had been glad to knock off early yesterday after retirees Mr and Mrs White cancelled their 5pm appointment, apparently they had double-booked and were 'both having our feet done, dear'. For once Tom could handle a cancelled appointment.

Polly had spent much of the day on the phone to Jody, whose parents had gone to Chester to stay with her. Nothing had changed, Craig hadn't turned up and Jody was in turmoil. Polly told Jody again and again she was here for her. Tom felt pangs of guilt, should he say anything? He couldn't.

At least Jill was in a better mood this morning and Emily was also back after her first sick day off in over a year.

'Let's take a shufty in the gods,' Tom said as Mark sat there open-mouthed.

Mark was early 30s, single and led a single life. He was always joking Tom had got married way too soon. 'There are loads of girls out there my man', he used to tell Tom. Although he had ended up admitting he would probably have tied Polly down to marriage himself, had he met her before Tom did! *'She's a cracker, Tom, lad!'*

'All looking good mate, now a quick look downstairs, you had any problems with your teeth?'

Mark shook his head, unable to say anything as Tom prodded around. Emily was fixing some paste for a quick clean up. She was quiet this morning and not her usually bubbly self. Tom suspected it was because she was still feeling unwell.

'So, you still whacking the old golf ball around then?' Mark sat up and rinsed out his mouth as he went to answer Tom's question.

'Yeah, mate, had a net 68 the other day. Playing off five now, the lowest I have been, you played anymore since we last met?'

'No, no chance, I just about get to go for a run once in a while these days. The chance of getting out for a day to play golf borders between none and as good as none.'

'Oh, come on man, you're your own boss, aren't you?' Mark laughed. 'Grab the chance pal, life is too short. You never know what's round the corner, you got any kids yet?'

'Um, no, not yet.'

'Well, you better watch out for that, when they come around you're really buggered.' He looked at Emily, 'excuse my language'.

'They'll be the end of you. My mate Pete has just had twins, poor guy. Used to be at the golf club twice a week, now his missus has him up feeding the kids at 3am, clearing the crap from the nappies at 4 and feeding them again at 6, he's like a walking zombie. Spoke to him on the phone last night, I bloody woke him up, didn't I? It was only 7 o'clock. Keep away from kids I say, nothing but hassle.'

Tom enjoyed Mark's take on life, it reminded him of his world 12 years ago.

'Well, thanks for that my friend, I'm still on that plan thing aren't I? The one I pay you about £25 a month to spend four minutes a year looking in my gob.' Mark patted Tom on the arm. 'Easy life, mate, still, you're the dentist.'

'And I'm always here if you need me in the middle of the night when you've got toothache. Don't you forget that you old bugger. Worth £25 quid a month of anyone's money.' He shook Mark's hand and smiled as they said their goodbyes.

'Keep swinging pal,' Tom shouted as Mark headed down the stairs.

'Oh, I like a bit of swinging.'

Tom washed his hands and looked at Emily as she cleaned the instruments, he had been building himself up for this all morning. It was a risky conversation, but he would work things out as it developed. It needed to be done.

He went downstairs to see Jill, who was just popping out for lunch and would be back in an hour. Tom closed the door behind her and locked it and went back upstairs. Emily was also getting ready to go out for lunch.

'Emily, have you got a minute? I want to talk to you, in here.'

'Sure,' Emily replied.

Tom walked into the small canteen where there were three chairs and a table. He sat down and pointed at her to sit down opposite him as he closed the door behind them.

She looked at him. 'Is everything alright?'

'No, it isn't, it's not alright at all.' Emily looked concerned.

'Let me tell you a little story that's been happening in my life over the past few weeks. Polly has been receiving abusive, threatening texts, our phone at home has also had people call up and say odd things, not nice things and all sorts of weird stuff, mainly about me. Stuff the police ought to know about to be honest.'

Emily's usual care-free demeanour was replaced by one of stiffness, her cheeks turning red.

'And I think I know who has been calling her. It's not a very nice thing for her to be going through, don't you think? As I said, I was going to go to the police about it and I spoke to a mate of mine who is a copper, he said finding the culprit would be easy, 'malicious communications' is an offence. I still might still go down that route, if people have nothing to hide, they won't mind their phones being checked. What do you say, Emily?'

She knew she had been caught. She had no idea how Tom knew, but she suspected. She looked at him but he wasn't going to accuse her. He wanted to watch, see and feel her reaction. When it came, Tom was shocked.

'I fucking hate her and I fucking hate you for this.' Her lips pursed as she exploded in anger. She stood up, Tom hadn't been expecting this.

'I've worked in here with you for a year and not once, not once have you paid me any attention.' Her voice got louder. 'I've done everything I can to get you to take interest in me and what have you done? Nothing, fucking nothing. That slag of a wife of yours, is all you talk about. She comes in here all flirty and mouthy, shouting and laughing, dressed like some teenage tart and you call that a wife.'

Tom went to say something, but stopped himself. If he wanted a confession, this was it and he was going to have to get it warts and all. It was dawning on him, Emily was jealous of Polly, because Emily had a crush on him! *Jesus!*

'I could have made you happy, Tom, but you have never given me a chance. I may be younger than you, but we could have been great together. I pictured it, it's all I wanted, couldn't you see?'

She sat back down and pointed at him, her voice quieter now.

'Karen told you, didn't she? She's a fucking cow as well. If she hadn't been so pissed that night, I'd never have known about any of your two's mess. How do you think she got hold of your mobile number? She pleaded me for it, oh, by the way, does Polly know about your baby together? Ha, ha. I bet she let out one of her big false laughs when you told her that, or did she just crash the car on purpose?'

'Okay, Emily, that's enough I've heard enough, get your coat and get out of here. You can leave straightaway, we have nothing more to say. I don't want to see you again. And if I do, I'll make sure everyone knows why I fired you, including the police.'

She put her head in her hands and began to sob uncontrollably, but Tom wasn't having it.

She looked up at Tom, who was standing over her, she shook her head.

'I'm sorry,' she said through the tears. 'I'm sorry, I just don't know why I did it, I know this sounds silly but I've just always seen you as someone I could love, could have, could hold. If you only knew what I'd been through as a young girl, you would maybe understand, but I don't expect you to. Please forgive me and tell Polly, I'm sorry. Don't go to the police, please.'

Tom wanted to take her by the arm and march her out, but he couldn't. As much as he wanted her out of his surgery, he did care about her. She had been a good worker and they had enjoyed many laughs together. He'd never noticed her affection for him, her crush, Polly would think him so naive. He could hear her now... *'You're telling me you never noticed she fancied you? Christ, Tom!'*

'I know I'll go,' Emily said, wiping her eyes. 'I'll find another job and I'll leave you alone, I know it was just fantasy for me. I've never been loved. You are one of the first blokes who has shown me any sort of kindness. I liked it here and look what I've done? Look how I've repaid you?'

He felt a tinge of sorrow for her. But it was all too late.

'Okay Emily. Well look, I'll pay you an extra month's salary in your pay packet next week, so you'll get two months, you'll soon have another job. But I can't forgive what you have done, you were so wrong. Let this be a life lesson and I'll tell people you left to get another job. But if you do continue to contact Pol in any way, then I'll come down on you like a ton of bricks and, as I said, that includes the cops, do I make myself clear?'

Emily nodded. 'I'm just so sorry, I'll get my things.'

And with that she walked back into the surgery, picked up her coat and bag and walked down the stairs. Tom followed her, unlocking the door. She never looked back.

Tom sat down. He felt drained.

He went downstairs and sat in Jill's seat on reception, looking at the appointments for that afternoon. He would tell Jill that Emily wasn't feeling well, not that Jill would believe him. But he couldn't think of any better excuse right now. He would tell her the full story next week, unless Jill got to Emily first.

He puffed out his cheeks, he was looking forward to seeing Polly tonight. She would never believe this. After that, he might nip over to the Queen's Head for a quick half or three, hopefully some of the gang would be there. That at least would release some of the tension.

Yet, still uppermost in his thoughts was *that* e-mail from the clinic in London.

It couldn't come soon enough.

SEVENTY SIX

THERE was joy and apprehension in Tom's steps as he headed towards the hospital. Although the worry over Karen and Lee was still hanging over them, at least he had found out who had been sending Polly the messages. And it had been dealt with.

He thought she would be relieved when he told her, but Polly was never the easiest to read.

'You're seriously telling me, those shitty texts and calls were from Emily and all because she is a jealous little kid who fancied you?' Polly was almost laughing as she sat in her hospital bed. Except she wasn't finding it funny.

'A spotty, piss-head of a tart like her, thinking she had a chance with you? Bloody hell. And you didn't suspect or notice a thing, I suppose? Working with her day in, day out for a bloody year and you didn't notice she had some sort of crush on you? Why am I not surprised? You are unbelievable.'

Tom took it on the chin. There was a perverse comfort he shouldn't have been surprised by her reaction. She was on the mend.

'It was definitely her?' Polly looked at Tom.

'Well, if it wasn't, I don't know why she walked out and took the fact I told her she was fired so easily. If she hadn't sent them she would have made more of a fuss than she did. Oh, and she asked me to apologise to you.'

'Apologise? Well she can fuck right off.' Polly leant across to pick up a cup of tea on her sideboard next to her bed. 'And before you say, *'Polly mind you language'*, you can shut up. If our marriage

430

ever wanted testing, you seem to be going about it in the right way, right now. First Karen, now Emily. Is there anyone else out there I should know about? Perhaps some woman on Instagram you've been have sex text with. Christ, I never knew I'd married such a stud.'

Tom just sat there. When she was like this, he knew it was best to let it roll.

'Look, I'm sorry about Emily, but I had no idea,' Tom held her hand. 'You're always saying I wouldn't know if a woman fancied me even if she stripped naked in front of me, that's because I only have eyes for you.' He gave a pathetic smile.

Polly shook her head. 'Pass me that sick bucket will you?' I'm going to throw up. The reason you wouldn't notice, my darling, is because you are more interested in teeth than tits.'

'Thank you dear, such kind words, you have a way with them. Anyhow, how's Jody?' He changed the subject.

'The same as yesterday. Upset, hurt, can't understand what's happened and why. She'll start to get angry soon when it all sinks in, I bet you. Her parents are furious with Craig, you know her dad and he isn't one to argue with. The only thing Jody has at least got is money, unless Craig suddenly files for divorce and wants half of everything, but I'd be stunned if he did that, seeing as he paid everything off.'

'How did he pay the mortgage off?' Tom said. 'Did they not have much of one?'

'£190,000 apparently,' Polly replied, a surprised looked on her face.

'Where the hell did he get that money from,' he added, before deciding not to pursue the question, he had a nagging feeling he knew where Craig got the money from.

'I don't know,' Polly said, sipping her drink. 'Jody might come down for a few days soon if she can find someone to run the shop.'

There was a brief silence. The lady in the bed opposite waved at them both, they waved back, before the conversation turned towards their baby to be, and Milky's wedding plans.

'I'll find out more from Milky tonight,' Tom smiled. 'Think I might go down for a quick beer or three. Hopefully a few of the gang will be there.'

'Wish I could come, I could do with a glass of wine, perhaps next week. Give them all my love, won't you? Especially Stu, give him a big kiss from me and tell him I love him.'

'Right, I've got to go, or I'll miss last orders, see you tomorrow. And if you are okay about it, I'm going to the footie in the afternoon. I'll call here in the morning and then come back later, but only if Arsenal win.'

'You better be here, win or no win.' She pointed a finger.

The pair hugged and kissed and Tom again put his hand on Polly's tummy. 'Love you my little babe. I can't wait to be a dad.'

The letter was from Craig. It was sitting on the door mat, addressed to Tom. He saw it as soon as he walked in. He opened the envelope.

Hi mate,

Well, you probably know the news. I've gone and I won't be coming back.

You probably think me a right tosser – fair enough. But the world can play tricks on you and it has with me. It's all too long a story but started with that night with that woman at that conference. But I'd appreciate it if you never told Jody, or anyone, what we spoke about. Maybe one day she will find out, maybe she never will. She'll rebuild her life.

Of course if you want to tell her, that's your call.

Up the Arsenal!

Craig.

Tom re-read it again. What a bastard. What an arrogant, arrogant bastard. No, he wouldn't tell Polly nor Jody, neither needed to know. '*Of course if you want to, that's your call.*' Craig could go to hell, he could read between the lines. He wanted Tom to tell Jody, make him feel better that she knew what had happened. He could go fuck himself. Tom read it one more time, before ripping the note into pieces and binning it.

There were huge cheers in the Queen's Head as Tom walked in, it was 10pm and most of 'the gang' had been drinking for a few hours.

Janie, Alison and Ann leapt to their feet to hug and kiss him. All asking how Polly was at a rate of knots, Tom was struggling to keep up with them.

'Let me get myself a beer, and I'll tell you the latest.' He knew none of them had been allowed to visit Polly while she was in Addenbrooke's. And she'd only moved closer to home late yesterday afternoon.

'There's my £20,' Tom put his money in the kitty.

'No, no, no,' Ben said. 'You're not paying tonight, plus the fact even you can't drink £20 pounds-worth of beer in an hour.'

'Can't I? I'll have a bloody good go, no, you leave that money in there, the kitty fund is sacred.'

Tom went to the bar, but stopped halfway and turned round and looked at his friends who were all chatting away to each other.

'Oh, just one thing before I get the drinks in,' he said. 'Stu, come here.'

Stuart looked around. He got up and began walking towards Tom, who met him halfway.

'This Stu, is from Polly,' Tom announced. And with that he held Stuart's face with his hands, pulled it towards him and gave him a big smacker on his forehead! All the friends roared with laughter, before he pulled himself back and smiled at his friend.

'And that's from me as well,' he said quietly. 'I know what you went through that day, I can't thank you enough.'

Stuart nodded and tried to make light of it. But you could see him getting emotional, he tried to laugh it off. 'Bloody hell, mate, that was a surprise, would have preferred it on the lips from Pol, mind you.'

Polly's accident had hit Stuart hard. Janie stood up and put her arms around her husband as he went to sit down.

'I'm just glad she's okay,' Stuart smiled. 'Okay, enough of this Tomfoolery. See what I did there? Tom... Foolery!'

'So, what would Pol want us to do now? That's right, get pissed. Come on Tom, get those bloody beers in.'

They all laughed and clinked their glasses to Polly's health as Tom brought them up-to-date with the latest, but not telling them about their baby.

The night finished with another game of 'round-the-clock' darts, with everyone taking part.

Ben was the victor, managing to take out the 25 and bull in

two darts. He did a quick lap around the bar after hitting the bull, much to the amusement of the other dozen or so drinkers in the pub, before a round of shots to celebrate.

'Even Pol would have been impressed with that,' he said, as he high-fived Paul at the bar on his way past.

Paul turned the music up as the clock hit 11 and for the next hour the chat got louder and the stories flowed. Milky's wedding preparations were apparently coming on a treat, Denise had even booked a chimney sweep, something that had confused Milky.

'I'm glad she's not here because I want to ask you guys something, I daren't ask Denise,' he said to the group. 'I don't understand, why do we need a chimney swept just because we are getting married? I don't have a chimney to sweep for a start.'

He shrugged his shoulders and waited for an answer. Scott explained the reasoning, a good luck charm and all that, you could see the relief and confusion on Milky's face.

They all said their good nights and Tom walked back to his cottage. It had been a week since the accident but it felt like a lifetime, he'd got used to not sleeping much in his own bed. As he opened the door and turned the lights on, he went into the kitchen, it was all very quiet and he decided to have a small glass of water before he went up to bed. At least he didn't have to get up early in the morning.

He hadn't taken his phone to the pub, which he scolded himself for when he looked at it on the kitchen table. What if Polly had wanted him urgently? He was so careless.

He went to pick it up and flicked to see if he had received any messages, he only had the one notification. It had been sent at 9.49pm.

An e-mail. From the clinic in London.

SEVENTY SEVEN

ARCHER and Cantwell had spent Friday lunchtime chatting about just one thing, Craig Baldini.

Cantwell wasn't a fan of prison visits and admittedly Archer would rather have kept a man who looks like your stereotypical ex-offender, away. Raising suspicion by meeting someone who looked like he should be in a prison with you was not a good idea, Archer felt.

'I was there over an hour, it was a set-up. I had the right address, I know that place like the back of my hand.' Cantwell was not happy. It had cost Archer £10K, £5K each for the two 'hit men'. Not that Archer was bothered about the money, but Cantwell was pissed.

'So, what do you reckon?' Archer said. 'Have you spoken to Liam?'

'Yeah. He says he hasn't spoken to his mum for a couple of days. I know you are close to your boy, but it wouldn't surprise me if he knows something, and I've tried to call Marie about 20 times.'

'Leave Liam out of it. This isn't his fight, he's a good kid. If he knows anything, he knows 'cause his mum told him, that's not his fault, I won't have him touched.'

'Your call,' said Cantwell, sitting back in his chair. 'Quite honestly mate, it's all up to you now. You know I'll help, but I won't be made to look a prick, you understand?'

Archer nodded.

'You reckon they might have gone off together?' Cantwell leaned back in his chair and looked at his friend. 'Or has Marie just done a runner? And by coincidence Baldini's just gone walkabout as well?'

'Gone off together?' Archer exclaimed, moving forward in his chair to get closer to Cantwell. 'Gone off together? Why the fuck would they do that? She's about 20 years older than him. They only shagged once and that was nearly two years ago, or so she says. Don't tell me you think they've been going at it all this time? Christ, I know I kept an eye on him, but I didn't put Baldini down as having as big a set of balls as that. No, she's gone mate, that's what's happened. She's been threatening to piss off for years, I don't blame her. I've said this before, if she's gone, then she's gone, and that's it. What's happened to Baldini I can't fathom? Perhaps he does have a secret life, another life. Maybe he was tipped off by Marie and he decided to run, I don't know. But gone off together? I can't believe that.'

'Well, I don't know what to think.' Cantwell looked as dumbfounded as he sounded. 'Something's not right.'

Visiting time was coming to an end. There were 20 prisoners with visitors in the room and one or two had already got up to leave.

'You know anything about Baldini's wife?' Archer said. Cantwell shook his head.

'Well, find her and find out where her husband is, once we've pinned him down, we can think of another way of getting him, he can't just vanish.'

'But what if he is with Marie?'

'Fuck me Charlie, do you know something I don't? Do you really think the pair of them have gone somewhere together? Give me a break, they are hardly a couple of love-birds. I'd have known about it. No, Marie has gone. She always said she would start up a new life one day. Perhaps this was her parting shot, fucking me over with all that cash.'

'Well, as I said, your call. But I ain't keeping coming back here to visit you mate, as much as I like you, I hate prisons and I'm not comfortable.' Cantwell stood up to go. Archer joined him.

'Well, go find the bastard, speak to his missus, his workmates. I want him found. And if you have no luck, or if he has pissed off, leave one of those DVDs of Marie and him, where Mrs Baldini can find it. I bet she hasn't seen it, I'd like to see him wriggle out of that if he does pop his head up again. You did make copies?'

Cantwell smiled. 'Yep. I made copies and I've watched it. Hope you didn't mind?'

'You dirty old bastard. That's my wife you've been watching shagged.

'Go on Charlie, piss off.'

SEVENTY EIGHT

TOM was up early on Saturday morning.

The drink from the night before had little effect on the way he felt. He made himself some toast, poured himself some orange juice, told Alexa to play Radio One and looked out at the garden as he leant over the sink. The sun was trying to peep through.

He turned his phone on, he still couldn't get out of the habit of taking weekends off from his mobile. He must try harder. The notification from the clinic was still there, as was a missed call from Karen and a subsequent voicemail, which he suspected would be her.

He dialled 121 and listened to it. His expression never changed.

Tom hadn't been for an early morning run for some time, but he felt now was as good a time as any to go and clear his head, he had much to think about.

Arriving home after a jog that lasted no more than 30 minutes, but was halted after just five when he bumped into Janie who was walking across the green. 'Give Polly my love if you are seeing her today,' she had called out. Tom had stopped and chatted for a couple of minutes, telling her he was off to see her as soon as he'd got home and showered. When Polly would be back he didn't know, but now she was at the Norwich & Norfolk, she was open to visitors. Janie liked the sound of that.

Back home and showered, he jumped in his car and headed to the hospital, he'd packed an extra coat for his trip to the football that afternoon. He'd thought about not going but Polly hadn't seem bothered about it. And he wanted to. He pulled up in the car park and headed into the wards. It was 11 am, an hour with her before he had to go to the match.

As he walked around the corner, he saw Polly being helped up out of her chair by two nurses. She had been putting weight on her ankle for a couple of days, lightly mind you. He could tell she was grimacing, her damaged shoulder meaning it was proving hard to balance with one crutch.

He stood back and watched her walk a couple of steps with a nurse supporting her, before she sank back into the chair next to her bed. She was changed and out of her nightie, which was nice. Blue shirt and blue trousers.

'Morning,' Tom said as he bounced into the ward. 'Morning, morning, morning.'

He leant down and kissed her on the cheek, then the head. He sat down beside her.

'And how are you today?'

'I've had another bath, it was wonderful.' Polly looked up to the sky as she spoke. 'They took my ankle and shoulder bandages off and I soaked for about 30 minutes. Mind you, it took the nurse about 10 minutes to get me out, my shoulder is still so painful.' She winched.

'Well, I must admit it is nice that you are smelling good again, you were starting to pong.'

'Bloody cheek. Pong? I don't pong'

He laughed and looked at her. He kept staring, saying nothing. The ward had five other patients in but none had visitors as yet. The lady opposite waved once more. They waved back. He looked around at the rest of the ward's patients, before returning his gaze to her. He grinned.

'What? What is it? Why are you grinning at me? What is so funny?

'I've got some news.' His face changed to a more serious look as he leaned closer to her and held her hands. Polly didn't need to ask what it was about, she knew, her stomach tightened. She'd tried to put this moment behind her since she had found out about Karen. She knew this moment would come. Oh, how would she cope with the bombshell she was sure Tom was about to drop?

He continued to stare. It seemed like an eternity before he

spoke.... 'He's not my son, Pol.'

'Lee, he's not my son, I'm not the father.'

She didn't know how to react, didn't know what to say. She'd played out a scenario in her mind so many times and it had always been Tom telling her Lee was his son. She had wondered how she would react. Would she cry? Would she shout at him? The one thing she'd never thought about was what she would do, or say, if Tom told her Lee wasn't his son.

'Oh, my God, oh, my God. You're not joking me are you? You're not kidding me? Please say you are not stringing me along. Don't mess about.' Tears began to well in her eyes.

Tom grabbed hold of her hands.

'I had the e-mail come through late last night, it's all there in black and white, and he's not my son. Don't cry, be happy, I know you're relieved, so am I. I've known since last night but I couldn't call you. This morning I even went for a run to clear my head, it's been crazy. This has been killing me as much as you. I have to admit I did think he was my son. But he's not and that's that. DNA results are not wrong, the result says it's 99.9% sure I'm not the father. That's it, it's over. Now we can concentrate on our little bundle of joy that's tucked away in that tummy of yours.' Tom patted Polly's stomach.

'I can't believe it.' Polly leant across and put her head on his shoulder. She was aware the other patients on the ward were starting to look across. But she cared little.

'Well, believe it, and I'm sorry.' Tom looked into her eyes. 'I'm sorry for this whole fricking episode, it's nearly broken us, but it hasn't. And that's the main thing, we are so strong. I love you and even when you are eight months pregnant I'll still say you have the best figure in Melsham.'

Polly pulled herself away from him, laughing and crying at the same time. 'Just in Melsham! Oh, thanks very much. But tell me this is true isn't it? It's all over.' Tom nodded. 'Oh, I'm sorry as well, I'm sorry for doubting you and leaving you and not being nice to you and shouting at you. And... Everything. I love you so much.'

Tom squeezed her hands. 'I love you too.'

Tom got up to move the flowers on the sideboard. They looked like they were about to fall onto the floor. He sat down and hugged Polly again, before she pulled back. 'Oh, by the way mum and dad are coming up later. I told them you were going to the football, they are going to stay somewhere overnight, and so I said they could stay with you.'

'What?'

'Only kidding.' She grinned. 'I didn't think you would like that, so they are staying somewhere in Norwich, they are going to go ballistic when I tell them I'm pregnant.'

'Come on, we were in a happy place and then you go and tease me about your parents staying with me. I don't think I could put up with your mum organising me in my own house. Which reminds me, I suppose I'd better call my mum and dad to tell them about the baby, does Jody know?'

'No, she doesn't, I'll call her today. I'll tell her all the news, I just feel so bad pouring our good news on her when she's so upset.'

'She'd want to know. You know she would, let her know before others find out.'

Tom stretched and pulled his shoulders back. 'So, there you go, girl. It's just me, you and bump. Family Armstrong. But...' Tom looked serious at her. 'There is something else and I've promised never to keep a secret from you again.'

Polly looked at him.

'Oh, no, what is it now? Don't keep doing this.'

He paused. 'I have had a voicemail from Karen, she left it this morning. You want to listen to it?'

She was quiet for a moment, then shook her head. 'No, just tell me.'

'Well, she spends most of the message talking through tears. She's not nasty, or unpleasant but asks if I would mind meeting her tomorrow, just to talk it over.' Polly's face looked like thunder.

'Hang on. Hear me out. Look, I had a chat with her in London after the test, not for long, but long enough to hear her story, it's not been a good one.' Polly's expression still hadn't changed. 'And that's my fault, is it?

'No, it isn't your fault, as I said, hear me out, Pol. She thought she was right about me being the father and I think she'd sort of started planning how it was going to work. But I had told her then to wait until we all knew the truth, now she is shattered. She's very vulnerable, I can text her back and tell her to piss off and don't come near me ever again, or I can talk to her and make sure she's okay with everything. That's just me being me. But you have the final say. I'll do whatever you want me to do, I promise.'

She looked up to the sky and breathed out, he was such a good man. He had a heart of gold and even though the last thing she wanted was for him to speak to Karen, she had to let it happen.

'Go and see her.' She leant across and put her hands on Tom's cheeks and pulled him close. 'You're mine, all mine, you are such a kind man. I'm so lucky to have you, but please, don't let her get to you. You know what I mean?'

Tom nodded as the pair touched lips.

'That, my little mummy-to-be, is exactly why I married you. Because under all the toughness, the rude words. And the excessive drinking... Is a wonderful woman. I'm so proud of you.'

The pair kissed again. 'Cheeky bugger, I haven't had a drink for a week at least.'

'Sorry are we disturbing something? Come on you lovebirds, time for the rest of us to kiss the patient.'

Polly looked up. 'Mum, dad, you're here already, I thought you were coming later this afternoon.'

'We were dear but your father put the wrong postcode in the sat nav, so we left Brighton this morning at 5am because the sat nav said we wouldn't be here until 1pm,' said Polly's mum, Margaret.

'He'd put NE in the stupid thing and not NR. And NE is for Newcastle, which is where we were heading, it wasn't until we went past Cambridge at 8 o clock this morning, and were heading north on the A1 he realised his mistake, didn't you Jonathan?'

Jonathan smiled knowingly. Tom smiled. He knew the feeling when you'd been beat, Polly and her mum were two of a kind.

'Anyhow,' her mum continued. 'How are you feeling darling?

'And what's been going on. Anything we should know?'

SEVENTY NINE

KAREN cried most of the night.

Never in her wildest dreams had she thought Tom was not the father. She looked again at the e-mail, headed 'Paternity Test' and the final line that cut so deep...

'Based on our analysis, it is practically proven that Mr Tom Armstrong is not the biological father of child Lee Harding.'

There were lists of DNA numbers and figures, similar to the ones on Lee and her DNA tests, that she could neither be bothered to look at nor try and work out. The e-mail said a 'Paternity Test Certificate' would be in the post in the next 48 hours but she would throw that in the bin.

Lee had been staying at friends on Friday night, so she'd cried alone, eventually getting to sleep at 3am, having finished off a bottle of red wine. She was feeling no better on Saturday morning, in fact she felt worse. The house was empty. Reality had set in, Tom wasn't Lee's father and the results were not up for disputing.

It was 7.30 in the morning when she called Jane to tell her the news. She was as devastated as she was. Jane had been the one person who knew the full story of all her sister had gone through, well almost the full story. Jane, and Emily.

Emily should never have known. If she hadn't said she worked at a dentist surgery, Karen wouldn't have questioned her that night as to what surgery and who owned it. Then the demon drink started talking and she said too much. Oh, well, it doesn't matter now.

After talking to Jane, she'd plucked up the courage to call Tom.

Jane had suggested she did so, but Karen was going to anyway.

She knew he was likely to say, *'get lost'*, if he had any sense, she'd caused him enough grief. But she wanted to call, although she ended up leaving a message.

Lee was going straight from his friends to watch a rugby game, so she had the day to herself, she would spend it at home. She felt a mess and no doubt looked one. She took herself off for a walk but her mind was spinning. Her dreams were shattered. It wasn't Tom. As much as she didn't want to admit it, she now knew the answer to a question she had never wanted to confront.

Later, while making herself dinner, she got a text from Emily. *'Cheers Karen. I'm out of a job now. Fuck you.'*

She looked at the message again, tough shit. She blocked her. Karen had never told her to send Polly texts, calls, or whatever she'd obviously gone and done. She was a stupid, immature child. Their days were over.

Her phone rang, and her heart skipped a beat when she saw who it was. It was Tom, she took a deep breath.

'Hi.' Her voice weak and quiet. She turned off the oven. Dinner could wait.

Tom's voice was strong. 'Hi, you wanted to meet?'

'Um, yeah. Well, obviously we know the news, I just wanted to meet up and say and well I don't know what really, just talk. But, you can tell me to piss off. I would understand.'

'I won't tell you to piss off. But you do know we can't continue to meet and talk, we can meet tomorrow if you want, for a short time. How about where we met at the park, near the cycle track? 11 o clock?'

'Okay, I haven't got to get Lee to rugby tomorrow which makes a nice change.' Karen staged a nervous laugh.

'See you tomorrow then.' Tom hung up.

She put the phone down and turned the oven back on. She went into the living room and sat on the settee. And cried once more.

Jody's parents had spent a couple of nights with their daughter.

They could do little more than console her, the fact her dad wanted to kill Craig meant he was not in the best of moods throughout and, while her mum was loving and comforting, his anger meant Jody was glad when they went home Saturday lunchtime.

She called Polly.

'Hi, are you okay?' Polly picked the call up on the first ring.

'Oh, darling I'm fine, how are you? I was about to call you, my mum and dad have just arrived. Are your mum and dad still there?'

'They've just gone, I don't mind to be honest. Mum has been great, but dad has spent much of the time threatening to kill Craig and wanting to know where he might be. In some ways, I'm glad he's gone, I know he means well, but it's very tiring, all his negativity.'

'Only because they love you, Jody.'

'I know. But I'm actually glad of a bit of space to myself now, does that sound strange? I won't keep you if your mum and day are there with you.'

'No, it's fine. And it doesn't sound strange about wanting space, so long as you are okay in yourself.'

'I am, I just can't still believe what's happened.'

'Don't try to think about it, please. Just think about the future, you have a great future ahead of you. And who knows? Craig may still turn up, perhaps something has spooked him. I don't know what to say to be honest, I'm sorry, I'm just waffling.'

'Don't worry darling, I know, it's all so unreal.'

'Well, I have got something to tell you, well, two things actually. I hope this cheers you up a bit..... Are you sitting down?'

Polly's parents walked back into the ward having taken a trip to the shop downstairs to get sweets and books.

'Hi, guys, you find everything?' Polly had just come off the phone from Jody. 'It's a nice shop isn't it? Tom said it is.'

'It is darling,' said Margaret, as she handed Polly a bar of chocolate. 'Are you feeling okay? Make sure you eat plenty of good food, in your condition, this is a treat.' She smiled at her daughter, then turned to her husband. 'Fancy us going to be grandparents, isn't that exciting, Jonathan?'

'Thrilling,' he said, winking at his daughter. 'All those dirty nappies.'

'Ignore him. He's only cross because I've bought him a map, he won't get bloody lost now, will you dear?'

Charlie Cantwell hadn't got much sense out of PJC Shipping when he called and asked to speak to Craig Baldini.

First of all he was given the tenth degree by some woman who claimed to be Craig's PA. She wanted to know why he wanted to speak to him and when had he last tried to speak to him, it was a weird set of questions, ending with the lady, who called herself Lisa, saying he wasn't in, she wasn't supposed to be in. And she didn't know when he would be back.

If that didn't confirm that Baldini was on the run, the call to Mr and Mrs Baldini's house the night before had left him thinking as much. The call was picked up by a man with a gruff voice, and when Charlie asked to speak to Mr Baldini, the man couldn't have been ruder if he'd tried — *'he's not here. He's pissed off and left my daughter and bloody good job. He's an arsehole. So, no, I can't help you and if I find him, I'll kill him.'* And with that the phone went dead.

Charlie hadn't even been given a chance to say who he was or what he wanted.

But it did confirm his hunch that Baldini had gone or was on the run, and maybe with Marie. Even if Archer didn't think that, he would make enquiries on that front. He had fingers in plenty of pies to help source that information, and as early as Saturday night, he had it.

It appeared Marie and Craig had left the country, and likely together, of that he was now 99% sure. The trouble is, where had they gone was a mystery, his sources had found Marie had purchased two plane tickets from six different UK airports to six different destinations. To back that up, she'd bought six pairs of tickets for connecting flights from all those destinations. He couldn't find out the name on the other ticket, but he was sure as eggs were eggs, Baldini was with her. The pair of them could be anywhere in the world, Charlie had to give it to her, Archer had taught her well... *Clever girl.*

He would need to speak to Archer to see what was next.

EIGHTY

<u>Sunday, May 10</u>

SHE was dressed in a pink blouse and white trousers, with a red coat. Karen held the umbrella above her head. It was raining quite hard.

As Tom approached she turned to look at him, there was no smile on her face.

'Hi, thanks for coming, you didn't have to.' She feigned a weak smile.

'It's okay, I don't mind. But as I said, this is it, now we know, this has to be it Karen. You do understand that?'

A tear ran down her cheek. 'I'm sorry, I'm sorry.'

He walked towards her and put his arms around her. She put her umbrella on the ground as she buried her head on his shoulder, the tears flowed as the rain came down.

'It's okay, it's okay.' Tom pulled her close.

She continued to cry before pulling back. 'I hoped Lee would be yours, not to come in-between you and your wife, I would never have wanted that, but so he had someone to talk to, a father-figure to confide in. This has always been about Lee, not me. I have never wanted anything from you, I've only wanted the truth and I still don't have that.'

He was stood back from her now and looking at her with sadness. Tom knew his life was set to carry on regardless. A baby on the way, a wife who loved him deeply. But he was still sore by this whole episode, the grief it had caused Polly.

'Is this what you wanted to say?' he said. 'Is this why you wanted to meet? To pour your heart out a bit more. I don't really have much to add, Karen. It's not been easy having to come to terms you may have a child you didn't know about. Watch your marriage heading to the rocks. And before you say anything, yes, I know it's been harder for you and Lee.

'So, what are you going to tell him?'

Karen picked up her umbrella and wiped her eyes.

'I hadn't told him anything up to now. All I've said is that I'll tell him one day. Maybe it's time to tell him I just don't know who his dad is.'

Something made Tom sense something wasn't right, however.

'Is that the truth, Karen? You really don't know who the dad is? Even now. Now you know it isn't me? You have told me everything, right?'

Karen stared at him. 'You can read me Tom, can't you? Bloody hell.' And with that she began to cry again, she got out a tissue and wiped her eyes. An elderly couple holding hands walked close by. Karen waited to say something until they had passed.

'I've never told anyone this Tom. And I mean, no-one. But you deserve to know, can we sit down?'

They walked across to a bench overlooking the cycle track. The bench wasn't as wet as many of the others, as it was hidden under a tree. Karen took a breath.

'Before I went on holiday that year, to Crete, something happened to me, something I have never told a soul, not even my sister.'

Tom just looked at her. 'A few weeks before we all flew out to Crete, there was a party at my friend's house in Woolwich. Her name is Tonya, it was the usual stuff, drink, a bit of weed, lots of dancing. Every week it was one party or another in my area of London.

'I had way too much to drink and I wasn't feeling great.' Karen had stopped crying now and was looking at the floor, then back up at Tom.

'Anyhow, I went up to a room to lay down and I must have fallen asleep, I was totally out of it. Then I was awoken by someone on top of me. I couldn't work out what was going on, it was all a bit of a blur. He had lifted my skirt up. I was petrified, went to scream but nothing came out. He was so strong, had his hand over my mouth. Then I felt him inside me, it was horrible. It didn't last long and I was still too out of it to do anything, I just lay there.'

Her eyes welled. Tom sat closer and held her hand. 'Oh, Karen.'

'Anyhow, when it was over, he got up and I think he thought I was still out of it because he made a point of doing up the buttons on my blouse. As he did I opened my eyes and I could see him. I recognised him.

'It was Tonya's dad.'

Tom was shocked. 'Shit Karen.'

'I knew it was him. He was a bit of chancer, had Tonya when he was 17, so he was not an older father. He couldn't have been 40. He loved himself and he'd been at the party. It was in his own house and he'd stayed. Everyone sort of played up to, *Tonya's dad. He's a right laugh'*. That type of thing.

'I saw him, Tom, saw him get off me. Me and Tonya had been friends since primary school, but what could I do? I just lay there, I must have been there another hour before I decided to get up and go back down to the party. And he was there, dancing and chatting, smoking and acting as though nothing had happened. I just went home soon after.

'Three weeks later we went to Crete and me and you met up, you were the only person on holiday I had sex with, honestly. I wasn't sure I wanted to meet anyone after what had happened that night. In fact I nearly didn't go on holiday, seeing as Tonya was one of the girls who was in the group. She didn't know then and she doesn't know now.

'When we met on that holiday, I liked you so much, you restored my faith in men. But I was silly, I told you I was on the pill, when I'd stopped taking it a few months previous because I'd been quite ill on it. When I found out I was pregnant, I just hoped it was you who was the father, and I tried to forget the rape happened.

'That's why I went to look for you, in London, convincing myself it was you.'

Tom was still holding her hand. 'That's terrible, Karen. That man shouldn't get away with it, you're stronger now. Get people to help you, he knows what he's done, I will help you get professional help, solicitors, whatever you need. Do you still speak to this Tonya girl? He needs to be held accountable for this.'

Karen looked at him and shook her head as she spoke. 'I haven't spoken to her in years, I think she is still about, we were good friends, don't know how I kept it from her to be honest. But don't worry about holding him to account. Two years after he raped me he was killed in a stabbing on a local park. Drugs related the police said, he's dead.'

There was a moment of silence. Tom felt so sorry for her.

'I can't imagine whether you're happy or not about the fact he's dead? On one hand you can't prove he's the father, on the other, at least the bastard is no longer about.'

'I know,' Karen said, nodding. 'I think overall I'm glad he's gone. But the fact you are not the father means he likely was. I don't want Lee to know about him, the bloke was a bastard. I don't know what I'll tell Lee..... You would have made a great father.' She smiled at him.

Again there was a moment of silence and Tom got up.

'But I'm not. And I have my own life to lead.'

She stood up and looked at him, tears beginning to fall down her eyes once more. 'Polly is one very lucky lady.'

And with that she leant forward and kissed him on the cheek. She picked up her umbrella and turned to walk off.

He watched as she headed off down the path, around the corner, disappearing from view... forever.

EIGHTY ONE

Three Weeks Later

TOM followed Polly into the Queen's Head to rapturous applause. It was if the whole village had turned out.

She had been home a week after her stay in hospital was extended when the doctors became concerned over the welfare of the baby, thankfully it proved a false alarm.

And while her broken bones were on the mend, she still needed one crutch to get around to take weight off her ankle.

All she had wanted to do was meet up with the gang down the pub on Friday night, even though she had only been home three days. Tom was all for it and had asked Jan and Paul to put some food on, but even Polly hadn't been expecting the reception she got.

A 'welcome home Pol' banner was flying from the bar and all the friends had got to the pub early, so as to be able to greet her in. Polly was beaming when she saw the banner as she walked in, as Janie stepped forward to hug and greet her. 'Polly's home everybody,' Janie shouted at the top of her voice. And everyone cheered again.

They all wanted to hug her and Polly, despite the inconvenience of the crutch, was happily doing the rounds, steady hugs, mind you.

After all the girls had had their turn, Polly came to Stuart.

He stood back from her as she came towards him.

The last time Stuart had seen Polly she'd been a bloody mess in a car crash he had to cut her out of. The friends quietened as the two smiled at each other. It was an emotional moment.

'Pol,' Stuart smiled at her. 'You have no idea how happy I am to see you.' As he went to finish his sentence, his voice cracked. He held one hand to his face to hold back the tears and stretched the other towards her. Polly walked over and hugged him tight, whispering in his ear, 'thank you Stu, thank you. I love you so much.'

There were few dry eyes in the pub as the pair embraced for some minutes. Janie was especially emotional, she knew more than anyone how that day had upset her husband.

Polly pulled back from him. 'Look at you, big softie. You're crying. I'm crying. Look, you've made your wife cry. We're all bloody crying.' She hugged him again, everyone was wiping a tear away.

'Okay,' said Tom. 'That's enough of all this blubbing. Let's get this show on the road. I've put money behind the bar and everyone's first drink is on me. Thanks for all your kind words and love.' He looked at Polly. 'It's great to have her back.'

Everyone was smiling and Polly grabbed hold of her husband's arm as Tom shouted above all the noise. 'Hang on though, quiet please, before we start. My wife has something else to say.'

The place fell silent and everyone looked at Polly.

'I just wanted to say how grateful I am to all of you for all the kindness you have shown me in the past weeks, you are such good friends. And thanks to all of you who have been looking after Tom. I've heard, bringing him round brownies and biscuits Ann, and was it you who made him a lasagne, Janie?' Janie nodded. 'He reckons that's the best lasagne he's ever eaten, thanks for that, now I'm stuffed trying to match it!'

Everyone laughed. 'But there is just one other thing I want to say, and that is a big thank you to someone who I've already hugged and kissed but I want to thank him again.... and that's Stuart.'

He put his hands up as much as to say, *'no need — please'*, and smiled at her. But she wasn't finished.

'I know we've had a little cuddle and kiss already, even though you wouldn't do tongues, Stu!'

'That's only because Janie is here,' Ben shouted as Janie walked across and pinched Ben on the arm.

Polly smiled. 'But thanks again Stuart, for everything, not just thanks from me, but also Tom.' Everyone clapped, smiles broad. 'And an even bigger thanks from...' Polly's voice stuttered for a second. Some of her friends looked worried, but she regained her composure.

'From.... my baby. My baby inside me here.' Polly put her hands on her stomach.

Jaws dropped. Janie looked at Stuart, Scott looked at Ann, Alison looked at Ben, Milky looked at Fourre the dog, before the girls walked towards Polly and hugged her, while all the guys shook Tom's hand.

'You're pregnant,' Janie said. 'How long gone?'

'Nearly 14 weeks,' Polly said. 'Take a closer look at my tum. Can't you tell? I was pregnant when I had the crash.'

'My goodness,' Janie said. 'Oh, my goodness, that's just sort of terrible and wonderful all in one go. I can't believe you are going to be a mum. Welcome to the club.'

As the girls continued their exciting chatter, Tom went over to Stuart who had gone to sit down on his own.

'Alright, Stu? Tom patted his friend on the shoulder.

'Wow. I'm fine, even finer now. I had no idea about the baby, that's great news.'

'Well, thank you, mate. You've helped save not just my wife, but our first child, I can't thank you enough. Might have to make you a godfather. Come on, let's get another drink.' The pair supped up and went to the bar as Paul turned the music up.

'Right, folks, grub is served down in the restaurant area, so help yourselves,' he shouted. 'Everything is down there, knives, folks, spoons, you name it.'

'What do you want to drink?' Alison said to Polly. 'You haven't got one.'

'Just a soda water and lime please Ally, got to cut back on the alcohol now. I'm not sure how I'm going to cope.' The pair laughed as they walked into the restaurant where Milky and Fourre the dog were already tucking in. Paul had handed Milky some dog treats as he went past him at the bar.

'I'm so pleased to see you,' Milky said as Polly walked up to him and gave him a hug and patted Fourre.

'He would say he was pleased to see you if he could talk,' Milky smiled. 'Wouldn't you Fourre?'

She patted Fourre again. 'Well, it's your turn for a celebration next isn't it Milky? When is the wedding?'

Milky frowned and his expression changed. 'The wedding is off.' Polly's face dropped.

'Oh, it's no big deal Pol, I called it off. We had a big row and she said something about how I put some things in life ahead of her. So, I said fine, there will be no wedding.'

'I'm so sad about that,' said Polly. 'Are you sure you are alright? What sort of things was she talking about?'

Milky took a sip of his pint. 'Well, I told Denise that at the wedding I wanted Fourre alongside us at the ceremony and in all the wedding photos. He must have his own place when we have our meal afterwards, if we have a sort of top table thing. She seemed okay with all that.'

'So, what happened?'

'I also told Denise that he had to sleep with us, in the middle of the bed because he always sleeps with me, and that if she was doing packed lunches for me to go to work, then she had to do one for Fourre. She asked me who I thought she was marrying, me or the dog? I said, both. She told me that was absurd and called me a big kid, so I told her she was acting like a baby. We argued and she moved out last Sunday.'

'You don't seem that bothered,' Polly touched him on the arm.

'I'm not. You'd have made packed lunches for Fourre, wouldn't you, Pol?'

Polly gave him a peck on the cheek. 'Of course I would Milky.
'Of course I would.'

EIGHTY TWO

One Year Later

POLLY was walking through Earlham Park in Norwich, pushing the pram, Jody alongside.

Oliver was six months old and had thankfully gone to sleep for a while.

'Well, come on Jode, you can't just say that, I want all the details.'

Jody had spent the last few days in London, with her new man. Polly wanted the gossip. She'd only found out about Richard 'the property developer' two days ago. Jody had kept it a secret, much to Polly's annoyance now she had found out. Then again it was her first serious foray into the world of dating since Craig had left, so Jody had been a bit coy.

The DVD that had been delivered to her house one night three months ago had, in a perverse way, helped her. At first Jody had ignored it, and the letter saying she ought to watch it. In the end, after a chat with Pol, she decided to take a look. It wasn't nice viewing.

It showed Craig and some woman. At first it had upset her and she felt humiliated. But the anger had already set in before then, the DVD was the final straw. She made sure all her friends and family knew what Craig had done. It was time for her to get back into the land of the living.

In the weeks after, Jody had gone out for a few drinks with

Pete, from the shipping company. Apparently Craig had moved £55,000 out of an account at the company into an off-shore business on the day he had vanished. It wasn't earth-shattering money for PJC Shipping, but it had left Pete and Jason with an unpleasant taste in their mouths. The Police had been informed but so far nothing had come of it.

Meanwhile, Jody had been out for a drink with a couple of other guys as well, but no more than that. Richard had proved different.

The pair met on Tinder and hit it off straightaway. He had no kids and had never been married. He was two years older than Jody, intelligent, sociable, good looking, and rich.

'Rich Dicky', Polly had christened him straightaway. He lived in London and after a few weeks of telephone chat, Jody had gone down to meet him. That was four days ago.

'You'll like him.' Jody was unable to contain her smile at the mention of his name, as Polly began the interrogation.

'He makes me laugh, he's just such a fun guy. Drives a Porsche, which okay, in London isn't that flash but his apartment overlooks the South Bank. He makes me smile, Pol, I so like him. We used to spend hours on the phone when we first started talking. I didn't want to leave London yesterday to be honest, we had such a great time.

'And you never bloody told me? Honestly, if you weren't my bestie, I'd be cross. Let's see a photo of him then.'

Jody got out her phone. It was a selfie of the pair of them standing on Tower Bridge. He had wavy dark hair and a broad smile, and looked like he had a suntan. Polly had to admit he did look dashing.

'He's 100 times better looking than that prick Craig.'

'Pol, that's naughty. We said don't mention his name.'

'Did 'Rich Dicky' behave himself?' Polly gave a little wink. 'You know what I mean?'

'Is that the most important question you can think of? Did he behave himself?'

'Yeah, it is actually.'

'Well, if you must know, he never made any 'come-ons', even gave me my own bed and then never sneaked into my room in the middle of the night, either. I was starting to get a bit frustrated to be honest.' Polly laughed as Jody pulled a disappointed face.

'That was the first night, but last night we went out for a lovely meal and when we got back he was ever the gentleman again, too bloody nice to be honest. Anyhow, long story short, I had a couple of drinks and was feeling a bit tipsy. He clearly wasn't going to make the first move, so I thought, 'fuck it', I'm going to shag you!'

'Ahhhhh!,' Polly screamed out loud, before remembering Oliver was asleep.

'You little hussy. Did you really? How did you do that? Was it good?'

'It was okay.' Jody was making a pathetic effort to hide a smile. 'I'd give it 11/10, it was bloody great. Three times bloody great.'

Polly stopped pushing the pram and the pair hugged each other.

'Three times! Bloody hell, Tom and I are lucky if we do it three times in six months these days. Isn't that right, Oliver *'I won't go through the night'* Armstrong?' Polly bent down and whispered to her little son, who remained fast asleep. She kissed him on the head.

The girls linked arms as they continued to walk, joggers overtaking them as they chatted away. Polly was happy for her friend, it had been a horrible year. Craig vanishing, the DVD. And she had sold the shop. She was still living in Chester, but working part-time for a sales company as a trainer, something she used to do before she met Craig.

The only saving grace was that money was no object.

'So, how is my little godson behaving?' Jody looked into the pram at Oliver. 'He does have Tom's nose.'

'So long as he doesn't have Tom's sense of humour, I don't mind,' Polly laughed.

'Don't say that. Tom's got a great sense of humour. How is the surgery by the way? I never dare ask in case he starts talking to me about molars and root canal things.'

'See, I told you, if ever you needed to have no sense of humour for a job, become a dentist. Real bore talk. Tom's right up his own street.' Polly grinned.... 'Only kidding, he's lovely really.'

'He is lovely and you know it. You're very lucky.' The pair

smiled at each other.

'Do you mind me asking, Pol. Do you ever think about her? That Karen woman?'

Polly shrugged her shoulders. 'Not really. At the time it was a shit show, but Tom knew her before me. I must admit there were times I felt like leaving him. So glad I didn't though. In fact I suppose I feel sorry for her, not knowing who her son's dad is. But she's history now. Tom wouldn't dare mention her name today.'

Jody put her arm around her. 'Anyhow, enough of her, how's the gym?'

'Oh, it's okay, in fact it's going quite well. The green area is up and running and you remember I used to tell you about James, the finance guy, as camp as hell, but really funny?'

'Oh, yeah, what about him?'

'Well, he's left. Left last month, went off to Cambodia with his partner, David, to open a shoe shop. How bizarre is that? I miss him. Apart from anything else there is no-one to take the piss out of Kevin. I'm working two days a week at the moment, but Andy seems fine with that.'

'Oliver needs a brother or sister soon,' Jody grinned, as the pair continued their walk.

'He may soon be getting one, Jode.'

'No, you're not pregnant again? Shit, how long gone? I thought you said you only did it once in about eight months. Jesus, he's got some super sperm that husband of yours.'

'Hang on, hang on. I just said he *may* soon be getting one, I'm not sure, but I've missed a period and I'm as regular as clockwork usually, I'm going to take a test at home in a couple of weeks.'

'Do it now. While I'm here. Please Pol, just in case. I didn't get a chance to celebrate when you found out about being pregnant with Oliver. Come on, I'm stopping over the weekend and if you're not pregnant, so what? You soon will be again.'

Polly smiled. Jody was back to her old self.

'You are so bad Jode. But, hey, okay, I'll buy a kit, but just between you and me, though,' Polly said. 'But if I am pregnant, don't tell Tom that you knew before he did. He'll sulk like crap.'

The two hugged again.

'Thanks Pol. It's what friends are for.'

EIGHTY THREE

Craig was standing in the hallway of the plush Caribbean villa he and Marie had been living in for the past year. His paradise life about to be shattered before his own eyes.

'I knew you were a fucking bitch. I knew I should never have trusted you.'

Charlie Cantwell was standing in the doorway, Marie standing alongside, smiling.

'Oh, come on Craig, have a sense of humour. It was fun while it lasted.' Her galling look sent a dagger through Craig's heart.

They'd had a year of sun, sea, sex, drugs and drink. It had been the perfect lifestyle with not a worry in the world. From the Caymans to Cuba, Jamaica and back, they'd been living the dream. But it was all set to change, right this very moment.

Marie had gone into town to 'pick something up' and returned with Charlie, who was now standing with a revolver pointed directly at Craig's chest. His menacing look saying it all. Craig had been stitched up good and proper. *'Dancing with the devil'*.

'Why Marie? Fucking hell. Why? I should have known. Fuck you.'

Marie smiled again as Charlie moved forward, keeping the gun aimed at Craig all the time. 'You're a little boy in a big man's world, Craig. How dare you stitch up my husband like that you piece of shit. From the moment you did that you were history.'

Charlie grinned as Marie spoke. She could be so powerful. Years of practice had made her hardened. Craig had never realised how way out of his depth he had been all along.

'All this time, Marie. All this time, this is what it was all about, revenge for your fucking husband. Why didn't you just hand me over the first time at that industrial unit? Why all the running away? Why all the dramatics? Why all the show? You had all this planned didn't you?'

'Family is all, lover boy. I enjoyed our fling and enjoyed our relationship, until I found out that it was you who had snitched on Stuart, you fucking lowlife. From that point on what you thought we were planning, I was planning something else. I didn't even let Stuart know I was going to get you back for what you did to him. Good aren't I?' She copped him a wink. Craig went to move forward but Charlie moved forward as well, pointing the gun ever closer to him.

'You see, Charlie here had an inkling, didn't you Charlie? Although I even had to string him along.' Charlie nodded, his bald head beading sweat.

'I even had to leave him pissed off that night I didn't bring you to him. Just me having a bit of fun. Not that all that matters now....'

Her face moved closer to his, as Charlie moved alongside. Craig was cornered and had no-where to turn.

'You're a bastard Craig Baldini and I hate you.' Marie's lip snarled.

'You committed the biggest crime in the book, grassing to the coppers. I hate you for what you have done to my husband and what you did to my family. Love you? You're joking aren't you? Great little sex toy. But now you have nothing. You were always going to end up with nothing. And you will pay for your deceit. Fun in the sun, hey, lover boy? Fuck off. Get it done Charlie.'

She turned and walked down the driveway of the villa, leaving Charlie staring at Craig.

Charlie moved forward, revolver raised, as he told Craig to turn his back to him and put his hands up higher.

There were two shots.

EIGHTY FOUR

<u>Three Years Later</u>

'OPEN wide'.

Tom had a lot on his plate. Not only was the surgery busy, but Christmas was almost here. He had three shopping days to sort out a mass of presents. He also had to get all the wine and beer.

Christmases had become very busy in the Armstrong household in recent years, even more so since the arrival of April, a sister to Oliver.

With both sets of grandparents heading to Norfolk this Christmas, it was going to be a busy one and he had to squeeze in lots of frantic appointments ahead of the holiday period, if he wasn't busy enough already.

There had been a bit of snow in the air and it had made for a festive feel. Jill had been wearing her Christmas jumper as early as the 14th this December. She was like a big kid again, her marriage to John, the taxi driver, earlier this year had brought her happiness.

The wedding reception had been a drunken affair at Hethersett Village Hall after the service in the village. Tom had offered to drive Polly, but in the end babysitters had been organised. It wasn't often he and Polly went out together, so she took it upon herself to get pissed and produce some outrageous and embarrassing dancing.

'I'll tell you what,' Mr Barton said as he sat in the surgery chair. 'If I had my way, I'd ban them, ban the lot of them. Lock 'em up if they don't take notice, it would be their own fault, roads are busy enough as it is.'

Tom frowned. 'Keep your mouth open, please. I can't see anyone banning cyclists to be honest, and as for locking them up, well, even I bike around my village sometimes. If you locked me up, who'd do your teeth?'

Mr Barton wanted to reply but couldn't, as Tom was poking about.

'Let's just have another shufty in the gods. All looks good, might just keep an eye on that one at the back, now rinse out.'

'And bloody traffic wardens, bloody jobsworths. Nothing better to do most of them, I'd get rid of them as well. Jumped up little Hitlers they are. Waste of money.'

Tom listened stoically, as he always did. Years of practice. 'Okay, Mr Barton, four months please for the next appointment. And Happy Christmas.'

'Ah, yes Happy Christmas old boy, love to the family.' And with that he marched out.

'Silly old fossil,' said Judy, Tom's assistant, who had been with him 14 months now. Tom shook his head. 'I know. I've had all sorts in this chair over the years.'

Mr Barton was Tom's last patient before lunch and so he was heading into town to sort out presents for the kids, as well as table presents for Christmas Day, Polly had sent him a text.

Yessssssssssss! Guess what? Jody, Richard and little Nathan are coming over for New Year's Eve!!!! Brilliant! I told Jody we weren't doing anything — neither were they. Ahhh! So excited!

Tom smiled. A bit like getting a good night's sleep these days, New Year's Eve celebrations had become a thing of the past. But at least he and Richard could enjoy a few drinks.

Tom walked briskly into Norwich, he picked up a meal deal from Tescos and a copy of the Daily Mail. He would take five minutes flicking through that and eating his lunch before embarking on his present hunt. He sat on a bench near one of the many mobile phone shops in the city. As usual, he started at the back of the paper, the sports pages. There was no Arsenal news and most of the football seemed to revolve around the Champions League, which Arsenal weren't in.

As he was flicking through, a rugby story caught his eye.

TEEN STAR HARDING SET FOR FULL ENGLAND CALL-UP

He put his food and drink down and read the article.

Lee Harding, the 18-year-old from Saracens, has been called up to the England squad for the Six Nations series.

Flanker, Harding, who has played at many England youth levels, is one of three changes to the 22-man squad, as England look to try to regain a Six Nations Grand Slam they last won four years ago.

Harding who hails from London, but lives in Norfolk, was snapped up by Saracens on his 16th birthday. He has made great strides since and many commentators were expecting him to get a full England call-up sooner rather than later.

'It's a great honour for me,' Harding said. 'I could never have thought I would be picked for the full England squad. But here I am and I'm determined to give it my all.'

Also in the squad are youngsters......'

Tom looked at the headline again, then looked at the photograph alongside the story, a photograph containing the three new players, with Lee standing on the left. He could see it was him.

He took another bite of his sandwich and smiled to himself.

Lee's mum must be so proud.

EIGHTY FIVE

New Year's Eve

TEN, nine, eight, seven, six, five, four, three, two, one.... Happy New Year!

Tom and Polly, Richard and Jody embraced, clinking glasses as they heralded in the New Year in front of the TV. Oliver had not long gone to bed, while April and Nathan had been out for the count since 10pm, thanks to a busy day at the park after Jody had arrived that lunchtime.

'Here's to a great year.' Tom proposed a toast. 'Whatever it might bring? Health, wealth and....'

'....Wedding bells!' shouted Polly, winking at Richard while giving her friend a big hug. 'The time is right, surely?'

'Thank you Pol, Richard can make his own mind up, he doesn't need your help.' Tom was quick to intervene as he could sense Richard didn't quite know how to respond, He was still getting used to 'Team Polly/Jody'.

Jody smiled and hugged Richard.

Baby Nathan had been born without the assistance of IVF. Polly had spent a week in London with her after the birth, Jody having moved to the Capital 18 months ago. In all the craziness she had gone through with Craig to start a family, it all came rather naturally in the end with Richard.

'I'd like to propose a toast, as well,' said Jody. The other three waited as she lifted her glass and pointed it in the direction of Polly.

'To Polly, my 'bestie', my rock.... My happy place.'

And with that the pair embraced again, as Richard and Tom looked on and smiled.

'Who wants cheese and biscuits?' Jody got up off the sofa, it was almost 1am, but the four were relaxing, a bit of Roxy Music in the background. Tom had opened a bottle of port.

All hands shot up and Jody went into the kitchen, followed by Polly. 'I'll do that Jode, you sit down.' But Jody was already up.

Once in the kitchen the pair of them busied themselves preparing the late snack.

'It's been a fun night. I'm so glad you could come, me and Tom would be in bed by now. He'd be snoring, I'd still be listening out for April.' Polly slouched her arm around her friend. The pair were now pretty drunk.

'Who'd have thought it? You and me with kids, bloody hell Jode, look how we've changed. We're getting old. Remember when we had figures to die for. I'm a bloody size 12 now. Do you think we are like, well you know, do you think the youngsters see us as 'yummy mummies?'. Or have we lost it?'

'Who knows, you never know, forget the 'yummy mummies'. Perhaps we are now full blown MILFs! Think of that, Pol?' Polly frowned.

'MILFs? What's that?'

'You don't know?' Jody cupped her hand to Polly's ear and whispered.

She shrieked! 'Shit, no, is that what it means? I'd take that as a compliment if it came my way. Especially if it came from Tom Cruise.'

'Tom Cruise? He wouldn't speak like that about women. He's far too decent a chap. And he's too old. MILF's are for the younger set.'

'Oh, no, don't know if I want a toy boy. All that huffing, puffing, strutting and over in two minutes. At least these days I get my money's worth from Tom. Well, not so much money, but those 'wham, bam, thank you ma'am' days have long gone!'

The pair laughed. Polly spilt some of her wine on the floor and went over to the sink to get a cloth.

'Where's the pickle?'

'Over there.' Polly pointed to the cupboard. The pair could hear laughter coming from the living room, Tom and Richard had got on well from the first time they had met.

As Jody opened the cupboard her phone, which she had stuffed in her back pocket, went off. She pulled it out and looked at the number but didn't recognise it.

'Who's that at this time of the morning?' said Polly, mopping up the wine. 'Someone wishing you Happy New Year no doubt. Why don't they just text like everyone else?'

'Don't know, I reckon it's my mum, she's got a new phone for Christmas. I'll give her a big New Year's shout out. Listen to this.

'Happy New Year to you, Happy New Year to you, Happy New Year dear whoever you are...... Happy New Year to you. Is that you mum?' Jody sung in a high-pitched fashion mimicking 'happy birthday to you'. Polly laughed and almost spilt her wine again, they were both well the worse for wear.

Jody listened for a few seconds to the voice on the other end, but her cheery expression changed.... She looked across at Polly, her eyes wide. She turned away and spoke into the phone.

'What the hell do you want, Craig?'

THE END

Printed in Great Britain
by Amazon

72504684R00281